JERRY HAYWIRE

By Forrester C. Fox

Deus Ex Machina

DEUS EX MACHINA PRESS

Copyright © 2018 by Ryan William Morgan

All rights reserved. No part of this publication may be reproduced, distributed, or transmitted in any form or by any means, including photocopying, recording, or other electronic or mechanical methods, without the prior written permission of the publisher, except in the case of brief quotations embodied in critical reviews and certain other noncommercial uses permitted by copyright law. For permission requests, write to the publisher at the e-mail address below.

Deus Ex Machina Press

rm@exmachina.group

@RealRWM

Publisher's Cataloging-in-Publication data
Fox, Forrester C.
Jerry Haywire / Forrester C. Fox.
1. Fiction

First Edition

Jerry Haywire is a work of fiction.

All of the central characters, incidents, events, and dialogue in the novel are fictional & imaginary. None of the things described in the book actually happened. That would be impossible, since everyone who speaks a line of dialogue in the book is a made-up, imaginary person. Obviously, the Paul McCartney in the novel, the Grasshopper, is not the same person as the musician from the Beatles – they just happen to have the same name. The companies, brands and products mentioned in the novel are all imaginary. They are all made-up – except for Grey Goose, the Grasshopper's favorite vodka. That's real!

- Forrester C. Fox, 2018

to Kellyjean,

Jerry Haywire would never, ever have been finished without the Joy, Energy, Hope and Love you brought right into my life. What a magical time — five in one!

A Special Thank You to

Sean Beagan,

John Crutchfield,

& Kate McLeod,

For the incredible psy-cho-log-i-cal support during the writing and editing process. The value of your encouragement is hard to put into words, and after writing this novel I'm out of those for now. But I couldn't have done it without you guys – I mean that!

to Paul McCartney:

JERRY HAYWIRE | Chapter List

Two Hundred Eighty-One Pounds of Disappointment
The Grasshopper & The Goose
Kuhhhmff
Bedbug Infestation
No Reverse
Fuck Jerry Maguire
Mucho Dinero
Middle Finger
No, It's His Sister
Dead Guy in the Living Room
Trail of Stupidity
Core Values
Spreading the Pozz
Festival de Jonron
Boomer Barbeque
Football Sunday
Marla's Wage-cuck
Baggage Free
Trifecta of Misery
Rise of the Bugmen
I Hate That Fucking Guy
Mattress King
Toxicity
Digital Facial
The Hoax Has Run Its Course
It Ain't A Little Problem Anymore
The Ebb and the Flow
Non Fregit Eum Sed Erexit
Lucky Horseshoe
Courage

Two Hundred Eighty-One Pounds of Disappointment

⁕⁕

Life is a series of disappointments. The disappointments come in different sizes and different shapes. The disappointments have different velocities, varying angles and disparate impacts. This particular disappointment, the one that so afflicted and so abused Maddox Malone on this day, weighed two hundred eighty-one pounds and it packed a major wallop.

Maddox Malone was enjoying a beautiful morning in Coronado, California at an amusement park called LegoLand. With Maddox were Laura and their children Thomas, Chester, and Felicia. Two little boys and a little girl out for the day, on a rare family trip. The kids went through Captain Cranky's Challenge and the Fairy Tale Brook at a breakneck pace. Their feet were little blurs as they motored along.

Maddox strolled up the walkway at LegoLand, taking in the beauty of the day. It was a typical – sunny – west coast day. As American as apple pie. The day, the crisp sunlight, brought back nostalgia for the old America — the clean America — before the country started its decline. Sunny days like this created a nice golden-blue light that reflected a soft and subtle glow. It was warm, but not too warm. It was perfect! Maddox looked around the amusement park. He enjoyed building the little toy Legos, because it was an activity he could do with his kids. He preferred the non-corporate toy sets. There was already too much Marvel! But never-mind all that.

The rides in the park were fun and clean. In fact, there was such radiance in the park! Every detail, down to the flowers and the plants, was tended to. The walkways ebbed and flowed with perfect decor lining the way. There was something soothing about the smooth yellow glow of the sunlight bouncing up and down on the property. There was something magical about this area of the country on a sunny day. And the temperature was perfect! Maddox felt himself very fortunate. This was first class fun for a family with small children. He enjoyed the setting immensely.

Thomas, Chester and Felicia pressed on, ahead of Maddox. Maddox didn't know where his wife, Laura, was at the moment. Laura and Maddox had been married for years. Laura was originally from Maine. Laura had jet black hair with blue eyes and was about five-foot-three. During her undergraduate years at Colby College, Laura played softball, even though she was smaller than the typical softball player. She had studied accounting during those same years. She followed up her degree from Colby by getting an MBA at Stanford. Laura was well-pedigreed and she was quite proper and very serious.

Laura and Maddox had met in Sunny Grove while Maddox was working at the large corporatist law firm of Decker & Formenter, and Laura had been working for one of Maddox's clients. Laura's parents, Gerald and Georgia, had also moved from Maine to Phoenix to be close to Laura, Maddox and the kids. At present, their kids were in the distance but they could still be seen. To Maddox, as he strolled up the walkway, the kids were just so lovely. They projected beauty. Light. Energy. Maddox was overflowing with positivity. Their hair was thick and straight like their father's, but darker, that is to say completely dark brown without the light highlights that Maddox had in his hair. Thomas was a tall, skinny kid. Chester was not short — but Chester was a scrapper with more stockiness. Their little faces - bright, beautiful and soulful! Happy! In their blue long sleeved tee-shirts, crazy camo-styled shorts — athletic ones — bright knee-high socks, they were, to Maddox, the perfect boys. Felicia, a few years younger, had the same color hair and was wearing a little mustard-yellow sun-dress over lime green tights — a perfect little girl. Maddox found the morning to be exhilarating. It was a beautiful day!

Maddox liked to observe his kids. This particular morning, Maddox was completely carefree — he wasn't expecting much work in his sports business - a sports agency called the Malone Agency. It was shaping up to be a relaxing Friday. He wore navy sunglasses with dark lenses, a blue-collared shirt, blue shorts with small black lines, midrange blue-striped socks and a pair of gray athletic shoes. Maddox had grown up in California, in an area north of Sunny Grove and known for its informality. Maddox had always embraced the casual lifestyle he grew up in and he loved the comfort of athletic shoes. It was hard to get him out of them! As usual, he was very casual today. Maddox's thick brown hair was combed but not styled with product so it was messy and wind-blown. He squared his strong shoulders and carried his head up high. He caught up to little Chester.

"Buddy, let me put some sunscreen on you. We're going to be here a while," said Maddox, addressing his little boy.

"No way," said Chester.

"Come on, little man, I don't want you to get sun-burned."

"No-oo-oo!"

Chester twisted his hips and strode away from Maddox with the agility of a little rabbit. Run. Run. Hop. Twist. Jam.

"No-oo, no way!"

Maddox gritted his teeth and abandoned his plan to protect his son from the elements. He could have caught the kid with serious exertion. But Maddox didn't want to tear a knee ligament in an impromptu bunny rabbit chase. Chester, un-greased, pressed forward towards one of the exhibits but then stopped suddenly and wheeled around.

"Daddy?" said Chester.

"Buddy?"

"Daddy, can we go to the park later?"

Maddox laughed out loud, just once. Chester just stood there looking up at Maddox. Curious, bright blue eyes. Beautiful skin. Tremendous energy. To Chester, it was a perfectly normal question. Maddox laughed again. Maddox's soul buzzed with warmth and good energy. It was the best feeling in the world.

"Of course we can go to the park. We have to find a local park. But we're at LegoLand now, buddy. I'm guessing you want to play football? Or baseball? Or hoops?"

"All of them. But what if there isn't a park here?"

"Well I don't know. But I guarantee there will be a park we can find."

"How do you know?" asked Chester.

"What's your name?" asked Maddox.

"Chester!" yelled the little fella.

"How do you know?" hollered Maddox.

This exchange made Chester break into a big, devilish grin. Chester was always trying to get to the park to play catch with a football and take his baseball swings. And shoot hoop! Even when they had just arrived at LegoLand and were scheduled to spend a good chunk of the day there.

"But what if there isn't!" Chester bellowed. He was serious and his face glared with annoyance. His eyes, usually light and bright and jovial, became piercing and intense.

"But there is a park, Bud. There's a park in Coronado. I guarantee it. So I can't tell you about no park."

"Okay," said Chester, a bit frustrated but finally accepting the answer.

Suddenly, it was good enough for Chester. He ran off. The kids reached Pirate Shores and were busy shooting water cannons at one another when Maddox's smart phone rang and buzzed. It whirred and beeped.

ii

The description included here of Maddox's caller might sound mean-spirited — but, unfortunately, there is no way to understand this story without being truthful about the type and quality of people involved. The caller was a semi-literate person from the third-world country of Colombia. He had a very low intelligence quotient. He seemed to have no personality. He was short and squat, weighed as much as a small black bear, dripped with perspiration, had disgusting halitosis, and had several moles and warts on his face. Those sprouted thick patches of dark hair.

Once, Maddox almost vomited in his sports car from smelling the caller's breath. Garibaldi Vascoso was the caller's name.

"Sooome-teeeng ees wrongg, Madd-ox! Sooome-teeeng ees ver-ry ver-ry wrong," said Garibaldi.

Speaking to Garibaldi was like pulling teeth because he lacked the intelligence required for cohesive and fluid interlocutory skills. And his English was poor. He was ugly, which made it difficult to watch him struggle with communication. To be honest, besides the warts and moles, Vascoso looked almost exactly like a shell-less terrestrial gastropod mollusk. A Slug.

The Slug struggled to communicate, but finally got the message across to Maddox that a big Malone Agency client, Pepecito "Pepe" Soliz of the Sunny Grove Big Boys, was unreachable. Pepe was not returning phone calls or text messages. Garibaldi had called him ten times with no answer. Okay, thought Maddox. That's not good, but let's not jump to any conclusions, he thought.

Pepe Soliz was an outstanding baseball player for the Sunny Grove Big Boys squad. He was affectionately known around Sunny Grove as the Poobah — the nickname was derived from a shortened version of Pooh Bear, since the sports media and the citizens and sports fans in Sunny Grove compared Pepe's physique to that of the vintage cartoon bear, Winnie the Pooh. He was called the Pooh Bear, Pooh, or Poobah more often than his real name. Now, no one could find the Poobah. A missing Poobah? This was a big deal!

"Okay, Garibaldi, let me make a few phone calls and see what I can find out," Maddox said as he hung up the call with the Slug.

Maddox just wanted to enjoy LegoLand with his family — but he couldn't avoid dealing with this. The Malone Agency, as was often the case, had very quickly taken over his morning.

The night before, the Poobah had been out partying, drinking and carousing with his brother, Roberto Soliz, and a Malone Agency recruiter named Ward Goldstein. Incidentally, Maddox would find out that Pepe had nicknamed the recruiter Party Wardy on that fateful night.

The clever reference, which showed the top line of the Poobah's creativity and humor, was based on the fact that Ward could start a party anywhere. Party Wardy!

Maddox suddenly worried about a drunken car crash. Or some other life-threatening catastrophe. So far, the information was not conclusively bad, as it was not known what had happened. Surely, though, nothing about it was good. Maddox was worried. Using his smart phone, Maddox sent a text message to the Party, Ward Goldstein.

The text message read, "Where are you? What is going on?"

Ward responded, "We are still here."

Maddox wrote back, "Where is here?"

Maddox felt a slow, disdainful suspicion. He stared ahead. Maddox pictured Ward Goldstein's thinning gray hair, and crooked, dysgenic ears as he read the ominous response that popped up on his smart phone.

"The Police Station."

Maddox blinked. They were at the Police Station? His fingers raced over his large, glowing smart phone screen, which hummed and vibrated.

"Why?" typed Maddox, sending the question to Ward.

"They are questioning the Poobah about a rape."

Maddox didn't respond to the final text message. Instead, he sent a text message to his high school friend. The friend, Ken, was a cop in Saint Cortana. He asked if he could help him find out what was going on with Pepe — and if there was any way Maddox could see the police report.

The beautiful golden scenery that glistened in the easy mid-morning California sun contrasted sharply with the awful details of the rape that emerged, slowly, over the course of the next few hours. It was strange, because Maddox was, during one moment, watching his children play in the warm, inviting sun. In the next minute, he was trying to find out the details of a rape perpetrated by an important client of the Malone Agency. A client that payed Maddox Malone a lot of money, every year, in contract commissions. Soon, Maddox was strolling through the LegoLand aquarium, behind his kids. He was looking at sharks and fish instead of little plastic toys. Things felt surreal and ominous. Maddox's face clenched. He felt hesitant; he felt disturbed.

Maddox's phone started buzzing, three calls at a time. The calls wouldn't stop. Maddox took the constant buzz of the calls like a boxer takes a glancing blow — a blow that touches but doesn't really connect. Meaning, he didn't answer his smart phone despite the fact that the machine pulsed, hollered and buzzed wildly. Buzz! Whir! Humm! He just kept moving, realizing quite well what all the calls meant.

The calls meant that the reporters, the press, the media — those buzzards - knew, somehow, that Pepecito was at the Police Station. The situation had shifted into overdrive. Reporters, seemingly every one of them in Sunny Grove, were frantically calling Maddox, looking for a quote. Maddox surmised, correctly, that someone had spotted Pepe's car at the Police Station and leaked the information to the press. The press knew that Pepecito was supposed to be rehabilitating from his recent collarbone surgery for connective tissue repair. Why was he at the police station? Was he being interrogated?

Maddox didn't have visibility into the media cubicles, obviously. If he did, he would have been shocked at what was going on in that sterile corporate wasteland. There were writhing, pot-bellied, balding, pale, silhouettes of nu-men in every media office, every newspaper, every blog, every magazine, in the Sunny Grove area - all trying desperately to reach Maddox Malone by phone to get a quote about the Poobah's situation. The callers were young men, mostly. White men and Jewish men, primarily. Each of them had paid tens of thousands of dollars — for multiple years — to go to journalism school. Having graduated, they now had their shirt-sleeves rolled up for the intense dialing session on their gleaming smart phones; pressing digital buttons, frantically, while grimacing intensely. Soy lattes were put aside, for the moment, as the bloggers hunted their personal version of big game. They were determined to get that quote about the Poobah from Maddox Malone. Some of them snuck back for sips of their soy, but others were just too focused on the Poobah story. Many were sweating profusely, from their bald temples and stank-pits. They were moving about, spinning, pacing in an agitated manner.

"Pick up the phone, please!" a red-faced graduate of the Northwestern School of Journalism screamed at his nine-hundred and sixty dollar smart phone. Northwestern was dialing Maddox's number, over and over. Maddox wasn't about to answer. In fact, each time Maddox's phone buzzed, he saw Northwestern's number on the caller ID. Maddox knew who Northwestern was, he had met him before. He thought, "Fuck that guy" - in exactly those words. Maddox didn't *want* to be mean to the guy. But he couldn't help himself and he still thought, "ah, Fuck that guy." After the sixth call, Northwestern pounded the rest of his soy drink. He drank it out of both thirst and frustration — two sips at a time. Feeling the soy settle right in his belly, he felt a little better, temporarily, and started dialing again. "I said pick up the God-damned call Maddox Malone. I know you always have your phone. I know you, man. Agents always have their phones. I need this quote, man. Maddox!"

Suddenly, Northwestern felt the twelve ounces of soy hitting him — hitting him hard, right where it counts — and he had to rush out of his little cubicle and into the bathroom to vacate his bowels. While he was in the bathroom, Northwestern's smart phone buzzed and throbbed with a reminder that after work he was to receive a delivery of groceries. He needed to go straight to his little apartment in the high rise two miles across the city so he could put the groceries straight into his refrigerator. He ordered the groceries packed in recycled cardboard, of course. After he relieved himself, Northwestern started dialing Maddox again and he poured himself some more cold soy for sustenance. "Pick up the phone, Maddox!" Northwestern raged.

A graduate of Syracuse University's School of Communications, who looked like he had multiple middles, was also frantically dialing Maddox's number. Syracuse just kept dialing while listening on the speaker-phone. "Oh fuck me, this dude ain't gonna answer his phone now is he. This is so disrespectful. How am I supposed to file my daily blog post if I can't get a quote on this story?" The Syracuse grad dialed his phone again and again. While he dialed, his smart phone buzzed and beeped with a reminder that his new seventy-five inch television was being delivered that day, to his apartment. Syracuse had to head straight home, because there was a new TV show out that he wanted to watch on the bigger screen. His current TV is only sixty inches, so this new screen represented a twenty-five percent increase in size. Meaningful! Syracuse was apparently happy about that message — he smiled — and, judging by his face, he had forgotten, at least for a few seconds, about Maddox Malone.

A graduate of the Colombia School of Journalism, who carried a miniaturized copy of his diploma in his wallet behind his driver's license, was also dialing Maddox from his cubicle on the eighth floor of a medium-sized high rise in downtown Sunny Grove. Like every other reporter in Sunny Grove covering the Poobah arrest, he was cursing at his smart phone while dialing Maddox on repeat. "Step up to the plate Maddox Malone, you asshole!" bellowed Colombia. "You think you're such a baller well guess what bitch you're wrong." His wispy little mustache moved a little bit as he snarled and yelled. He looked like a little attack dog. Colombia pushed his black-rimmed eyeglasses up on his nose. His fingers poked and poked at the digital buttons on his smart phone, and his muscle-less forearms almost dangled above the fingers. The only justification for Colombia's weak and docile physique is that it was perfectly emblematic of his self. "I know you Maddox, I've seen you around at the Big Boys' games — gimme somethin' to chew on here, Maddox. I need this! I need to break this story about the Poobah!"

Maddox picked up one of the calls, at random. He had received over three hundred calls in just a few short minutes. He answered with a "Hello?"

"Yeah, Maddox, this is Atticus with the Sunny Grove Big Boys' Bar-Talk Blog. Thanks for answering. What's happening with Pepecito? Where is the Poobah? Has he been arrested?"

"Atticus, wait, what is your blog called?" asked Maddox.

"Sunny Grove Big Boys' Bar-Talk Blog. We're one of the biggest blogs in the sport. Some of our users spend over two hours on our site every day."

"Oh. Yeah, well, I don't have a comment. No comment," said Maddox.

"Come on Maddox. What is happening with the Poobah?" asked Atticus, who was talking to Maddox from his nine hundred square foot apartment in Sunny Grove. It was considered a smart apartment, fully wired and connected. All of Atticus' meals were delivered to his door, managed by a big corporation that predicted his tastes based on a complex algorithm which used his feedback, his conversations, his appliances and his location data to feed him with maximum efficiency. His toilet was even wirelessly connected to his smart phone which was wired to his refrigerator and cupboards — by measuring and weighing Atticus' waste product and remaining rations, the appliances worked together, seamlessly, to re-stock his provisions via a grocery delivery service. In fact, right before he called Maddox, Atticus had been snacking on a perfectly-portioned serving of tofu covered in an orange sesame sauce with a hint of a spice that Atticus could not quite recognize. Considering the food to be Japanese, Atticus, judging by his facial expression, felt himself to be quite cosmopolitan and this fact appeared to increase his current regard for himself.

"Listen, unfortunately, I don't have a comment at this time," Maddox repeated himself.

Maddox hung up the phone with Atticus. Maddox didn't think it was possible, but time slowed down even more. Maddox winced. He shook his head slightly. He puffed out an exaggerated breath. Huuuuuh. He kept walking. He tried to bring himself back to the sunny day in Coronado, back to his family trip. He couldn't do it. The whole story felt really bad. Maddox told himself he would try to keep the big picture in mind. He told himself that he hadn't heard Pepe Soliz's side of the story yet. The only thing he knew with certainty was that Pepe was being held after being reported for rape.

Maddox couldn't make his mind slow down. He wondered if the Sunny Grove community groups had heard about the Poobah attack yet. How outraged will those advocacy groups be at this terrible crime? Will they attack Pepe and come to April's defense?

Maddox's phone buzzed again. He had received an e-mail from a guy named Donald Keyballs. He looked at it and saw that there was a digitized document attached to the e-mail. It was the police report! "Wait a second," thought Maddox, "Donald Keyballs must have been a fake name." An alias! Ken came through, this was the document that Maddox needed to see!

Maddox immediately scrolled through the document. Oh shit! Oh fuck! The story was so bad. Maddox's face was flushed from excitement, but it was a bad excitement brought about from anger and disappointment. He kept reading, quickly going through page after page.

Time, which had previously only slowed down for Maddox, now screeched to a halt. It stopped. Maddox was horrified on a personal, human level. And, he had the added pressure of having so much money involved because he was Pepe Soliz' agent. The famous Poobah from the Big Boys baseball squad had been accused of rape! "What a disaster," thought Maddox. In fact, Maddox was certain that the rape would spark a chain of chaos in Maddox's agency. Maddox felt that, viscerally. But, logically, he couldn't be sure of how things would play out.

Again, Maddox's smart phone buzzed and dinged. He looked at it and it was his friend Chris Black, one of Maddox's retired football clients, calling. Maddox had been Carl's agent for seven years. Chris was a great guy.

"Hello?"

"What the fuck man, have you seen the sports news on TV?" asked Chris.

"Nah, I'm not in front of a TV," said Maddox.

"Fat boy all up on that screen," Chris said, referencing Pepe.

"Yeah?"

"What is wrong with that guy?"

"Man, I don't know. He's a fuckin' idiot."

"Are you pissed?"

"Well, hu-uuh, I'm not fuckin' happy," answered Maddox Malone.

"Man I can see your eyes poppin' out of your head. Who was Pepe with?"

"His brother and Ward."

Chris knew Ward Goldstein, and Chris didn't respect Ward. He knew, instinctively and also from personal observation, that Ward was a degenerate piece of shit.

"Of course that Goldstein guy is there. He's always right in the middle of bad shit."

"Yeah, man. Fuck!" Maddox fumed.

"Well, you sound fuckin' pissed. Where are you?"

"I'm at LegoLand."

"Madd-man just tryin' to enjoy some God-damn legos with the fam and Pepe has to go mess everything up."

"I know, man, it's a beautiful day here."

"Not no more it ain't!" said Chris, emphatically.

"Not no more is right. I gotta go, I'm out of here."

When he ended the call on his smart phone a wave of anger and revulsion came over Maddox again. He was angry and disappointed. He felt defeated.

"Not no more it ain't," echoed Chris's voice in Maddox's head.

iii

Maddox's mind went straight back to April's rape. He started reading the police report again. He wanted to stop, but he couldn't.

Maddox couldn't put the description of the rape out of his mind and, sadly, there is no way to understand this entire story without first understanding exactly what happened that night between Pepe Soliz, Ward Goldstein and April Tilney.

The three of them had left McConney's Irish Bar in good spirits — drunk, high and rowdy - and they asked April Tilney to come along and hang out with them. April was drunk and high - and a fan of the Sunny Grove Big Boys - and she had agreed to go. They had all been at the bar for about three hours, drinking, playing darts, playing pool, shooting the shit, chasing tail. Pepe's brother, Roberto, who was more than half in-the-bag, drove them to Ward's mother's spare condominium in Saint Cortana. It was only about ten minutes away.

After they arrived at the condo, they continue drinking vodka and smoking marijuana while playing music in the background.

iv

Time starts to slow down. Party Wardy and Pepe glance at each other with a knowing stare. Eventually, Party Wardy Goldstein takes the initiative with April and leads her into the bedroom. April looks taken aback, at first. After a while, though, her face shows some excitement! Once they are in the bedroom, Party Wardy catches April around her waist. He kisses her firmly. She gives a couple seconds of token resistance, then kisses him back. The Party draws April to him and guides her to her knees. Even without the alcohol, the marijuana and the confusion, the experience and exhilaration might have prevented her from being able to block his advances! She has become excited, judging by her face. The Party presses forward, taking down his zipper and shoving something in April's face. She looks shocked, but not for long. Nature grabs her and she suddenly looks aroused! Her face looks primal! Her face shows some shame, but less shame than wild exhilaration. Her face looks like a burning fire! She takes the Party in her mouth and she begins using one hand to pull off her skirt and panties. Her face now shows a wild desire, even though paradoxically she isn't physically attracted to the old man she was now in bed with. That craggy old son of a bitch was twice her age! He was old and gross - but something was happening anyhow!

With her skirt and panties off, April feels the Party's hand push to divide her thighs, and two of his fingers rub and then penetrate her special place which caused her so much pleasure. Her face looks conflicted but she can't, and doesn't want to, stop the Party. The Party keeps celebrating in her mouth. His Party favor, short and stubby, proves long enough to hit the back of her small mouth. It knocks on the back of her throat like a one-armed drummer, tutt, tutt, tutt, banging into her tonsils. The one-armed drummer gets on a roll, tutt, tutt, tutt, tutt, tutt. April seems to wish that the wrinkly grey-tinged balls in her face were instead pink and, further, she seems to wish they belonged to a young, handsome actor, instead of the old Party. The Party withdraws his fingers from inside her, pushes her back further onto the bed, and strips off her top. Her little bottoms are already strewn on the floor. All her charms become fully exposed to the world. April makes no further token resistance, still buzzing from the effects of alcohol and stoned on marijuana. She had greedily taken twelve hits of ecstasy-laced weed over the course of four hours. The Party's lascivious fish-lips draw back tight, with a lustful expression. April feels his naked body join hers and her lips become glued to his. The Party is really getting started. April's face shows a wide variety of emotions. Confusion, fear, pleasure, excitement, happiness, withdrawal — all at the same time! He enters her, then goes in and out. In and out. Time goes by. It might have been one minute, and it might have been ten. Her insides are filled by five torrents from the Party. Goldstein grunts "oh fuck!", "God!," "oh fuck..." The Party is, temporarily over, as Ward collapses on top of April Tilney. Thirty seconds later he rolls off her and walks out of the room.

Time goes by. April is in a daze as she watches Party Wardy Goldstein walk out of the room. She looks like she is consciously trying to sober herself up. She takes a breath. Then she takes another. She looks like she is trying to calm herself and recoup.

Instead of being able to calm down, April becomes startled as she sees a silhouette entering the room. It was Party Wardy. Does he want another round? April's face suggests that she doesn't. She looks worn out. She looks tired. Party Wardy turns a little bit and waves his hand from left to right, motioning to someone to enter the room. Someone else walks in the room. It was the Poobah, Pepe Soliz, of the Sunny Grove Big Boys! April's face shows surprise and intrigue. Naked, he doesn't really look like Winnie the Pooh. In fact, he more clearly resembled a caterpillar that had gorged itself on leaves and other rubbish. Pepe's rings of fat jiggle as he steps, bug-like, into the room. Two hundred eighty-one pounds of Pepe! What is going to happen here? Before April, or anyone, speaks or does anything, Pepe climbs into the bed. His penis, shaped like a small soda can, is already erect, pointing at two-thirty. Next, Pepe Soliz simply turns little April over onto her stomach and stuffs himself, his entire soda can, into her tiny pink-ish butt-hole.

April's face shows pain and shock. "Oh my! Oh shit! That feeling!" April says, reflexively. Her face suggests that April had not expected Pepe to do that, she had not expected that particular point of entry. It feels so wrong! Her little butt-hole had never been penetrated before. She hadn't even realized that Pepe had walked in fully erect and ready to go. April, despite her haze of intoxication, had been open to more sex — even open to a session with Pepe. But not that way, not in her little butt-hole! And not without some affection. She was not okay with that — and it shows on her face. Soliz pounds away, hammers away, keeps driving the little soda can into her and smashing away at her, all while biting April's back and tugging mercilessly on her hair. Then the dam bursts. The first few spurts go inside her and the last couple go on her lower back.

Pepe Soliz, groans, closes his eyes, breaths hard and then laughs, loudly, with the noise emanating mostly from his belly. "Ooh-hoo-hoo-ha-he-he" groans and grunts Pepe the Poobah. It is a laugh and groan of unfiltered pleasure.

The Poobah climbs off of April, shakes his torso, and then he gives an enthusiastic high-five to his friend, Party Wardy.

"Oh baby that's right!" yells Party Wardy. "Got some! Got some ass!"

The Poobah and the Party both smile and laugh. They walk out of the room, with the Poobah exiting first and the Party following right behind. Once he makes it back into the kitchen, Pepe grabs his smart phone and casually scans the text messages he had received while he was inside April. There were messages from a couple other girls. The Poobah smiles.

April, still in the bed, looks as if she is struggling to come to grips with what happened. She couldn't call her sex with Party Wardy rape. She may have been drunk and high, but she had wanted to do that. She consented to it. She was into it. But after to the incident with Pepe Soliz, she now looked like she had been violated. Disgust shows on her face. Pepe had bitten her neck and almost chewed through her pretty little body. He had gone in violently, tearing the lining of her anus, bleeding her, leaving it prolapsed, and bruising her small buttocks with his powerful pelvic thrusts. He smashed her!

"I just got raped," April says, quietly. "I just got raped."

She gasps with fear and resignation. After a while, she leaves the condo, calls the police and tells them about the rape.

V

Still at LegoLand, Maddox's mind raced. Maddox wondered if Pepe Soliz would get deported back to his home continent of South America. In the United States, Pepe was like a rat that lives in a stable. A rat can live in a stable but that makes the rat an interloper, it doesn't make the rat into a horse. Pepe just didn't belong! Yes, he was good at baseball, but traditional American culture - traditional American society - was completely foreign to him. He didn't have the capacity to understand even the basics. He fit in well, much better, at home in South America. Of course, if Pepe were actually deported it would cost Maddox a lot of money in commissions. Maddox had no way to predict the fallout from this incident. For himself, for Pepe, for the Malone Agency as a whole - Maddox couldn't predict what would happen.

Maddox had started the Malone Agency with unused vacation money from his old law firm. He created the Malone Agency with seven thousand bucks and a big set of balls — he just went out and did it. At the time, many people said he was crazy for leaving a big, prestigious law firm like Decker. Maybe he was? But Maddox had made it happen in a rough and tumble business, even scrapping for deals in fringe sports without large followings. He wasn't scared. He did deals not previously thought possible.

Maddox kept dwelling on the rape. He wished he could compartmentalize better than this. But this was crazy! It overtook his mind - it was the only thing he could think about. There would be fallout from having a client do something this violent, this evil. Maddox's mind just kept racing. He didn't want to panic. Calm down, he told himself. Wait, he could just cut Pepe as a client, right? Why not? Maybe he should? He thought about it, but indecision - rising around him like steam - and then paralysis overcame him. His skin may have been tough, but Maddox Malone's core was still soft. He was torn! He was caught between an awful rape and the financial interests of his agency, his company that he had built from nothing. He froze, mentally. He couldn't flush the topic of the rape out of his mind, so the topic took up residence in his head, just spinning around and around. He felt the slow, mellow intoxication of a merry-go-round. Time moved slowly. Sound was amplified. A feeling of constant dread overtook him. He didn't know what to do. He couldn't predict what would happen. To make matters worse, he knew he would be wide awake all night.

At the moment, however, with the California sun shining softly, things seemed fine on the surface. It was still a beautiful day. The colors were so vivid. The park attendees chattered happily as they walked along. Many thoughtlessly sipped soda and ate processed food without a worry in the world. Everyone was so carefree! Everyone, that is, except Maddox Malone. Not no more, he wasn't.

The Grasshopper & the Goose

❋❋

Paul McCartney was a degenerate.

Or perhaps he was a paragon of virtue?

Paul McCartney was a nihilist.

Or was he a lover of beautiful and good things?

Maybe he was just the eccentric heir to the PartDok fortune? He did have a big trust fund, after all. Doesn't that type of thing tend to make people a bit eccentric? Maybe Paul was a good guy, but a bit jumpy?

Paul McCartney happened to have the same name as the famous British or Irish musician. But he wasn't the same guy. He wasn't the singing, musical Beatle named Paul McCartney. He was no relation to the musical Beatle at all, and he didn't look like a beetle. Instead, McCartney looked a lot like a grasshopper. The long, skinny shape of his straight face was the same as the little green bug's, his eyes sat in the same manner, and, although McCartney was not green, one quickly got the feeling that he might hop off at any given time. He was jumpy, hyper and seemed strung out.

Paul McCartney had no taste. Or did he have such refined taste that it was hard for normal people to gauge?

Paul McCartney, like the grasshopper he resembled so closely, had no soul. Or was he the first grasshopper to have a soul?

Paul McCartney was a successful investor. Or, did he never actually make any investments at all?

ii

On this notably cool evening in Phoenix, Maddox was getting the Malone Agency football client Aeon Laysett settled into a rental home. Maddox had returned from LegoLand and Coronado late the prior evening. He was happy to have something to occupy his time. He had been dwelling all day on Pepe Soliz and the rape of April Tilney. He fretted for April's little torn up butt-hole. Pepe had been released from the Police Station and was already back playing baseball for the Big Boys. Maddox had estimated that he had several million dollars in future commissions on the line — meaning, if Pepe Soliz was deported to his home country, or incarcerated in the United States, Maddox would lose all that commission money from Pepe's current and future contract. What would that do to the Malone Agency?

Paul McCartney was across town from Maddox in North Scottsdale, but he was heading towards the rental house as well. McCartney wanted to meet Aeon Laysett. Paul McCartney was a huge sports fan. All sports, didn't matter which. So, McCartney wanted to meet Aeon and sniff his jock strap. He wanted the scent to go right into his nostrils.

Maddox was using his smart phone's mapping application, trying to navigate to his destination while having trouble with his reception. Some rock music was playing in his sports car. Maddox sang along.

> It's all right ... I know
> You're the only one ... who can show us at all

Maddox and Paul pulled up at Aeon's temporary house at roughly the same time. They walked up to the door together. McCartney was blasted. Loaded! Or was he? For certain, his eyes were darting and he was moving a mile a minute. Maddox wasn't sure why. Maddox hustled to keep up. McCartney was jumping from spot to spot like his small green brothers and sisters always did. The Grasshopper was living up to his name! Maddox noticed McCartney sniffling, and his eyes darting frantically. He didn't know what to make of it, so he ignored it and he looked away.

"Hey Aeon," said Maddox as Aeon let them in the door.

"Hey man, good to see you!" said Aeon with a big, infectious smile.

"Hi, I'm Paul McCartney," said the Grasshopper.

"Nice to meet you, man," said Aeon. They shook hands.

"I could definitely block you," Maddox jabbed at Aeon.

Aeon was an outstanding football player. He was a dominant pass rusher at six-foot-five and two hundred fifty pounds. He was a beast! Maddox Malone, at six-foot-one and roughly two hundred pounds, could definitely not block Aeon. But Maddox liked to tease him to make him laugh.

Sure enough, Aeon laughed, "Ha-ha, okay Madd-man, whatever you say."

McCartney didn't understand the interplay between Maddox and Aeon and therefore he just ignored it. Or did he understand it so well that it was below him?

"Congratulations on all your hard work getting ready for the draft. Take no prisoners!" said McCartney. "I can't wait to watch the draft on the television. I just can't wait. I love hearing everyone's opinions and analysis. I love watching sports news, I watch it religiously. Every day, and I always have it on in the background, even if I'm not watching it. Let's do this!" said McCartney.

McCartney had a reedy voice and spoke in a weird manner. Sometimes choppily, sometimes formally. He sounded as if his thoughts about what he was going to say were disjointed from what he had actually said. He looked like he had a fucking stick shoved up his ass. Totally stiff in his lower back. Strange haunches! He had square jeans and a blazer on. Loafers. He was carrying an attaché case, of all things. His face, nestled below his curly brown hair which was grotesquely overridden by a grey skunk-stripe right down Broadway, was contorted in a weird plastic grin and his eyes darted back and forth.

The Grasshopper had a prominent scar below his mouth. The scar was shaped like a boomerang and came from a time when the 'Hopper was playing an intense doubles badminton match. He had taken an inadvertent hit - a hit from his partner - who had swung wildly, desperately, at the plummeting birdie. Instead of hitting the birdie, his partner had connected with McCartney, right in his face. It took eighteen stitches to sew his face back up. It looked strange — shiny and jagged.

Everyone noticed the scar immediately, right when they looked at his face.

"I appreciate it, man. I'm looking forward to it," said Aeon.

"Are you feeling good? I know you were having an issue with a hamstring injury a couple weeks ago. You got yourself right? You gonna run a good time next week?" Maddox asked Aeon.

"Yes-sir! They've been giving me good stretching and physical therapy and I'm feeling great."

"Fantastic. When does your mom come out here?" asked Maddox.

"She's coming out next week. I can't wait," said Aeon. Laysett was a momma's boy, raised by a strong, single woman. When he spoke about his momma, his face lit up and he glowed.

"Okay, great. I'm looking forward to meeting her," said Maddox.

"This is a fantastic house. I hope you're comfortable here," said McCartney. The house belonged to one of McCartney's friends, who had purchased it with an allowance from his rich father.

"Oh yeah, it's incredible! I love the view," said Aeon.

"Paul was the one who set up the house for you," Maddox told Aeon. Maddox could tell that the Grasshopper wanted to brag about his friend's house. It was a really nice place.

"Oh, really?" asked Aeon.

"Take no prisoners!" McCartney hollered. "Yes, it belongs to one of my friends, his father is the owner of the Flaming Timber Dogs, the local hockey team. He's out of town, so I figured it would be a good place for you to stay for a couple weeks while you train for the draft. I've been up here many times with the owner, this is a great place to entertain. I sip my Grey Goose, that's the vodka I drink by the way, and look out over the pool and the city lights. I'm sipping Goose here all the time. Let's do this!"

Everyone thought the Goose reference was bizarre, except

McCartney. McCartney often casually sipped on Grey Goose, a corporate vodka which McCartney felt was a great association for him. He mixed it with cranberry or pineapple juice and viewed it as a very personal vodka. He drank that particular vodka because he felt that being associated with Goose made him exude high class. There was a French flag on the bottle! Paul tried to drink Grey Goose exclusively. Drinking Grey Goose, that exact brand, made him hold himself in higher regard than he otherwise would have. He loved the brand!

"That's cool," said Aeon.

"I've only ever seen this guy drink Goose and he always, always, wears Roman Laredo blazers and those same square jeans, the ones he has on now. He's one of those preppy types I guess," Maddox teased.

"I went to Our Lady of the Lake College for a year, man, I know exactly what you talkin' about," said Laysett.

McCartney looked sheepish, but his eyes still darted and he rocked from side-to-side, balancing his weight on one foot, then the other. Maddox wondered why he was moving like that, and was a bit embarrassed, but didn't say anything about it.

"Well, we're going to do some incredible things together," said McCartney. "I don't know if Maddox has told you about the TENACIOUS Training Facility. Have you, Maddox?"

"No, I haven't," answered Maddox with a half shrug. If Aeon had looked carefully, he might have noticed an ever-so-slight look of trepidation on Maddox's face. A tinge of uncertainty that kept growing as seconds passed.

"Let's do this!" McCartney shrieked, oddly. "Okay, well I'm funding a world-class training facility that we are going to establish in Phoenix. It's called TENACIOUS. Maddox came up with the brand. The facility is going to have first class training for athletes, plus things like TENACIOUS wrestling, tennis, and golf. We've already acquired a golf tour called Philly Hole Fanatics and we've acquired TENACIOUS wrestling from a guy named Tony Capote. Core values!" said McCartney.

Paul McCartney spoke fast, and he sounded very robotic. His little speech was met with an awkward, temporary silence, which Maddox broke.

"Paul is really connected in Philadelphia," said Maddox, "that's where his grandfather started the company that now belongs to Paul. The company is called PartDok. Isn't that right, Paul? He's a busy guy, a heavy hitter."

"Cool! That sounds great. Gonna be awesome to have your own facility to go with the agency. The future is bright for TENACIOUS," said Laysett. Aeon Laysett looked interested and excited, like he was happy to be part of the Malone Agency that was growing in this manner. Explosive growth!

"That's true, we're so proud of the TENACIOUS brand," said McCartney. "When people think about elite sports, they're going to think of TENACIOUS. TENACIOUS will be the biggest name in sports. It's going to be legendary! Core values!"

"Yes, we have to really push the gas on those projects," said Maddox. "We need to get the bid in on the site for the TENACIOUS facility. We have to get TENACIOUS moving this week."

"Well, money is not the issue," said the Grasshopper. "It's going to move. TENACIOUS is going to be huge. Take no prisoners!"

Maddox had been working hard on the TENACIOUS brand and business concept for well over a year. When McCartney made statements like this, it made Maddox feel good – at first – because McCartney sounded so excited about TENACIOUS. But after that initial feeling wore off, it made Maddox feel bad because McCartney hadn't yet delivered on any of his commitments. Not a single one. Maddox worried for this specific reason: if McCartney could float bullshit out so easily, what guarantee did Maddox have that anything the Grasshopper said was true? Maddox was frustrated with the commentary, he was frustrated with McCartney's style. But, Maddox greedily wanted the growth that would come with the TENACIOUS facility. So he made himself be patient. He told himself there was nothing else to do but be patient and plug away, to work hard on the projects.

"Well we are going to let you do your thing, Aeon. Paul just wanted to come through and say hello," said Maddox.

"Sounds good man, great to meet you, Paul. Good to see you Madd-man," replied Aeon.

"Okay, Aeon, nice to meet you as well, I look forward to seeing you soon. I'm gonna go drink some Geese. Let's do this!" said the Grasshopper with wild eyes.

The conversation wrapped up. It was a crisp night. As Maddox walked to his car he said his goodbye to McCartney and then walked past him. He glanced at McCartney's phone and noticed that McCartney was ferociously, adamantly, scrolling through pictures of naked women. "What the fuck?" thought Maddox.

Maddox had seen Paul McCartney doing the same exact thing on his laptop computer the week before. He saw it while they were sitting in the same conference room that McCartney borrowed from a friend for use by **TENACIOUS** for meetings and planning. At the time, Maddox thought it was weird and inappropriate to do that in the conference room. "What was McCartney doing?" thought Maddox. The other day, Maddox didn't say anything to Paul McCartney about the naked pictures — and he didn't say anything on this night, either.

Maddox roared off in his sports car, "Woke up this morning, got myself a bee-aar! Woke up this morning, got myself a bee-aar" Maddox sang along, with his car stereo pumping. Before he could push the thought of McCartney checking out naked women out of his mind, his smart phone rang and glowed with a call from Paul McCartney.

He heard McCartney's rushed voice, almost fumbling for words, say "Hey, uhh, Maddox could you do me a huge favor? If my wife asks you anything, tell her that I'm still with you."

"Wait, what?" said Maddox.

"If Emma calls you or texts you, please tell her that I'm still with you. Okay?"

"Ummm, okay," said Maddox as he scrunched his nose and squinted his eyes.

"Okay, thanks Maddox. Core Values!" said the Grasshopper.

Maddox thought the call was weird. It was shady. But he didn't want to know what Paul McCartney was up to. Maddox was blinded by TENACIOUS and his quest for more growth, more deals, more money. Maddox, continued to speed off, heading north. The phone call with Paul McCartney was already out of his head. Totally compartmentalized. The music kept playing.

Oh no! The thought of the phone call popped back into Maddox's head. What was that guy up to? But Maddox didn't want to think about it. He didn't want to think about anything relating to Paul McCartney other than the fact that Paul was funding the TENACIOUS Training Facility. Maddox could picture the growth of the Malone Agency that would result from this project. He pictured more deals, more clients, more success, more money. More private jets, more vacations, his kids could have anything they wanted! Same with Laura. Heck, same with him, Maddox Malone. Thinking about the phone call, or even McCartney's eccentric mannerisms, was just a distraction from the projects and these goals.

So, Maddox Malone didn't stop to think know why Paul McCartney made that phone call, and he didn't care.

ii

In fact, there were a lot of things about Paul McCartney that Maddox Malone didn't know. One of them was that Paul had recently spent three weeks in a substance abuse facility. Twenty-one days!

The story, the one that Maddox didn't know, went something like this. McCartney had checked himself in to a facility with maybe five or six dozen fellow addicts. The rehabilitation clinic was very upscale, as McCartney was using his grandfather's money – the money from PartDok. He wanted to attend the best rehab facility. The Pinkerton Clinic! Every so often during his stay, the clinic had everyone come together for community healing. It was the only time that the customers were not able to use their smart phones at their leisure. Besides this time, they would never be seen without their little digital devices right in their hand.

When community healing happened, the chairs were arranged in a huge circle, with no tables to sit at. Many customers were pounding coffee after coffee to get a nice caffeine buzz. Some of the repeat customers, the people who had been to the clinic before, even remembered to bring their own espresso capsules so they could enjoy hot water filtered through their favorite premium roast during their stay. In group session, many of the customers were very willing to share the different ways that heroin, cocaine, crack, meth, marijuana, mushrooms, acid and alcohol had ravaged their bodies, minds and spirits.

Often times, during community healing, from a window on the second floor overlooking the recovery room, the owner of the rehabilitation facility — a fine-looking gentleman named Rudolph Pinkerton — would gaze out over his current crop of customers. Mister Pinkerton was, as a matter of fact, gazing down at this very moment in time. He was counting the heads of his customers, making sure everyone was paid up and in the system. That was capitalism! His business was very strong — and he loved repeat customers because they didn't require as much orientation - he even offered them a discount for return stays. The money from the Pinkerton Clinic came in handy for Mister Pinkerton because he, himself, had an expensive hobby. Rudy Pinkerton always bet on the ponies. He always bet on sports. He played poker when he could. He played blackjack in Vegas, in Atlantic City, at Indian casinos. He played roulette with his customary flair. Oh, how he loved to shoot craps! So the money from the Pinkerton Clinic came in, then it went out, then it came in again, then it went out. The cycle repeated itself over and over again.

The group sharing went on, as it had the day before, with all the customers sitting in the main room. McCartney's mind was elsewhere. But his attention was re-focused back on the room when John Roberto, a guy who looked like the quintessential degenerate loser, and was a long-time customer of the Pinkerton Clinic, interrupted a speaker who was going on and on about marijuana dependency by letting out some excess gas.

"Woooonnnnnnnk!"

The blast indicated that John Roberto had no respect for the rehabilitation program. It seemed that John Roberto didn't give a fuck if everyone knew that he didn't care about his own rehabilitation. He had already been to the Pinkerton Clinic three times, anyway. This was old hat. Three times! Even so, he told everyone who asked that, when John Roberto got out, he planned on taking all the drugs and drinking all the gin that he could find. Most customers either frowned or ignored John Roberto and his rude antics.

But not Paul McCartney. He laughed. He loved the action! He sniffed hard while opening up his nostrils. He imagined the smell. Would it make him gag? Would it make him vomit? What had John Roberto eaten, wondered McCartney, anything good? Those may have been unpleasant things, but, still, he wanted to know! Sadly, Paul was too far away to get the texture of the stinky cloud into his nose. The speaker kept droning on and on about his marijuana problem. Talking about appetite, mania, depression, nightmares, dependence, buzz, even hot-boxing. McCartney was bored.

John Roberto looked around and noticed that nobody – not a single person – had the balls to say anything to him about his rude gas expulsion. So he let another one rip, with even more enthusiasm, with gusto. He even lifted his leg! The customers in the rehabilitation clinic couldn't fathom John's actions. They had their own problems, for sure, but this behavior was vile and unacceptable. But not to Paul McCartney, who thought it was funny. He laughed uproariously and let himself really enter the moment.

"Ha-ha-ha-ha-ha," laughed the Grasshopper.

McCartney dwelt on the moment. He wanted to freeze time. Both John Roberto and McCartney looked around the rehabilitation room to see how the other customers in rehabilitation reacted.

On the far side of the room, sitting at a table alone, a small, ant-like man named Bert was drinking coffee with sugar and cream. He didn't do anything other than drink his coffee, he showed no reaction at all. His hair stuck up in two places, giving a subtle hint of antennae. His eyes were active, moving fast from side to side. He wore a stained Chicago Grizzlies tee-shirt. He had never played football in his life, but he was a super fan. He watched for twelve hours on every Football Sunday. Many of the men at the Pinkerton Clinic were like Bert. Little skinny men or little dumpy men, stout or gaunt, all with short legs, shuffling feet, and inscrutable faces with insect-like eyes – all invested in their own particular pastimes.

Fred Pankston, unlike Bert, had heard John Roberto's rude release and he did react. He scowled. Fred made a gun shape with his fingers, pointed it at John and jerked his hand slightly backwards. After that, he blew on the tip of his second finger. John Roberto stared back at Fred, trying to instill dread into Fred. He tried to scare him, using only his face. He stared so menacingly! The tension escalated.

John, also scanning the room, saw Fred make the gun motion, so he got up and yelled, "You gonna take a shot at me, Fred? You want some of this, big boy?"

Fred, who was, in fact, a big boy, barreled out of his chair and faced John down. McCartney, hopped up out of his chair and then scurried over into the fray. Paul McCartney clipped John on the back of his calf with his expensive loafer. John Roberto stumbled but he did... not... go... down. Rudolph Pinkerton, up above, looked on with urgency as the rehabilitation counselor paced over and positioned his body between the two men to try to end the fight.

McCartney laughed and screeched "Let's do this!" with a higher pitch than usual. He hopped up and down. A couple of random customers shook their head. A few people stood up to get a better line of sight to watch the pathetic scuffle. Most people didn't even get out of their chairs.

Soon, order was restored. There was no further disruption as the rehabilitation meeting churned on. Mister Pinkerton was concerned, but not alarmed. The meeting resumed.

When it was finally McCartney's turn to stand up and speak about his addiction problem, it was apparent to all who noticed that he was built almost exactly like a grasshopper. Grasshoppers have a head, thorax and abdomen — McCartney had the exact same format. His legs resembled the thorax shape due to the fact that McCartney always wore square jeans - perfectly square - that seemed to touch together at all times. Like a grasshopper, McCartney's head was held vertically at only a slight angle to his body and with his face pointing forward. Both McCartney's mouth and the mouth of a traditional grasshopper are situated at the bottom of the long head. A grasshopper's head features a pair of eyes, like McCartney. A grasshopper has a pair of thread-like antennae that are sensitive to touch and smell, which was slightly different than McCartney's electronic earpiece that focused exclusively on wireless network communication. A grasshopper had more legs than McCartney (who had merely two), and also featured wings. McCartney didn't have wings.

McCartney stood up and cleared his throat.

"Ahem!"

The Grasshopper's haunches billowed.

"Hello everybody, I'm Paul McCartney. Like the Beatle but... not ... him. I'm here because I lost sight of my values. My core values. Ahem. My wife, my sweetie, caught me staying at hotels I shouldn't have been at. The hotels were situated really close to our house so she wondered why I would do that. Why would I do that? She found out things that I was doing, a lot of dumb things. I was drinking too much Grey Goose, usually with pineapple juice, and I was back on the powder. I was riding the tiger."

McCartney didn't go into more detail regarding his drinking and drug use than that. That was it. And he completely glossed over the fact that his wife had caught him contacting numerous working girls - sex workers, prostitutes, e-girls, thots - on his smart phone to set up trysts all around Phoenix, while giving the women some of his grandfather's money in exchange for access to their bodies.

McCartney continued, "I just want to recommit to my sweetie. To my honey. I want to get back to my Core Values. Core Values! I just really want to make this happen, I want to make my sweetie happy. I have to get back to what my grandfather taught me."

It was, in fact, not his grandfather but, rather, his grandfather's money that taught him all of the lessons that made him who he was, today. But he didn't admit that. The Grasshopper may not have even known that.

"I'm going to make it back. I'm going to turn the corner. I'm going to be a big success! Let's do this!" hollered McCartney, concluding his speech.

McCartney's short speech went over poorly. In rehab, most people, to the extent they are listening, can almost instantly smell bull-shit. You can't bull-shit a bull-shitter, as they say. McCartney tried for a crowd-pleaser type speech. A jubilant return to sobriety. A jubilant return to his wife. It was all Balderdash! Claptrap! Humbug! Phmmp Phmmp Phmmp, went his square jeans as his prominent haunches exerted themselves.

"Nice speech," said John Roberto with a knowing smile as McCartney walked by.

"Thanks John. Checked that box!" said the Grasshopper. His scar glistened and his skunk-stripe gleamed. His haunches bustled a little more than usual under his square jeans.

Maddox Malone didn't even know that McCartney had been in rehab. Maddox thought that McCartney was eccentric. Rehab was the furthest thing from Maddox's mind. When he saw McCartney, the only thing Maddox ever thought about was growth, revenue, success for his agency. He thought about the coming expansion with TENACIOUS!

Maddox had already made it home and he was sitting in his leather chair. He was relaxing and reading a book called *the Revenant*. He was at the part when Hugh Glass was surviving by eating a mostly-rotten buffalo carcass while trying to heal up wounds inflicted upon him by a grizzly bear - at least enough so he could go get his stolen stuff back. Maddox was thrilled by Hugh's fortitude! Maddox even, just for a brief moment, imagined being a settler like Hugh instead of a sports agent and lawyer. Rifles, knives, horses, adventure - no smart phone!

But how did settlers make money?

Maddox imagined forging a country, in this case the United States, out of nothing. Settlers facing down incredible odds. Surviving amidst incredible savagery. Maddox thought about the whole context of the story, the big picture. But really, *the Revenant* was just a simple tale of revenge. Hugh Glass wanted his shit back, and he was gonna go get it. Maddox was reading in his big leather chair, relaxing and taking his mind off of the Pepe Soliz rape, off of the TENACIOUS projects, off of the struggling sport of Platform Volleyball. He took his mind completely off the Malone Agency, which was often hard for him to do - he was obsessed with growth! His boys were playing with their Legos, his daughter was playing with her dolls, and his wife was on the phone, talking to her mom, most likely, or one of her girlfriends. So, Maddox wasn't thinking of Paul McCartney at all, not at that moment.

When he put the book down, the topic of TENACIOUS did pop back into Maddox's head. Things relating to the advancement of the TENACIOUS projects seemed to get delayed quite often, he thought. Given the scope of all the TENACIOUS projects, it would be okay if a few of them were delayed or fell through entirely, Maddox allowed. In fact, that would help allow for greater focus early on. This was how the sausage was made, he told himself! When he entertained, ever so slightly, ever so fleetingly, the thought that the TENACIOUS projects might be fake, a hoax, he felt apprehension. Queasy, even! No way, that couldn't be the case. Why would the Grasshopper perpetrate a hoax? No one would do that, thought Maddox. These projects were real, very real. He knew it! He went to bed shortly after putting down his book. He had a recruiting trip coming up, and he had a lot of work to do the next day. After all, he wanted the Malone Agency to grow!

Kuhhhmff

❊❊

"Hands, hands, hands!" bellowed Otis Ballard.

Otis, a former Private in the Army who went by the nickname Major O, was enthusiastically re-telling Maddox Malone how he used to take Obadiah Ballard — or O-Bad — to the park to play catch with a youth football. All this happened when O-Bad, Major O's son, was a little boy. Presently, Maddox was out in New Orleans working on getting O-Bad to sign with the Malone Agency. He was keeping in touch with O-Bad and his dad. Major O was telling Maddox a story about how he would take O-Bad out from their home in Mississippi to the park whether there was rain or shine. Major O would yell "hands, hands, hands" at O-Bad to get him to catch the football with his hands away from his body. Whether or not the advice made any difference is unknown, but it made for a great story. It was a chance for dad to take some credit. And, either way, O-Bad became a fantastic wide receiver. A really special player — and an important recruit for the Malone Agency. The football skills themselves came pretty easy for little Obadiah because not only was he a natural athlete with speed, quickness and jumping ability but he also was gifted with huge hands for snatching the ball out of the air. Consistently! And consistency was key. O-Bad rarely ever dropped one!

Major O was a charismatic guy. He was handsome, about six-foot-one, trim but not too skinny. Women found him to be sexy on the occasions that he stayed just sober enough to interact. He kept his haircut high and tight, real clean. Real clean. He was an African-American guy, originally from the south, Mississippi to be exact. Maddox liked Major O a lot. Major O was genuine, he was authentic. What Maddox saw was what Maddox got. Maddox liked that. He was articulate and funny. He had a good heart and was an open book. Maddox could tell Major O enjoyed his cocktails, and maybe even a swig and a swag of vodka straight out of the bottle here and there, and that was fine with Maddox. It had to be. Maddox would roll with that.

Major O's stories went on forever — so, Maddox was thankful that the stories were fun to listen to. He was telling Maddox, for the second time, stories from when he was on the intramural football team during his short, three-year stint in the United States Army. Maddox figured that must have been in the seventies or eighties, but he didn't know for sure. Major O had been a running back for the Army intramural squad, and he scored a huge touchdown in a scrimmage against Air Force. Maddox loved the part about the chant that the wild, raucous crowd did every ten minutes or so.

> Hey Ho! Hey Ho! You can't stop fuckin' Major O.
> You got the planes but we got the Mo', you can't stop fuckin' Major O.

Major O's story about the chant made Maddox widen his eyes with amazement and realization. He just sat there, processing the story, enjoying it. Major O told the story with so much enthusiasm and emotion that it echoed in Maddox's mind. The story made the intramural game seem like it was bigger than the Super Bowl. It was so funny, so real, so vivid!

At that particular moment, Major O and Maddox were shooting the shit in a little dive bar in New Orleans. Maddox had flown in at the crack of dawn, and he was hustling around all day. Nonstop. Contacting clients and sponsors on his smart phone, which constantly buzzed and whirred and glowed with digital activity. It was a little data center! He had been working hard to try to line up several meetings with key sponsors of his main Platform Volleyball client, Lacy Stratton. He was scheduled to attend a Platform Volleyball event the next day, and had a lot of coordination and preparation to take care of. The Platform Volleyball Tour was struggling financially, but Maddox wanted to try to hustle up some sponsorships anyway. Maddox figured that all of the key sponsors would be there the next day. Maddox was heading out to close some deals!

At present, Major O looked like he was in a good mood — he looked like he was buzzing from a few cocktails. Well, to be more precise, Major O had downed six cocktails and he was still going strong. The alcohol made him mellow and talkative at the same time. The stories flowed freely! Cocktails were poured and drank, poured and drank.

Major O was smiling at the moment because a fellow named Zaine Fuller, a recruiter for the Malone Agency, had handed Major O ten thousand dollars, cash, a couple of hours earlier. A recruiter is, simply, a person whose job it is to bring new clients into the agency. To help Maddox sign them. And Zaine was recruiting with O-Bad by giving him and his family stacks of cash. That was Zaine's method! The stacks of cash made Major O smile. Maddox didn't know that Zaine had given Major O that money — and, what's more, the payment was highly illegal. Meaning, the payments were against the law and, if prosecuted, carried heavy penalties, including potential jail time. This type of thing happened a lot in the dirty sports agency business! Buying clients for future fees! But Maddox Malone didn't want to operate that way, and, if he knew about the payments he would have freaked out. Zaine and Major O had met up two hours earlier, before Major O was set to meet up with Maddox. The cash drop looked like something out of a spy movie.

They were secretive because both of them knew the Malone Agency could get shut down for illegal payments! They could all get thrown in jail!

For Maddox Malone, ignorance of the cash payment was bliss — for now at least. The stories went on, the drinks kept flowing and the laughs continued for another hour. In between stories, Maddox took Major O through the plan for the rest of the season for Obadiah. Obadiah was still playing football at his college in Louisiana. When they weren't telling stories, they were discussing training and preparation for the Football Draft. That was only a few months away, and time was flying. They talked about building a brand and some of the marketing associations that Maddox had in mind for O-Bad. All in all, it was a solid recruiting meeting. They spent two more hours talking football, drinking, and shooting the shit. As usual, they got along really well, laughed a lot, and their thoughts meshed well in terms of the process and the plan for

Major O's son, Obadiah.

"We're going to do something really special. It's going to be special. I'm really looking forward to it. I've got to ask you, though, man to man. Is Obadiah gonna sign with me?" said Maddox.

"Let's ask da boy himself," said Major O. He picked his smart phone up off the table and pressed a few digital buttons on the shiny screen. The phone glowed and shone and buzzed. The phone was set to loudspeaker mode, and it rang.

"Hey dad," said O-Bad as he answered his smart phone.

"Just one thing little O — you gonna sign with the Madd-man and the gang at the Malone Agency?" asked Otis.

"You know that's right. You know that's what I'm gonna do," answered Obadiah Ballard.

"Okay, that's all I was callin' about. Have a good night and get some good rest for the game."

"Okay dad, I'll catch you later."

Major O turned toward Maddox.

"See, Madd-man, that's a done deal. He's gonna sign. Done deal."

"Awesome," said Maddox with an expression of happiness on his face.

"Coming back to what you said, Madd-man — special is cool. Maybe that's a good word for O Bad. I like it. I raised him from the time he was little to be special. He deserves it. But it's not everything for him to be special.

"It's not?" asked Maddox. "What else?"

"That's not all. I want him to be kuhhhmff. Now is the time for him to get kuhhhmff," said Major O.

"Kuhhhmff?" said Maddox, quizzically.

"Yeah man, that's the next level above special. That's family, that's respect, that's style, that's charity, it's love. It's when you're absolutely rockin'. It's the full deal, homey. That's Kuhhhmff," said Major O, flashing an enormous smile with blazing white teeth. He was drunk, but Maddox could hardly tell because he was coherent and funny. He was engaging.

"Okay, cool, I get it. I understand. But what is the word from, where did you get kuhhhmff from?" asked Maddox.

"Brother, it's for kuuuhhhhhmffortable. Comfortable, man. Comfortable ... KUHHHMFF," said Major O, smiling.

They both laughed! They both smiled broadly and clasped hands in a high five. They held it for two seconds then pumped their fists. Big grins! Wide grins! Maddox was going to use this term from now on, he loved it. It was kind of stupid, but it was funny. Kuhhhmfortable!

The subject changed and they started talking about old football games again for a minute, when suddenly a fight broke out in the bar. There were two rather large women, one white, one black, who had commenced hair-pulling and frantic screaming. The black woman had a fist full of the white woman's brown hair and the white woman had a fist full of the black woman's dyed-blonde hair. It was confusing and exhilarating at the same time. Maddox and Major O both looked around the little dive bar — there was no security present! No one whose job it was to break up the fight!

What was going to happen? Due to the strong grips that each had, they were in the midst of a brutal stalemate. Moments passed. Seconds seemed like minutes and minutes seemed like hours. Both had fistfuls of hair and since they were in an even position in terms of leverage, time crept forward without final result. Neither one could land a decisive strike! Each one of them used their other hand, their free hand, to chicken fight the other woman. The chicken fighting was neutral, just smacking and jostling. One of the women did manage to land a painful crab pinch.

"Feel the burn!" she yelled as she clamped as hard as she could, using her thumb, forefinger and middle finger to create the vice.

Both women topped out at about five-foot-three or five-foot-four. And they tipped the scales at roughly the same amount as one another, approximately one hundred ninety pounds, maybe one ninety-five. Their reach was similar. So, on paper at least, it was an extremely fair fight! One woman had a tee-shirt on that said "Calm the Fuck Down". But clearly she paid no heed to her own shirt!

Neither could gain the advantage, so the struggle continued. The fight kept going, with no end in sight. The women screamed at each other. Both women were with men who had brought them to the bar as dates. The men, Barry and Jake, awkwardly stood by for a moment, but then Barry stepped in to the circle of conflict. Barry walked in without a plan, though. He hadn't made up his mind as to exactly what he would do, but still he entered the fracas as if he had been rallied by none other than King Henry. Barry was the man who was dating the white woman. Once he was close enough, he made an impulsive decision. Barry aggressively slapped the shit out of the black woman, whose name, incidentally, was Maxine. Barry slapped Maxine right on her cheek, just above and to the left of her mouth, with three successive loud phwwwpttt phwwwpttt phwwwpttt sounds. Maxine was stunned. Barry, finished with his slap attack, bowed up his back, pivoted and took three steps diagonally towards the wall while surveying the scene to watch what would happen next. What now?

The other man, Jake, the boyfriend of the black woman, took five purposeful strides and then socked Barry, the bitch-slapper, in his face. Jake socked Barry right on his fucking mouth. The punch, when it connected, sounded like a wet rag being thrown into a barrel of oil. He threw a right cross and Barry never even moved, he just ate the punch. Barry's mouth was a mess. His mouth was busted! Jake had taken revenge for the three slaps on his girlfriend. The melee raged on.

"Why you hit muh girl?" yelled Jake, enraged.

"Ima kill yo bitch!" Barry yelled back with his mushed up mouth. It looked like one of Barry's teeth was completely dislodged and three other teeth were bleeding profusely at the root. His lip was so puffy it looked like a raw hot dog was attached to his mouth, sideways. A few seconds later as the swelling continued, and the hot dog, connected to the bottom lip, now looked as if it had been cooked! Barry looked hurt and crazed at the same time. Barry was furious.

"I'ma fuck up that bitch, oh yeah, she gonna get it!" yelled Jake.

"Who you callin' a bitch? I already slapped yo' big bitch in her mouth. I showed her what was what!" yelled Barry. He was so mad, he kept yelling even though he had been getting his ass kicked by Jake.

"I'ma fuck you up!" Jake yelled as he charged and bear-hugged Barry while launching a flurry of weird wrap around punches that were hitting Barry's lower back with no meaningful effect.

"You tryin' to kidney rap me now?" Barry yelled.

"Mother fucker! You gonna get it!" Jake kept yelling.

"Here it comes mother fucker," screamed Barry. Barry, already bleeding from his mouth, threw what was supposed to be a straight right punch but it didn't connect. It didn't have a chance. Maddox couldn't believe that Barry told Jake that the punch was coming and then threw a sloppy, looping punch with his right hand. Maddox laughed while trying to muffle the laughter. He wanted to enjoy the fight with Major O but he didn't want to get involved in it, not at all. The other guy, Jake, took a step back then bounced forward like an angry bear. But he had no plan! So, this time he caught a punch right on the side of his throat. He went down like he was shot, but somehow managed to spring back up before absorbing any more punches or kicks. It was the first punch Barry had landed. Maybe the fight was finally evening out!

Was anyone going to stop the fight? Maddox looked around and he didn't see anyone rushing in to do anything. This thing might go on forever, Maddox thought.

Pandemonium broke out! Another man, who looked like he might be of Mexican or Guatemalan heritage, grabbed a beer bottle, broke it on the bar and started brandishing it. This fight was now fully diverse, fully post nineteen-sixty-five American! The two original brawlers traded more punches, with Jake landing a decent right hand to Barry's face. The women stayed locked on the hair, but the white woman had finally released both hands from Maxine's hair and began punching Maxine right in the medium-sized nook of her face between her cheek and nose. She drew blood. But then the black woman's date, Jake, got a solid kick in on the white woman, whose name was Farrah. Jake kicked Farrah right in her huge, flabby ass!

When Jake's size twelve-and-a-half shoe connected with Farrah's rear end, the fat on Farrah's ass flowed upward, away from Jake's foot, away from the earth's gravitational pull, like melted rubber. The kick startled and upset Farrah so much that she forgot to keep punching Maxine. She stopped inflicting damage on Maxine's face, and Maxine took only one or two seconds to gather her wits about her and started punching Farrah. What ensued was a flurry of rabbit punches to Farrah's face. Rat! Tat! Tat! Rat! A Tat! Tat! Six little vertical rabbit shots right to Farrah's nose and mouth. Individually, the punches were not very powerful, but when Maxine ratcheted them together, they did some meaningful damage. Three of them, in fact, caught real solid. It smashed up Farrah's face and fattened her lip — it wasn't as bad as Barry's hot dog lip, but it was blown up and bloody. The lip kept puffing up for the next ten seconds, then it leveled out. Farrah started crying. Tears were flowing!

"Dat bitch fucked up muh face! Go finger bang yourself!" Farrah screamed, blubbered and cried hysterically. Tears and snot were flowing down her face. "Go finger bang yourself!"

Major O and Maddox sat, frozen. There was still no security, no one to break up the fight. The guys were frozen with amazement, not fear. They both thought about breaking up the fight, but with Jake, Barry, Vicente, Maxine and Farrah all involved, they just decided against it. Too many bodies. Too many pounds! The dudes were big and so were the ladies. "Not my problem," thought Maddox, and Maddox could tell that Major O thought exactly the same thing. Not my problem.

"These mother fuckers are crazy!" Maddox hollered at Major O.

His face became big with excitement. This was a pretty good fight!

"You right about that. You right about that, my brother!" Major O hollered back. His face showed excitement as well, but he had somehow channeled all of the excitement into his mouth, which moved rapidly as he yelled at Maddox. It reshaped with every syllable! The rest of his face stayed strangely fixed. It was uncanny.

"I hope they are all drunk if they acting like this! This don't hurt now but it gonna hurt in the morning!"

"It will numb the pain!"

"Numb it! Numb that shit!"

"Oh shit!"

"Hey Major, did you see that? Oh man no way! She buckled, she buckled!"

Farrah's knee had buckled under her weight after she tweaked it during the fight. Actually, it was more than tweaked, her anterior cruciate ligament had snapped in two. The entire knee, therefore, had become completely unstable and it showed in her gait, which used to be a lumber but had morphed into an unbalanced lumber. Her walk was lopsided to the left and it was hard to watch. The yelling continued throughout the bar. There had been no security in the little dive bar, so the fight had raged while the bartenders tried desperately to call for help on their smart phones. Finally, two guys showed up from somewhere, and they were acting as bouncers by aggressively removing people such as Jake, Barry, Farrah, Maxine and the bottle-wielder, Vicente. Maddox and Major O were far enough away from the melee to feel comfortable sitting back and observing. They saw a man, in the back right corner of the dive bar, filming the entire episode on his smart phone. Maddox guessed that the man was streaming it onto a social media feed.

And Maddox was right! The guy filming was an actual content-creator on digital media — a twenty-nine year old guy named Larry Hare who lived with his parents just outside of New Orleans. He had sixty-seven thousand followers on his digital media video streaming account.

He was live-streaming the fight right from his Endless Content Super 6G smart phone, with a big shit-eating grin on his face. He was receding, early! He was always filming just in case he stumbled into some great digital content! Then Maxine and Farrah gave him what he wanted.

Maddox and Major O weren't quite smiling, but they weren't quite frowning either. Both held their eyes open about thirty percent wider than usual. Maddox took another sip of his vodka and soda with a lime, his fifth of the night. The guys had also done a couple shots of whiskey and tequila. Maddox savored it then swallowed. In addition to all the drinks with Major O, Maddox also had two Bloody Marys at the airport in the morning and two more vodkas on the plane — so Maddox was drunk. Not hammered, but buzzing. That was the nature of recruiting, it seemed.

Maddox and Major O hadn't done a damn thing so neither felt like they would be attacked. They figured the fight would stay contained. Stay aware! The guy that brandished the bottle got swarmed by the two guys, whoever they were, that came in to help the bartenders. The makeshift bouncers did an excellent job of neutralizing the weaponized bottle without incurring any damage to their persons. Because Vicente brandished the weapon, everyone seemed to forget about the way the brawl started. The poor, little, squat, flat-faced guy with the bottle had found himself in the hornet's nest. Everyone hated him for escalating the brawl. Originally, the fight was a curiosity. No one's life was really in danger based on the fight between the two, immobile land whales. Vicente lost perspective, he lost control and took the fight to the next level.

Vicente really paid the price for doing that. The two makeshift bouncers had ended up beating Vicente's face in pretty good. They didn't want to, but Vicente kept brandishing the bottle and he wouldn't - or couldn't - calm himself down. He had a black eye and a bloody nose and his neck was radically misaligned. His neck was locked in a severe and painful-looking crink to the hard left. He tried to rock-crank, to jack-crank, his neck back to center alignment, to normal alignment, with his right hand by pulling on his forehead but that neck was locked in place.

That neck wasn't gonna move, not tonight. That guy was out of alignment and bent up! He limped out, bleeding from his face, staring to the left, and with a severely sprained or broken ankle. It was crazy because he wouldn't have even been involved in the fight if he didn't brandish the bottle. It was going to be a long road to recovery for Vicente.

"That guy's not kuhhhmff!" exclaimed Major O. Maddox felt like he might die laughing. Not so much at the injuries to Vicente, but at Major O's timing and his expressive face.

"He's not kuhhhmffortable! Muh bottle. Muh bottle, oh no what happened?" said Maddox while cracking up. Maddox was laughing so hard he could barely speak. Major O was laughing hysterically. His head bobbed up and down.

Without the fight, Maddox and Major O might have called it a night earlier. But after the fisticuffs broke out and were subsequently resolved, they were energized again. It was invigorating. They didn't have a hog in that fight — but it gave them an adrenaline rush. Soon enough, the drinks started flowing again. The live music started back up at the dive bar. The little band was rocking again. The bass guitar was pumping. Maddox and Major O were energized. The small dance floor started buzzing again. Women with bare backs and high heels went back over to the dance floor. All of the fighters had been removed. Booze was flowing again. The bartenders were mixing vodka drinks, three at a time! Asses were shaking again. The energy was back!

A blonde named Katarina approached Maddox and asked for a dance simply by staring at Maddox, looking him up and down, and then glancing over at the dance floor. Maddox quickly and subtly signaled to see if she had a friend for Major O to dance with. For that purpose, he used a quick hand signal from left to right with a clear message. Bring a girl for my friend and I'll happily dance with you. Out of nowhere, a slinky brunette appeared and approached. Her name was Celeste. Tight top, short skirt, high heels. A lot of attitude, too. Very pretty! When Maddox got up to dance with the blonde he strutted out to the dance floor, showing high energy. The brunette grabbed Major O's hand and led him out to the dance floor.

Major O was grooving on the way out. Strutting and bucking! Putting on a show! Maddox smiled as he thought back to the chant, "Hey Ho, Hey Ho you can't stop fuckin' Major O!" It was true!

Major O kicked his left leg forward three times like he was jitterbugging. Maddox laughed heartily. They were having a great time. Major O smiled knowingly. Then he put his right hand in the air with two fingers extended. With two more steps he was in the middle of the dance floor giving everyone what they wanted to see. And that, of course, was a modern version of the mashed potato! His feet moved in and out and he added some unique hand and arm grooves that people from the nineteen-fifties could never comprehend. He added technique that was previously undiscovered, never before seen! The women glanced at each other and kept their bodies moving. The band was playing a mix of blues and classic rock, with the current song a classic jam. The women shook their asses and kicked their heels. Katarina and Celeste were fun. They were magic!

"Brown Sugar, how come you taste so good?" the singer boomed.

They danced and danced. It was a great time, but then it was over. It ended suddenly, as Major O said goodbye to Celeste with a kiss on the cheek, walked over to Maddox and said "Yo Madd-man, I'm beat. I'm going to hit the sack."

"Okay brother I'll touch base with you tomorrow. Good times!"

"All good, all love! I'll talk to ya when I talk to ya," said Major O with a big shiny smile.

Maddox laughed to himself. This is how you do it! This is how you recruit! This is how a sports agent built relationships! Maddox was feeling really good about the night spent drinking, telling stories, recruiting — recruiting was the lifeblood of any successful sports agency. Maddox wanted to grow! He knew Obadiah Ballard was a great recruit for the agency. A sure superstar. A difference maker. Maddox and Major O both left the bar, with Major O turning left out of the front door and Maddox turning right. Maddox was heading back to his hotel.

Combining the momentum that Maddox had from McCartney's financing commitments to the TENACIOUS training facility, and his other recruits, numerous active deals, revenue growth — things seemed to be going well. But suddenly the thought of Pepe Soliz and the rape of April Tilney stormed back into his head. What was going to happen with all that? Would he lose all the commissions from Pepe Soliz? That would be millions of dollars! That negative thought precipitated another negative thought, starting a spiral.

Maddox then remembered how much the Platform Volleyball Tour was struggling and he worried about his trip the following day. What if none of the sponsors would commit to new deals for his clients because of the instability of the Platform Volleyball Tour? What if more Platform Volleyball sponsors bowed out and the entire Platform collapsed? Maddox knew that if that happened, many of his contracts would be flushed through the bankruptcy system. He would lose revenue. The Malone Agency would shrink, and he wanted growth. Maddox was leery, he just had a bad feeling about the Platform Volleyball tour. Platform Volleyball had been flushed into bankruptcy before, several years prior.

Maddox became apprehensive. Suddenly, the old New Orleans balconies hung over Maddox like clouds. There was a storm of dread and disappointment, degeneracy and dissatisfaction. Maddox blinked, breathed in, winced, breathed out, and shook his head slightly. He kept walking toward his hotel.

Maddox arrived back at his hotel, stripped his clothes off, and took a scalding hot shower. He climbed in bed, grabbing a book out of his work bag on the way. Reading, even for five minutes, helped him shut his mind down. He had to fly out early in the morning to get to the Platform Volleyball event. He had opened *Captain Blood* by Rafael Sabatini, a book that his mom had sent him a while back — but he only got a few lines into the book before he fell asleep. He just passed out! He was extremely fatigued from travel and the long day working, drinking and socializing. He slept soundly for almost six hours, then was awakened by the smart phone alarm that he had set in order to get ready for his travel to Los Angeles. A new day had arrived, and he needed to head out to the Platform before it collapsed!

Bedbug Infestation

❋❋

Carlton Duffer felt like he had been caught in a glue trap! When Carlton Duffer finally woke up, he looked around. "Oh fuck! Where am I?" he muttered. By way of background, Carlton Duffer is Lacy Stratton's husband. Lacy Stratton, of course, is the top Platform Volleyball client of the Malone Agency.

Platform Volleyball is a sport that was invented in the late nineteen-nineties. It is, essentially, an offshoot of beach volleyball. Beach volleyball is played on the sand directly on the beach. Platform Volleyball is played on an artificial beach created on top of an actual platform built out over the ocean, balancing on massive steel and cement columns. Sand is layered, carefully, onto the Platform for the events. The Platform was initially conceived of as a direct marketing ploy. The founder, Harry Oswald, set out to create a spectacular, televised series of events so that he could use the eyeballs that watched the sport to market his product. His product was Efficient-Pop. First, he made strainers for popcorn that had been popped — but still contained un-popped kernels. Harry recognized, before anybody else, that nobody likes it when there are un-popped kernels in an otherwise tasty batch of popcorn.

Those things cause misery!

Harry had solved that specific problem and had become a millionaire, many times over, from the sale of his popcorn strainers, which were manufactured by Efficient-Pop very cheaply in a remote region of China, a region that did not even have the benefits of modern sewer systems. His tax subsidies were pushed through Congress by a sneaky friend of Harry's who had won a seat in the House of Representatives by campaigning with lofty, but ultimately meaningless, patriotic speeches, causing the boomer burger-fats to vote for him by playing to an over-the-top rah-rah fascination with the military industrial complex. Rah, rah America! Amazingly, thanks to the tax subsidies from the same burger-fats that voted his friend into office, Harry Oswald actually made money on the manufacture of his strainers - even before he sold them! Mister Oswald kept pocketing his tax subsidies and then selling his strainers while also steering the company to be the market leader in pre-popped popcorn – they never, ever bagged an un-popped kernel. Once he was the market leader in strainers, all Harry had to do was expand his business by pushing his bagged and flavored Efficient-Pop on the Platform. That, right there, is how Harry Oswald became the world's first Popcorn Billionaire.

Everyone had to hand it to Harry Oswald, since the Platform created an incredible visual effect for television and for those watching the Platform Volleyball matches live. He had created a day out by the beach, actually out over the water, above the ocean, combined with some competition. There were sharks! Dolphins! Whales! Sea Otters! All of these wonderful creatures would swim around the Platform while the fans enjoyed the competition, drinking soda and eating Efficient-Pop.

The late Mister Oswald was such a stickler about the Platform. If a person played beach volleyball, even once, that person was ineligible to compete on the Platform. For that reason, many of the best beach volleyball players, such as Sinjin Smith, Karch Kiraly, Todd Rogers, Kerri Walsh, and Misty May, were never able to compete on the Platform. They weren't even allowed in the stands. Either you were on the Platform or you weren't!

Face it, Harry Oswald was an all-or-nothing kind of guy. About ten years ago, Harry Oswald, tragically, had committed suicide by hurling himself off of the Platform during a televised match. Before the suicide, he made one of the most anguished faces that had ever been seen. He yelled "Vegetable Oil Kills!" and then jumped right off the Platform, into the water. He didn't leave a note, so there was much speculation as to what he actually meant. On the one hand, it was a clear statement. On the other hand, there was vegetable seed oil everywhere – all the big food companies used cheap, unhealthy vegetable oils in their processed foods to keep their costs low and their profits high. The corporations didn't care if they made people fat and sick – they were focused on profits. So who knows what he really meant? Everyone was horrified, but of course life had to go on without Harry. Anyway, the Platform's current management was having a hard time matching Harry's magic touch. It seemed that no one wanted to watch the Platform Volleyball events, not anymore!

Lacy Stratton, Maddox's client, was scheduled to compete on the Platform that day. Unfortunately, though, at the moment, she was dealing with a huge distraction. Lacy couldn't find her husband, Carlton Duffer.

Carlton was missing!

Even though it was getting towards mid-morning, Carlton was still hammered from the night before. Drunk on cheap tequila and beer — and also high from hitting the Dragon and the Moose — Carlton was scared. He had totally lost track of the time. He hadn't even gone home yet. Instead, he was with a girl, and the girl wasn't Lacy Stratton. Lacy didn't know how to teach yoga!

Lacy was walking around looking for Carlton as if he were a lost dog. Her head swiveled left then right. Then left, then right.

Suddenly Lacy's phone rang. It was a caller from a private number. The caller didn't identify himself by name, but, rather, with a muffled and rushed voice informed Lacy that Carlton was in room one-oh-eight of the Beach Comber Motel. Lacy's eyes went wide.

In many ways, Carlton Duffer was similar to a bedbug. This similarity, though, wasn't exactly the same type of similarity as existed between Paul McCartney and a grasshopper. In Carlton's case, his similarity was less physical than McCartney's. Carlton's similarity to the bedbug was almost purely behavioral. The behavioral similarity was simply this: once Carlton had infested Lacy's life, some years before, he was very hard to get rid of, just like a bedbug.

Now, Lacy hadn't tried to get rid of Carlton herself — it was Lacy's family that wanted him gone. They simply didn't like him. They tried to run him off, to chase him out. To squish him. They hated Carlton Duffer! They schemed, in so many ways, to get rid of the Bedbug.

One time Lacy's uncle told him that he and a few of Lacy's other uncles were playing golf at Windy Forest Golf Club when they were really playing at Pointed Hills. The foursome had laughed the whole time they played and screened fifteen phone calls from Carlton when he was desperately trying to find the group. Another example, her family would take Lacy aside and point out his personal flaws and his lack of character. The family did everything short of trying actual violence or poison. But there was a significant problem. Bedbugs are incredibly robust. Once a Bedbug infestation sets in, it's really hard to root them out. The Bedbug, Carlton Duffer, like his little brothers and sisters, was a survivor.

But his survival, marriage-wise, was most certainly not guaranteed this time. Not at all. Carlton had to work his way out of this trap!

"Carlllll-tooooonnnnnn!" Lacy screamed as she burst in the room using a key that she had lifted off of a housekeeping cart. Her face was bright red.

Carlton Duffer just lay there with his bottom lip crooking out at a twenty-seven degree angle. He was caught. He couldn't move. After a minute, the Bedbug got dressed and Lacy walked him back to the car.

"How did you find me?" asked the Bedbug.

"Someone called me," said Lacy.

"Who?" asked Carlton Duffer.

"I don't know. Maybe someone from the Beach Comber. Why does it matter? Why would you do that to me?" she asked him, point blank. Her bottom lip quivered, even though it didn't crook, since she was about to cry. She tried to keep it locked in. She stared at his crooked lip, which she often mistook for a look of sophistication and thoughtfulness.

"Baby, I was drunk. I don't know what I was thinking," replied Carlton Duffer with an exaggerated grimace. His crooked bottom lip flared out quite a bit more than usual, the flare was about thirty-eight degrees. He then crooked it more for extra effect - extra sophistication — and now it hit forty-four degrees. He shook his head slowly, pretending he was in a sad scene in a movie.

"Do I not satisfy you? Is that woman better in bed than I am?" Lacy asked, pleading.

When Lacy had retrieved him out of the bed there had been a brunette, named Summer, approximately five-foot-six and one hundred twenty-three pounds, sprawled out naked in the hotel bed. Summer's face was looking very satisfied at the moment. Her ripened, split apricot had, from the look of things, been worked over in just the right way by Carlton Duffer. Clothing and bedding was strewn all over the room! Summer didn't even stir when Lacy walked in the room, she just lay there looking relaxed.

"Of course you satisfy me, I love you more than anything. I love you, I love you," Carlton said, making puppy dog eyes as he responded. He looked down, then up, softly. He was trying to push her buttons!

"Then why did you sleep with that yoga instructor? Why would you sleep with that bitch? Why?" Lacy asked. She was still pleading with him, begging to understand.

"I was drunk and I made a mistake. I just kept making mistakes. It was so wrong!" said Carlton. It was so right, said Carlton's face. It was so right!

Carlton continued, "I was drunk and I couldn't stop myself. I need to quit drinking. It wasn't me, it was the alcohol," Carlton said, desperate to find a way out of this trap.

"I can't believe it. I can't believe you did that," said Lacy with a tear streaming down her face. Then another. She was crying. She started crying even harder.

"Baby, I love you so much. I love you more than the sun and the moon. You are like the stars and the ocean. Like a dove. Like a whisper willow," he said, using the most sincere voice he could muster up for the occasion. His face looked like he was searching his mind for more random comparisons. His lip was crooked. But he didn't mention any more, apparently that was the kitchen sink and it would have to do!

"Awwww, thank you baby. Am I really like the stars?" Her eyes looked dreamy as she responded. It didn't even occur to her that she didn't know what a whisper willow was.

"I love you baby, I don't know why I did what I did. I want to be with you. I am going to stop drinking. I am going to stop hitting the Dragon and the Moose," said Carlton.

The survival instinct of the Bedbug was kicking in with full force. His face showed that he sensed an opening. He looked determined to burrow his way back in.

"How can I believe you?" Lacy asked. Carlton could probably tell, from past experience, that she was ready to take the bait, but she still needed to be sold.

"I'm going to go to rehab!" proclaimed the Bedbug.

Here was the hook! He made the announcement bravely, as if he was setting off on an extreme adventure. Carlton Duffer, a fucking idiot, had never read a single book. If he had, he might have realized that he fancied himself, at that moment, as quite similar to Kurtz in *Heart of Darkness*. Uncharted territory! Maybe there would be hot chicks in rehab? Maybe there would be personal massages? Suddenly, Carlton was looking forward to this whole rehab thing.

"You decided that on your own?" Lacy asked. "That's so responsible!"

"Yes, I need to get clean. I can't believe I did that. I can't believe I gave her the special D. Damn it," said the Bedbug. He was totally into his act!

"Wow, I can't believe you called it your special D. Also, you need to go get tested. I can't catch a sexually transmitted disease. That would be horrible. Word about that always gets around in this city. What would people say?" said Lacy.

"Baby, okay, I'll get tested," said Carlton, who, judging by the angle of his lip, had no real intention of getting tested for anything. His lip was a tell – a tell that he was thinking of how special his D was and replaying the night's action with Summer, and her apricot, in his mind.

"Where are you going to rehab?" asked Lacy.

"That place Alicia, uh, uh, I mean Oscar went. It's supposed to be really good. It's down the coast, you know. It really sucks because Coachella is coming up next weekend and I wanted to go. I really wanted to go to Coachella. The vibe at Coachella is so groovy."

"Okay, but that rehab place is expensive. It's super expensive."

"I know. I know it is."

"Do you have the money to pay for it?"

"Uhh, no, uhg, no, no," said the Bedbug, wriggling. "No, only if you help me. I can't ask my family, my mom is broke and I think she's using again, maybe even hooking. My brother has that adopted boy, you know, I forget the kid's name, oh yeah, umm, Carter. Ner, ner, ner! None of them have any money." Carlton laughed, with his unique style, as he finished speaking. "Ner, ner, ner."

Lacy winced, expressing displeasure with what she heard.

In addition to the adopted nephew, Carlton had at least one other rather strange familial relationship. That particular relationship demonstrated his early aptitude for getting himself out of sticky, nearly-impossible, situations — and therefore needs to be recounted here.

Before he left Providence, when he was in his early twenties, Carlton had impregnated a young girl, a freckled nineteen year old he called Barb. The Bedbug, of course, had no ability to support Barb and the child that was on the way. He had no job and all he did was hit the Dragon and the Moose all day.

The Bedbug tried to plan, day and night, for a way to wriggle out of this situation. He was panic-stricken! Would Barb agree to an abortion? Carlton couldn't be sure. But, one night, while he was at a family barbeque, a cookout featuring burnt mystery-meat and hot dogs imported from Mexico, fortune finally smiled down upon Carlton Duffer. Todd, Carlton's father, had divorced Carlton's mother many years before and was living unhappily with a wildebeest named Wanda who seemed to grow meaner and nastier by the hour. Carlton also just happened to notice that Todd had a bright twinkle in his eye when he looked at young Barb. Using a few strategically-offered shots of cheap tequila, and offering Todd three or four puffs off the Dragon, Carlton had managed to pawn Barb off on his own father.

Todd had given Barb the old jingle-jangle later that night. Twice! The next day, Todd evicted Wanda from his home. Todd and Barb were soon married. Todd assumed all responsibility for Carlton's offspring, Danny Duffer, who was born later that spring. It was a huge relief for Carlton — whose son Danny magically became his brother!

"Ner Ner Ner" he had laughed at the time. His face was so celebratory! His lip had gone crooked, more than a thirty-two degree bend this time.

As his conversation with Lacy concluded, Carlton continued to blame the alcohol — and the Dragon and the Moose — and left later that day to an expensive rehab facility. It was paid for by Lacy, of course. To get there, the Bedbug took a driving service to rehab — and he made sure it was a luxury ride, not the economy model.

Carlton immediately integrated himself into the rehabilitation and recovery program. He burrowed in, ready to enjoy the time. The rehabilitation environment was similar to the one that the Grasshopper, Paul McCartney, participated in. For Carlton, though, there was no chaotic event similar to those precipitated by John Roberto, Fred Pankston and Paul McCartney. No gas release, no finger pistol, no shriek, no scuffle. There was also no flamboyant owner watching over Carlton's rehabilitation facility, which was owned by a faceless multi-national corporation based out of Belgium.

All the same, people gathered together chasing something, often looking for a fresh start. They hoped that the Belgian-owned facility was exactly what they needed. Some of them genuinely wanted to get off the shit they were on before it killed them.

When it was his time to speak, he cleared his throat.

"Ahem. Ahem." The Bedbug stood up. Patients were expected to speak for roughly three minutes, but Duffer wasn't feeling that today.

Three minutes was too fucking long. He wasn't Abraham Lincoln. He was Carlton Duffer, God-damn it, and he would do exactly what the fuck he wanted to do.

"It takes a strong person to admit that he is weak," said the Bedbug with his signature twang. "I am weak. I am such a weak man."

Carlton paused and smiled, involuntarily and mostly on the right side of his mouth, bottom lip crooking comfortably and a bit provocatively.

"But now, guess what? Now I'm strong because I admitted it. See how that works? Ner ner ner," he said as his lip crooked out sharply.

He paused, and he looked so satisfied with his speech.

"So, I drank thirteen beers and three margaritas the other day, plus seven and a half shots of chilled Tequila and ended up in bed with my yoga instructor, Summer. I am married but not to Summer. Sometimes, I realize that I need to learn more from myself. There is so much that I can teach myself! I have to realize that I am the smartest person that I know. The smartest! I can't function in solitude. I need a woman in my life but that woman needs – needs – to be my wife. I think about that all the time. I am weak but I can be strong. I am my own man and I am not living off my wife. I'm also good on the Platform. You want to get on the Platform with me? I don't think so. Ner. Ner. Ner! Thank you. Ner, ner."

Carlton crooked his lower lip, as usual, blinked his eyes deeply, twice, and sat back down. When he sat, he realized that he had crooked his lip a little bit more than the normal twenty-seven degrees, and, as if to underline a point, he aggressively crooked it out some more. On purpose! He let out a long, slow breath and then followed that up by licking his lips a few times, re-crooking the bottom lip, and finally folding his arms across his chest and leaning back. He breathed out, dramatically. Whooooooosh.

One minute, Carlton was in Los Angeles and the next minute he was gone. Just like the Danny Duffer derby, Carlton knew that it was a great idea to head to rehab. It might have been the only way he could convince Lacy to keep him around. Carlton's survival instinct was strong! A few weeks? For a Bedbug? That's nothing! Bedbugs can survive for years, in the harshest conditions. Carlton knew he would make it home, he knew he would feed again!

ii

When Maddox landed in Los Angeles, he took a driving service to Manhattan Beach. He ran into Lacy's dad, Tobias P. Stratton, a retired, Italian-born, commercial fisherman living in South Florida, as they were both grabbing a coffee. Tobias told Maddox that Carlton had been shipped off to rehab.

After they spoke about rehab for a minute or two, Tobias pulled Maddox close. He leaned in.

"Hey Maddox, don't say that I said anything, but Carlton is trying to get Lacy to make him her agent. Replacing you."

Maddox laughed, just once.

"Wait, what?"

"Yeah, she told me. Carlton wants to be Lacy's agent. I just have so much respect for you that I wanted to let you know."

"Okay, thanks Tobias."

Maddox immediately put that conversation out of his mind. Carlton Duffer was a fucking idiot. Maddox couldn't get bogged down with Carlton's bullshit, he had to focus on the soda endorsement contract extension he was negotiating for Lacy. The current contract had involved a protracted discussion, a painful process, taking several months. Maddox had held out for more cash in the deal — after a hard fought negotiation, he got the extra money. It was a great contract, a huge win for Maddox and the Malone Agency. It was the first advertising campaign ever negotiated in the specific product category at issue — soda for not only a mother but also for her babies. Maddox had pulled off a high-paying endorsement for Lacy with XtraShoog Soda, a soda company that made a product, on purpose, with double the sugar of most of its competitors. It paid really well and it was the first advertising campaign in the entire soda category that featured a mother and her young children. In the advertisement, they all just stared out into the distance while standing on the Platform, staring at the ocean, looking happy, guzzling XtraShoog!

Maddox was personally skeptical of the product itself — Maddox had wondered, for a minute or two, if doubling the sugar was a health hazard — but Maddox had the magic touch on these deals! Money talks — it was as simple as that — so he put the deal together and got it done. But the original contract expired in a couple months. And the soda company was ducking! Maddox couldn't get them on the phone. He wanted the money from that extension! But, in the back of his mind, Maddox knew that if the Platform collapsed into bankruptcy, the soda deal, even an extension, would go away.

Maddox had been working hard, scrapping, and pulling off deals for the underdog. Like Lacy, who at five-foot-seven was one of the shortest players on the Platform. Lacy made up for her height with a wiry, strong, springy build and incredible quickness and toughness. She was a great Platform Volleyball player --- one of the best ever.

Lacy was cute, especially when she was younger. Lacy was a mix of Italian and Korean. She had mostly European features with a few Asian traits. For example, she had the plump lips of a Korean chaperon. She was pretty! And that, in the past, really helped Maddox with sponsors. Lately, sponsors weren't returning calls relating regarding Lacy. Maddox feared that the sponsors were starting to regard Lacy as old news and what's more, he feared they knew that the Platform might collapse.

He wished Lacy played a more popular sport. It was getting harder and harder to get the big multi-national corporations to do deals in third-tier sports like Platform Volleyball. The big corporations wanted more eyeballs on their product than Platform Volleyball could currently provide! In the past, before the ratings declined, Maddox had done major marketing deals with the companies that made soda, computers, phones, search engines, candy, sunscreen, clothing, sandals, backpacks, and athletic supplies, others— Maddox pulled off deals with them all. He was pulling off deals that nobody else could do! But he fretted about the downtrend. It was becoming impossible to ignore.

He had an interview scheduled with a reporter from the Los Angeles Journal named Peter. Maddox walked in right on time.

"Hey Maddox," Peter said when he saw Maddox first.

"Peter, how are ya?" said Maddox with a grin and a handshake.

"Good, it's just another day in paradise."

"Fantastic. That's what's up."

"I know you are pressed for time. I wanted to sit down with you and get a handle on some of the sponsorship deals you have done for Lacy. You broke new ground, man, congratulations. I really never thought I would see these kinds of deals happen. Not on the Platform, with Volleyball at least. I know there's a rough patch now, though, with sponsors leaving the Platform. How is that going to affect you and Lacy?"

"Thanks. Yeah, it's been a fun ride. As to the question, I'm not avoiding your question, I just really don't know. Obviously anytime a major sponsor leaves, the Platform crumbles just a little bit."

"What is causing this wave of sponsor defections?" asked Peter.

"It's really simple, Peter. Not enough people are watching the Platform Volleyball events. It doesn't move the needle for a true megacorporation, a powerhouse brand. It's not worth their time to advertise. They can't push enough product, not lately."

"That's so sad. On a better note, what's up with Lacy's personal sponsorship situation? I see that two logos are on her visor, the soda logo is on her suit. The cable TV service also has a small logo on her suit as well."

"We're kind of maxed out in that regard, so we have to be a little creative. I got some temporary tattoos on her computer deal and her potato chip deal — so that we could increase the space available."

"Wow, has anyone done that before?"

"Ha-ha, I have no idea. I never watched Platform Volleyball

before I started working with Lacy. Someone would have to look that up," said Maddox. Maddox immediately regretted the comment because he thought it was overly honest. He should have just said no.

"Got it. Do you think you guys have struggled lately with Platform Volleyball largely being viewed as a niche sport with limited viewership? Do you think the Platform will survive another year?"

"I wouldn't say we have struggled overall. We have done some great things. We really have to fight hard against that perception, though. Sometimes the toughest thing we have to do is get our foot in the door and get people to understand that the athletes on the Platform are good athletes, not bad basketball players. They are not tall people who suck at hoop. They are not wiry people who aren't good at tennis. Because of Lacy's winning track record, I've been able to leverage my relationships with the big brands and get some great deals done."

"I really appreciate you taking me through this, Maddox. Anything else you can add?"

"I'm just trying to help the Platform. We need to pull together to get through this economic downturn. We need to find a way to get more eyeballs on the Platform. That being said, the work never ends, as the financial difficulties on the Platform never seem to go away."

"Cool, Maddox. I got it. What do you have on tap for the rest of the day?"

"Watching some Platform Volleyball, and I'm going to meet up with some sponsors and then I fly up to Sunny Grove tonight."

"Got it. It was great to catch up. Thanks for taking Platform Volleyball to prominence, man. I love this game! It never would have happened without you blazing the trail. Even if it never gets back to where it was, it's been a fun ride," said Peter.

"You're too kind and you flatter me. And I don't know if we ever really pulled off prominence, but we definitely tried. Hell, we're still trying. Anyway, thanks. Text me if you need anything else," replied Maddox.

"Sounds good, I appreciate it."

With the interview complete, Maddox walked back to his hotel. He had a bit of time to kill before the tournament resumed and decided that rather than answer e-mails or make phone calls, he would take a mental break and read a book. When he arrived back at the hotel, he pulled Roberto Bolaño's *2666* out of his travel bag. He sat down on the hotel sofa and picked up where he left off. Maddox was at the part where Bolaño, a gifted writer, just kept describing murder after murder. It was chilling. Maddox had to force himself to continue reading. At one point, though, when one of the murder victims was strangled after being vaginally and anally raped, Maddox had to put the book down because the passage made him think of Pepe Soliz. It seemed as if he could not get away from thinking about Pepe Soliz for more than a couple hours at a time. Maddox couldn't help but think of the physical and mental condition in which Pepe left April. He also couldn't help but think about the large commissions Pepe paid to him. And he didn't want to think about any of that stuff, not right now! He had to get out to the Platform and make some deals. He wanted to grow his revenue.

Instead of opening the book back up, Maddox placed it on the table and walked out of the hotel, heading north towards the Platform. After walking for thirty minutes, he took a little water taxi out to the event for five bucks. Maddox had to admit that it was beautiful out on the Platform in the middle of the Pacific. Gold-colored sky, with a white streak of clouds right down the center. The heavy Platform support columns were so impressive, so imposing. The over-sized bag of Efficient-Pop sat on the horizon, promoting itself.

Maddox looked around. Wow, he thought, there were hardly any fans on the Platform. That's not good. That's bad! He looked in the sponsor tent and it was empty with the exception of a marketing representative from Efficient-Pop. He was the only guy in the entire tent, and he was just sitting there in his two-tone, white and yellow, Efficient-Pop shirt with a dour expression on his face. Damn-it, those guys had a free lifetime sponsorship on the Platform. They were grandfathered in by Harry Oswald! Maddox's heart sank. Efficient-Pop would never make a sponsorship deal with Maddox Malone. And there was no-one else to talk to in the sponsor tent.

Maddox's face reflected perfectly his feeling of gloom and doom. Maddox grabbed a bag of Efficient-Pop and opened it up. He stuffed a handful of the popcorn in his mouth. No Kernels! But, wait a second, thought Maddox, the popcorn tasted awful. It was swimming in cheap-tasting vegetable oil! Maddox scooped the Efficient-Pop out of his mouth with his right index finger, tossing it on the sand. He looked at the bag. He didn't know that Efficient-Pop was popped, strained and seasoned half way around the world. He threw the rest of the bag away. He walked to his right and sat down in one of the empty seats.

Maddox Malone just sat there on the Platform, looking out into the ocean. He was forlorn! He didn't even watch the Platform matches. The attendance was a disaster. How was he going to make money on Platform Volleyball endorsements and commercials if no one cared about Platform Volleyball? He just looked at the ocean.

At least the ocean was still full of beauty and wonder.

No Reverse

❀❀

Thhhh-waaaaack, thhhh-waaaaack, thhhh-waaaaack. The wheels on the little four cylinder green coupe were pumping hard as Kalli and Darcy made their way north on the four-oh-five from Long Beach towards Hollywood. Neither of them knew what part of the car made the thwaaaack sound and neither of them had time to worry about it. Kalli was driving Darcy's car, even though she didn't have a driver's license and was only fifteen years old. This was strategic. Darcy was trying to teach Kalli to drive so she could transport herself to auditions independently of Darcy sometimes. Cars were threading through traffic, buzzing in and out of the green coupe's lane. The green coupe was beat up. Darcy had driven it heavily when raising her sister's kids, Barret and Maryanne. Years before, Darcy's sister had become hopelessly addicted to crack cocaine and the kids had nowhere else to go. The crack epidemic was real and Darcy's sister had been a user and in a sense a victim. A victim of accessibility and a society that was so stacked against her that she had said why not? And once she was hooked, it was basically over. Darcy, a lady with a big heart, took her sister's kids in and gave it her all. She raised, great, successful kids when it was all said and done.

Kalli and Darcy sang along:

> Can you pay my bills
> Can you pay my telephone bills
> Can you pay my automo-bills

Darcy was belting it out. As a matter of fact, so was Kalli. Darcy had been a backup singer in Los Angeles and Las Vegas for a number of years. Originally from Mississippi, Darcy had the same exact birthday as Kalli in June. She had a big voice. She was a pretty woman, around five-foot-nine. Slender but feminine. She was part African and part Japanese and she always lightened her straight hair. She was a fun loving person with a big smile. Their music selection, while annoying to most people, was normal for these two. They loved that shit!

A few months before this outing, Kalli finished in the top five in the Miss Teen California pageant as the reigning Miss Teen Sunny Grove. She was happy that she didn't win the pageant because she thought it was a boring dog and pony show. She hated standing there in different outfits answering ridiculous questions in the way that the panel wants to hear. She thought the way the mothers and daughters treated each other was ridiculous. She thought the other contestants were rude bitches (although she didn't think it using that specific word). One girl had even cut the straps on Kalli's dress in an act of sabotage — while her mother watched. Kalli had still won that competition. Too bad her new dress didn't make her ugly!

At the time, a few months ago, Kalli's parents, Patty and Raymond, had been loading up their silver Cadillac Coup Deville for the long drive back to Petaluma. They hesitated, then looked over at Kalli, who was standing nearby with her photographer friend, Matty.

"Mom, I'm gonna go with Matty to Hollywood. I'm gonna do modeling and acting full time. I'll catch up with you later." Kalli had a bag of clothes and ninety-seven bucks in her pocket. She went on to get emancipated and drop out of high school a couple weeks later, when she was preparing to read for a feature film audition.

Her parents, despite the gravity of the comment from a fifteen year old, took it in stride. There was some stress, to be sure. But there was no gnashing of teeth. They knew she was a beautiful, vibrant girl and they thought that her best opportunity may have, in fact, been to do what she was deciding to do. To go for it in Hollywood. Who knows? Had their path been perfect?

"Okay, honey," said her mom. There was a look of concern but her parents weren't completely opposed to it. Kalli was five-foot-eleven inches tall and striking. Swedish and Irish. She had a beautiful, friendly smile. She was a bit mischievous, though. She was impulsive. Every day, her plans changed. She would be about to do something and then she would just go and do something else. Now, she was fifteen and she was headed to Los Angeles for modeling and acting.

"I'll talk to you soon. Love you," Kalli said as they wrapped up their conversation and started to go their separate ways.

"Love you."

Kalli jumped into Matty's car, a faded red shit-tier sedan that she thought was a five series but may have been a three series. It was beat up. They dropped off a little Mexican gay dude that Matty had met the night before after the beauty pageant at a gay bar in Fresno. They had nicknamed the little Mexican Border Patrol. The little gay Mexican didn't speak a word of English, but Matty, who was also gay, thought he was cute. Border Patrol had slept on the floor in Patty and Raymond's hotel. Kalli thought the whole thing was goofy and hilarious.

When Kalli was getting into the car, she was quite a sight. In fact, she looked like something from another world. So beautiful! She was wearing denim overall shorts with a yellow tank top on underneath. She had no jewelry on. She didn't need it. She was a sight to behold. She didn't walk with a model walk, not now. She was being herself, a young, athletic girl that grew up riding horses in Northern California, north of Sunny Grove. She could put her nose up and walk like a swivel-hipped tall model when that was required. Right now, though, she was having fun. Her life was right out in front of her, like an open road. She wanted to press the gas and drive. She was ready to go! Matty, wearing a black tank top and running pants over flip flops, trim and little, hopped into the driver's seat of the red sedan. He sped off, bringing Kalli safely to Los Angeles.

Returning to present time and the ride with Darcy, there were a stream of vehicles racing beside and ahead of Kalli. They were still singing, and Kalli had to admit that Darcy looked just a little nervous riding along with the young aspiring model. The girl was impulsive and also was distracted by things like the car radio. One minute she might be driving along and the next minute singing and dancing in her chair. It seemed that Kalli wasn't always concentrating on the road when she was singing along with the radio.

On the side of the four-oh-five, past Inglewood, Kalli and Darcy saw a Mercedes sedan smashed up against a retaining wall. Cops and ambulances were everywhere. The traffic hadn't completely stopped yet, so the rubber-neckers hadn't taken over. Traffic was still moving. The Mercedes was smashed, and whoever was in it was probably dead or otherwise close to it. Kalli and Darcy rolled on, towards Hollywood.

The green coupe's speakers were continuing to pump out music for Kalli and Darcy. The little car was buzzing along. Kalli was pressing the gas, trying to get to Hollywood on time. Thhhh-wackkk. Thhhh-wackkk. Thhhh-wackkk. The green coupe sounded bad but it was still moving along. Darcy was juggling her phone. She was lining up auditions for Kalli while making little comments to correct and monitor the inconsistent driving.

They were nearing Santa Monica Boulevard, where they would need to cut over to Hollywood. They passed a truck that had blown a tire. Kalli wondered for a second if the noise she kept hearing was the tire on the green coupe. If not the tire, a belt? She put the thought out of her head. They kept moving. Brake lights were everywhere as traffic ebbed and flowed. Kalli hit the gas, though. She hated hitting the brakes.

"You know something, Kalli?" asked Darcy. "You did a great job in that shoe advertisement audition. You were fantastic."

"Thank you Darcy," said Kalli, wondering a bit what Darcy's angle was for giving her complements on her recent shoots. Darcy chattered on. Darcy had, about two years before, given up her career as a backup singer to become a manager for models and actors. She represented mostly ethnic kids, but had met Kalli through Matty. So, she represented ethnic kids plus a tall pretty blonde looking for work with big brands.

"If you keep doing what you're doing, you're going to be a big star," said Darcy.

Maddox told players the same thing all the time. Darcy meant it, as Maddox did almost all of the time.

Kalli appreciated the pep talk. It helped, because sometimes she was scared and worried about work and money. Kalli hit the accelerator and moved to the right. She exited on Santa Monica Boulevard. They were heading to an audition. An audition for yet another modeling contract. This one for a big clothing company. She had to slow down. She veered to the East, heading to Hollywood. The world stretched out in front of her! Hollywood, no less ambitious than old Paris. Old Rome. Old London. The irresistible destination for all those with the looks, talent and moxie to try to make it on the silver screen. Ah, entertainment! Kalli was determined to live among the victors and she knew she would be successful. Never-mind the fact that she lived in the living room of her backup-singer-manager's house in the ghetto of Long Beach. She had no money, but she had her head-shots and she had her dreams.

She was not discouraged to be at the wheel of a five hundred dollar green coupe trying to get a contract worth maybe ten grand. She took one hand off the wheel, a brazen act for a fifteen year old.

"There it is, babe!" said Darcy. "How could you not find that place?"

Kalli looked to the right. She ignored the question with a little smile. She kept pressing the gas. They were barreling through Beverly Hills. Darcy was pointing out that particular hotel because Kalli had been there a week before, modeling for a well-known shoe company. Kalli had been lost, arrived late, and had a disastrous day. She kneed her dresser in the head, not on purpose, but while trying to give him a better angle to put clothing on her naked body. He absorbed the knee to his face without complaining out loud, but Kalli could tell he wasn't happy. She looked great, but the shoe company never called her back.

Kalli felt uneasy. She had been so stressed for the shoe ad event. Arriving late, because she had gotten lost, then having a terrible experience across the board. An uneasiness was seeping into Kalli's mind again. Heading up Santa Monica Boulevard for the clothing company audition, she didn't want a repeat of the shoe ad event. She didn't want to be late and stressed. It was enough for a young girl to have to look pretty and bubbly, she couldn't handle the additional pressure. She was having some anxiety, although it was limited at this point.

She was feeling okay, because she knew the area and was comfortable navigating. Darcy was on her phone, trying to secure additional opportunities for Kalli and also for a little boy with a sugar cereal company. Kalli was heading northeast on Santa Monica Boulevard, as the audition was in Hollywood Heights. She was feeling good about getting to the right place, on time and with no incidents, until she suddenly remembered one thing. The green coupe could not reverse.

"You doing okay, Kalli?" said Darcy. "You look tense."

"Yeah, I'm good."

"You stressed about the audition?"

"Not at all. I wanna park somewhere where we don't have to reverse to get out. It's too embarrassing to put it in neutral and push."

Darcy didn't say anything back. Darcy usually wouldn't take the green coupe to an audition, but with Kalli not having a car, she didn't have a choice.

Kalli glanced to her right at Darcy.

Darcy was looking straight ahead, grimly.

Off to the right was a billboard with a girl in an ad for a line of swimwear. Kalli checked it out — the girl looked great. Kalli got distracted and swerved to the left.

"Kalli!"

"Sorry."

The scenery in West Hollywood was like any other day. Crowds of locals and visitors, rolling around doing stuff. They're gasping for breath. They're soaking it in. They are loaded up with tourist gear. Tee-shirts. Shot glasses. Fridge magnets. Knick knacks. Consuming everything they can! Kalli headed northeast some more. Then she turned left on Highland to get to the audition. For a second she couldn't tell which street she wanted but it came back to her quickly. The audition was right by a big hotel that she had been to for an audition before. She knew she needed to head north. Even at fifteen, she knew that.

Even though she was not close to needing to park yet, Kalli started to get nervous. Here she was, a model, and if she parked in the wrong spot, they would have to put the green coupe in neutral and push it out to get going again.

"What's wrong?" asked Darcy. "You're gripping the wheel tight and your face is flushed. What's wrong, girl?"

"I'm just thinking about parking. If we can't find a spot where we can pull straight out then we have to push it out and everyone will be looking at us like what the fuck?"

Kalli turned right onto Yucca, which was adjacent to where she needed to be. As she turned, her attention was grabbed by a woman wearing a tank top and some tight denim shorts. She staggered off the sidewalk and looked like she might collapse. There were two men close by in baggy jeans and football jerseys. They were laughing at the woman. Kalli didn't like the scene. She thought about stopping to help the woman, but she knew if she was late to the clothing company audition it would be a disaster. She drove on. She sped up through the Hollywood jungle. She was approaching the moment of truth. Could she get a parking spot by the audition that let her drive straight out without having to push the car backwards in front of everyone?

"Well, you think we're gonna be able to park okay?" Kalli asked Darcy with a pretty little smile. She still looked nervous!

There were cars parked all along the street. The Los Angeles sun shone down brightly. The closer they came to the location of the audition, the more people they saw out on the street. In cars, on sidewalks, milling around. There it was up ahead, the space for the audition. Kalli kept rolling forward. She needed to find a parking spot that didn't require reverse. She eased by a few standard spots. No chance they could use those without the reverse gear being operational. She breathed out. Darcy was absorbed in her phone.

Kalli thought she saw a spot to the left where she could pull forward out of it after the audition. She'd take it! To the left! Oh shit, that one wouldn't work. To the right, there was one! Oh no. That wasn't one either! She kept rolling. She reached the next intersection. Then she started through.

"Where are you going, Kalli?" asked Darcy, looking up from her phone.

"I'm still looking for a parking spot that will work for us. I don't want to push the car out after the audition."

"You're right about that, I would die from embarrassment."

Up ahead the sun-kissed glow of the Hollywood streets beckoned. Bright. Glorious. Wait a second. Up there, a spot? The light was green. Kalli didn't know what to do. Someone was honking a horn behind her in a blue luxury car. Kalli looked in a rear-view and it was a fifty-something year old lady who obviously had a ton of plastic surgery. The lady looked so upset! She was shaking her fist at Kalli and screaming obscenity. All because Kalli hesitated momentarily? Darcy also looked back and had to laugh.

"Wow, she's mad!"

"She mad, she mad!"

Kalli and Darcy laughed at the weird lady. Kalli pressed the gas through the intersection. "What is that?" she said, urgently. She thought she saw an animal in the road.

"It's a bag, probably a bag of clothes or something. Don't stress," said Darcy.

Kalli lurched the car forward. At this point she was full of anxiety. She was fifteen, driving in Hollywood with no license -- and no reverse gear. She veered the green coupe to the right. She was breathing in big gulps. Her chest was heaving in and out. She had pressed the gas a little too hard, and the back of the green coupe fishtailed. Kalli fought the urge to panic. She pressed the gas again and tried to even out the back tires. Neeeeer! Vroooom!

The green coupe straightened out, as Kalli caught the left turn to circle back around to the audition. She was clinging to the wheel. Pressing the gas. Barreling ahead.

"You okay?" said Darcy.

"Sort of. I have of anxiety. The parking situation, you know."

"Okay, just breathe. Okay, we're coming back around to the audition. Slow down now, girl."

"Okay."

Kalli's heart was racing. In her side pocket she had six pages of sides that she had memorized for the audition. Now, she was worried that she would catch a case of can't-remember-shit disease because of the driving and parking fiasco. They looped back around and now they were directly in front of the audition site.

"There it is, Kalli! You see that! That's the spot! We can pull straight ahead and we won't have to push our way out." It was like they found the lost Arc of the Covenant.

"Yeah. I got it. We got it."

Kalli was desperate to park. She pulled into the spot with the straight ahead pull out access. They made it! Kalli threw it in park and climbed out of the green coupe. She was wearing a tight red v-neck tee-shirt, some black cigarette pants and some casual low cut converse tennis shoes. She had a bracelet on her wrist. Her blond hair glistened in the sun. She was flushed from the stress associated with finding an unrestricted parking spot. She was good natured, though, so she laughed it off and tried to forget about it. In her hand, she clutched the six pages of sides that she had memorized the day before. Did she still remember them? She hoped so.

She strode into the audition with Darcy at her side. Several people gasped audibly when they saw her. She was a beautiful girl, tall, slender but not weak and emaciated. Her weight was only down a bit because she was struggling to consistently find money for food. She had successfully gotten modeling contracts with a number of companies but money was always touch and go. Even with the contracts there never seemed to be enough money. In fact, she was sleeping in Darcy's living room a lot of the time. Darcy's living room was also Darcy's office. So Kalli was up at the crack of dawn getting ready for auditions or helping Darcy to deliver her headshots around Los Angeles.

As she walked into the clothing shoot audition, she saw the typical setup. The mass of young girls vying for the same modeling job. The workers herding people in the right direction. The camera folks taking test shots for the company. Kalli was breathing heavily as she entered the room. The parking situation was stressful. She took a breath, though, and composed herself. There was a panel of six people in the room. One of them had a camera, and it was immediately pointed at Kalli. She had a counterpart, a feminine man named Frances, reading the sides with her. The casting director was set back, observing everything. It was fast! Five minutes later, she was finished. It was a wrap. Now, all that was left to do for this particular audition was to see if there would be a callback. The casting director would either call Darcy to look at Kalli again — or she wouldn't. Either way, life would go on.

After the audition, Kalli and Darcy headed to Miyagi's on the Sunset Strip. It was a spot where people could get terrible sushi on the ground floor and head up to the second floor for celebrity karaoke and cocktails. Kalli walked in, with the glow of the Sunset Strip hitting her back as she walked in the front door. Darcy walked behind Kalli. They skipped the bad sushi and headed straight upstairs for cocktails and Karoake. Kalli was fifteen, but Miyagi's didn't card the young girl and she was soon sipping on an apple-tini. Darcy always wanted to limit her to one or two, and this worked, at least once in a while.

A woman named Billie was singing some old school Janis Joplin, and was doing a good job. She had high energy and knew the song well so she was good to listen to. Kalli and Darcy both sang along.

> Freedom's just another word for nothin' left to lose
> Nothin', don't mean nothin' hon' if it ain't free

As the woman finished singing there was a bit of a hush and a gasp that overtook the crowded bar. Whitney and Jamie had walked into the bar. It was as if the needle scratched and the music stopped, for a second. There was a good bit of chatter for ten seconds or so and then everything was back to normal. Whitney was hanging out in the corner and Jamie had brought a little handheld video camera and was talking to people and filming the conversations. He was a ham.

After the small disruption from that celebrity entrance, the party regained its focus. There was a buzz in the crowd as Whitney was handed the microphone. The music started to play and people realized she was going to sing one of her own songs! The crowd was loving it!

Whitney really hit her groove on the second verse, belting it out:

> Oh, I wanna dance with somebody
> I wanna feel the heat with somebody

There was cheering, and even some squealing and shrieking while Whitney went through the song. The crowd gave her some warm applause as the song finished. Two men in silk suits ordered a round of vodka shots for the entire bar. Cocktail servers started pumping out shots ten at a time and they flowed throughout the room.

As Kalli and Darcy walked through the room, they heard a very drunk patron say, "Whoa! Come on in, you never know what you gonna get at da famous Miyagi's. Guarantee one hunnerd percent entertainment. Drinks flowing like Niagara Falls. You might find Whitney Houston singin' one of her own songs. Nobody never seen a spot quite like this. It's fucking Miyagi's like the Karate Kid except no Mistah. That's what I'm talkin' about!"

They both smiled and kept it moving.

Kalli was on her second apple-tini, but also drank one of the shots from the mystery men in the silk suits. She buzzed with energy and a bit of tipsiness. She was too young for this lifestyle, in many ways, but she was enjoying it tonight. She saw Jamie and his handheld camera. He was walking around in the crowd, talking with people.

"Hey girl how you doin'," he said as he walked up to Kalli. "Speak into the camera would you?"

"I'm at Miyagi's on the Sunset Strip. What could be better than that?" Kalli said with a smile. With her heels on, she was about six-foot-two, and as she answered Jamie, she looked down at him. He was struck by how pretty she was. He kept walking, though, like an old man should.

Kalli had a soulful worldview. She wore her heart on her sleeve. She always showed her feelings. She expressed herself brightly. She had no formal education, but she was smart and she was perceptive. She had dropped out of high school at a very young age to pursue success in modeling and acting — although singing was what she really loved. She was going to go wherever the road took her, because, let's face it, she was floating with the tide. She had no idea what would happen the next day, the next week. Her plans always changed! She had to adapt! She was impulsive - she recognized no limits! She had gone to Hollywood with a makeshift support system. She had Matty, Darcy and some other agencies helping her with opportunities, but she was relying on her looks and personality more than having a solid plan. Truthfully, she was winging it at fifteen! Dropped off on Hollywood Boulevard, with no parental supervision. Emancipated. She finished the night by singing a karaoke song herself.

> Worry
> Why do I let myself worry?
> Wondering
> What in the world did I do?

She had a nice voice, with depth and power. She had no formal training as a singer but she wasn't scared when she sang. She just went for it. She loved Patsy Cline!

When it was time to go, she and Darcy got into the green coupe again. They had parked in a space on the Sunset Strip parallel to the sidewalk, so they could pull straight out without backing up. This meant that they were practically home free! Darcy was driving, despite her poor night vision, because Kalli had a couple of cocktails as well as a couple shots of vodka. They barreled down the four-oh-five back towards Long Beach. Thhhh-wacck. Thhhh-waack. Thhh-waaaccckk. That sound again! They made it home safely.

The next day would be more of the same. Heading to an audition, delivering headshots and probably ending the night at a bar again. Kalli had made her decision to go to Hollywood and there was no turning back. At times, she would question herself. At times she was scared and lonely. At times she loved it in Hollywood! She was fiery and could stand up for herself, but was still young and inexperienced. Even scared. At times she would miss seeing her parents on a daily basis. Same for friends and other family members. But she never really questioned her choice to go for it in Hollywood. Others, some of her friends, couldn't believe it. They couldn't believe she could take that kind of risk without a safety net, without more support while she was trying to establish herself. She didn't care about all that. She thought that she had the natural tools to make it. And the energy. Looks, personality, toughness and energy. And besides, she had no reverse!

Fuck Jerry Maguire

❋❋

After leaving the Platform Volleyball event in frustration, Maddox Malone did end up staying the night in Los Angeles, at his hotel on the ocean. A surprisingly pleasant group of seagulls chirped, wailed and cawed outside. He had been too tired to take the late flight back. Instead, he got up early, at four thirty a.m. to hit the airport for the first flight out so he could head up north to Sunny Grove. Maddox was happy to be off the Platform — what an embarrassing sponsor turnout. What a waste of time! And that Efficient-Pop popcorn tasted horrible!

As Maddox got his rental car, Maddox thought about Pepe Soliz. But this was different. This time, Maddox was thinking about Pepe as a baseball player, not as a rapist. Maddox was thinking about Pepe's new contract. It was going to be a huge commission! Pepe Soliz, Maddox figured, had something rare in the technique-oriented, specialized world of upper-echelon baseball players - he had more mojo than precise skill. Pepe Soliz was one of those guys, rare in the sport of baseball, who could swing at bad pitches and still be successful. Most guys with no plate discipline could not hang around the majors at all. Pitchers would toy with those guys. But Soliz was different, partially because he had such a tank-like body and such aggressive hands that he could still clobber pitches outside of the strike zone. That was an anomaly. That was amazing!

His Poobah physique attracted such attention! In fact, during a game the prior season in Sunny Grove, Pepe's uniform belt broke under the stress of trying to hold his flowing belly fat inside his baseball pants. The belt had snapped right in two. All the fans thought it was so funny! The Big Boys' social media feeds had exploded. How can his belt break? How can his belly be that big? The Poobah! We love the Poobah! On the day that the belt broke, the relatively small strap of material simply had no chance to contain the momentum generated by a tidal wave of belly fat. The belly fat flowed from left to right as it followed the torque from his wide hips turning aggressively during his swing. The belt snapped like a twig under a bear's paw. It snapped like the neck of a cat being prepared for Vietnamese cuisine. It snapped like the neck of a chicken sacrificed in Mali in a ritual designed to give the answer to a specific question. If the chicken fell to the right after its neck was snapped, the answer to the question was yes. If it fell to the left, the answer was no. In Soliz's case, the question was, is his belly too big for his uniform? And the belt, well, it snapped to the right.

The Poobah didn't care about the damn belt. He just wouldn't back down. This made him who he was, it made a chubby guy who looked like a Caterpillar into the Magical Poobah. Who else could hit three home runs in one Fall Classic game? There were only several other players to do that in the history of the sport of baseball. In the rich history of the sport! Reggie Jackson of the New York Yankees. Pablo Sandoval of the San Francisco Giants. Albert Pujols of the St. Louis Cardinals. And, the Babe! Babe Ruth of the Yankees did it as well. For Pepe, the Poobah, he was able to join this group and help the Sunny Grove Big Boys win a World Series. He didn't acknowledge any personal limitations and actually seemed to bend the laws of physics. It was a recipe for success!

Maddox was so happy to have the Poobah as a client. Big contracts! Big fees! Money! He was happy to have the Poobah as a client — as long as he could keep the rape of April Tilney out of his head. The rape, though, gnawed at Maddox Malone, whenever he thought about it. He hated that story. The mere thought of it chewed him up. He wondered when they would hear more from the police. He wondered when they would hear more from April Tilney's lawyer. Maddox he turned the music up, some outlaw country, to overpower those thoughts.

> Clyde plays electric bass,
> plays it with finesse and grace
> Set on the porch ain't got no shoes,
> pickin' the bass and singin' the blues

He hit the freeway hard. Maddox floored it up to eighty miles per hour right away. He was moving!

A few minutes later, Maddox exited the freeway and turned right then left, parking about ten minutes early for his planned visit with Grover Giles. Grover was a business acquaintance that Maddox knew from his time at Decker & Formenter. Grover was very successful — he ran a two billion dollar private equity fund that specialized in investments involving natural resources — and he was well-connected. Grover wanted to visit and catch up, and he also wanted to see if his son Niko, a student at the University of Southern California, could intern with the growing Malone Agency. Grover pulled up a few minutes later and fumbled through some stuff on his passenger seat before walking in and sitting down with Maddox.

Maddox was seated at a table close to the edge of the coffee shop and the rays of the sun were striking the window at an angle that generated a perfect level of warmth. Some air that was being pushed out of the vent hit Maddox, but it wasn't too much. He loved this part of Sunny Grove.

Maddox's phone buzzed with an e-mail from Donald Keyballs. The same account, Ken's alias, which had sent him the police report. It was a fresh e-mail message which read.

"The Rape charge is still awaiting review by the Detectives. The Rape Kit was accidentally destroyed by female officer. Big Boys Fan. Coffee spilled on Rape Kit."

"Are you kidding me?" thought Maddox. "A Sunny Grove Big Boys fan spilled coffee on the rape kit? Is that even possible?"

Maddox turned his head at the revelation from Don Keyballs' e-mail. When he turned, he noticed that the rest of the tables in the small coffee shop had a total of six people at them. Five were tenderly holding their buzzing smart phones and either looking intently at the screen or typing something into it. The sixth person had a box strapped onto their head with his or her smart phone strapped right to his or her face. The body connected to the smart phone in a box was sexually ambiguous. It was impossible to tell if the body was male or female. It was a coin flip! Everyone else in the coffee shop was deeply entrenched in their digital world, their digital content, and they didn't look like they were coming back any time soon. The barista brought Maddox's iced Americano in a large plastic cup.

"What would you like?" the girl asked Grover.

"Let me get a large latte with an extra shot, please," Grover said.

"Okay," said the girl as she walked through the doorway with a bounce in her step.

"So what's up, Maddox? I saw the stuff in the papers about Pepe Soliz. Sounds horrible! What was the Poobah thinking?"

Maddox looked up in the air, quickly. Not again! Not this story!

"Anyhow," Grover continued, "you must be busy, thanks for taking the time to meet me," Grover said with a unique half-grimace, half-smile as he sat down.

"Good to see you, Grover. Yeah, it's crazy. But of course I'll find time to meet about Niko's internship, no problem. Plenty of time to worry about all the other stuff. To be honest I don't mind getting a chance to take my mind off of the Pepe Soliz news," Maddox responded with a blank expression, a countenance that did not project any emotion to Grover.

"Well, we can ignore it, or if you feel like you want to vent, that's fine too," Grover ventured.

The girl brought Grover's latte. She also put two coasters under the coffee cups. Maddox was looking out the window. He trusted Grover, but he was still wary of sharing his thoughts about the Poobah. Maddox hated the rape, but also wanted the Poobah's fees, and didn't want to say anything that tipped the apple cart, even privately.

"It's a good iced Americano," Maddox said after he took a sip. His breathing slowed as he relaxed. He felt good. He looked over at Grover.

"I've never had one here," Grover said as he sipped his latte.

"Well you're on that dairy, unlike me. I drink almond milk quite a bit, but I don't really drink any regular milk and never soy."

"I hear you. I love whole milk lattes. So filling."

"I used to drink them."

"Hey, before I forget, if you ever need any help in the financial world, just let me know. I'll do what I can to help. I've been running my private equity fund for twelve years now and we have good reach. Not bragging, but we're big," said Grover. "I'll help you if I can, as a thank you for letting Niko work with you."

"I appreciate that. I'll keep that in mind," said Maddox.

"What the heck was Soliz even doing in Saint Cortana?" Grover said. "It seems so weird."

Maddox stared out the window. He decided that he would open up and talk to Grover about the incident. He hadn't spoken to anyone about the incident really. He never talked about business, especially bad news, with Laura. A couple people had called him and asked him about the incident but he didn't say much at all. He felt bottled up. He felt disconnected from himself and from reality.

"Well, he was on the disabled list recovering from a collarbone injury and made plans with his brother and a recruiter from my agency. A guy named Ward Goldstein. A rotten guy."

When Maddox said that, he thought about Ward Goldstein's disgusting case of colitis — his stomach was literally rotting inside him — but he didn't want to talk about that with Grover.

Maddox continued, "Somehow they thought it would be a good idea to go out and get smashed in Saint Cortana and then bring a girl back to the house and run train on the girl."

"Oh, man."

"It was insane. I was at LegoLand with my family when I found out."

"Wow, that's unforgivable. Ruining a trip to LegoLand. You said they ran train?"

Maddox wondered for a split-second as to how Grover knew

about that term – but dismissed the thought.

"Technically it was Ward first and then Pepe. But basically, yeah. And it wasn't so much LegoLand as it was the fact that we hadn't been on a family vacation in a long time. I've been so busy with work. I haven't had the time to do stuff like that. I've just been pushin' that boulder up the hill," Maddox said bluntly.

"Yeah, I hear you. So Pepe Soliz had sex with her after Goldstein?" asked Grover. "That's the way this whole thing went down?"

"Well, ahem, well... she was anally raped after she was with Goldstein if you call that sex. It sounded pretty brutal and invasive. His position is that she invited him in and consented."

"Oh, man."

"Either way, the sex has already been admitted. I just found out a few minutes ago from my friend that the police have bungled the investigation because they contaminated the crime scene and spilled coffee on the rape kit. It's like a bad movie."

"Really? Wow. I didn't see that in the news," said Grover.

"Yeah, that part has been kept under wraps. I just found out from an anonymous e-mail," Maddox didn't tell Grover his source, his friend Ken, called himself Don Keyballs.

"And she accused Soliz only in terms of the rape? Not Goldstein? Isn't that weird?"

"Sort of, she accused Goldstein of facilitating the rape. But she acknowledged that the sex with Goldstein itself, which occurred a few minutes before the rape, was consensual."

"Unbelievable."

"Yeah, you could say that. And the story is real bad. Between you and me, the recruiter is a real dirt bag. I was naïve to think he would be professional around my clients. He's a scumbag. A parasite," Maddox frowned and shook his head, slightly, as he spoke.

"I see. The whole thing is crazy to me. I mean, this was a violent rape! What are the prosecutors waiting for? What are they doing all day?" asked Grover.

Maddox paused for a full ten seconds. He thought the same thing. What was going on? But he had a sense of dread, because if Pepe was convicted of rape or deported Maddox would stand to lose millions of dollars of fees and several years of work. The Platform was collapsing. TENACIOUS was moving slow. He couldn't afford to lose that money from Pepe Soliz!

"I don't know. It's like the girl doesn't exist. It's like the incident didn't happen. It's like people don't care about what happened to April. That bothers me even though I am supposed to look out for Pepe. And even though Pepe pays me big commissions. I can't afford to lose Pepe Soliz's commissions — that would really hurt the Malone Agency. I've been growing so fast and I need that revenue. But it kills me because I don't need this kind of shit in my life. It's been keeping me up at night."

Grover paused and nodded slowly and Maddox looked thoughtful.

"That's tough. What a sticky situation. Let me ask you this, Maddox, on a separate topic. Is Pepe Soliz a smart guy or no?"

Maddox was still processing what Grover had said before, and he was also lost in his own thoughts. Maddox snapped back into the conversation.

"Well, he has a flash of brightness in his eyes when he talks about baseball, a buzz and energy. But that's the only time, the subject of baseball."

"I see."

"There's a language gap since his English is bad and that makes it harder to tell about his overall intelligence level. But overall, no, I don't think he is intelligent. Between you and me he's pretty stupid. He's just really good at baseball."

"I see. Obviously, that's what I would have guessed," interrupted Grover.

"Why?" asked Maddox.

Before Grover started to answer, Maddox thought Grover gave him a look like Maddox's question was very naive. Grover responded, "Generalizations obviously don't always hold true but, yes, of course I figured him for having a low IQ — not trying to be mean, I'm just saying that based on the averages — he looks like a third-world Colombian or Venezuelan with aboriginal features and an African mix. There were a lot of African slaves pumped into South America and their ancestors are still there, genetically. The ones in Mexico, incidentally, were mostly killed off when slavery ended. The Mexicans were tough on the Africans when they stopped working. Anyway, I took some classes on genetics in graduate school. He's most likely got a really low IQ."

"I don't know about all that," Maddox said with a grimace.

"It's true, he's most likely got a low IQ, just going by the averages," said Grover, very matter-of-factly.

Was this type of discussion even kosher? Maddox took Pepe Soliz as he was, he didn't really care where he came from or what race he was. Did Grover really think he could know that Pepe Soliz was stupid based on his genetics? Maddox was amazed. How was Grover getting away with this? Those opinions!

Maddox engaged him, just a bit by saying, "A lot of people would say it's racist to say the whole country of Colombia or Venezuela or Brazil has low IQ people? How would we even know that? It's so backwards down there in a lot of areas, how do you even measure IQ? Maybe they are smart but untapped? Maybe they have more of a magic-based culture, less rational. Just different, you know."

"Yeah. Yeah. I definitely don't know for sure. But what if it's true and those people are stupid and can't be changed? We don't know that it's not true," said Grover.

"Hmmm," Maddox didn't like it but he didn't know what to say.

"And intelligence usually taps itself — it just happens that way. Singapore has no natural resources to shake a stick at and they are a rich country. They are smart people. I would venture to guess, without being sure of course, that most Venezuelans are stupid. Just to use that example since I think that population is more homogeneous than Brazil," Grover replied.

"You guys need anything else?" asked the barista, Maryn.

Grover looked at Maryn's cute little round butt with a quick glance that Maddox caught. Maddox laughed to himself at Grover's quick peek.

"We're good, thanks."

"Look. I didn't come here to talk about racial differences. I spent years studying that stuff, I know it inside out. So, I just wanted to touch base about that internship for my son Niko. He'd love to work at the Malone Agency," Grover said as he took a sip of his latte and breathed in.

"Yeah, and by the way, congratulations to Niko for getting into USC. That's a nice accomplishment, a good school," said Maddox.

"Thanks. I was looking at the statistics, he did it even though he got a racial penalty for being white from the admissions department."

"Wait, what?" said Maddox.

"They subtracted more than two hundred points from Niko's SAT scores to, ummm, I guess, ummm, to level the playing field for everyone else who doesn't benefit from, umm, white privilege. Asians get penalized too. Niko still got in, even with the penalty, so it worked out."

"Wow. They really do that? Why?" asked Maddox.

"It's kind of amazing to think about. I don't know. They just give a penalty to certain people and a boost to others."

They both sat there for a few seconds.

"Anyway, as to your other question, even if, for the sake of argument, Pepe is not one of them, there are plenty of smart people in Venezuela," Maddox shot back.

Maddox's professors at Berkeley would be proud of his push-back. Feel the sting of the counter lash!

"Sure there are. It's a curve, not a flat line. There are real differences between groups of people, though. Some are dumber than others. I studied this in Cambridge. I studied it for years. I'm not making it up and I'm not saying it to be mean. Frankly, I don't care if the people of Venezuela are smart or dumb, I'm just trying to be honest and speak clearly."

Maddox didn't want to debate whether intelligence quotient was racially-based or not. He didn't see any upside to it. He preferred to avoid the topic entirely. Isn't it racist to notice stuff like that? Aren't intelligence tests themselves racist? He sat silently and took another sip of his iced Americano.

Grover continued, "Races are different in all sorts of ways, and probably the most important way is in intelligence quotient," Grover said. "Decades of psychometric testing indicates that you have Jews with the highest average intelligence quotient, usually followed by Asians, then you have whites, who are still high IQ, then Latins and blacks weighing in with low IQs. These are clear differences that affect people and society. Look around, you can't help but notice it. It's real and the data supports it. The test data."

Maddox paused and considered what Grover said.

"I haven't studied this stuff. If you said that in a class at Berkeley peoples' heads would explode. They teach that everyone is equal, that everyone is the same. Things like that. All the Berkeley professors would argue that everyone has a blank slate and if they are stupid it's because they didn't have a good environment to develop in. Every professor there believes that. They all believe the same thing, and they enforce their opinions."

"Uh-huh."

"And who is to say if they are wrong? They don't want people to focus on differences. You're not supposed to notice that — it's safer that way, and it's better for everyone. It's not nice to tell someone they are stupid," said Maddox. "It's not nice. I would never tell Pepe that."

"Yeah. I hear what you are saying. I just have no idea why you wouldn't address something if it's true. How can what they say be true? People are different. Look around."

This conversation was going nowhere because Maddox didn't want to give in and agree with Grover. He made his face go blank and he just didn't respond.

"So what's up with Niko? We were e-mailing about that internship. What does he want to do?" Maddox blatantly changed the subject.

Grover had studied the topic for years, formally, and Maddox was just getting exposed to his thoughts. He couldn't process what Grover said. It didn't fit with the movie that was playing in Maddox's head. And who cares if Pepe was stupid? Maddox already knew that.

Grover said, "Niko is a great kid. I know I'm his dad but he really is. He wants to tag along with you and follow you around when you will let him. Sorry to bring up that other stuff, let's forget it and try and have a great time."

"Oh it's no problem. I just haven't looked into that stuff. I haven't studied it," said Maddox. "Yeah Niko can tag along with me to some stuff. You think he really wants to do this shit? You haven't seen the latest demand letter from April Tilney's lawyer in the Pepe Soliz rape case. It's brutal. The police report, too. Sickening. Because of what happened, now the girl is asking for more than a million dollars to settle her civil claim for sexual battery."

Maddox had viewed the demand letter on his bright smart phone screen before he started driving over to the coffee shop. It gnawed at him because he knew Pepe Soliz spent his money immediately upon receiving it. After all the cars, clothes, baby mommas and child support, nightclubs, girlfriends and other stuff. He knew that Pepe wouldn't have any money to give to the girl as a settlement for the sexual battery claim — it was pretty amazing since he made millions of dollars playing baseball. Maddox hated the thought of paying off a rape victim for the Poobah.

But he also hated the thought of losing Pepe Soliz and the large fees that he paid to the Malone Agency. Maddox frowned, slightly. He had no idea how to predict what was going to happen.

"He thinks he does want to do it. He really wants to be a sports agent. His mind is set on it. You know? Show me the money! SHOW ME THE MONEY!"

"Showing the money is old news, man, the new thing is to be kuhhhmmf," said Maddox.

"Kuhhmf?"

"Kuhhhmfortable. Kuhhmmff."

They both laughed even though Grover had no idea about the origin of the term with Major O.

"Everybody loves Jerry Maguire," said Grover. "What a classic movie!"

"Man, fuck Jerry Maguire!" bellowed Maddox.

"What?"

"You heard me. Fuck Jerry Maguire."

"Whoa! That's the first time I've ever heard anyone say something negative about Jerry Maguire!"

"Fuck Jerry Maguire. Jerry Maguire ruins lives — it might ruin Niko's for example, if he's interested in sports because of that movie. A lot of people don't know what you have to deal with to represent professional athletes. It's like you're handling all their problems and the problems never end. Drugs, booze, painkillers, rape, women, baby mommas, injuries, steroids, fights, a corrupt business, low-level recruiters, cracked-out cheating spouses who think they can be agents, hustlers, trainers, they want this they want that. Constant issues and drama. And fuck that little kid with his stupid facts too, little pumpkin head," Maddox said with an angry smile.

Grover sat there, looking stunned. Maddox had actually surprised himself with the rant. Maddox loved the Malone Agency! How could he attack the sports agency industry like that? How could he attack the patron saint of sports agents, Jerry Maguire? Maddox loved the hustle, he loved making deals. He loved the Malone Agency brand he had built to prominence. But maybe the Pepe Soliz rape, the collapsing Platform, and the TENACIOUS delays were getting to him? Maddox was lucky that he didn't know about Zaine delivering stacks of cash to Obadiah and the others. He might have melted down!

He had years into the business, and Maddox didn't know yet that the only way out for Maddox was further in. Way further in! So, further in he must go!

Maddox took a breath and looked out the window. The Marin landscape was the perfect level of green, soft sun, and inviting scenery. The light wind blew the trees outside enough so that they swayed softly.

"I like this location, it's a good coffee shop. A good latte," Grover said.

"I'm glad you like it, I do too. I'm so addicted to coffee it's sad. The rest of my life is under control," Maddox said, chuckling.

"I've never tried it."

"So you really believe that stuff about IQ?" Maddox was genuinely curious. He wondered why most people were so afraid to have that discussion, but Grover didn't mind.

Grover responded, "I know it's true. Look, there are clearly high IQ people and low IQ people. We can see them and talk to them. We can look at their achievements. We can look at their problem solving skills. We can look at their inventions. We can look at what they say and what they do. We can look at their societies. We can look at their children. It's actually simple, it's actually common sense."

Grover pressed forward, his face projecting his belief that his argument was irrefutable. There was a pause in the conversation.

"Hmm. I don't know. I think you're out there. I don't think that's right," said Maddox, squinting and grimacing.

Grover continued. "I've studied this stuff for years, the biggest problem is that people naively project their own abilities onto people who don't have the same gifts that they do. They can't imagine that some people have limited capabilities. They can't accept it, they can't fathom it. You know, the equality meme. But, people are different," said Grover, firmly.

"Yeah, I can see that. It took me a while to realize that if Pepe was here for something other than baseball it would be ridiculous. Even bringing him here for baseball is a little weird if you think about it. Why not just let an American play? Of course, I don't want that because I want the commissions," Maddox admitted with a greedy smile and a bright flash in his eyes.

They both paused. Everything sank in.

"Definitely interesting. Hey, Grover, I appreciate the visit. Okay, so we're settled on the internship for Niko and we have to leave open the question of racial IQ differences for now? We didn't solve that puzzle!" Maddox said with a laugh.

"Yeah that's about right," said Grover with a friendly smile.

"Alright then. Text me if anything comes up with your son and we'll be in touch. Let's grab a coffee after I go to Venezuela in a couple weeks. I'll try to figure out how smart the people are down there. Haha," Maddox wrapped up the conversation with a big smile, a laugh, and a handshake.

Grover also laughed. He was a smart man with a good soul, but at the same time the things he said seemed very controversial to Maddox. How could he say those things? But Maddox also recognized that Grover had a keen eye, and he was discerning and noticed things. He spoke honestly about things that he noticed. Maddox liked him. Maddox didn't know why, but he got the sense that Grover couldn't believe that Maddox had fought his way to be competitive with billion-dollar companies in an industry known for bare-knuckle brawling. A dirty, cut-throat business. Maddox could tell that Grover was so impressed with that. But Maddox thought that Grover had hinted that Maddox needed sharpen his elbows and stop being naive — and Maddox was embarrassed that he never paid attention to news or political events. He was too busy with the Malone Agency. Suddenly Maddox felt soft and naïve. They shook hands and parted ways.

Maddox really enjoyed the meeting, because it made him think. Maddox couldn't believe what a discrepancy there was between ideas and thoughts, which could be neat and clean, and living, which always seemed to be messy and unforgiving. It seemed like there was always a permanent dislocation between a genuine exploration of ideas, meditative thinking, and then looking off in the landscape and finding problems, exceptions, counter-examples, or outright confusion and controversy. Things got messy. Things got muddy. Things blurred. A beautiful idea is like a still life painting of a flower pot sitting on a window-sill. Real life is like the actual flower pot getting knocked over and breaking on the ground, causing a big mess all over the place. But that's no reason not to have ideas. And it's no reason not to live. Maddox was happy. It was an excellent conversation! For the rest of the day, Maddox would not be allowed to spend so much time in the world of ideas; he was off to the Big Boys' stadium to see the Poobah play and then he would have to go to dinner after the game. For better or worse, after a small escape, a chance to think, during his conversation with Grover, he was firmly fixed in the mess of real life.

MUCHO DINERO

**

"Oh shit, this might be another one of Pepe's women," thought Maddox as he sat down in his seat at the Big Boys' Stadium. "Is this another baby momma?" Maddox sat down in his chair with a bag of peanuts and a bottle of water – his standard fare for a ballgame. Maddox was, unfortunately, seated directly next to a plus-sized woman who looked like she might have been in her early-to-mid-twenties. It seemed like she took up her own chair plus half of Maddox's chair! The woman looked exactly like a potato bug. She was bulbous, she was round.

It was immediately apparent that the Potato Bug didn't speak English. She had no real differentiation between her limbs. Her head blended into her neck which blended into her torso which blended into her poofa which blended into her legs. Also, she was quite pregnant to top it all off. This had to be one of Pepe's conquests, thought Maddox! Maddox shook his head, slightly. Maddox was growing tired of Pepe's antics. The random pregnancy upset Maddox! There were already at least six random girls in the country that had been sired by the Poobah – each with a different mother.

Yes, Pepe was enriching the country with his baseball abilities. But Maddox couldn't help feeling that it was weird for there to be this many of his offspring running around. They were everywhere! If Maddox knew about six of them, there could be ten of those little rug-rats running around! Hell, there could be a dozen of those little fuckers running around! "What about the environmental resources that small army would use? What about climate change? Overpopulation is really hard on the planet – and Pepe's offspring would probably eat more than the average person, if they inherited his size and proclivities. So, if he had twelve offspring it would be even worse for the planet than normal people who ate less food," thought Maddox. For Maddox, it was a lot to think about. The conversation with Grover also weighed on him. What if the Poobah was single-handedly lowering the IQ of the country with his progeny, who would almost certainly lack intelligence? What would that do to the gross domestic product?

Enough of this! Maddox didn't want to be mean. And, he reminded himself that he hadn't even confirmed that the woman was one of Pepe's baby mommas. Of course, it was highly likely when you considered her physique, the language that she spoke, and the fact that she was pregnant – her cooch seemed like it would be a good fit for the Poobah's adventurous tool.

Unfortunately, pushing the thought out of his mind wasn't working! Maddox couldn't take it anymore. He wanted to know truth about the situation. So, Maddox used his smart phone to ask the Slug if Pepe Soliz had knocked up yet another woman. "Yessssss" came the immediate response from the Slug, Garibaldi Vascoso. For a Slug, he sure was fast on a smart phone.

Of course he did, thought Maddox. Of course he did. Suddenly, a wave of serenity flowed over Maddox. Maddox stopped fighting the circumstances. He stopped worrying about the environmental impact of random offspring sired by the Poobah. He just accepted things. He accepted the woman. He accepted the baby. He accepted the Poobah for what he was. Pepe was enriching the land — who knows, maybe one of his daughters will cure cancer. Acceptance relaxed Maddox for a minute, and he looked out over the field. It was another beautiful day in Sunny Grove.

Aurelia was the Potato Bug's name. She was twenty-four years old. Born in Mexico. Aurelia snuck across the border with her mother when she was eleven. She had worked odd jobs since childhood. Restaurant service, hotel service, grocery stocker, parking attendant. She did a lot of jobs that, face it, no one really wanted to do. She had a slight limp. She had a tattoo just above her rear end that said "MAMI." The lettering had a red heart next to it with an arrow through it. Maddox couldn't detect any stress or worry on her face. She just sat there, blank, sort of smiling, mostly blank.

Aurelia lived with her mother and her mother's boyfriend. Her mother's boyfriend, Carlos, was an alcoholic day-laborer, also from Mexico. He had six or seven drunk driving offenses on his record — only one of those had a fatality, though. Carlos was a menace on the road! He only drove the wrong way when he was drunk, but when he was sober he was still a speed demon, a lead foot. Incidentally, Carlos was always trying to feed Aurelia's kitty when Aurelia's mother, Isabel, wasn't around. So far, Aurelia had been able to fend off his advances. Carlos had never entered her castle!

Maddox did not know all of that backstory, of course. He knew nothing about Aurelia, her mother Isabel, or Carlos — other than her connection to Pepe. A minute later, Maddox and Aurelia glanced at each other and Maddox realized he would be sitting in close proximity to someone with whom he had absolutely nothing in common — not culture, not experience, not learning, not habits, not literature, not art, not travel, not a shared view of humanity, not even language. Maddox wondered if Aurelia was thinking the same thing. Then the moment was gone, as the warmups continued on the field. Aurelia was looking at Pepe out on the field, and Maddox wondered, briefly, if she was flashing back to the session a few months before in which Pepe got her pregnant. Maddox guessed that Aurelia had told Pepe something like "Dame tu gran pene duro, papi!" He smiled to himself.

Some old school rock and roll was blaring out of the stadium's speakers, and Maddox sang along.

> Rags to riches or so they say
> Ya gotta keep pushin' for the fortune and fame
> You know it's all a gamble when it's just a game ...

Maddox looked out on the field and saw Pepe Soliz warming up for the game. He looked heavy. Maddox flashed back to the time that he had gotten Pepe Soliz to trim down. He had chaperoned him to workout sessions and helped him lose more than seventy pounds. Of course, Maddox only did it so that he would be in a better position to negotiate the Poobah's contract with the Big Boys. As a result of getting Pepe in condition, Maddox had been able to negotiate a twenty seven million dollar contract for Pepe Soliz. Over three years. It was a real feather in Maddox's cap, and Maddox's commission was over one million dollars. Maddox was pleased with himself. No one else had ever gotten the

Poobah in shape before.

The game was uneventful, but it ended up as a solid win for the Big Boys. Pepe Soliz was two-for-five with a double off the wall in right center.

After the game, Maddox walked down to the player tunnel to wait for Pepe Soliz because they had agreed to go to dinner after the game. Maddox hated the dead time, just waiting around. He stood there for what seemed like forever! And the payoff? Dinner with the Poobah, a boring schlub who would probably just stare at his smart phone the whole time. Maddox grimaced. He gritted his teeth. He had to do it though, it was the nature of the business. Pepe was a big commission, a big fat walking dollar sign.

Pepe Soliz was always one of the last players out of the clubhouse. It was no different that night. He lumbered out after about thirty five minutes.

"Hey Papi," Soliz said, giving Maddox a hug.

"My man," Maddox replied with a smile. "You wanna go eat?"

"Cheese Town Restaurant. We goin' to Cheese Town."

"Oh Fuck! God-damn it," muttered Maddox, not loud enough for Pepe to hear.

Maddox hated the Cheese Town Restaurant and its salty, heavy food. But there would be no negotiating on this one. Maddox knew that if there was one place Pepe loved it was Cheese Town.

"Okay. Cheese Town it is," said Maddox with a forced smile. "Good game. You feeling good?"

"Yeah, I feel good Papi."

"I thought that ball you hit to right center was gone."

"Me too. Me too. Hey Papi, if I keep hitting good I want a new contract."

"I'm with you. You gotta keep hitting, Pepe. Hit the ball, Pepe!"

"That's what I gonna do. I gonna hit."

"That's what I need you to do."

"Can you get me that new contract if I hit Maddy?"

"I'm ready to do that. We can do that."

"You sure Papi?"

"Yeah, I'm sure. Just hit, baby."

"You gonna get me a nuevo contrato, Madd-man?"

"Yeah, Pepe, I'm gonna get you a Nuevo contrato!"

"NUEVO CONTRATO JAJAJAJAJAJAJAJAJ" Pepe howled.

"NUEVO CONTRATO!" Maddox yelled back. He thought he smelled money!

"Dinero?"

"MUCHO DINERO, PEPE!"

"MUCHO DINERO!" yelled Pepe back at Maddox.

Maddox and Pepe loaded into Pepe's truck and cruised over to the Cheese Town Restaurant in the United Temple section of Sunny Grove. Pepe Soliz was blaring some South American rap-type music. It was terrible and it made Maddox miserable. It affected his physiology negatively. It rattled his brain.

> Bum bum bum bum bum arriba bum bum bum bum bum arriba. Bum! Arriba!

Pepe and Maddox parked and they trudged into the Cheese Town Restaurant where they sat down at a table for two. Soliz kept sending messages from his smart phone, which constantly dinged and buzzed throughout the dinner. Maddox didn't really care, he didn't have much to talk about with Pepe anyway. Passing the time was fine. Maddox, looking for something to do while Pepe was engrossed in his phone, checked his digital and social media feed, which usually featured sports-related news. Tonight, for some reason, there were several articles about bathrooms. Maddox squinted. His smart phone was featuring several opinion pieces which argued, quite adamantly, that men dressed up as women should be able to use whichever bathroom they please. Maddox scratched his head. "That's weird," he thought. "That's really weird. Why is this information getting pushed into my phone?" thought Maddox. "Who has time to argue about that stuff? Why is this on my phone?"

The waiter came over and introduced himself. Maddox and the waiter made a little small talk while Pepe Soliz stared at his smart phone.

"I know what I want," said Pepe. "Bacon pizza, large."

He wasn't joking. Maddox could picture the grease and the calories going straight to Pepe's massive belly. Maddox guessed the pizza contained ten thousand calories. Maybe more? He didn't know.

"I'll get the chicken cacciatore," offered Maddox. He dreaded the salt and all the mystery additives Cheese Town would put on the plate.

"Anything to drink for you guys?"

"Whiskey," said Pepe.

Maddox ordered a soda water. Maddox stared at Pepe. He thought about April's little butt-hole. He thought about the commissions Pepe paid to Maddox's agency. He thought about Aurelia. He thought about the next contract Pepe was going to get at the expiration of his current deal. He thought about his agency. He thought about the police report! He cursed Don Keyballs for sending that thing to him in the first place! He thought about Pepe's statistics — boy could the Poobah hit the baseball. Maddox blinked and tried to bring himself back to the dinner. But, Pepe was focused on the screen of his smart phone anyway. It didn't matter if Maddox paid attention or not. It was a digital dinner.

Pepe continued sending text messages, or doing whatever he was doing, on his smart phone, so Maddox just looked around the restaurant. A few fans were lurking around the table, but no one approached. Maddox tried to get Pepe's attention, and he also felt like he needed to ask about the rape case.

"So, have you talked to the defense lawyer in the last couple days? You know, about the girl, April Tilney?" Maddox finally asked. Bringing up the rape made Maddox feel queasy, but he felt that he had to. He couldn't spend hours with Pepe and not say something about it.

"I don't wanna talk about dee rape," said Soliz. "Better to relax. Better to enjoy food. Better to enjoy dee whiskey."

Maddox leaned back. "What can I do?" he thought.

The food arrived and the waiter refilled Maddox's water. Pepe ordered another whiskey and then started demolishing his Bacon Pizza, two bites at a time. Maddox scanned the restaurant for a second. He just looked around. When he looked back, Maddox realized that Pepe had eaten the entire pizza — in what seemed like seconds. Maddox could see bacon grease dripping off the side of Pepe's mouth and down to the v-neck collar of his tee-shirt. Maddox just looked at Pepe, watched him eat.

Maddox could see the record spinning in Pepe's head and it was obvious that the needle wasn't touching. Maddox was reminded about his conversation with Grover. Maddox cursed Grover, internally, Was this real? Was this real?

Maddox glanced around the restaurant and noticed that most of the diners were staring intently at their smart phones, while the big screens glowed with information, messages, pictures, whatever. Some of them were staring and scrolling. Some of them were staring and typing. Some of them just staring. It was a digital dinner!

Maddox struggled through his salty chicken dish. Soliz had his smart phone out, as usual, and it looked like he was sending messages to people.

"I'm texting Party Wardy. We gonna have another Parddddyyy," said Pepe. He gave a mischievous smile to Maddox. He was rubbing it in!

Maddox flew into a rage! Did Pepe's actions from Saint Cortana even register? What was wrong with this guy? How can he joke about

Party Wardy and Saint Cortana? Maddox didn't say anything back.

Instead, Maddox felt a sudden need to vent the frustration that was building inside him. So, he took his smart phone out of his jacket pocket and fired off a text message to Paul McCartney which said, "We need to get the bid in for the TENACIOUS facility NOW. All these projects are moving forward and we don't even have the facility and the rest of the funding. We need to get this done or the whole plan is going to fall apart." He sent the text message and put the smart phone back in his jacket pocket.

"Did you hear me Madd-ox, I'm texting Party Wardy. We gonna Parddddy."

"Shit, man," Maddox said with a sarcastic tone. "After the rape case I'm not so sure you guys should go out together ... ever."

"Ah, don't be borrrrr-ing, Maddox. Let's gooooo! Parrrrrddddy Warrrrdddy."

"Not again," thought Maddox.

Maddox's body tensed. He became hyper-alert. He was frustrated, angry. But he didn't want Pepe to see that emotion on his face. He sat there, stone-faced. Pepe made a loud swallowing sound as he finished his whiskey and breathed out. "Ahhh," Pepe wooshed, expressing satisfaction and refreshment with his cocktail. This signaled that they were all finished at Cheese Town, so they closed out the check and walked out of the restaurant.

"Can we go to dee wine bar?" asked Pepe.

"Sure, Pepe, but I can only stay for a couple hours. I need to get some rest," said Maddox.

About thirty minutes later, Pepe Soliz had already hammered back two more whiskey shots, and was holding a double whiskey with cola. Maddox didn't know, but Pepe had used his smart phone to send a message asking a baseball groupie to come to the wine bar. The baseball groupie, Gabby, had been sending Pepe nudes by text message while Pepe and Maddox were at Cheese Town. The Poobah told Gabby, in different words, that he wanted to do some interior decorating with her.

Just then, Ward Goldstein, the Malone Agency recruiter, walked into the wine bar. Maddox smelled a disgusting, foul, odor, and turned away, gasping for some fresh air.

"Parrr—dddy Wardddy!" bellowed the Poobah.

"Hi Pepe. How's my Poobah," said Ward Goldstein, giving Pepe a quick embrace. Garibaldi Vascoso, the Slug, oozed in, just a few minutes behind the Party.

"Go get me con-doms, Pardddy," Pepe had said. "And hurry dee fuck up!"

Pepe only needed to tell Party Wardy to jump and Ward would ask, "How high?" That's what jock sniffing recruiters did — they lived to serve professional athletes like Pepe. Ward would do anything Pepe asked, with a hop in his step. Ward was fifteen years older than Pepe Soliz but he lowered his eyes and shuffled his feet out the door.

The Party mumbled, under his breath, "should I get some extra-large condoms to stroke Pepe's ego or some smaller condoms that actually fit Pepe's stubby little rod?" His face showed distress over this dilemma! On the way, he opened his valve three different times release some of noxious gas. Hisss. Hisssss. Hisssss. Ward was wracking his brain for what to do! He couldn't settle on one or the other decision, so he got both types. Two packs of each! Now, the choice of which condom to open up, if any, would be decided by Pepe. Gabby, the cute little groupie, had arrived in a loose black romper with pink underwear underneath. She had three inch heels on as well, black. Without the heels, she was about five-foot-four with b cups and a tender little behind that looked as if it tasted like fresh ginger.

"Hey mami," Soliz said while staring at Gabby's body.

"Hey Pepe," the girl responded with excitement showing on her face. "Good game tonight big guy. I love the Big Boys."

Gabby was a super Big Boys fan. She was always happy when the Big Boys won a game. She even had alerts sent to her smart phone, which throbbed and pulsed every time the Big Boys scored a run.

"How you doing tonight, mami," Soliz replied as he kept looking Gabby up and down. He licked his lips. His right hand absent-mindedly rubbed his obscene belly fat. The second and third finger on his left hand rubbed his thumb, back and forth.

"I'm doing good. How are you?" Gabby said as she looked at the tubby Caterpillar.

"I'm fine. Fine. I'm sore from the game. Uhhhh, muh shoulder, muh hip."

Soliz looked at the ground for a moment then back up at Gabby, staring at her chest.

"Nice win today," she said with a cute little smile and an inviting giggle.

"Thank you, mami," that giggle was the only opening he needed, he grabbed her hand and walked her to the restroom. On the way in, Pepe gave Gabby a little grab on her butt. She fluttered and floated into the restroom. He locked the door right when they entered. Pepe kissed Gabby on the mouth, one time, and then opened his belt — he hadn't broken this one — and took down his pants and boxers. Gabby stripped off her pink panties but left her romper on, just angling it to the side so Pepe could enter her from behind.

The whole scene was remarkable! In the little bathroom, the Poobah was holding onto a metal bar above his head while going at Gabby. To be sure, the fact that the Poobah was having sex again wasn't particularly interesting. Pepe mated all the time. He mated every week, a few times, at random. That part was routine — if that were the entire story it would be gratuitous, it would be boring! But this was anything but boring! This was very interesting, due to the particulars and the physical logistics of this mating session.

It was interesting for this reason: during their mating session, Pepe and Gabby looked almost exactly like evergreen bagworms — the bagworm is a type of caterpillar, or at least a similar species. That particular bug forms a cocoon-like bag with its head and legs protruding and always dangles from a branch as it prepares to mate. In this instance, Pepe had left all his baggy — yes baggy — clothes on and just dropped his pants around his knees. Gabby, also, had left her baggy romper on. All the baggy clothes created the exact same visual of the bagworm's cocoon-like bag. And, Soliz hanging from the metal pole was very similar to the evergreen bagworm and his branch. The female bagworm, while mating, morphs into a larviform creature. Gabby, apparently, morphed into a larviform creature anytime she got close to a Big Boy. She had already mated with three other members of the Big Boys team! Five more and she could claim enough notches from Big Boys to actually field a baseball team. There was a real life nature show taking place in that Sunny Grove bathroom!

Pepe was filled with lust and, as usual, he was fully-invested in the present moment. He was pumping like an oil drill. He was churning butter! Schlmmpft. Schlmmpft. Schlmmpft.

Gabby was incredibly enthusiastic in the bathroom. This was her fourth time with a Big Boy, but the first time in a bathroom with a Big Boy! She was moaning loudly as they continued to work things through in the bag. Pepe's belly was making a loud popping sound on Gabby, muffled only a little bit by her portion of the bag, meaning the romper.

Gabby turned around, bent down, and continued to work on the situation. Soon, the bagworms were finished with their task. Just like that, Gabby fixed her romper to cover herself and left the bathroom with Soliz right behind. Soliz laughed and gave Party Wardy a high five on the way out of the bathroom.

"Oooh Baby! Got Some! Got some pussy!" yelled Party Wardy.

After the wine bar, the gang walked toward the waterfront. There was the sound of music and drunken shouts. A panhandler petitioned everyone, one by one, for a couple bucks. A shady guy on the corner just gazed over at the group. A police officer watched from a distance. A redheaded lunatic with a t-shirt that read "Urban Viking" yelled "guess what, now I'm sober so you can suck my dick" at the police officer.

"Why would he say that?" thought Maddox. "Maybe he was drunk earlier?" The police officer turned his head slightly but didn't move. Ward Goldstein was sending messages to a man who dressed like a woman, while releasing his valve every five or six minutes. Hiss.

Garibaldi, the Slug, limped along, his knees having a hard time supporting his over-sized, oozing body.

Pepe Soliz was starting to snap back from his bag session. He just looked like he was perking up again. His eyes were re-focused. Maddox was walking behind, thinking that he didn't really want to be there. He was one of the top young sports agents in the country and he wanted nothing to do with these degenerates.

Maddox was lost in his thoughts and ideas, but stuck in the reality of the moment. There was no alternate realm for him between reality and his ideas. No middle ground either. It was always the still life or the broken flower pot.

The gang walked into a new bar, close to North Post. There were about half a dozen girls in the room, all dressed provocatively and all beautiful to look at. They frittered about like doves. Pretty doves. Maddox made himself at home and casually started talking to a Russian named Veronica. She looked like Ana Kournikova, the tennis star, but with a hint, perhaps ten percent, of Asian ancestry. And what manners Veronica had! She was so polite to Maddox! She spoke so sweetly and so pleasantly it was like music to his ears. She was so attentive to him and stared at him when she talked. They spoke for a while and then Maddox walked off, looking around.

Pepe Soliz, with Gabby gone, walked off into the corner with a pretty Latina woman. Party Wardy Goldstein was hunched over his vibrating smart phone, still sending message after message to the man who dressed up as a woman. The way he was hunching made Maddox think it looked like Party Wardy wanted to block anyone from reading his screen. "What was he sending?" thought Maddox. Goldstein, who had major stomach problems related to rotting intestines, kept releasing his gas valve every few minutes. Hisss. Hissss. Garibaldi Vascoso was off to the side, by himself, his breath reeking. He kept looking at a much younger girl, whose name was Carlita. She was thirty feet away from him across the room. Garibaldi never approached her.

Maddox thought to himself, "You can feel the degeneracy. It's rising, like bread baking. It's thick, like curdled milk." Maddox shook his head with a barely noticeable grimace. He was disappointed in himself — he couldn't pinpoint exactly why but the feeling nagged at him. He checked his watch, wishing that he were home or at least back in his hotel with a book or a movie. He loved the money that Pepe paid to the Malone Agency, but deep down he was coming to despise Pepe. With rare clarity and honesty, Maddox thought long and hard about the rape of April, pregnant Aurelia, and sex with Gabby in the bathroom — and that was just the last few days? What in the heck was going on here? "Pepe was just a piece of shit," thought Maddox. He lived like a wild animal. What would the Poobah do tomorrow? Maddox didn't want to know.

Maddox backed up his thoughts. He cleared his mind for a second. He thought about his work at the Malone Agency. Why was he doing this? Why hustle like this? Why was he here, walking through Sunny Grove with Pepe Soliz and the rest of this group of people? He asked himself this question, in those exact words, and then just let himself think.

He walked and thought.

Well, he was working with Pepe to earn the commissions for negotiating his contracts — so he could grow his business and support his family. That was the nice way to put it — really Maddox just wanted the fucking money! For a second, that answer felt fine. But then he got down on himself. He was catering to Pepe's obnoxious whims, and being associated with Pepe's behavior, to earn a five percent cut of Pepe's high-paying contracts. Pepe had no standards. This thought made Maddox feel cheap — maybe he was cheap hired help who would do anything, tolerate anything, support anything. Maybe he would do anything for Pepe's money? Maddox hated this feeling! How did this happen? How had he gotten here, to this exact point? How was this his life, his business?

Maddox said his good-byes to everyone and started walking back to his hotel because he had an early flight to Miami the next morning. As a matter of fact he had to be at the airport at five in the morning. He was dreading the early wake-up, he was dreading the travel, the flight. The dread, like the degeneracy that surrounded him, was heavy and it was relentless. It was just a flight, but this particular travel, for some reason, really weighed on Maddox. He didn't want to go! But, he couldn't walk away. Could he? That would be insane! What about all the money?

Suddenly, his smart phone rang and buzzed. It lit up. Interestingly, it was Paul McCartney calling him. Really? That was a bit of a surprise, since McCartney had been very hard to reach for quite some time — weeks, really. Hopefully, thought Maddox, the Grasshopper was ready to hop over to the bank to transfer over some of grandpa's money to TENACIOUS.

The TENACIOUS business funds McCartney promised long ago were way overdue!

Middle Finger

❋❋

Propriety can cause society to rot. Darkness and silence are friends of degeneracy. It festers. When direct truths are evaded, and replaced with fake-speak, a shabby temple of tolerance is erected. Speech is constrained and behavior changes. Conformity is called for and the new behaviors thrive. Challenging this framework, and speaking clearly, is not easy.

Right as Maddox was walking back to his hotel, Paul McCartney, the Grasshopper, was starting to hop up a flight of stairs. He was also dialing Maddox's number. The stairs were pointing towards the door of a young girl who said her name was Chanel. Chanel was lying in her apartment on a queen-sized bed with nothing on but an over-sized white tank top that said "I'm in 3D" right across her big breasts. She was laying on her back, and, at twenty-two, she still had a nice body. Voluptuous breasts, similar in shape to butternut squash, except more round and less long. Chanel's nipples were pencil erasers that made guys crazy. Her legs were muscular but not bulky, she looked like she worked out on the stair-master but not too much and not too little. She had a nice caboose. Her face was rough, though. She always looked strung out, with drawn eyes and a blank stare. She was openly advertising and selling sex on a publicly accessible website, the same one that Paul McCartney, the Grasshopper, frequented. She sold sex to pay her bills and to support her drug habit, which she picked up a few years before, after enduring a shitty childhood with no dad. In a parallel universe, she was a pretty young housewife with two kids, living clean. But in this universe, the real one, Chanel was a hooker. She sold access to her wares on a website that operated right out in the open. Right in front of society. Nobody did a damn thing about it! Except the customers, like McCartney. McCartney, having made the appointment an hour and a half before, hopped up to Chanel's door with two explosive jumps while finishing his conversation with Maddox Malone on his smart phone. McCartney's skinny right arm raised up and he knocked on Chanel's apartment door. He looked green under the tint of the porch light. His buggy eyes bulged. His haunches brimmed. One particular zip code tingled. It tingled!

While his right hand knocked, his left hand pressed his shiny white nine hundred and thirty dollar smart phone to his ear. His hair was gelled, it was curly. His curly hair was mostly brown, but he also had a dramatic and unique gray skunk-stripe running down the middle. The gel made the brown part of his hair shine and it made the gray part glisten.

On his call with Maddox, Paul McCartney was talking fast, as usual. "Well, Maddox, I'm really excited about all of our TENACIOUS initiatives. I will send an e-mail summary about all of the projects tomorrow. I just hung up the phone with the real estate agent, and I instructed him that we are ready to buy the building for the TENACIOUS facility. We're ready to move forward! He's bringing the paperwork for the offer to my house tomorrow and I am going to sign everything then. I'm excited that we put the bid in on the building for the training center and I can't wait to make progress on golf, tennis and wrestling as well. Money is not an issue! Let's do this! Core values!"

After weeks, months even, of unrest and stressful uncertainty — of regarding Paul McCartney as unreliable — this conversation was music to Maddox's ears. A rush of positive energy hit him like a bolt of lightning.

"This is great news, Paul. I'm so excited! TENACIOUS is going to be huge. Core Values!" Maddox replied.

Maddox couldn't stand Paul's stupid sayings, but on this occasion, he was so happy and excited about the long-awaited facility bid that he repeated one of them back. He breathed in and out. His energy buzzed, it flowed. Suddenly he did not dread his trip to Miami any longer. His enthusiasm for work and for the Malone Agency skyrocketed. The dread lifted. Life, lately a series of disappointments, became bright again. Maddox felt light, he breathed easy. He paused and laughed to himself for a second. He thought to himself that this level of elation may have been a bit excessive — but then he reminded himself of what a struggle it had been to get Paul McCartney to focus on TENACIOUS. Maddox had thought it was business travel and the eccentric activity of a trust funder that had made the 'Hopper hard to pin down — not drug rehabilitation and other vice — but all the same Paul was hard to contact. All that didn't seem to matter anymore, the long-anticipated deal was finally happening. The flagship training facility was coming as envisioned by Maddox Malone. Core Values!

Paul McCartney had promised, over and over, to fund the purchase of a training facility in North Phoenix. Now he was finally formally signing the paperwork for the offer. Maddox was thrilled. "Thank God," he thought. A wave of relief flowed over Maddox's entire body. They were finally going to have the site for the TENACIOUS facility. Maddox just kept dwelling on it, he just let the conversation linger in his mind. Thank God. The bid was just shy of two million dollars for a large building on a nice lot that would house the TENACIOUS Performance Institute and, eventually, the adjacent TENACIOUS Tennis Academy would be added to the site. He felt vindication where there had only been frustration and worry. The cash bid on the facility, the cornerstone project for TENACIOUS, gave Maddox great assurance. Long overdue assurance! Comfort. As they were about to hang up, Maddox overheard part of McCartney's odd conversation with a woman.

"Is the doctor in?" McCartney asked. The Grasshopper's antennae were up.

"Honey, you know she is," a young girl's voice, Chanel's voice, responded. She artificially lowered her voice an octave and continued. "The head doctor is in, Paul."

"Oh baby I'm coming in then! I need some treatment! I got a mild condition!" McCartney exclaimed. His skunk-stripe glistened and he had a massive smile on his face as he hopped forward.

ii

Following the call, McCartney moved on to a far different activity, one that had nothing to do with TENACIOUS. He put his gleaming smart phone in the back left pocket of his square jeans, and with his other hand he pulled five hundred dollars out of his front right pocket and put the cash on Chanel's dresser. Shortly afterward, he walked behind Chanel into the bedroom.

Besides Chanel, McCartney had exploited a variety of types of women that he found on this particular website, the one where prostitutes advertised their wares. Young, old, skinny, fat, tattoos, nose rings, blond, brunette, Mexicans, Haitians, Africans, big breasts, small breasts, saggy breasts. Once, McCartney tumbled with a hooker with a missing tooth. Once, he got into a hooker with part of her nose eaten away by a flesh eating bacteria. Once, he did so much with a hooker who had a tuft of thick hair growing out of her left shoulder. Because his wife was so ornery, so plain and disagreeable, he had a jaded appetite and all of these things added spice and exhilarated him. In this world, Paul McCartney found deformity and infirmity to be a turn on. In the case of Chanel, she was one of the most beautiful people, physically, that McCartney had ever been with. She was beautiful, but she had empty eyes and no personality. It was sad. Chanel was in a bad place, selling sex, and as a result she needed to self-medicate, which she did with a combination of Xanax, crystal meth, wine and a healthy dose of citrus-flavored vodka.

The night before, McCartney's working girl of choice had been an African woman, originally from Martinique. Her given name was Yasmine, and her hooker name was Vixen. She was powerful. Big frame, big derriere. Strong hands. She had a purplish wa-wa that, with any honest assessment, was big and sloppy. So sloppy! Other than that issue, she was as beautiful as a lioness. McCartney had only to look at Vixen to get fully excited. McCartney had walked up the stairs behind the African and could not resist grabbing her chooch. He got a whole handful and squeezed firmly while making sure not to lose the full grip. She looked back with a seductive smile and she waggled it exactly where he had grabbed her. When they got into the bed, Paul and Vixen passed the gravy. They passed it left and right, up and down, hard and fast. Then again. After a total of an hour, McCartney abruptly kissed Vixen on the mouth and left. He had hurried home that night because he told his wife he was meeting with Maddox about TENACIOUS and he knew that excuse wouldn't hold forever. His wife had Maddox's phone number. What if his wife sent a message to Maddox on his smart phone to ask what the 'Hopper was up to? What if Maddox said that he didn't know?

At present, Chanel was all worked up. Distracted? High? She was wringing her hands and striking sexy poses, but awkwardly. Then she focused in and her performance tightened up. Her body was so nice! McCartney caught her behind again and squeezed it and rubbed it. His pinky dragged firmly over her bare way-woah. At first, Chanel showed a look of alarm when that happened. When he drew his hand up, though, it seemed to loosen everybody up. "Oh you bad, bad boy. You gonna get at me?" she asked.

Chanel was good in bed. She said the right words. She had the right noises. When she had a client, she lay there with her legs apart and moaning. It's true that it was choreographed and she used lube rather than actually being physically aroused and wet, but she really got into the performance as much as she could. Obviously, she did this for everybody, but she didn't make it feel that way. She made it seem like she was tailoring this specifically for McCartney. She didn't stare up at the ceiling, pretend to be somewhere or someone else, or look over her left shoulder and count bedbugs on the sheets. She talked about the things a man wants to hear — and she tried really hard to be good at it so that she could make her men climax quickly. She used a breathy, husky voice to say "fuck me, fuck my pussy. Get it! Get in there!" That always worked very well, every day, to speed things up with her clients!

McCartney started making a noise with his tongue. Click, click. It was strange. Chanel's face tightened and her head tilted. The Grasshopper started to stridulate, rubbing his lower leg against his forearm. It made a chafing noise. He tried to make a percussion sound, but it was more of a fleshy thud. He started to flap his arms like wings. It looked like he was trying to crepitate and create a loud slapping noise while flying. It was wild. Chanel's face scrunched up with concern.

"You can take a shower, honey, if you like. There's a fresh towel in there," said Chanel.

"No, that's okay, I'm clean. I showered before I came over. Let's do this! Ha-ha-ha-ha-ha!" said McCartney with a high-pitched laugh.

There was a beautiful photograph of a child, a little boy holding a toy truck, on the dresser.

McCartney paced back and forth, jerking around, hopping. Turning, pacing, hopping. Another hop for good measure. Chanel, circled the 'Hopper and dropped to her knees and took down McCartney's square jeans. She started earning her rent with her mouth. Enthusiastically! She needed regulars like McCartney. She licked and kissed and was touching herself and moaning softly. McCartney was turned on quickly. He was ready to spring inside her. For some reason, McCartney was sticking his middle finger in his own sprat while she worked on him with her mouth. He tried to strike a powerful pose when he was standing above her. He guided her up by the shoulder and then he started doing work on her, reciprocating. McCartney suddenly hoped, urgently, that he was Chanel's first client of the night. He had no way to be sure because even if he asked her there could be no guarantee that she would answer honestly. She was tight and wet. But, did she taste like semen? Fuck, who knows? McCartney stayed really hard because he was focused on her body and not so much on her rough face. Also, he was hopped up on a combination of cocaine, Grey Goose and Viagra. He wished he didn't have to neglect his sprat, but there was nothing he could do at that precise moment. He only had two hands! He lifted her up and felt like he could keep giving her the business forever, but Chanel wanted to keep things moving so she could watch a movie later. Or go to the mall. So, McCartney acquiesced and raised up off the bed and reached over to the dresser for a condom.

"Are you ready for me?" Chanel moaned as she pulled her legs back opening herself up to him.

"I'm going to rock your world," claimed McCartney. "I'm going to pile drive you. Take no prisoners!"

McCartney climbed on top of Chanel. There was so much lube involved in this process that it was like a slip and slide up in there. McCartney looked down into the eyes of what he viewed as a beautiful young girl. The eyes that looked back were those of a fucked-out whore. It was sad! It is uncomfortable to speak the truth like that, but it was true. Chanel was used up, and she was in the process of being spit out by the degenerate society she was born into. Digital advertisements for selling sex. On top of Chanel, McCartney had a desperate, hungry look. He was wild with desire. Chanel looked back up at him. She tried to feel some desire, tried to pretend that she was in love with the old man, but she couldn't. She was disgusted by his long Grasshopper face and bulging eyes. She would have laughed at his skunk-stripe but she didn't feel like making the exertion. She wasn't in love, obviously. Not at all. As he was moving in an out, the look on his face indicated that he felt as if he was on top of the world. He must have felt so powerful and all-important. As she took him in and out of her, she felt like she was being crushed, lied to, destroyed, used. She moaned, but not out of pleasure, she just wanted to speed him up and get the job done. She despised him. She wanted her insides back!

"I'm putting everything I have inside you!" McCartney grunted. "I can't give you anymore. Can you feel that hammer?"

Everything in McCartney's heart, everything in his body, everything in his existence, was nothing. He was truly worth nothing. He was a walking zero. From a distance, McCartney appeared happy and interesting; he had his grandfather's money from PartDok after all, and with that he bought nice things. He had several fast cars. He had a big, beautiful house. He appeared successful. It was textbook privilege! The close up, the reality, was ugly, dishonest and malicious.

He kept his head to the side of Chanel's and angled his eyes down, only focusing on her face when he kissed her. His left hand pawed at her right breast, while he stabilized himself with his right elbow and continued on. Then, he stabilized himself with his left elbow while plugging his right middle finger back inside his sprat. Deeper now. His finger was up to his second knuckle and he was still pressing it further. Paul McCartney tasted his own finger. Why the fuck did he do that? What the fuck! Suddenly he was more than ready, and then the whole thing was over.

"What is it?" Chanel moaned. "Are you okay?"

The Grasshopper dismounted and took a couple hops to the

bathroom.

"Seriously are you okay?" Chanel called from the bedroom.

"I'm fine that was awesome. That was great! I'm cleaning up."

His mind hopped to other subjects, seemingly at random. He thought of a record player, spinning a vinyl record playing a slow love song. He thought of a vase, holding flowers. Then everything was spinning. He kept moving.

"Oh my God," she said back. "Okay, cool I was worried that you got up so fast. It's like you jumped out of bed. Ha-ha."

Chanel laughed. She just stood there, laughing, even though she had just been throttled by a guy thirty years her senior in exchange for five hundred bucks. Perhaps she was lost in the moment. She smiled.

The reason that McCartney had jumped out of bed so quickly was that he started to have hallucinations. He looked at Chanel again and saw fire ants crawling near Chanel's wa wa. They weren't really there. To McCartney, they were devouring her one bite at a time and the bites were causing her to swell and turn a bright reddish purple — reminiscent of Vixen. In a mere ten seconds her little cooch suddenly looked, to McCartney only, like a seven or eight pound grape. For a quick second McCartney leaned toward her to taste the grape. He loved grape juice! Apparently distracted by something else, he looked to his left. He loved pomegranate. He heard music pumping, but it was his imagination. The whole scene was a hallucination. The music kept pumping. Phwump, Phwump, Phwump. He was going nuts. He had to get the fuck out of there!

"It was great," the Grasshopper hollered back, fighting to try to get control of his mind. "I don't want you to worry. Hey, I know I'm a great guy. I have core values. Like everyone, I have my own problems but I want to be able to communicate with you. I want to be open with you. We have our own relationship, you know! My wife thinks I'm a cunt-chaser. She's so shallow. All she does is sit around all day with other women who don't do anything productive and they gossip. Maybe you have it right. Maybe you're right. I know I'm rambling, but I need to get some stuff off my chest. I feel like I'm in rehab again, except I can be more honest around you. In rehab I say what they want me to say. I just throw out some bullshit. But I say it so well, they believe every word! I mean, jeesh, we have a relationship."

"Ummm, yeah."

"Wow! You're a good listener. You're paying attention. It's the full experience. Listen, I don't mind whatever my wife gossips about. She never does shit. Me? I'm driven for success, like my sports company TENACIOUS. My dad, Steve, who lives in Philadelphia, took his dad's money and chased fast women every which way. Hey Chanel, I have to run along. Chanel? I have to bounce out of here."

"Okay, love," Chanel said.

The Grasshopper was really fucked up.

"I'll see you next time," she continued.

"Let me know if you want me to bring anything for you next time. Love ya."

"Maybe champagne?" she volunteered.

"Of course. I'll bring the best. Money is not an issue! See ya."

McCartney stuck his lips out in a hard, gluttonous way and at the same time hopped, feverishly, back to his sports car and sped off. He had to get back to the McMansion before his wife got suspicious. Shit, the real estate agent was coming over first thing in the morning. He had to sign all of that paperwork for the bid! What a headache. Would he use grandpa's trust fund to finance the TENACIOUS facility? Who the fuck knows! Maybe he would talk to his Uncle Marty and Marty would fund them for him? Maybe he would fund the projects from his allowance. Maybe he would tell the real estate agent to fuck the hell off? Maybe he would hop along to some other project. Who knows? Fuck Maddox Malone anyway, what was he going to do? No, he thought, he would sign the offer for the TENACIOUS facility. He told himself he was going to do it.

McCartney laughed again, loudly "ha-ha-ha-ha-ha."

It was a piercing, high-pitched cackle. It was just another day for the Grasshopper. He didn't care about anyone other than himself. And, when he was honest, he glimpsed his true self — a lazy, degenerate, dishonest, amoral, weak, lecherous bug. He kept driving, pressing the pedal in his turbo-core sports coupe to go faster. The engine responded with a whirr and a buzz and the powerful German sports car clipped along, tearing up the road.

With these negative thoughts creeping into his head, he had to shut it down. So he yelled "Let's do this!" even though there was no one else in his car. He brought his mind back to Chanel for a minute. He had wanted her so bad. He got her so good, used her. Yet, driving away from her apartment when the appointment was over, he still felt so empty. So empty that even he, the soul-less Grasshopper, could recognize the feeling was emptiness. Since he felt empty so often usually he didn't notice. It wasn't his ordinary day-to-day meaninglessness, this time. This wasn't the same emptiness he felt every other God-damned day. It was a more aggressive emptiness than usual.

To block that feeling, he shut down his mind. To do that, he turned up the music and pumped his fist to the beat. The last time Maddox had rode in Paul's car, he had changed the satellite radio station to nineties rock. It was still tuned to that station. McCartney, drugged out of his mind but with the booze wearing off, was rocking to the music.

> I have to get it
> Get it right
> What I need
> It's what I need

McCartney was dirty. He hadn't showered after the sex. He hadn't even washed his hands. He had his own fluids on his stomach. His fingers smelled like either wa-wa or sprat, depending on the exact finger. He could still taste Chanel on his lips and tongue. Now, as he drove, it was the taste of disappointment. At the time of the tryst, at the time of the action, it was the taste of excitement, of exhilaration. If he had any introspection at all, he would have learned long ago, from hundreds, even thousands, of experiences on that particular website, that having sex with someone you don't give a fuck about feels emptier than not having the sex in the first place. After the sex is finished, the only thing left is the big empty.

McCartney was so empty, he was full.

STACKS OF CASH

✤✤

On the other side of the country from McCartney and Chanel and their sexual transaction, the cocktails were already flowing at the hotel bar and grill in the South Beach section of Miami. Maddox had spent the morning flying across the country. On the plane, he read Jules Verne's *a Floating City*. The book was really flat, to be honest, but there was an intriguing plot background that caught Maddox's attention. A woman on a boat to New York, from Paris, doesn't know that her husband, whom she hates, and another man, whom she says she truly loves, are both on board the ship. Maddox was working through the novel and he noticed himself anticipating some good, old-fashioned violence with, possibly, a dash of heartbreak mixed in.

Maddox hailed a cab outside of the airport and jumped right in. His energy was extremely positive because he was still buzzing from the news that Paul McCartney told him the night before. The TENACIOUS training facility purchase was going through! Maddox's system was functional, as he was living mostly on black iced coffee, almonds and fiber. His vodka intake was way up, though, as that was always directly proportional to his level of recruiting activity. And right now, he was recruiting eleven football players to the Malone Agency, including O-Bad and E Fear. It seemed like every recruiting meeting was a boozy, cocktail-filled affair.

His mindset was myopic in that he was focused intently on the Malone Agency's business. No time to think about more important things – and no regard for more important things as, in fact, more important. It was a roller coaster ride, since one minute he might be in despair over thoughts related to Pepe Soliz and his rape of April. He worried about losing his commissions with Pepe in jail or deported. The next minute, he might be worrying about the financial problems on the Platform. Then, he might flash to some positive news, such as the TENACIOUS facility bid that was being entered on this very morning.

It was hard to stay steady. It was hard to stay level, to keep his foundation. Maddox really focused on doing that, though. Despite the peaks and valleys, overall he was fine. Maddox was still cruising over to the hotel where he was supposed to meet up with Elk Fearghus, Senior, and Major O. The ride from the airport would be at least thirty minutes, possibly longer. Big Elk and Major O, had already been at the Clevelander for a while. They had been with Zaine Fuller, a runner and recruiter for the Malone Agency.

Zaine Fuller had, just a couple of hours before, filled the pockets of Big Elk and Major O with ten thousand dollars cash, each. He handed both of them an envelope stuffed with hundreds. When he passed the money to them, he held the envelope with his right hand, passing it to the left hand of each of the other men. With his left hand, he patted the right shoulder of the receiver. On his face was a curly smile. The left corner of his mouth curled a little higher than the right, and his left eye squinted about twenty percent more than the right to accommodate the curl. Major O had immediately stuffed the money into a pocket of his windbreaker. His face was relaxed and knowing. Kuhhhmff. Big Elk had stashed his envelope in a travel pack, made to carry passports, that was strapped to his waist. He laughed to himself with a little squeal. Tee hee hee. His face, outwardly, just looked excited. He didn't look crazed or tense — just excited and enthused. After the cash drop, Zaine, Big Elk and Major O had started drinking at eleven-thirty in the morning. Why not? That's what they had thought. So, Zaine had spent an hour and a half in the early part of the day having cocktails with the guys, but he had to head to the airport because he was going to deliver stacks of cash to another undergraduate football player. The other player was in Louisiana and went by the name of Jeremiah Raspico.

Maddox was unaware of Zaine's morning activities, unaware of the cash delivery. Maddox had been busy for a couple of days paying attention to Platform Volleyball and Pepe Soliz. Zaine had been e-mailing him with expense requests, but Maddox just approved them because his thoughts were elsewhere. Maddox's music feed was playing and the song was mid-stream as Maddox was in the stretch run arriving at the hotel and the adjacent bar.

I wanna feel the change consume me
Feel the outside turning in
I wanna feel the metamorphosis and
Cleansing I've endured within

Maddox handed the driver some cash, said his thanks, and stepped out of the car. He scanned the terrain. The familiar colors of Miami presented themselves spectacularly. The oranges, the yellows, the pinks, the light blues, the whites and off whites. Sun baked - rays of sun everywhere. It was glorious. Maddox felt blessed! This was pure Miami, the colors, the essence, the feel. It reminded Maddox, ambiguously, of Athens. It reminded Maddox of the Mediterranean lifestyle, which he appreciated - the bright whites, the pinks, the yellows and oranges, the blues. It was a couple hours before sunset and it was not too unpleasant even though it was most certainly on the hot and humid side. Maddox had worn climate-appropriate clothing in the form of a light cotton collared shirt and linen trousers. He encountered no resistance as he strolled through the hotel entrance, making his way to the bar. He saw Big Elk and Major O and he approached the table.

"Time to get this party started!" Maddox roared. Maddox was happy to see the guys, and he was still riding a wave of enthusiasm because Paul McCartney had resurfaced and updated Maddox on the timing for the TENACIOUS facility bid. Maddox was buzzing with energy from that great news.

"Maddox Malone in the house!" squealed Big Elk. "Tee hee hee tee hee!"

Big Elk was a hefty guy, probably three hundred pounds, but despite his size he had a cute high-pitched voice and a very distinctive laugh, a little titter. Raised in the Virgin Islands, he was a jovial fellow. He had a big, infectious smile. A great guy! Maddox really liked him and they embraced as they laughed and kept exchanging greetings.

"Yo, yo, yo, you Kuhmmmmfortable right now? Your face ain't smashed up, is it?" said Major O with a huge smile. Major O's comment brought back a wave of memories from the night in New Orleans when the fight had broken out in the bar. Maddox smiled. Then he laughed. Major O laughed. They clasped hands for a few seconds and both clearly enjoyed the moment of recollection.

The guys all kept exchanging little remarks. A guy rode by them on a beach cruiser bicycle. He made a huge impression on the group because of his outfit. He had on a tank top, a tight bathing suit, flip flops and a tri-colored little red beanie cap. He also had a pot belly and a goofy mustache. The guys hollered with laughter.

"Let's get some shots going up in here what do you guys say? Let's get this rolling," said Maddox.

"Man, I don't know about all that. We did two shots while Zaine was here and we also been having cocktails. We gotta slow ourselves down. I'm buzzin' my brother. I gotta admit, I'm buzzin'!"

"Yeah, but that was Zaine. We haven't had the chance to hang with Madd-Man. We haven't hung out with Madd-Man in what seems like weeks let's get this going, tee hee hee tee hee," said Big Elk with his trademark squeal.

The waitress came over and she was a sight to behold. She had dark brown hair, piercing green eyes, olive skin.

"How are you today? You are a little late to join this rowdy crew," she said, teasing. "I'm Alessandra, by the way. I've been helping these guys so far today."

"I'm good, I can't complain. I'd love to get a vodka and soda with a lime. Hey can we also get three shots of silver tequila, chilled? I've got to get these guys to learn how to have a good time, obviously they don't know how to do that," Maddox said, laughing.

"You got it," Alessandra replied with a friendly smile.

Alessandra walked off with her ass jiggling from side to side. Everyone in the party watched her walk off.

"What's good Madd-Man?"

"Man, I've been flying around working on stuff. Pushing the

boulder up the hill. The Platform is struggling for money again so I'm trying to make contingency plans. You know, for Lacy Stratton and everyone. That's a mess. Been working closely with Pepe Soliz on a couple of things. And here's the big news," Maddox continued, "We put in a bid, a two million dollar bid, for that training facility I told you guys about. TENACIOUS training. It's gonna be in Phoenix and also have a tennis academy attached. So things have been busy. It's good to take a breath and have a cocktail with the boys."

"Holy shit, that's big time!" said Major O. "That's fuckin' big time."

"Woah, Maddox, that's why we call you the Madd-Man. That's what's up! The Malone Agency all the way, tee hee hee," exclaimed Big Elk.

"You know how O-Bad used to be a really good tennis player before he gave it up to focus on football. That's great news!"

"I've seen O-Bad play tennis. That dude can fuckin' hit a tennis ball," said Big Elk.

"Fuck yeah, he can," said Major O.

"Guys, tennis is a sport for gentlemen. You can't cuss when you talk about it," Maddox joked.

"Tell that to John McEnroe," said Major O and everyone broke into laughter.

"So, Maddox, what do you think about signing Raspico? You think he's good enough to play at the next level? Zaine been giving him some cash. Stacks of cash, big stacks, to be honest," Big Elk said, smiling as he sipped his cocktail after changing the subject back to football. "Tee hee hee," giggled Big Elk.

Maddox paused and processed what Big Elk had said.

"Stacks of cash?" Maddox's face went blank, then it flushed red as he asked Big Elk to repeat himself.

"Yeah, man. Zaine been givin' Raspico stacks of cash, fat stacks, every other week. Says he's expensing it to you. He says he puts the expenses in an email invoice to you every couple weeks. He's been giving money to players all across the country," said the Big Bahamian.

Another pause ensued. Maddox just sat there, staring at Big Elk. Big Elk was trying to process the look on Maddox's face. Everyone took another sip of their cocktails.

"I gotta be honest with you, he's been giving money to me and to Major O also. It's not the reason we are signing with you, but it's a big part of it because it's a huge support for us right now and of course all the other agencies are offering the same thing. All the agencies be givin' stacks of cash! You didn't know that?"

"Really?" asked Maddox after a long silence.

The statement screeched the party to a halt, at least temporarily. Big Elk realized that he had made a significant disclosure. He was genuinely surprised that Maddox didn't know about the stacks of cash. Now, the cat was out of the bag! He let it sit there for a second while he assessed Maddox's reaction. Maddox's face stayed blank but was still flushed, just a bit. Elk could tell that he had registered a decent shock to the system. "Mother Fucking Zaine," thought Maddox. That mother fucker! What was he doing?

"Yeah. I can't believe you didn't know that," Big Elk said, matter of fact.

"How many stacks of cash is Zaine giving everyone? How often?" Maddox asked. "You say fat stacks but how much does that mean?"

Big Elk swallowed and then spoke. "He gives him three stacks of cash every other Tuesday and he gives his momma two stacks of cash a month also. I'm not trying to get the guy in trouble, I thought he would have told you. I didn't mean to rat him out. I was asking because I want to be a part of the Malone Agency and it's only gonna help me if we sign the best players. I'm in this thing for the long term," said Big Elk. Elk had been requesting a job with Maddox's agency as a recruiter. "He gave me and Major O ten stacks of cash each, today. I got it right here in my travel pack."

"Wow," said Maddox. "I have to think about the whole thing. It's news to me. That's news to me," Maddox offered up a bit awkwardly. "We'll work through it, though. It is what it is. I'll call Zaine later today and find out what's going on. Let's just talk about it later."

"That sounds about right," chimed in Major O as he took a sip of his cocktail. Major O could tell Maddox was uncomfortable and jumped in to help change the subject.

Maddox processed that part of the conversation internally. He didn't want to talk about it anymore until he spoke with Zaine. Maddox steered the conversation away from the cash payments. Those were illegal! He didn't know what the penalties would be for the agency and, possibly, him personally. His mind raced. He felt stunned. He felt unsettled. He wanted to sign O-Bad and E Fear, of course. But he never thought his recruiter Zaine would break the law to do it. Maddox sat there, feeling paralyzed.

"Well, anyway. Raspico looks good to me at the level he's playing at now but I haven't talked to any scouts about him," Maddox said, trying to bring the mood back around to a carefree visit.

"Yeah, he looks good to me too. But you're right, a lot of guys look good," said Elk while shaking his head slowly. "Zaine can't be giving money to everybody. It's illegal and it's not a good look. I get it when some guys need help. But come on."

Right then Alessandra arrived with more shots of silver tequila, which helped Maddox push the thought of the illegal payments out of his mind. She passed them out with a smile and said "I'll be back in a minute to check on you boys" and then she walked off. The men raised a toast and downed the shots. Big Elk laughed his customary "tee hee hee tee hee." After he took his shot, Maddox gave a playful grimace and breathed in deeply through a tight mouth. Major O just wore the shot right to his face and then sat there, looking relaxed. He looked happy, he looked kuhhhmff.

"Those pass rush guys can really be in demand. But he's got to be able to play the run too," said Elk, restarting the same conversation about Raspico.

"What is that dude wearing over there?" said Major O, changing the subject.

"Bro, I think it's a furry fedora," said Maddox, squinting his eyes in the direction of the man.

"You got to be kidding me," said Major O.

"Not kidding."

"That thing looks like it belongs on an Italian in Brooklyn. Maybe on a dude that looks like Joe Pesci, tee hee hee tee hee."

"Listen to Big Elk makin' fun of Italians. What do people do in the Virgin Islands anyway? Go to the beach and eat coconut? Man, I wanna move to the Virgin Islands," said Maddox. "I wanna run up and down the beach in a loin cloth with a big machete and chop up and eat fresh coconut! That's living man."

"No joke, that's kuhhhmff!" said Major O.

"Fuck yeah, eating coconuts and then grabbing coconuts on the beach!"

"Grabbing coconuts."

Everyone laughed. When it died down, Maddox sat at the table. Then he sipped his vodka and soda. He flashed back to the conversation about Zaine giving stacks of cash to Raspico, Big Elk and Major O and also E Fear and O-Bad. How long had this been going on? How much? These players both said that they were signing with Maddox, but what effect would this illegal activity have on the process? He was very disappointed that he had to find out this way. He was very disappointed that he learned about the payments from Big Elk instead of the recruiter himself. He would have to put it out of his head and deal with it later, after he talked to Zaine.

"Hey guys, let's have one more drink and one more shot and then hit the strip clubs," said Major O.

"Man, you like the old Richard Pryor joke that you don't like cocaine you just like how it smells, tee hee hee, that's how you are about the strip clubs, tee hee," said Big Elk.

"That don't even make no God-damn sense Big Elk," said Major O, laughing.

"Why we gonna go and do that? We're having a good time here," said Maddox.

"Why we gonna go see naked women? Do you really have to ask that? Let's go see some tits and ass. Come on now! We in Florida!" said Major O.

"Yeah they will totally love us, three drunk clowns."

Maddox ordered another round of drinks. The last round, finally! The shots came back first.

"Who wants to do the toast?"

"You do it."

"Why me?"

"You just flew in, you late to the party," said Big Elk. "Tee hee hee."

"So what?" asked Maddox. "What the fuck does that have to do with anything?"

"Well, you got them good words. You got that vo-cab-u-lary! Tee hee hee, tee hee."

"Nah, man, Major O made up 'kuuuhhhmmff.' I got all the boring words. Major O has art. Major O is a word artist," said Maddox. "Let's make Major O do the toast."

"Let's go Madd-Man! Stop fuckin' around and make the fuckin' toast!"

"Okay, here goes," said Maddox.

Maddox raised his glass. He cleared his throat. He paused. He looked at Big Elk. Then he looked at Major O. Then he spoke.

"I'd rather be with the people in this bar than the finest people I know. Cheers!" said Maddox.

It was one of those generic toasts and Maddox didn't think it was that great, but it always drew a laugh from the people on the receiving end of the jab. And today was no different.

"Tee hee hee." Big Elk just sat there and laughed. "Tee hee hee." Then he sipped his cocktail.

"Ha-ha I'll drink to that!" said Major O.

"Cheers, brothers."

"Cheers."

The other drinks arrived and the guys sipped on those. The Miami sun shone down. The party just kept going. The guys relaxed and shot the shit. They gave each other hell. Fifteen minutes later they paid the tab and jumped into a cab to a cabaret that was a short ride northwest, heading inland from South Beach. Maddox, Big Elk and Major O walked right in to the joint.

Maddox ordered three more shots of tequila and another round of vodka and sodas for everyone. Maddox was pretty drunk, yet again. Recruiting was always a boozy process. With Major O and Big Elk, especially. Maddox always ended up taking the guys out drinking. He took a deep sip of his vodka and soda. The guys clinked their shots together and drank them. Tootsie's was the largest strip club in the world, at least according to them. The music was loud and the place was clean, which was a plus. On the main stage, the stripper Destiny was dancing to Buck Cherry, and the guys were enjoying her dance. Destiny was about five-foot-seven, and she had brown hair and green eyes. She had small, b cups with metal bars pierced through the nipples. The sexiest thing about her was her mouth, and a close second was her little butt. She bleached her wa-wa once a week and her coochie was freshly waxed. She was fun to watch, for those who enjoyed the repetition of the titty club. Her music blared.

> But I got a girl who can put on a show
> The dollar decides how far you can go
> She wraps those hands around that pole
> She licks those lips and off we go
> She takes it off nice and slow

Destiny was writhing around the pole and also gyrating certain parts of her body. Half of the guys in the club were watching her intently. The other half were doing something else entirely, and not even paying attention to her. Maddox, Big Elk and Major O were talking football, but they kept glancing up at Destiny every few seconds.

"Where do you think E Fear gonna be drafted, Maddox?" asked Big Elk. Maddox was buzzing from the vodka and tequila. He hated talking football and business when he was out drinking with the guys. He would rather just shoot the shit. But draft projections always came up, every time the recruiting process took place. Maddox looked for his crystal ball — it was nowhere to be found, so he just started talking.

"Uhh... Well, I think it could be anywhere from the first to third round. I know that's a big range but I'm saying that is what is possible. Let's see how pro day goes. He has the prototypical size and he can really move. He's like a big cat."

"Oh yeah a big cat I like that tee hee hee."

"A big, powerful cat. The scouts that I've talked to are all infatuated with Arlo Dawson, though. So I don't know man. I have a crystal ball but I left it at home."

"Yeah, I hear you. I know it can be a range. I haven't heard about him creeping into the top twenty picks. So I'm thinking second round, even though I'm hoping for late first round."

"We'll have to see what happens. We're doing all the right things. We made the right plan."

"That's what we have to do with O-Bad," chimed in Major O. "We have to see. Everything gonna be fine."

"Hey, why don't they put some more comfortable chairs up in here?" asked Big Elk.

"I know. My ass feels like it's sitting on a turtle shell. I'm gonna need a massage to be able to fly home. My ass feels like raw beef. I hope there's not a butcher here," said Major O.

"Seriously? What the fuck does that even mean?"

"What are you guys talking about?"

Everyone laughed. Elk with his customary, wild "tee hee hee tee hee." Maddox and Major O with more standard, but still enthusiastic, laughs.

"We're talking about the football draft. The football draft," Maddox deadpanned. Then he let loose a big, exaggerated smile.

Maddox didn't think it was that funny, he was just goofing around. But the guys laughed, they loved it. Drunken revelry!

"Hey boys, anybody want a dance?" A stripper named Angel said as she came by and rubbed up on the boys to try to tempt one of them into a private room. Angel was about five-foot-nine and blonde. She had a Mohawk haircut. She had a nice round ass and big tits. Great calves. You could tell by looking at her that she would make her money stripping and then spend it on some other bullshit. Who knows what? Angel was hot but everyone passed on the private dance so they could keep talking. The look in her eye was seductive, but everyone could tell that she was only stripping for the money. Same as all the girls.

"In a bit, probably. We're talking now," said Big Elk.

"Okay, thanks sweetie."

"Anytime, baby."

The night finally wrapped up, a couple of hours later, around two in the morning. In the meantime, the guys had watched at least fifteen young strippers dance up on the stage, three minutes at a time. There was exposed coochie everywhere! Guys were having a great, superficial time. A bleached blond with big cannons who went by the stage name of Amaris, sat on Maddox's lap and ground herself into him. They managed to make some small talk while she rode on his lap. Amaris was nineteen and hailed from northeast Florida. She had never seen anything outside of Florida, she had no knowledge of the world. Every boyfriend – every single one – promised her big things but always eventually left her after doing nothing productive. The boyfriends always rearranged the furniture but they never made any home improvements! Once they had been inside enough, they just moved on to a different location.

She seemed nice enough to Maddox. But Maddox didn't see how she would ever be able to get off the pole — at least until she hit the wall in her thirties. Then the pole wouldn't be there for her. He didn't have time to worry about all that, so he just enjoyed the lap dance as much as he could while staying married. Afterword, Maddox, Major O and Big Elk parted ways. It was a long recruiting and partying night. Both of the recruits' dads had a great time. O-Bad and E Fear were completely committed to the Malone Agency. That was huge! Maddox disregarded the revelation about Zaine making illegal cash payments to the players and their families. He blocked it out of his mind. He would just have to figure out what to do about all that later. Besides, Maddox was riding a wave of good news with the TENACIOUS facility bid officially in. But, he was tired from all the work and travel. As soon as Maddox made it back to his hotel room, he crashed, face down. He was exhausted and needed to get a little bit of rest.

He had to fly to Los Angeles in four hours!

No, It's His Sister

❋❋

The alarm on Maddox Malone's smart phone went off a mere two hours later. It was blaring right in his face! Maddox woke with a start and tried to clear the cobwebs. He wasn't hung over, really. Was he? He told himself he wasn't. He didn't know how much vodka he had drank. He lost track. Same for tequila. After further consideration, he realized that he was definitely hung over, but all things considered he told himself that he was fine, besides being tired from getting only two hours of fitful sleep.

Maddox trudged down to the lobby and jumped into the waiting car. He arrived and made his way through security, stopping for two Bloody Marys. Both of them were doubles. Maddox headed into the stand-alone, full book shop. It wasn't just an airport convenience store with a few books in the corner. It had an excellent selection! Pressed for time before his flight, Maddox settled quickly on a hardcover copy of the complete short novels of Anton Chekhov. Right before takeoff, his smart phone rang and buzzed. It was his client, Lacy Stratton, calling.

"Hey Lacy."

"Hi, Maddy. How are you?" asked Lacy.

"Great, here. You?"

"Not so good. I know we need to catch up about the Platform Volleyball Tour and all, but I was hoping we could do that another time. Hopefully they don't go totally broke. Anyway, I have a question."

"Go for it, Lacy."

"I need a referral for Carlton's adopted nephew, Carter. Carter broke his arm in a bad fall. They want someone who has experience in sports medicine to handle it because they are grooming Carter for an athletic future," said Lacy.

Maddox absolutely hated hearing anything about Carlton Duffer. That guy was a fucking idiot! Apparently, his brother and his brother's wife were as well. Grooming Carter for an athletic future? Maddox laughed to himself. Did she really say that?

Maddox vaguely recalled the story of Danny Duffer, Carlton's son who had become Carlton's brother through his adoption by Todd, Carlton's father, which was facilitated by Carlton and his tequila shots, so Maddox asked, "Lacy, we're not talking about Danny Duffer, are we?"

"No, Maddy. Danny only just turned eighteen. He hasn't adopted anyone. Besides, he transitioned a couple years ago. He's Danielle now," said Lacy.

"Wait, what?" asked Maddox.

"Yeah, he transitioned."

"Huh? Transitioned? Like that Olympic guy?"

"Oh yeah, you didn't know that? I guess she hasn't been out on the platform much since she became a girl."

"No, I never heard that," said Maddox. "I didn't know."

"Well, anyway, yeah. She did. She's a girl now. Danielle's the name," said Lacy.

"So, Carlton has a daughter?" asked Maddox.

"No, it's his sister. Remember, Carlton's dad Todd adopted Danny," said Lacy.

"Okay, so he was his son, but then his dad adopted Danny and he became Carlton's brother?" asked Maddox.

"Exactly. Then Danny transitioned and became Carlton's sister, Danielle," said Lacy.

"Got it. But Danielle was never Carlton's daughter?"

"No, because Danny already had been adopted by Todd, Carlton's dad. So Danny Duffer was already not Carlton's son by the time that Danny became Danielle. He went straight from brother to sister, Danielle never looped back to daughter," said Lacy.

"He never made the loop to daughter? I think I get it."

"Well, she didn't."

"Who?" asked Maddox, since he had become confused.

"Danielle. Straight from brother to sister. No daughter."

"Okay, I understand that. So Danny has been everything besides Carlton's daughter?"

"Exactly."

"Alright," said Maddox, taking a deep breath. He stared straight ahead, forcefully. "Back to the other kid. Carter. How old is he?"

"Carter is eight."

"They're grooming him for what, exactly?" asked Maddox. He was trying to be diplomatic!

"Well, Carter's, ahem, not super bright, so the best chance he has to go to college is if he's good at football or something like that. They have him wearing a helmet and practicing by chasing after a chicken in the back yard, like Rocky. If he catches the chicken, he gets candy."

Maddox waited for laughter but none followed. She wasn't joking! Maddox thought, slowly, because he was stunned. A dumb kid in a football helmet chasing a chicken in the backyard?

"Are you kidding?" Maddox asked.

"No."

Three seconds of stunned silence ensued.

"Okay, let me hang up and try to find an arm guy. I'm about to take off on my plane so worst case I'll send you the info when I land. But I'll do it before I take off if I can. Lemme see what I can do."

"Thanks, Maddy!"

Maddox called his friend who was a trainer in Phoenix and asked for a referral to a sports-related orthopedist. The trainer said to give him a couple minutes and he would text a name. He did, and

Maddox sent the name and number to Lacy for Carter.

Maddox had seen the boy, Carter, one time in Los Angeles on the Platform, during a volleyball event. When he met the boy, Maddox felt very sorry for the boy. It was a heartbreaking circumstance! The boy didn't look well. He had a poor physique, a snotty, flat nose, dull eyes and strange visage. Carter's belly was protruding almost unnaturally and he was chewing on a mangled hot dog that was undoubtedly brewing dangerous germ cultures. Maybe he was immune? The boy's belly was distended. Maybe he wasn't immune? The belly looked like a bowling ball on the front of his torso. For a brief second, Maddox contemplated what a damaged and empty soul Carlton Duffer's brother and his wife must have had to chase down that boy in his home country, take him to a foreign land and then groom him for football. How could they deprive the boy of his heritage, his home, his family, his traditions, his culture? They just ripped the poor boy out of his home country of Ghana and brought him all the way across the world and tried to make him act like someone he just wasn't. To Maddox, that sad adoption was a clear symptom of the emptiness of American techno-democratic society. He hadn't fully articulated the concept to himself, but he thought that exact thing, very clearly. He just didn't know exactly why he thought that.

If Maddox had taken the time to lay out his thoughts on the matter, he would have done it this way. One day, not too long ago, people decided that they cannot live their lives without a smart phone; all of a sudden everyone *had* to have one. They would buy these fancy smart phones, these hand-held computers, made by Endless Content or some other manufacturer. It became, in fact, rare to see a person not staring at a smart phone screen. Some years earlier this need for a smart phone and constant connection to digital communication and digital media would have dumbfounded the same exact people who now stared at their phone constantly. All the time!

Once the smart phones were everywhere, and there was a network, the average wage-slave and his cubicle-dwelling girlfriend started to consume more and more digital media on their Endless Content smart phones, and many people began producing this type of content as well.

Everyone produced content! The people provided the product to each other, and they consumed each other's product, which was content they posted - pictures, videos, messages, memes - in a new technological ecosystem. It was hard to tell the fresh content from the waste product! It all sort of tasted the same. But no one cared what it tasted like, they just consumed everything! In many posts, they would see celebrities with their adopted children! The celebrities all adopted children from destitute places like Africa or Haiti or Cambodia. The celebrities plucked these wonderful little cherries from their native countries, brought them to America, and gave them everything.

This was a wonderful thing, thought the social media consumers! They wanted to emulate the stars in their own personal life! This was what happened with Lacy's brother-in-law and the adopted boy that they called Carter.

ii

Maddox landed in Los Angeles, and half an hour later, he opened the door of Nathan's Manhattan Beach and looked for two familiar men. Dave Olson and Omar Matish both worked in marketing for a large corporate-side agency. Maddox had done a couple big deals together, made a lot of money together. Dave and Omar both wanted Maddox to bring them business in the future, and Maddox typically enjoyed their company. Dave and Omar were seated at a high table in the bar area.

"What's happening, guys?" Maddox asked them.

"Nothing, man, good to see you," Dave said. "You hungry?"

"I don't know what I want to eat. Just getting my feet underneath me. How are you doing, Dave? What's up, Omar?" said Maddox, nodding his head as he finished speaking.

"Not much Maddox, working today."

Outside, it was a typical Southern California day. The plastic sunlight came in through the window. Where the sun hit directly, it felt warm. It felt good! The view of the beach was impeccable. There was a soft wind. The scenery was crisp. Los Angeles may have been wildly over-populated, but the weather was perfect! The guys read the menu and shot the shit.

"What are you going to be doing in Las Vegas?" Omar asked Maddox at one point in the conversation.

"I'm recruiting a golfer that's from there. I have a partner out of Phoenix who is funding a training facility, a golf tour, and a wrestling league. So we're moving towards doing some more golf stuff on the rep side. We just put in the bid to purchase the training facility. TENACIOUS. I'm pretty excited."

"That's awesome. Congratulations on that, it sounds great. Cool name, TENACIOUS. How did the last Platform event go? Wasn't that last weekend or something?"

"Fuck, Omar. I'm worried. No-one was there. No sponsors attended. The Platform is not well kept up. Efficient-Pop has gone down the tubes. I tried to eat some Efficient-Pop the other day and it's horrible. It tastes like shit. It tastes like cardboard swimming in shitty vegetable seed oil. Like canola oil or something. No wonder Harry Oswald yelled that when he jumped off the Platform. At least the ocean, the overall setting, was still beautiful."

"Oh wow," said Dave. "That sucks."

"To top it off, Lacy's husband — Carlton Duffer — got shipped off to rehab. Also, Lacy's dad told me that Carlton is angling to become Lacy's agent. He wants to replace me."

"Homey gonna replace Maddox Malone? The original Maddman? I don't think so! On that other stuff, rehab and stuff, don't get dragged into that shit. That's a no-win situation for you."

They ordered their food.

Omar had a shaved head and was wearing a light blue golf shirt. His face was round, caramel colored as he was a mix of black and Latino heritage. He had round eyes, a flat nose and medium-sized lips. His khakis were too big for him.

Dave was about the same size as Omar, maybe five-foot-eleven. Not too fat, but definitely soft. He looked like he was German or something like that. Their faces were the same shape, but Dave had some hair, a more protruding nose and tighter lips. He also had a golf shirt on and some khakis. They sat leaning forward, with their forearms on the round bar table.

"The weather's been nice here, that's for sure," said Dave. "Besides the bullshit you mentioned did you have a good time?"

"No. I'm not gonna lie, I'm really worried about the Platform. Like I said, it was pretty bleak and pretty grave. But the weather was beautiful. I don't know what's going to happen."

"That's crazy. Well, one of the reasons me and Dave wanted to catch up with you today is to make sure you keep us in mind if there's any way we can help you or your clients on the Platform," agreed Omar. "Even though it's struggling, you never know."

"I'll do that," said Maddox. "I'm not sure what's gonna happen, I'm not even sure what I'm gonna do regarding the Platform but I'll definitely keep you two guys in mind. You know I will, we pulled off some big deals together."

"You remember what we did with the Pogo Back, bro," said Dave. "If we can move that product, we can move anything. You know what we can do with our advertising system. Eyeballs, man. We can help reach a lot of people. We can move a lot of product. We can shove any product, no matter how shitty it is, right down people's throats."

Maddox, Dave and Omar had put together a deal to promote Pogo Back with one of Maddox's action sports clients. A snowboarder. Pogo Back was basically a pogo stick that attached to its owners back — no hands required! The company's slogan was "Good Luck!"

It was terrible!

It was dangerous!

But Maddox, Omar and Dave managed to sell tens of thousands of Pogo Backs before Pogo Back's parent company became hopelessly mired in product liability litigation. The owner of the Pogo Back Holding Corporation fled the country, ending up somewhere in East Asia, with all sorts of rumors, mostly about drugs, sex and money, shadowing him. But Maddox, Omar and Dave — outside consultants — walked away unscathed, with full pockets. In fact, they each made a couple hundred thousand dollars on the Pogo Back deal. In the back of his mind, Maddox knew that the Pogo Back was a lousy, dangerous product. So did Omar and Dave. But they all wanted the money, so they pushed it anyway. In the business community, it wasn't even frowned upon at the time. They were featured in some glossy marketing journals. It was a feather in their cap!

"Oh, I remember Pogo Back well. I can't believe we got away with that," said Maddox with a smile and a wink.

Everyone laughed. They laughed and laughed.

A few minutes later, the waiter navigated through all the tables of customers staring at their smart phones and put the turkey sandwich, salmon salad and breakfast burrito on the table. He brought refilled waters and then walked off back again through the digital lunchroom. The conversation lulled as the men ate. Omar ate his salmon salad with a high level of ferocity.

"So Lacy's husband is really gonna try to represent her?"

"I guess," said Maddox. "I don't really care, the Platform is so shaky right now everything might fall apart."

"What's her husband's name again? I thought I remember hearing that guy played Platform Volleyball too," Dave asked Maddox.

"Carlton Duffer."

There was a pause.

"Why is her name Stratton?" asked Omar.

"She didn't like the name Duffer. She thought Lacy Duffer sounded like an antique chair."

"What did he go to rehab for?"

"Not a hundred percent sure, but I heard he was hitting the Dragon and the Moose and then got caught, you know, caught, with the yoga instructor. He's still in rehab."

"She should ditch that Duffer," said Omar.

"Omar thinks he knows everything," said Dave.

"Well?" Omar said, smiling.

"You act like you're the coolest guy, married to the greatest woman on the planet. You're not. You're a bald, single Latin mulatto or some fucking mystery-meat guy who has a smashed face. I honestly can't believe anyone would date you. Who are you?" Dave said, laughing.

Omar was laughing even harder.

"Go fuck yourself!" Omar hollered. "You're mad because you told Diana about your undying love for her before she left your ass." Omar raised his voice to a high pitch and continued, "You complete me! You are everything to me!" he squealed, mocking Dave. "Bro, she left your ass anyway."

"I did do that, I did. I hate talking to Omar about this shit because he knows everything. He knows everything," Dave said as he laughed hard and his face turned beet red. Everyone was still in good humor despite the strong needling.

"Man, Diana didn't want to complete you – she wanted to follow your lead, like any good woman wants to," said Omar. "If she's the center of your existence then you ain't got shit to offer her. Do something, man. Not just selling Pogo Backs. She's like 'why don't you have other shit going on too? Why are you so clingy on me? What the fuck is wrong with my dude?'"

Dave gave a shrug in Maddox's direction as if to deflect the content a bit, but the reality is that both Dave and Maddox were listening intently. Omar was getting on a roll.

"Just because she does it doesn't mean she really wants to walk all over you. She just can't control her emotions, it's really that simple.

Listen to me. She can't control her emotions. You have to be the rock that doesn't get moved by that shit."

"It might be true, man. I never stood up to Diana," said Dave. "I thought giving into her would make her happy. Or maybe I thought it would appease her. She left me anyway," Dave said. "She worked me like a dog, she worked me for years, and she took my shit at the end. If I had it to do over again I would push back. I used to just let her win and never press anything. Then, later, she would come over and kiss me on my head and call me a little fuzzy rabbit or a cute little puddle bear."

"Woah, she called you puddle bear?" said Maddox.

"Yeah. The Puddle Bear."

"What is a Puddle Bear?" said Omar.

"No idea!" exclaimed the Puddle Bear.

"Oh, fuck!" Maddox exclaimed.

"Fuck, man," said Omar, shaking his head.

"Yeah pushing back sounds good in theory, Dave, but arguing and fighting all the time blows up a lot of marriages. And that sounds like where that would go," Maddox said. "So I don't know... I think it could be that you're damned if you do and you're damned if you don't. But at least it probably feels better to push back than to sit there like a little bitch. Ah, who knows, man?"

Talking about Dave's divorce made Maddox think of his own parents' divorce. Maddox had a good childhood. Almost ideal. He had a great family, with four brothers and sisters. All talented, nice people. Often, it's hard to say what causes the end of a marriage, and Maddox didn't necessarily know what caused his parents' marriage to break down and end in divorce. Over time, his mom began to despise his dad's opinions, and vice versa. This contempt then extended itself from opinions to thoughts to mannerisms to personal characteristics. Everything started to annoy. Everything broke down. Communication waned and then stopped. The more each of them felt this way, the more they despised one another. The mutual discontent with one another grew greater every day, every year - sometimes the growth could be measured in hours or even minutes. They began engaging separately in their own activities, hobbies and pastimes. Maddox's mom threw herself into her children's activities. Maddox's dad spent his free time as a sports fan or with other pursuits, including supporting his children. The domestic harmony of Maddox's family steadily declined over a long period of time. Nobody in the house was fully aware of this because of the intense focus on academic and athletic achievement and other activity — the daily routine, the daily grind, school activities, social lives. Then one day, it was all over. Maddox was a natural optimist who was usually very resilient. He was always a high achiever, bright eyed, funny. But the end of his parents' marriage had a negative effect on Maddox. It wore on him, every day. He wasn't emotionally equipped to process it and react to it. He walled himself off as much as he could.

Around this time, Maddox's angry twin was created. This was a side of Maddox marked by anger, disappointment and brooding. And stubborn-ness. He could chase the twin off for long periods of time, but the twin always came back. The angry twin grew whenever Maddox was forced to take sides with one parent over the other. He loved his mother, but often times he was in the uncomfortable and sickening position of being split in two parts. His thoughts might agree with his father, while his heart sided firmly with his mother. This split fed the angry twin and helped the twin grow strong.

Maddox's soul bounced back and forth between happiness and anger, between love and hate. It was destructive! Maddox didn't like the angry twin, not as much as he liked his normal self. But life went on, it had to.

Soon after, he had dived into his work at the Malone Agency, head first. He started to build a family of his own — that was a solution, Maddox thought. All of these thoughts raced through his mind while Dave kept speaking. His mind was racing! Maddox snapped back into the conversation when Dave spoke.

"Well, Omar knows everything about everything. He knows fuckin' everything. Let's ask him," Dave said with a chuckle.

"Yeah Omar what's the solution?" Maddox asked.

Omar's round face just sat there, hovering above the table. His head looked like a helium balloon. He looked like a round-headed smiling cat. Omar was hovering!

"The solution is the Chill Factor, my friends," Omar said with his face still hovering over the table and featuring a wry smile. "You have to give your woman a fraction of everything she gives you, that's the Chill Factor. It can be two-thirds, or it can be three-fourths — but no more than three-fourths, that's for God-damned sure. This has to do with everything. Messages, calls, gifts, nights out, declarations of love, signs of affection, kisses, even fighting and arguing. Also you have to maintain your own activities — mine's lifting — but it can be hunting, fishing, shooting, riding, basketball, whatever. It shows restraint and elevates your status. So what Dave did in terms of pushing back — not at all — was a huge mistake and probably helped end the marriage. But pushing back more, arguing more than she does, is also a huge mistake. You can't do either, you have to use the Chill Factor. If you don't, you're fucked."

Maddox had studied Ancient Greek at Berkeley for a time, before he went to law school there. He had read a lot of Ancient Greek philosophy and history. Omar's little speech triggered something in Maddox's mind.

Maddox chimed in, saying "Once, there was a philosopher, in ancient times, a Greek guy, I can't remember which one, that was being asked if he had a wife. 'I have her,' he said, 'but she doesn't have me.' That sounds like Omar's Chill Factor." Maddox smiled broadly, then laughed. The others laughed as well.

"Yeah, that's the Chill Factor! You nailed it!" said Omar.

Omar paused. Everyone absorbed his comments. Maddox had no idea if he agreed with Omar or not but he found his thoughts interesting. Omar was opinionated and expressive. Maddox also reminded himself that Omar, with all the aggressive opinions, was single. Hmmm.

"Talk to me, Maddox," Omar said. "Not specifically about your marriage because that's none of my business, but about these topics we are touching on. I like learning new things," Omar said, finishing with a little smirk.

Maddox did not say anything for a full ten seconds.

"Yeah, my marriage to Laura ... I don't even know what to say about that. We're so busy day-to-day we are just going along. Getting through the day, getting through the week. I feel like all I do is work on the Malone Agency and that TENACIOUS facility project I told you about. But, I'll tell you this," Maddox said, "I agree with a lot of what has been said. And I see people make mistakes with women all the time. Young guys, my clients. Young athletes. Older guys too. They let the women run crazy game on them. They have no plan — they're not thinking with their head."

"Uh-huh," said Omar.

Maddox continued, "They have confidence in their sport or their job but not in other things. Sometimes they are surprisingly scared or shy. So they get what they get. But controlling the process has to do with some of the stuff you touched on earlier, Omar. Like setting your own agenda as a man, setting a plan."

Maddox paused for a second. He noticed that the guys were listening intently.

"So here's the thing, guys... here's the thing," Maddox continued. "The guys make the mistake of not working on themselves. I see it all the time. They work hard at their sport or a skill or whatever — they have to do that or they couldn't be professional athletes — but they are not working on themselves. On themmmm-sel-vvvves! You gotta do that or you have no value, no chance." said Maddox, not realizing that he was sharing some really good information.

The long lunch conversation wrapped up as Maddox promised to keep the guys posted about any developments on the Platform. Everyone enjoyed it and felt good about what they learned. After the lunch Maddox got in his rental car, made sure his bags were in the trunk. He went and parked by the beach. He walked across the sand and took a water taxi out to the Platform. He sat in the sun and watched Platform Volleyball matches. Just like the last Platform event, there were only a few people in the stands and no-one, not a soul, in the sponsor tent. Nobody was making deals, not at the moment! It was a ghost town. Maddox thought about the old Platform, the beautiful Platform out on the ocean, the Platform's potential. "Maybe the Platform itself was fine but the sport of volleyball wasn't the right fit?" thought Maddox. But those days seemed long gone, so Maddox wrapped things up and headed to the airport. He had the radio tuned to an outlaw country station and he sang along with Waylon.

> I've been down the Mississippi,
> Down through New Orleans, Yes, I have.
> I've played in California,
> There ain't too much I haven't seen.
> No, there ain't.
> Well, I'm a ramblin' man,
> Don't fool around with a ramblin' man.

Whenever he heard that song, it made Maddox think of his travels. He was born in Oklahoma, but only lived there for two weeks. Then, he was moved to California. School in Boston. He thought back fondly to his time teaching high school and coaching baseball in Louisiana – when he would travel to New Orleans from Baton Rouge for live music and nightlife. He had been everywhere in the country, everywhere in the world, most places several times, except Africa. He had no penchant for magic and disease. And, while the concept of hippos suited Maddox just fine, he was not fond with actual hippos! Was his experience worldliness? Cosmopolitanism? Or rootlessness & wanderlust? He shut his mind off and just enjoyed the music.

Soon, Maddox turned in the rental car at the airport and buzzed onto the shuttle over to the airline ticketing window. He went through expedited security and fifteen minutes later he was at the airport bar. Two vodka and sodas with a lime later, he was about to board his plane to Sin City. But then he decided to slug down yet another cocktail. After that, he boarded his plane.

Once in his seat, Maddox opened the Chekhov book that he purchased at the last airport. He read the first novella in the hardcover volume, which was, coincidentally, called *the Grasshopper*. It was the story of Dymov, a physician, and his marriage to Olga. Dymov got cucked by Ryabovsky, who gave Olga the business in numerous positions. Olga wanted it from Ryabovsky, who she found to be more exhilarating, more sexual, more exciting, than her husband Dymov. Soon enough, Olga got it good from Ryabovsky. She got blasted from behind, from the front, on bottom, on top, on all fours. Soon after his cucking by Ryabovsky, Dymov caught diphtheria. Then Dymov died. It was that simple, and it was all over. Reading the novella was a shock to Maddox's system. Shocking to see the fragility of life. Shocking to see the false permanence of marital bonds laid out on the page — even though Maddox had seen that in the real world with his parents. First, life and marriage were there. Then, they were over. So fast! And Maddox was terrified by the intimate view Chekhov gave him, the view into a destructive marriage. He couldn't get over the fact that Dymov got cucked by Ryabovsky who seemed like a pretentious piece of shit. A shittier artist! How did Dymov get cucked by that guy? The whims of Olga! After quickly reading the novella, despite being amazed by the story, Maddox grew weary and fell asleep. He woke when his plane landed, a short time later, in Las Vegas. He was in Sin City!

Dead Guy in the Living Room

❋❋

The house had to have been built in the nineteen-fifties. It was painted blue, but it was not kept up well and the blue paint was peeling and otherwise fading due to the harsh Alaska weather. There were white spruce trees lining the street and the sidewalk, they grew high enough to shade the second story of the house when the sun was strong. A cat sat on the porch rail, making a difficult balancing act look easy. The birds in the trees were chirping. An enormous black raven flew down and grabbed something out of the street and then flew back up into its tree. The raven had to weigh at least four pounds. He had shaggy throat feathers that made him look like a bearded, miniature dragon. The raven was feasting in the tree, enjoying a nice lunch.

A silence overcame the street, even the birds stopped making noise for a minute. A man's body was being carried into the house. He was placed on the living room table. His eyes were taped shut because there was a risk that they would pop open at any given time, and that would be very disturbing for everyone, except the dead guy. His mouth was slightly open. The opening looked black, it looked eerie. It was unclear as to whether the corpse had a full set of teeth.

The wind whistled through the spruce trees. A car horn honked in the distance, rare for this little town. There were children, Native American children, playing in a vacant lot about two blocks away. They could be heard at the faded blue house, because the acoustics in the area were so clean.

The two men that dropped off the body walked back out the front door. The house belonged to a woman named Betsy, who handed the men twenty dollars each and said thank you for the help. One of the men pocketed the money while the other slipped it into his wallet and put the wallet back in his jeans pocket. The woman, Betsy, took off her shoes and left them on the little porch.

She was wearing a knit cap and a gray coat, together with jeans. The men drove off. Betsy walked into the house and glanced around.

There was no one else there. It was just Betsy and her brother's corpse. Her brother had hanged himself the day before. Betsy looked at the marks on his neck where the rope had gripped him and slowly, then all at once, extinguished his life. He was a heavyset fellow. Short, squat. Flat face. Long black hair. A pointed nose. His eyes were taped shut but of course Betsy, his sister, knew that he had brown eyes resting under his eyelids. His body was dressed in Native American garb, consistent with what his tribe, the Hydah tribe, traditionally wore. His body was on a piece of wood that was covered by a sort of canvas stretch cloth and it was propped onto a table in the living room and the poles that stretched the canvas out, the ones by his feet, were also propped onto a small chest of drawers to give his body the proper balance. He wasn't going anywhere.

The plan, for Betsy, was to display and mourn his death for three days, according to and consistent with tribal custom. He was surrounded by debris, junk, garbage, dishes, magazines, knick-knacks, and anything else that someone could possibly collect and accumulate, because Betsy was a hoarder.

Betsy tossed back a shot of cheap gin. She looked around the room but left all the shit where it was. Betsy needed to go to the airport to pick up a young girl from Los Angeles, who was coming up for the summer to help Betsy's husband, James, run his bar and she was planning to help promote and organize a fishing expedition business as well. She had been a model and aspiring actress in Los Angeles, but, according to James, had sort of burnt out – and there were rumors that she actually flamed out. The girl's dad was friends with James and had suggested that there might be good opportunity up in the Alaska area. It was untamed land by modern standards, to be sure.

The girl had grown tired of the modeling grind and the hustle, the feast and famine of advertisement shoots, auditioning, and the Los Angeles lifestyle. She was living too fast. She had never landed a feature film role, despite being a finalist for several major ones. Life would have been so different. But it didn't happen. She would make money from modeling contracts in spurts, and sometimes the money would be really tight. She was always on the party circuit, running around looking for gigs and networking. She didn't want to live like that anymore, and, even though she was now only in her early twenties, she had dropped out of high school and gone to Hollywood at the age of fifteen. It was time to try something else.

Why not try something wildly different, she had thought? The great outdoors during the day, fishing, boating, adventure, and helping to run a bar at night? What could go wrong? What could be more different than the plasticity of Los Angeles? She just decided to go for it.

Betsy rushed off in her silver, four door truck to grab the girl, Kalli, at the airport. Betsy was not thrilled at the idea that Kalli was coming up to stay with them, as they already had tight quarters in their house. But she went along with it as it sounded like they were going to be in position to create a tourist attraction with the boating business — which would help the bar and grill make more money. Betsy wanted to make more money.

Kalli was young and impulsive, and had stayed up the night before in Los Angeles, drinking with her friends and reminiscing about old times. Years had gone by in Los Angeles and she was ready to get out of there. She caught her plane and made the three hour flight up north. When she landed, she couldn't believe the smell that was in the air. Crisp. Clean. Salt. Wild. Open. A fresh breeze, no smog, no plastic smell. Micro plastics? Not here. It was so different from Los Angeles!

Kalli walked from the airport in Ketchikan, Alaska to the ferry. She was out of Hollywood. But her life still spanned before her like the open road. Modeling and acting didn't define her. They never had. Maybe she would do something else? Maybe she would work in fishing. Maybe she would sing — she always wanted to sing, she loved it. Maybe she would find a husband and start a family. Her thoughts and her plans constantly changed. She had no idea what she wanted to do. In a strange way, she did everything and nothing at the same time.

Kalli walked off the plane in Ketchikan, Alaska, and had been told that she needed to take a ferry over to the island. She stood at the edge of the ferry as it started the voyage and she saw a pod of killer whales. As they neared land again, she saw a bald eagle doing laps above, looking for prey.

As she reached the pickup zone in the ferry port, she looked over and saw a short, round Native American looking up at her. She had green eyes, laughing. Laughing energetically, almost wildly! Kalli had no idea why she was laughing like that. Based on a picture her dad had sent her, Kalli figured out that it was Bestsy.

Kalli jumped in with Betsy and they greeted one another. Betsy told Kalli to go ahead and pick some music she liked. Kalli tuned the radio to some country music and sang along.

> These outlaw women, first of their kind
> Outlaw women they got you right on time
> Outlaw women don't need any guns
> Outlaw women just out for fun

Betsy pressed the gas pedal and steered the truck toward her house. When Kalli walked in, she almost fainted when she saw the corpse of Betsy's brother on the living room table. A chill ran through her body and she suddenly felt that she was in danger. Not because of anything that Betsy did at that particular moment, and not really because of anything specific at all. She caught the scent of danger, a sense that something was not right, and with that came fear.

"Ummm, who is that?"

"That's my brother, he killed himself two days ago."

Kalli was silent. The brother had taken the blessing of death, of freedom, of having nothing left to lose, from nature, which, in turn, gave it to him when he choked off his air supply with a corded rope. In a way, it was natural. Did he think as deeply about the topic as did Seneca or Socrates or Hamlet? Of course not.

"It's tribal custom to display the body for mourning for three days. I'm going to do that, starting today, since we got back this morning. Everyone is coming over later for food and drinks," said Betsy.

Kalli looked at the body and could almost see it stiffening on the board. She was happy that her stomach was empty, so that if she heaved or wretched nothing would come up. She felt weak. This was too much! She wanted to go back to Los Angeles all of a sudden.

"Let me show you where to put your stuff, Kalli."

Betsy walked Kalli up a flight of stairs to a bedroom area. There was no bed. Kalli figured out that, like other members of the tribe, she would be sleeping on the wood floor. That's how they did it. Betsy was putting Kalli in the room where she and her husband slept, so that Kalli would be safe from any of the younger tribe members who thought they might try to explore the insides of her body without invitation. Her husband could be trusted, at least a little bit, if only because Betsy also slept in that room.

"Betsy, would you like help around the house since people are coming over?" asked Kalli.

"Sure, that would be great."

"Okay, I'm going to get started. Let me know if there is anything specific that you would like help with, otherwise I'll work on clearing space."

"Can I ask you a question?" said Kalli.

"Of course," said Betsy.

"What happened to your brother?"

"He hung himself."

"That's awful. Did something happen? Let me know if you don't want to talk about it."

"No, it's okay. Let's see, he was on drugs and he drank a lot. He didn't have much money. There was nothing he really liked to do. Women weren't interested in him, he was just a short and squat little man. He had very little money. Look at him. He didn't want to do it anymore, I guess. Just didn't want to be alive. I found him dead when nobody heard from him for an entire morning at his work."

"I'm so sorry," said Kalli.

"Well, everyone is going to come over to mourn him and eat food. Then, life will go on again, as before. He's gone."

"I would be crushed if I lost anyone in my family. I'm sorry that this happened," said Kalli.

Kalli made trip after trip to the dumpster. She cleared out a massive amount of clutter in the house. It was almost three, and the mourners started flowing in. What followed was an incredible feast, with booze flowing like water. Betsy was the daughter of the Chief of the Hydah tribe — so it seemed that every member of the tribe came to pay respects. Wine, Vodka, Rum, Whisky and Gin — all cheap brands — were flowing.

"I want to get drunk!" Betsy told anyone who would listen. "Kalli, have a drink!"

Kalli decided to have a couple of cocktails. After all, there was a dead body on the table. The alcohol relaxed her almost instantly. Betsy bustled around, sipping on her whisky and the occasional flute of champagne. It was a strange mix. She looked like she was intent on getting drunk.

There was so much chatter in the house that it was sort of a chaotic confusion. Everyone was catching up, telling stories, drinking, eating food and bustling about. A couple of the young Native Americans kept staring at Kalli. At five-foot-eleven, she was taller than everyone in the room, including the men, who were mostly five-foot-eight or so. Everyone, it seemed, was either drunk or beginning to get drunk — the mourning event provided a reason on this day, but to be honest most of them would have gotten drunk anyway, for no reason.

"Why did you come all the way up here?" one of the Native American girls asked Kalli.

"Well, I needed a change. I was tired of living in Los Angeles. It sounded like it would be so pretty up here, and the fishing expedition business sounded exciting. Honestly, I just made a quick decision. So who knows? It sounded right. I didn't feel like chasing commercials and modeling gigs anymore. I didn't want to keep acting. I just got tired of all that. I hope this works out. I'm not sure what I'll do if it doesn't," said Kalli, flashing her eyes open just a bit.

"Oh, that makes sense. Cheers!" The girls clinked their glasses and took a sip.

The Chief had arrived an hour before and he was, in fact, drunk. He sat down on a sofa, looking bored and sad. He looked incredibly sad. He fell asleep.

Betsy, who at first had been loud and jovial and partying, was crying now. She had drank just over half a bottle of gin and also a couple of shots of whiskey. Maybe even more than that, she lost track. She was very drunk and became very emotional. The others went on eating and drinking.

"Don't cry," a Hydah man said. "This is a celebration of your brother's life. We must enjoy the memories. Crying makes it too difficult."

"But he is my brother. My only brother. I lost my brother. I hate this," said Betsy, crying.

"We are all Hydah. We are all from the same tribe. We must come together and fill the gap and the sadness left by your brother."

"I don't understand, why?"

"Well, he had a deep pain and sadness that nobody could help him with. That is why he is with the Spirit."

Kalli was listening. She still couldn't believe the turn of events and the whirlwind travel in the last twenty four hours. What had she gotten herself into? The only part of the equation that had worked out so far was the natural beauty of Alaska. It was fantastic. The views, the smells, the landscape. But the rest? Cleaning House? Drinking cocktails next to a dead body? And where was the boat for the fishing business? Did they really have one? She couldn't be sure! If they did, how would they advertise and attract business? All of a sudden she felt despair, because she felt that the boat expedition business wasn't the greatest thing in the world.

"How do you know he is with the Spirit?"

"I just know. The Great Spirit is always with us. He has made himself into a bear or a fish or another animal. I am sure of it."

Betsy did not answer, but she took a sip of her drink. The man chewed his food until he was finished and he walked away, sipping a whiskey.

As the day wore on, the wind picked up and was whipping through the trees. It was getting cold out. The raven still sat in his tree, as he had been doing most of the day. Kalli looked around the house. Numerous drunk tribes-people were sprawled and strewn throughout the house, and now there were dishes and glasses everywhere.

Kalli felt scared and sad. She felt like crying. But instead, she sipped more vodka and soda water while she tried to calm herself down. She just kept replaying her decision in her mind. Over and over. She had just arrived and she was already thinking that she wanted to get out of Alaska!

Kalli's thoughts were heavy as the day wore on. She was gloomy, and questioning everything. This state assumed an air of permanency. She had suddenly bolted, like a wild horse, up to Alaska. Now, she thought she had been too impulsive.

All these thoughts hit Kalli at once. She reminded herself that she needed to get out of Hollywood. She reminded herself that wasn't going to work, not any more. Kalli had expected a triumphant and dazzling career in Hollywood. Instead, she got some sporadic success and a lot of empty promises. She reminded herself that going back there was not a solution.

Now, in Alaska, all that was gone but there was a different issue. If the fishing and bar business weren't in fact as attractive as she had thought they would be, where would she go to next? How would she get home, off this reservation, off this island? She had almost an out-of-body experience as she pictured how she could remove herself from the situation. She was growing cold to her surroundings. She had recently arrived and her instincts told her she needed to get out — this was a bad decision.

Days went by, then weeks. Before she knew it, she had been up there for a couple months, in a rut. It was clear to her that the boating business was not going to materialize anytime soon. That had been a pipe dream - there was not enough money for promotion and developing the business idea. Kalli knew that she had to get out of Alaska!

ii

There was a guy in Alaska that Kalli had known for some time who had always been flirtatious towards Kalli, she knew him from when she lived in Northern California. She thought he was pretty cool, and he was tall and handsome as well, so she decided to pursue this next time he hinted at his interest. The day came as he flirted with her during a conversation at a friend's house. For the first time, Kalli showed interest back. She flirted back. He told her that the job that he had been trying to pursue in Alaska was not panning out for him. He had some family money, and told her that he was thinking about getting set up in Washington or Oregon and pursuing work as a chef instead of working on an oil rig. During the course of the conversation, they held hands. A few days later, they kissed quite a lot. Half way joking, she told him that she would move with him, to Oregon. But he said that he loved the idea. It was an impulsive decision, yet again. Just like that, they were a couple.

A few days later, it seemed like the relationship was going great! What could be better? They were getting along. They were combining their lives. Her boyfriend, whose name was Michael, seemed like a great guy. Some more time went by and Kalli had decided that she wanted to make love to him, it was the right time for her to be with him. She was thinking that she would be with him, forever. She was in love. When the time came, later that night, everything was perfect. Some dinner, some wine, some relaxing music. Michael had kissed her tenderly and they made love, first on the yellow tan leather couch, where Michael was touching Kalli gently then more enthusiastically with his thumb and forefinger, and then in the bed where they listened to music playing in the room and made their own music as well.

Kalli was happy with the relationship! Michael had been very nice to her. He seemed grounded and motivated. Soon afterward, they moved to Seattle and got set up in a happening neighborhood. Everything seemed great.

But that didn't last long. He became controlling. Jealous. He began drinking a lot, most likely because he wanted to overcome his brooding, jealous mindset. He couldn't handle the thought of Kalli stepping out on him – something she hadn't even thought of doing. He was drinking out on the town, drinking at home. Michael drank everything he could find. It seemed like he had a bottle of vodka stashed in every cupboard and a bottle of whiskey in every cabinet.

Kalli felt boxed in, suffocated. Michael wouldn't let Kalli have a car. He was even jealous and frustrated when she bought a bicycle and started riding it around town. He bitched about her having the bike. He brooded on it day and night, non-stop. What was she up to? He couldn't even handle when she would ride her bike to the store to buy food or something to drink. He worried that other guys would try to steal her from him. He obsessed, he stewed. The obsession was poison, slowly accumulating in Michael's mind and body.

Kalli was bar-tending enough to get by, to contribute to offset the couple's expenses, when combined with the money that Michael had from his family and from his work as a chef. Her dreams of performing – of acting, singing, modeling, whatever – seemed long gone. They seemed dead. Acting and modeling seemed like a distant memory. As far as singing, she couldn't even entertain the notion. How could she get that balloon off the ground? She didn't have a band. She didn't have a guitar player. She could write lyrics, but she couldn't put them to music. Therefore, she didn't have any songs written. She had a good voice, but it was still very raw.

She needed to learn how to control her voice. But she didn't know how. She didn't know how to relax when she sang. Kalli was good at a lot of things, but she didn't know how to do anything at an expert level, really, other than ride horses. And now she was stuck in Seattle with an alcoholic boyfriend who was becoming more and more controlling every day. His pathology was increasing.

The diminishing relationship led Kalli to over-eating. Kalli gained weight as the days and weeks in this new relationship went by. There were still some good times, for sure. But they grew more sporadic as each month went by. They tried to get by, pay rent, have fun here and there. Time flew by! Michael kept drinking, all the time. Kalli kept gaining weight, and instead of five-foot-eleven and a pretty, lean one hundred thirty pounds, she ballooned to one eighty-five. One eighty-five! She had gained over fifty pounds and she hated how she looked. She was depressed. Because her time modeling and acting was over, she felt like a failure. She felt regret. She felt like she could have done something better with her career. She could have worked harder, worked smarter, she thought. Something! Unless she was heading out to work, she stayed in bed or on the couch. Based on mutual frustration and a stagnant relationship, they decided to leave Seattle and move to Bend, Oregon. So they did!

The relationship ebbed and flowed in a positive direction with the move. At first, there was renewal, then there was rebirth. Michael cut back on his drinking for a couple of months and Kalli stopped stress eating. She trimmed down a bit, but not to her modeling weight. Soon, again, Michael was getting hammered every day. Michael was putting down vodka or whiskey two sips at a time. He was always hammered, or so it seemed. Michael was blackout drunk on many nights by nine p.m. With the increase in drunkenness came a decrease in shared interests, in shared time, and then came something unexpected. Violence.

At first, Michael started to grab her, just here and there. It wouldn't physically injure her, these grabs. He would strong-arm her. It didn't really hurt. But he would modify her direction, move her around, use his strength and higher level of physicality to move her or reposition her or put her on a new path. To show control over her. Kalli didn't like it. He would bump her and wrestle her. He wanted to let her know that he was bigger and stronger than her. That he could physically control her. From there, it moved on to throwing her around. It was scary, but never really left a lasting injury. Same with the pushing. He would shove her when angry or frustrated with her. Or in an argument over something. She lived with all the escalation because he was physically dominating her but not inflicting injuries on her. And, what's more, she didn't really know what to do.

That all changed one night when Michael and Kalli took a cab out to dinner. Kalli thought Michael was getting out through the door on the other side. Instead, he was following her out of the same door. Without looking, and unintentionally, she and closed the door on his hand. He had to struggle to get his hand out of the cab door as the cab drove off. When he wrestled his hand free, he ran back over to where Kalli was, screaming at her.

"What the fuck, you fat bitch? You slammed the door on my hand!"

After he screamed that, he punched her in her face with his right hand as hard as he could. She was stunned and bleeding.

"What the fuck, bitch? Why you gotta slam my hand in the door? Fuckin' fat bitch! You deserve that," he said after he punched her in the face.

Kalli cried. She just stood there and cried. Once a beautiful fashion model and now a heavy punching bag.

No one else saw the punch. Kalli didn't know what to do. She wiped the blood off her face and kept crying. She had no support system in Oregon. No family. She was getting no exercise, she had no productive activities other than her work. She began drinking too much, to cope with her unhappiness in the relationship. She was drinking grape vodka a few times a week. Two sips at a time! It wasn't healthy, and she knew it, but she didn't know, yet, how she could fix things. Although she had not articulated it, even to herself, at the time, she decided at that moment that she would leave Michael when she could. It wasn't going to be easy because she didn't have any money put aside. In fact, she had less than two hundred dollars set aside that Michael didn't know about. She needed more, or she needed to catch a break to be able to get out of there somehow. Her face had healed by the time her mom visited in October. But she was still fat, for her, and incredibly unhappy. Her mom was older, and wasn't in the best of health. Her mom didn't have any extra money to help her. Kalli didn't even tell her mom about her problems. Kalli didn't want her mom to be upset about what was happening to her.

Kalli reinforced the idea, in her own mind, in her own thoughts, of needing to leave Michael. In the meantime, she resolved that she would just try to give Michael as much vodka as she could so that he would pass out, drunk, as early as possible. Then he would leave her alone, she thought.

iii

Fate was soon helpful to Kalli for the first time in what seemed like ages. Kalli had made friends with a young woman named Ashleigh at work and, by extension, Ashleigh's husband Billy. Something very strange, and very interesting, happened with Ashleigh and Billy that caused Kalli's fate to overlap, to intersect, with Ashleigh's in a convenient manner.

Ashleigh went through Bill's smart phone and caught text messaging, romantically, with another man. Ashleigh had been checking Billy's smart phone to look for messages from other women. But, Billy, in a surprising development relating to the details of his extramarital affair, was receiving explicit messages from a man, including pictures of the man's hairy, lumpy penis. That thing was disgusting! Ashleigh had checked Billy's phone because his interest level in entering, and thrusting in and out of, her vagina was so remarkably low. It was non-existent! So, she had grown suspicious of an affair. But a gay affair? When Ashleigh saw the messages she just slumped over. Billy was from one of the most religious families in Oregon! What was he doing with that penis?

Some messages had gone back and forth in order to set up a meeting for later that night! Ashleigh reviewed all the messages and then put the phone back where it was.

"I'm gonna hit the gym, baby," said Billy, casually, an hour or two later. "I'm gonna lift and then do some cardio. Then I'm gonna grab a couple of things at the store and I'll be back. I'll be a couple hours."

"Mmm-hmm, okay Billy."

Billy bent over and gave Ashleigh a kiss on the forehead before he walked out to his car. Ashleigh waited for him to back out of the driveway, then she hurried to her car. She followed Billy, from a distance. At the first intersection outside of their neighborhood, he made a right. The gym would have required a left turn! Her heart was racing and her face looked tense. Sure enough, Billy turned into a cheap motel and shuffled his short legs into room one nineteen. The room was on the ground floor and it was unlocked. Someone was waiting for Billy in the room. Ashleigh parked and waited in her car. After five minutes, she made her way over to the window and peeked in.

When Ashleigh arrived at the room, Billy and his lover, a man named Tanish, were still in the conversation stage. They had each rested their smart phones, which were used to set up the tryst, on the end tables. Tanish's was set up and aimed at the bed so that he could record a video of what was about to happen.

"So, are you still married?" asked Tanish with a casual laugh. "I want to live openly with you and be with you."

"Ha-ha, yes, but my wife and I haven't had sex in over three months. Last time we did it she stuck her ass out and let me dock up for a minute. Which I did, of course. Then I went to sleep."

Tanish laughed, and he laid down on his back while still laughing and smiling.

When Tanish laid down, something clicked in Billy. Here it comes!

"Billy," Tanish moaned as he took a deep breath and licked the skin behind Billy's ear. Billy moaned with pleasure as the saliva remained behind his ear. It felt cool in the crisp Oregon air.

"I love having you to myself," said Tanish. "I need you to myself. You're so fucking hot!"

Billy kissed Tanish on his hairy chest. Tanish stroked his own hairy, lumpy penis a few times. It was hard and a dis-colored combination of brown, black and yellow with a few hints of pink. Several gnarly bumps protruded from the starboard side of his swollen member. They looked like Stonehenge, but on a small scale. In contrast to Tanish, Billy's penis was youngish looking — pink and red — with hints of orange and blue where there were veins.

Ashleigh, took her time to approach the room, and was peeking in the window through a three inch crack in the curtain. She could see everything. Her face showed a mix of outrage, anger, disgust. Ashleigh took a quick picture through the hotel window, using the camera on her Endless Content smart phone. Both men were too lustfully engaged to notice anything. The picture captured the men kissing each other. During the kiss, Tanish's hand was on Billy's erect penis. Billy's hand was on Tanish's chest.

Ashleigh locked her smart phone and walked away. She took two deep breaths to compose herself. She looked ill. And who could blame her, she was getting cuck-queened, and not in the most customary manner.

While Ashleigh was driving, the action between Tanish and Billy kept progressing. They kissed, passionately. Suddenly, the time came. Tanish flipped Billy over. Billy was on the bottom, with Tanish on top. Billy's eyebrow raised and he made some extremely graphic and provocative comments. More things happened and then Tanish entered Billy and pushed down, hard. Other things happened. Soon, Tanish had Billy's face was crashing into the headboard of the cheap motel bed. Bwomp! Bwomp! Bwomp! Bwomp! Billy's face was red, especially on the right side. The whole right side of his face had been mashed into the headboard. He angled his mouth to the left to try to take the brunt of the bashing against his right cheek where there was a little bit of padding. The cheek absorbed the shock and his lip crooked out and he dragged his tongue through his mouth and out into the open air. More things happened. Bwomp! Bwomp! Bwomp! Bwomp! After a while, Tanish was done. He finished while moaning and yelling something about being a wild Turk.

By the time Billy got back home, there was no lingering sign of the fact that, when she returned home, Ashleigh had vomited for ten minutes straight. Violently. Then she had dry-heaved for another five minutes. She had cried and vomited while Billy was still getting railed by Tanish, but every once in a while she let out a crazy, disbelieving laugh. Woah-ahaha-woah-ahaha! The loud laugh was therapeutic. She was still in shock, still absorbing the trauma in her brain like Billy had absorbed Tanish.

"I'm so tired, Billy, I think I'm going to go to bed early," said Ashleigh. She muffled her strong emotions. She locked them down!

"Okay, I'm going to be in the home office, working. So busy. I feel energized after the gym, though," said Billy, with a deep satiety to his voice.

"Sounds great. Night," said Ashleigh, while she suppressed a gag reflex.

Ashleigh went in the Kitchen and called Kalli. Kalli, who was at work, serving cocktails, answered the call.

"Hey, Ashleigh."

"Hey, Kalli. Remember that one time we talked about how we both wanted to move away from Oregon? Not sure how things are with you and Michael, but I'm ready to get out of town," Ashleigh said. "I need to go."

"Is everything okay?" asked Kalli.

"Well, yes, no. I'm safe. I just need to get out of here," said Ashleigh.

"Me too," said Kalli. "Me too."

"Okay great we'll leave next week."

"What day?"

"Monday."

"Okay, pick me up Monday. I've been saving gas money. Let's talk tomorrow if we can. Love ya, girl."

"Okay great. Love ya."

Kalli's face bubbled over with excitement as they hung up. She had saved a few bucks for gas, food and incidental expenses on the trip south. The key was that Ashleigh had a car. Kalli suddenly had a way out of town. The rest would work itself out. Kalli was confident of that, she was certain. She couldn't wait to get on the road!

Trail of Stupidity

✳✳

Maddox Malone did the recruiting meeting in Las Vegas, which was standard fare, and flew home immediately. He took a driving service home, then hopped into his sports car and floored it, heading up north. He was traveling sixty-five miles per hour in a fifty-five mile per hour zone, trying to get into the office as fast as possible to get a jump on his day. His sports car was rocking:

> Ain't found a way to kill me yet
> Eyes burn with stinging sweat
> Seems every path leads me to nowhere

Maddox sang along during the drive. He had a large iced Americano in his cup holder and a pile of almonds in his hand. He worked his way through the almonds methodically. Flip, chew, chew, swallow. The almonds weren't tasting great, but they needed to hold him over until eleven-thirty, when he would shoot out to lift weights and eat. He was hungry! Maddox entered his office, walked behind his desk and immediately logged onto his personal computer.

Maddox Malone had a lot to do this morning. Catch up on sports news, transactions to finish, sponsors to call, clients to message. His digital media feeds buzzed and whirred with notifications hitting his smart phone. He needed to find out the status of the TENACIOUS facility bid. He hoped that the purchase had closed! He just had a lot of shit to do. He took a sip of his iced Americano, then another.

His assistant, Eleanor, and the Slug were both next door in the other office. Elite Baseball Rumors was always one of Maddox's first stops on his computer's web browser. That's where he got his baseball industry news. They had their finger on the pulse of the scouting and agent community. It seemed like they got all the contract news, first. They had good takes on the sport and on the business related to it. He popped the website open in his browser.

The top headline on Elite Baseball Rumors blared "Salcido

Duran Signs Worst Contract Extension in Baseball History."

"Woah! Wait a second! What in the fuck is going on here?" thought Maddox. "Woah! Woah! Wait, What? What happened?"

Salcido Duran was a client of the Malone Agency. Elite Baseball Rumors had to have this wrong. But how would they make this mistake? Oh fuck, what did the Slug do? Maddox's heart started pounding away. This was grim. He kept reading on the website. Oh God-damn it! Holy Shit! This can't be real! His heart pounded even more. His temperature rose.

Maddox continued to scroll down, scanning the blurb and the comments on the website. Fuck. Shit. No Way.

"Garibaldi Vascoso of the Malone Agency could not be reached for comment."

Maddox's eyes were pulsating. His fingers tensed as he scrolled down with his mouse. He kept scanning the article. The author called the contract the most "team friendly" contract in the history of the sport. Maddox swallowed. In the history of the sport? Holy shit. Obviously, if the contract was team friendly that meant it was bad for the player.

"Oh no!" thought Maddox. Maddox swallowed. He had put down his iced Americano because he suddenly felt queasy.

For a moment, Maddox felt horrible for Salcido Duran. Salcido had grown up in difficult conditions, but with a loving, stable mother, outside of Caracas, Venezuela. He loved baseball. He was also personally very diverse, which was nice. Strong, flexible, quick. His arm was special and the release on his throw was as fast as a frog's tongue launching towards a fly or some other insect. Maddox thought of Salcido and felt sorry for him.

But, "wait a minute," thought Maddox. Forget about Salcido Duran for a second. What about the Malone Agency? Agencies that do deals like that cannot survive. It's too competitive and agencies that make bad deals don't get clients. Those agencies die, they close, they go out of business. This contract was a major disaster for the agency!

Maddox glitched, he flickered like a television screen with a bad connection, then he boiled. The Slug had nuked the Malone Agency! He felt an energy rush, but it was bad energy. It was anger. It bordered on hatred. He felt inclined to violence. He tried to suppress that feeling. His smart phone buzzed and buzzed, it whirred and beeped and stirred. He closed his eyes for a moment. His head felt heavy. He felt another rush of energy, then a wave of fatigue and remorse. His stomach rumbled since it was empty, but he felt no hunger.

His smart phone just kept buzzing so he finally checked it. Most of the activity was related to the Salcido Duran disaster, but the latest buzz was caused by a text message from Paul McCartney that read "Hello Partner, I can't wait to get to work on our list of open action items for TENACIOUS today. We are ready to get the Spanish Tennis Academy deal in place. Let's do this! Take no prisoners!"

Maddox was angry. He didn't want to deal with responding to McCartney right this minute, but he did anyway. Since the Grasshopper was hard to reach much of the time, Maddox always tried to communicate promptly with him when he surfaced.

"Thanks Paul, is the TENACIOUS training facility purchase closed?" Maddox wrote back.

Maddox told himself to stay calm. He told himself that anger would not help things in any way. He took a big breath in.

Maddox buzzed next door, using the office land line. Garibaldi answered. "Garibaldi, can you come over to my office?" said Maddox.

A couple minutes later Maddox saw Garibaldi ooze through his door and towards his office. Maddox, who had planned to stay calm, lost it. He lost his composure. He lost his shit.

"You dumb mother fucker. What the fuck were you doing?" Maddox yelled.

Maddox hadn't even waited until Garibaldi walked all the way through the door. He started yelling. Maddox was shaking his fist and stomping his foot. Before Vascoso could even respond, Maddox smashed a smiling bobble-head through a framed, autographed photo of Maddox's client, Chris Black.

"I said no God-damned option years! How did you agree to those option years? What were you thinking? You gave away Salcido's whole career, for nothing. You fucked that kid."

Maddox said this despite the fact that he was actively trying to contain his anger, trying to calm himself. He tried to bottle his fury up inside. But his rage had no way to be controlled. He had no filter and soon he was just letting his anger out, in the form of a tirade directed at the stupid, hapless Slug.

"Umm well dee team kept asking me... Salcido, he want to do it you know to take care of his mom... his mom," Garibaldi stammered out a reply in broken English, "Salcido, he, uh, he care about his mom so much. He love her. He love her."

"It's the worst contract that I've ever even heard of. It's so fucking embarrassing. Everyone in baseball is talking about it."

"Umm... but Salcido Duran he want to do eet to take care of dee theengs."

Maddox kept yelling. Maddox's veins in his neck were throbbing. His eyes were bulging. His fist was pounding on his desk. Bam! Bam! Bam!

Maddox glanced back to his screen which still had his digital media feed open and it seemed that every member of the baseball media was making a crack about the terrible contract engineered by the Slug. The digital media kept streaming in. With each one that he read, Maddox became angrier.

"Could Salcido have signed a worse contract?" said one post.

"The Razors just abused Duran's agent. I didn't know anyone could bend over that far," said another post.

"I can't believe all those option years, Duran signed away his whole career. How did that happen?" the posts just kept popping up on the website's digital media feed.

The Karat Town baseball blogs were on fire, mocking the Malone Agency for taking the deal. He took a breath and tried to calm himself down.

"Garibaldi, before I left for Miami, I specifically reviewed the market value of the contract with you. I said that under no circumstances should you include any option years in the contract. Not a single one. I said do the same fucking thing I did for Pepe Soliz. The Big Boys asked for option years a million times and I said no. You just swallowed the Razors' load. You gave away that kid's whole career. You fuckin' idiot."

Remarkably, the anger and frustration at the contract kept building as Maddox spoke. He was getting angrier by the second, which seemed impossible since he was furious from the moment he saw Garibaldi oozing toward his office. At first, it had been a cold fury that entered Maddox's mind. But the fury had become hot!

"You're a moron," Maddox kept yelling. "How stupid do you have to be to do that deal? I should shove that contract down your throat, you fucking idiot. You fucked Salcido. You fucked the Malone Agency!"

The Slug surreptitiously slid, sideways, sliming silently out the office door. He left behind an invisible trail of stupidity.

"Oh, Madd-ox, I don't know what is dee matter," mumbled the Slug.

"How am I ever going to sign another player when I have fucking idiots working here? What is wrong with that guy? Who does that fucking deal?"

The Slug had already made his way next door, and Maddox was pretty sure he didn't even really understand why Maddox was angry. Then, Maddox was hit with a wave of frustration — this time with himself. He was the guy who hired the Slug, after all. Maddox sat in his chair and put his face on his desk for thirty seconds. He just sat there in misery. Finally, he sat up.

When Maddox started the Malone Agency he planned on doing

something special. He wanted to make deals. Make money. He didn't know where the windy road would take him, but he hoped and expected it would be somewhere good.

Now?

The horny Poobah was raping, impregnating woman after woman, defiling bathrooms, crushing Bacon Pizza and demanding mucho dinero.

The Platform might as well be crumbling into the ocean. And to top it off, Efficient-Pop was horrible.

The Grasshopper was late on his TENACIOUS Commitments. He just hopped around yelling "Let's do this, Core Values!"

Zaine Fuller was making illegal cash payments to recruits like Obadiah Ballard and, seemingly, every other recruit in the country.

The crooked-lipped Bedbug was plotting to represent his wife, Lacy Stratton, once he got out of rehab. The fucking Bedbug, a guy whose son was also his sister!

And, this, the latest disaster — the worst contract in baseball history was now negotiated by an employee of the Malone Agency.

Maddox breathed. He needed to get out of there. He felt like either drinking vodka or going to the gym. He chose the gym. He jumped into his sports car and headed south, stomping on the gas much harder than usual. He turned the music up on his car stereo, but Maddox didn't sing along.

> Hope this is what you wanted
> Hope this is what you had in mind
> Cause this is what you're getting

His gym was pretty nitty-gritty, a bare-bones operation frequented by muscle-heads and bikers. The general manager was a lunatic – but that didn't matter to Maddox. He just wanted to lift some weights. It was a cool Phoenix morning. Maddox changed while he was parked outside the gym. He grabbed his weightlifting belt, wrist wraps and earbuds and walked into the gym. Walking in, he looked at his reflection in the glass on the building. He looked okay — but when he was honest with himself, he knew that he wanted to take his fitness levels up two notches, maybe three. He felt too soft, too corporate. He wanted to invigorate himself, strengthen himself again, but always seemed to go in spurts and get interrupted by events. Well, today was a good day to start fresh, he thought.

Maddox hit the squat rack to warm up. He needed to get a good pump going to free his mind. Because of the frustration with the Duran deal, Maddox wanted to move some serious weight around. So, after he did five sets of squats, he hit his chest with seven sets of between eight and twelve repetitions on incline bench press, working the weights up from one hundred thirty five to two hundred forty five and back down for the last two sets. In between sets he rocked out fifty push-ups, and a few dumbbell curls. He finished with one hundred dumbbell squats, sets of twenty. The workout gave him a good physical buzz, and that took away some of his anger and frustration about the botched contract.

Just then, Paul McCartney sent a text message to Maddox that read "I am following up on the facility bid. We are locked and loaded for the Spain Tennis Academy trip, we will attach it to the **TENACIOUS** training facility. I have all the funding. Money is not the issue! We're going to replicate my grandfather's core values! Let's do this!"

Following up, thought Maddox? Maddox shook his head slightly. What did that even mean?

"Fuck this text message shit," thought Maddox. Angry from the disastrous Salcido Duran deal, he dialed the Grasshopper from his smart phone. The 'Hopper answered.

"Hey Paul, when is the facility bid going to be finalized?"

"I'm following up on that right now. Take no prisoners!"

"Umm, okay. So it will close today or another day?" asked Maddox.

"I'm not sure but I'm calling the real estate agent right now.

Money is not an issue. Let's do this!" hollered the Grasshopper.

"Okay, Paul. Let me know when it closes."

"I will, Maddox. Core Values!" responded Paul McCartney as the conversation concluded.

Maddox had to leave for Spain early the following morning. Which meant that he would head home to see the kids and Laura and then he would have to pack his shit. The workout was essential based on the frustration from the Salcido Duran disaster, but he was excited to get home. He completed the triangle from the office to the gym to his house and walked through the front door.

Chester was running around with a nerf gun, Thomas was on the personal computer playing a video game, Felicia was playing with a blonde Barbie doll, and Laura was on the phone talking to her mom. Again. It occurred to Maddox, as it did every so often, that he had not had sex with Laura in, well, in as long as he could remember. He shook his head, slightly. He stifled a grimace. He felt a fresh wave of disappointment. How did that happen to him? At least his kids seemed great.

"Hey kidders," Maddox said to the kids as he walked through the door of their McMansion.

"Hi daddy," said Thomas.

"Hi daddy," said Chester.

"Hi daddy," said Felicia.

The kids were off in their own little world, so Maddox went into his home office and dropped off his computer bag. He put on a pair of comfortable sweatpants and an old Platform Volleyball sweatshirt. He went to the fridge and cracked open a soda water, dumped a couple ounces out and then poured a couple ounces of cranberry juice in. He walked back into his home office. He took a sip of his little soda water drink. He sat down at his computer. He checked his flight information. He was on the six o'clock flight to Barcelona, stopping through the airport in New York. That meant he needed to be at the airport in

Phoenix at four or four-thirty in the morning, which meant a three a.m. wake up call.

He grabbed his travel laptop and attached it to his office laptop. He transferred over a couple of files that he would need for Spain. One was a form term sheet and the other was a planning and strategy document that Maddox had prepared during the prior month. With that completed, he walked into his bedroom. He grabbed his suitcase, and filled it with two suits, two pairs of shoes, five pairs of socks, five boxers, three tee-shirts, three dress shirts, a couple belts, his shaving kit, a spare phone charger, some gym shorts and topped it off with an extra laptop plug. He zipped up the bag and set it in front of the door. With that out of the way, he went back out into the kitchen and heated up a chicken burrito in the microwave. Not good, but passable.

Laura had gotten off the phone with her mom, Maddox's mother-in-law. They talked on the phone for at least an hour every day, and they also spent a lot of time together in person. All at the expense of time available to Maddox and Laura to share in their marriage — which was already limited because of Maddox's over-commitment to the Malone Agency and his generally misdirected priorities. Both were to blame, to be honest. But it had gone on for so long it didn't really matter anymore. Maddox ignored it at this point. So did Laura. What could they do?

"Hi, Maddox," said Laura. Her face was dour. Her eyes looked tired. She looked away from Maddox. She seemed down-trodden to Maddox.

"Hi," Maddox answered.

"How was your day?" Laura asked, checking a box in her mind.

"Fine," said Maddox, checking a similar box.

"You look stressed. You look tired," said Laura.

Maddox didn't think he looked tired, but he probably couldn't argue about the stress. He figured it showed on his face after he yelled at the Slug. He thought, briefly, of the contract for Salcido Duran. He felt some rage bubble up, again. He pushed those thoughts out of his mind.

"I'm fine. Had a good session at the gym. Did the kids have a good day?" Maddox said.

"Good. Thomas is playing a game and I think Chester is off playing basketball or whatever. Felicia is coloring or playing with dolls. Did something happen?" She seemed to be able to tell that something was bothering Maddox. So she asked.

"Nah, a guy that works for me did a shitty deal. A really shitty deal. You know, Garibaldi Vascoso. I'm just mad about that. Livid. I left the office early and lifted. I have to get up at three in the morning to get to Spain tomorrow. For the Tennis Academy we are going to attach to the TENACIOUS Training facility. I'm going with Paul McCartney."

"Of course I know Garibaldi. I've had him and his wife Roberta over here for dinner a bunch of times. Spain, again? How is that going? How's Paul McCartney doing?" she asked.

"I didn't mean do you know him. I meant, you know. It's a figure of speech. McCartney's the same as always. He finally put the bid in for the facility. Says he's following up on that. It's really bothering me."

"What? Oh, well. Whatever. I know him, I know. Yeah, I thought that the training facility was purchased a long time ago? That's been going on forever."

There was an awkward pause. Maddox looked at Laura.

"No, it was supposed to be but it's not. He did put the bid in the other day. I guess those things just take time. I was getting really frustrated, but at least the bid is in. Maybe things will start to move like they are supposed to. I'm working on an Academy deal to bring an Academy run by Sporting Barcelona to the TENACIOUS training facility here in America. Here in Phoenix. I'll get it done."

"Yeah, we both saw Paul McCartney's huge house. That place is a mansion. He's got the money. He's probably just busy with that company his grandfather started."

"I'm on top of it. It's just a big project. I'm sure his commitment is still strong. I spoke with him today."

"Spain, that's a long trip. That stinks."

"Tell me about it."

"You've been working a lot lately. When do you come back?" Laura spoke with a rapid-fire monotone and she seemed distracted. She didn't really seem to care. Was she just sniffing around to see if the TENACIOUS stuff was grating on Maddox too much, or causing financial stress for Maddox's business, the Malone Agency? But, thought Maddox, at least she asked.

"Yeah, umm, well I have a lot of shit to deal with. I'm there for almost two days. In Spain. After that, I have to stop in Venezuela for Pepe Soliz's home run derby and then in New York to meet with Benjamin Cohen, my PR guy, on the way back. We have to talk about that thing with Pepe Soliz from Saint Cortana and I'll watch Pepe play the Metropolitans. I can't really say that I'm looking forward to the trip. Long flights and the schedule is brutal. But there you have it. That's what I've gotta do."

Laura didn't say anything back. So Maddox walked away. He turned his head about an inch to the left and sharpened his eyes.

Talking about all of that travel made Maddox apprehensive. He wanted a few hours away from dwelling on the trip. To actively think about something else. He ate his chicken burrito, which he regarded as pretty nasty, and continued sipping on his soda water, savoring the cranberry flavoring. At least he was ready for his flight.

Feeling relaxed, he went into his home office and opened up his copy of *Fathers and Sons*, by Ivan Turgenev. He loved that book! He was reading the part where Bazarov offered to help the doctors perform an autopsy on a man who had recently died of typhus. Maddox got to the part where Bazarov cut himself in the process. Maddox felt horrible for Bazarov and knew that there was a decent chance that Bazarov would die. Twenty minutes later, Maddox was having difficulty keeping his eyes open. So he put his book down. He crawled into bed and passed out almost instantly! He was flooded with dreams. Almost spinning with dreams! After two hours of fitful sleep, which included a couple of times that he woke up completely, the dreams started to settle down and he began to get more restful sleep. He needed it! He had a long trip on the horizon, and only a few more hours to rest before it began. A new day was dawning soon.

Core Values

✹✹

Maddox woke up with a start. He had slept solidly because of his workout, but he certainly could have used a couple more hours of sleep. In fact, when his alarm went off at three a.m., he sat up in his bed and greedily longed for two or three more hours of sleep. His body felt tired. He woke up a little hazy and didn't immediately turn off his alarm. After thirty seconds of buzzing and beeping and begging, the alarm finally jarred him fully awake. The alarm was ruthless, unforgiving. Maddox took a second to remember where he was. Ah, his home office, where he slept when he had odd sleep hours! In fact, it was where he slept most nights. He stared at the ceiling and then took a few minutes before gathering himself and getting out of bed.

He thought of the Salcido Duran contract immediately, but flushed it out of his mind. No time for that! He had to get to the airport to travel to Spain for the TENACIOUS Tennis Academy meeting. His ride would be there in forty-five minutes. Plenty of time! He stumbled into the shower. Soaped up with some body wash, shampoo and conditioner in his hair. He scrubbed his ass and soaped and rinsed his undercarriage. Armpits, then everywhere. He was clean and bounced out of the shower and draped a towel around himself. He ran a razor over his entire face when he got out of the shower. Clean shaven! After towel drying and then air drying for a minute, he put some deodorant on, bracing himself for the long flight to Spain. He threw on a tee-shirt, jeans and some comfortable tennis shoes. He put a little bit of styling product in his clean-cropped brown hair. He would travel casual and comfortable and then change into a suit in Barcelona for the meetings.

His driver, a cute young Eastern European girl named Katarina, arrived. Maddox walked softly out the front door, without waking Laura, Thomas, Chester or Felicia. Even the dog kept sleeping. He would message or call them later to check in, that much was for sure. Maddox placed his brown suitcase in the trunk, placed his black computer bag next to the suitcase, shut the trunk and hopped into the back of Katarina's car.

During the end of the ride, as he was starting to wake up a bit, he took out his smart phone and sent a text message to Paul McCartney.

"I just arrived at the airport in Phoenix. I'm flying to Barcelona to do the meetings regarding the TENACIOUS Tennis Academy deal with Sporting Barcelona. Hopefully you are en route as well. The Spanish folks will want to see your face since you're providing the funding. That's important for the letter of intent. Thanks."

The Grasshopper responded immediately. Maddox wondered why he was up, unless his travel schedule was the same as Maddox's.

"I'll be there, Maddox. This is going to be very important trip for TENACIOUS. TENACIOUS is going to be the biggest name in sports. I am so driven to finish this project successfully. Let's do this!"

Maddox walked briskly into the ticketing area. Maddox grabbed his smart phone and sent a message to his wife Laura.

"I made it to the airport. Tell the kids I miss them and love them. I'll be back in a few days. Intense travel but I'll have my phone on when I can. Maddox."

He didn't get a response but figured, correctly, that his wife was still sleeping.

Maddox boarded the plane and took his seat, sipped on his iced Americano, and opened up one of the books he had stashed in his laptop satchel, VS Naipaul's *Among the Believers*. He was at the part where Naipaul was writing about Shafi, a thirty-two-year-old Malay who lived in Kuala Lumpur. Maddox was intrigued by Naipaul's interplay between anti-modernity and faith. How can anti-modern people survive in the modern world? Maddox admired Naipaul, who led a wild personal life, for getting off his ass and looking for answers. Physically looking. Talking to people.

Before long, the rest of the plane started to fill up. Maddox did an exaggerated double-take at the woman who boarded the plane to sit next to him. She was stunning. After a second or two, he realized it was not just any woman, it was Halle. She was prettier in person than she was in the movies. Maddox enjoyed watching her in *Swordfish* during the scene where she sat topless in the lawn chair. Her freed breasts looked glorious out in the sun. Maddox didn't feel like small talk right now, even with Halle, so he kept his face tucked in his book. Naipaul could really write!

Maddox and Halle disembarked and went their separate ways. Maddox went to the airport bar and ordered, then drank, a vodka and soda with a lime while he waited for his connection to Barcelona. Then another one. Then one more. He did it out of boredom as much as anything. At least that's what he told himself! But, he had to admit that all of the Malone Agency issues were nagging at him. He wanted to disengage from that feeling and that's where the vodka and sodas came in.

Maddox was anxious about this trip!

He received a text from Laura, responding to his earlier text. It read "Travel safe we'll see you in a few days."

Maddox wasn't happy with the text because it seemed impersonal and he missed seeing his kids, but he read it and kept his mind moving along. He had other things to worry about.

An e-mail also popped up on his smart phone's shiny screen. It was more paperwork and confirmations from TENACIOUS' real estate agent regarding the facility bid. That made Maddox feel good. The formal bid, placed by Paul McCartney on behalf of TENACIOUS, was just under two million dollars. The real estate agent sent several more e-mails, with document after document attached. This was great news and it gave Maddox some comfort regarding the time, energy and money that he had spent on TENACIOUS. Now things were moving, thought Maddox. TENACIOUS was real!

He wanted this trip to be over, and it had barely begun. He boarded his connecting plane, to Barcelona, Spain.

He sent a text to McCartney, which read "I'm boarding my plane to Barcelona. What is the status of the facility bid, has it been accepted by the seller yet? I saw the documents come in from the real estate agent before I took off, but we need to make sure that is locked down and completed ASAP. WE NEED TO FINALIZE THE PURCHASE OF THE FACILITY. All these things tie together." There was no response, not right away at least, but it felt good for Maddox to press the issue of the facility closing.

The bid was great — now TENACIOUS needed to finalize the deal, pronto. They needed a cornerstone building. That was the plan all along. They needed that deal done in order to proceed with the rest of the TENACIOUS brand concept. Maddox read for another two hours or so. Then, some travel-induced fatigue hit him and he slept the rest of the way until he landed in Barcelona.

Following a cab to his hotel and a shower, Maddox put on a suit and made his way over to the Sporting Barcelona headquarters. Inside the team's headquarters, there was a crowd gathering and the meeting was expected to start at one o'clock in the afternoon. All the right people were there, all the decision-makers that would be required to sign off on the TENACIOUS Tennis Academy letter of intent.

It was a big moment for TENACIOUS! The TENACIOUS Tennis Academy would be a world class addition to the training facility.

Maddox walked in, projecting a certain confidence. Outwardly, Maddox smiled. Inside, he was grimacing.

The club's director, Pedro Der Sentinel, walked into the room.

"So," he asked. "How's it going, Maddox?"

"Great Pedro. I trust you are well?"

"I am, thanks."

"Everything is moving along nicely back in the States," Maddox said. "This academy is going to be amazing. We are going to take our facility in the United States, add your know-how, and create the best tennis development program in the world."

"It is a great match," agreed Pedro.

"We know that you guys know how to create players. We know

that. I know how to build brands in sports. That's what I do. I've done it many times, often with less to work with. This is a match made in heaven," said Maddox as he lifted his hand and squeezed his thumb against his index and middle finger in a gesture of enthusiasm.

"Great. Everything sounds constructive. Now," Pedro chided, "if we do this, this international academy, I want you to be fair. I'm going to tell our people to be fair, too."

Maddox assured Pedro that he would be fair, and noted that there would be plenty of money to go around based on TENACIOUS' pricing model. Maddox joked that he would be on his best behavior. He wanted to make a great deal for everyone.

"Let me make you rich," Maddox joked. "Let TENACIOUS make you a rich man."

"I hope you do my friend. I hope you do. And Maddox," Pedro said, "I hope this isn't going to be bullshit, because if it is, you can do it with Sporting Madrid instead of Sporting Barcelona."

Pedro and Maddox both laughed at the joke! Right when Pedro articulated the word "bullshit", Paul McCartney entered the room with two steps and a hop. Then one more hop and two more steps.

"Hi Everyone, I'm Paul McCartney and I'm really excited to be here on behalf of TENACIOUS Sports. Let's do this!" exclaimed the Grasshopper, with his eyes looking buggy and his mouth rounded in a weird shape.

The Grasshopper's haunches were brimming. He looked plastic, he looked strung out. His brown, curly hair with the dramatic skunk-stripe right down Broadway was gelled but misshapen. His mouth rounded again, then went oblong. Then it rounded again. The jagged, reddish, shiny scar on his chin glistened in the light. His pale face housed dull eyes. His Grasshopper haunches went from brimming to fully laden. They were billowing!

"Hi Paul, welcome to you and Maddox from Sporting Barcelona. Welcome to Spain!" said Pedro.

"With everyone arriving from overseas, why don't we break for fifteen minutes, give everyone a chance to get comfortable, have some coffee, use the restroom, whatever, and then we will start with the meeting to finalize the Sporting Barcelona TENACIOUS Academy deal. Does that sound like a plan?" asked Pedro.

"Perfect!" said the Grasshopper, still brimming.

"Sounds great," said Maddox. He had to take a piss, so he loved that idea.

Before Maddox could head over to the restroom, the Grasshopper jumped over his way and they spoke, privately.

"Hi Maddox. I've spoken with Bernie, you know, the guy in the states that can help us run the TENACIOUS Tennis Academy with Sporting Barcelona after this deal is done. He wants to do it. He wants to run the Academy and the related camps. He knows that we can be successful. What do you think?"

"Sounds great. Did you get my text message about the TENACIOUS Performance Facility building bid? We have always discussed attaching the Sporting Barcelona TENACIOUS Tennis Academy to the main training facility. I'm doing all this work on this brand, I want to make sure that you are following through on the facility bid. We need to close immediately."

"Roger that. Take no prisoners! I am waiting to hear back about the bid. If they don't accept it and they counter, we will either accept their counter or counter back. TENACIOUS demands success! Let's do this!" said the 'Hopper.

"Okay, I wanted that assurance. We can't do all these projects without that capital. Remember we have Tony Capote and George Korpine and others standing by. Relying on TENACIOUS. You know?"

"I know! I know! Oh, it's not bullshit. It's anything but bullshit," said McCartney. "Money is not the issue. Let's do this! Take no prisoners!"

"Great. Hey, I'm going to take a leak and grab a cup of coffee," said Maddox. "I'll see you back here in a few minutes."

Maddox hit the restroom and grabbed some coffee. Paul McCartney fiddled around on his smart phone, looking a bit surreptitious. Maddox caught a quick glimpse of the Grasshopper's screen. Naked women again! "What the fuck is wrong with this guy?" thought Maddox.

Seconds later, Pedro walked back in to the room, and the meeting started up again immediately.

"Look, Maddox," Pedro said. "If we're putting the Sporting Barcelona name on this tennis training academy in the United States, we need to be absolutely certain with respect to the quality of the facility."

The Grasshopper perked up and chimed in.

"Pedro, you can ask anybody about me. You can ask about my Grandfather's company. My Grandfather was from Philadelphia and started a big company called PartDok. We would never do anything less than first rate. Not second rate, my friend! In fact, I put a two million dollar bid in for a location just before I came here to Spain. It's a prime location! Let's do this!" said the Grasshopper.

Maddox swallowed, undetectably. Paul McCartney and his catchphrases.

"Paul has been steadfast in his commitment to fund TENACIOUS since I met him. And, as he said, his Grandfather started a company called PartDok that Paul inherited so he has the resources to fund TENACIOUS, which is an expensive project. I was there when he placed the bid to purchase the facility, so I can personally let you know that process is taking place. We will stay diligent and close the purchase as soon as possible. I'm underlining the importance of that with Paul."

"I'm so excited about the TENACIOUS brand, it's going to revolutionize sports," said Paul McCartney, while practically bouncing in his seat.

Pedro looked satisfied with these statements. Maddox felt like they were offering explanations of TENACIOUS' deficiencies and that the Sporting Barcelona folks could probably detect some uncertainty and some chaos. Maddox couldn't believe that McCartney was getting by with these general, lofty statements. Yet somehow he was! The Spanish were taking the Grasshopper at face value.

Other issues came up. Sporting Barcelona wanted firm control of how its trademarks and copyrights were used. They wanted to be involved in the creative output made up to promote the Academy.

"That makes perfect sense," Maddox agreed. "The more we can collaborate and come to agreement on creative, the better it will be. We will do those things together with a great process."

"Perfect, we are happy with being co-pilot and co-adviser, we understand you have a strong vision for the complementary TENACIOUS brand that fits so well with Sporting Barcelona. We understand that the business thesis is to create the association between TENACIOUS and Barcelona to be known as the best Tennis trainers in the world. We want to be part of that association, and we want to make money along the way. The United States is a sleeping giant in the sport of tennis. This will be a worthwhile project," Pedro said.

With most of the preliminary issues out of the way, McCartney's face showed excitement. He buzzed with energy. Maddox guessed that he was envisioning the TENACIOUS Tennis Academy five years out, thriving. Maddox knew that McCartney didn't know how to do anything relating to building that vision — but, Maddox justified, he didn't need the Grasshopper for that. Maddox and the Sporting Barcelona people knew how to do everything. He just needed the Grasshopper's for his grandfather's money. The facility and academy together would require millions of dollars in funding. Let him babble on about his Core Values, thought Maddox. TENACIOUS just needed the money to get going.

Pedro paused, then spoke again, saying "Gentlemen, we have covered quite a lot. I think we are in agreement on most things, the last requirement is that we discuss the financing and the distribution of profits between partners. I would propose that we take a fifteen minute break and come back to discuss and finalize this issue. Then we can update the draft letter of intent that Maddox circulated and we can finalize this deal. Does that sound good?"

"Perfect. Let's do this!" shouted the Grasshopper. "Core values!"

"Sounds good, Pedro," said Maddox.

As they all headed for the conference room door, there were big smiles all around. On the way out, McCartney sidled up to Maddox.

"I'm so excited. This is going to be huge, this is going to be absolutely huge," said the Grasshopper, sniffing through his nose in rapid, short bursts. Hmmmmphh. Hmmmmph. Hmmmmmphh. "I can't wait for this Tennis Academy to be the greatest in the world. Core values!"

Maddox didn't say anything, but thought "something is off with this guy. Something is wrong." Maddox felt queasy at this thought. He had put his reputation on the line for this TENACIOUS expansion. He was having second thoughts about the Grasshopper. Fuck this guy's Core Values, Maddox needed the facility purchase to be finalized. Everything was in a logjam! Maddox felt a sharp twang of brief panic, again. It was almost like he had been punched in the face. What if McCartney didn't follow through on his promises?

Impossible, thought Maddox, as he tried to calm himself down.

In fifteen minutes, everyone returned to the conference room to finish up the deal. There was a new person from Sporting Barcelona in the room, who introduced himself as David and said that Pedro had updated him on the previous discussions. He told everyone that he had the document open on his laptop and could make the changes to the letter of intent in real time. Once the discussion was finished and the document was updated and finalized, they could sign and then the Sporting Barcelona contingent wanted to take the TENACIOUS contingent for appetizers and a cocktail or two, David said.

"Wow, that sounds great!" said McCartney.

After thirty minutes things were going smoothly in the conference room. Everything was discussed carefully, and everyone was in agreement, with a system whereby TENACIOUS would cover the costs to get the Academy up and running and then, after the costs were returned to TENACIOUS, the profits would be split between TENACIOUS and Sporting Barcelona, equally. It was a clean deal! An equal partnership. Both bringing significant assets to the table, in the model.

"This is a great day for the worldwide Sporting Barcelona brand. We want to become the world leader in training young tennis players. We know how to do this and TENACIOUS can help us with the entry into the local community. We look forward to this program's success and to continued growth in America. We look forward to sharing in your core values."

McCartney chimed in, unexpectedly. "This is our capital, TENACIOUS' capital. We got it from the success of my grandfather and PartDok, both from Philadelphia, both with core values, his core values that he brought," McCartney said. "We're prepared to put in the amounts necessary to build Sporting Barcelona's brand throughout the world. This is a groundbreaking day for TENACIOUS. We are so happy to partner with Sporting Barcelona. Take no prisoners!"

Maddox was not impressed with the rambling speech. Instead, to be honest, he was irked and embarrassed. It was Maddox's turn to speak.

"Sporting Barcelona has done a first-rate job training players," Maddox said. "There is no denying this. You gentlemen know how to do this, you have the magic touch. You have built players like Randolfino, one of the greatest tennis players in the history of the world. I am so thrilled that TENACIOUS has this opportunity and it's heartwarming to get Paul McCartney's assurance regarding the funding from his grandfather and PartDok. We are lucky to have the Spirit of Mr. McCartney in the room and looking out for the new TENACIOUS brand."

David had made the simple edits to the letter of intent and now printed four copies of the final document on bond paper. He passed two to Pedro and one each to the Grasshopper and to Maddox. Everyone took a few minutes to review, confirmed the terms regarding the equal profit share were clear enough and acceptable to all the parties, and they were ready to sign.

"Paul, please do the honors of signing this letter of intent for TENACIOUS," said Maddox.

"Why don't you do it, Maddox? You put in so much hard work to get us to this point where the document is final and the agreement is reached? Take no prisoners!" said the Grasshopper as he hopped away, metaphorically, from something that he didn't want to do.

"Well, your commitment on the funding side is so important, Paul. We couldn't do it without you and your grandfather's achievements. We can't do it without your grandfather's blessing, in spirit. Here's to PartDok. You sign!"

"That's nice of you to say, Maddox. But you are the chief executive officer of TENACIOUS. You are making this brand the international powerhouse that it will be. Let's do this! You sign!" McCartney's pale white boomer face twisted and scrambled into a jumbled mess as he finished speaking. His mouth flattened, then went circular, then flattened again. Finally, it settled in a tubular shape with a slight uptick on the left side.

It looked ridiculous for them to argue back and forth in front of the contingent from Sporting Barcelona, so Maddox just agreed that he would sign. He gave in. Pedro signed the two copies in front of him. Maddox signed the two other copies. They exchanged papers, and each counter signed the other's documents. They held the final, signed copies, two each and every one shook hands.

"Here's to a hundred years of partnership!" said Maddox.

"I appreciate that and I wish everyone the greatest success with this venture. We look forward to working with TENACIOUS," said Pedro.

"Let's go get some Goo-oo-ooose!" hollered the 'Hopper.

Everyone glanced at him, surprised, but then everyone turned away, ignoring the comment. Maddox was embarrassed. It was, in fact, time to go get some appetizers and cocktails. The Grasshopper had a ridiculous way of pointing that out.

Maddox walked over to his hotel, stopping to buy a decorative plate for Laura that featured a dapper Spanish bullfighter stabbing a bull. On the walk back, Maddox Malone thought about all of the promises that McCartney made. The training facility, the tennis academy, the golf tour, the wrestling league. It hit him like a ton of bricks that there was no way all of that was going to happen.

Or would it happen?

McCartney had seemed so enthusiastic and genuine in his commitments! He seemed sincere about the two million dollar bid, right? Maddox didn't know anymore. The Grasshopper seemed like he was full of shit.

Or did he?

The Grasshopper's chaotic existence had stripped Maddox of his ability to think clearly about TENACIOUS. If it was all going to happen, it would have happened already. Or was it that these were big projects and they were going to take time to finish? Maddox didn't know, not anymore. He couldn't be certain. He would go round and round in his mind. They have to be real? How could they not be real? They seem so fake? Why would anyone fake these projects? They are taking so long. Is that normal? Maybe they will be funded now? He asked himself the same questions and the answers vacillated. He had never encountered a character like Paul McCartney before. Whenever Maddox tried to pin him down, Paul managed to hop away. Maddox sat there, naked on the hotel couch thinking about all that stuff. And the more he thought about it, the angrier he became. He started thinking that he should go confront the Grasshopper right this minute. Or, more practically, after getting dressed. The more he thought about it, the more his headache worsened and he grew more depressed, he was mind-fucking himself, spinning in thought.

"How did I let this happen if this project is all fake? How did I fall for this? It has to be real. Right?"

Maddox's eyes were heavy and tired and that made everything worse. His eyes felt dry and sore from lack of sleep combined with careful reading. He felt like he was getting a cold, in addition to the headache. Maddox had enough of this negative line of thought, so he decided to spring into action. He pulled two headache pills, ibuprofen, out of his shaving kit. He popped them into his mouth and washed them down with a swig of water. Okay, that should take care of the headache, he thought. He put on some jeans and a black sweater and some black rubber-soled loafers. They were dressy enough but almost as comfortable as sneakers because of the style of the sole. Now he was ready for the Red Frog Speakeasy, no matter what his thoughts were about the celebration. It was premature, in Maddox's eyes, but he needed to head over there. He had to do it, he had to see TENACIOUS through.

When Maddox got back to his room after the celebration of signing the letter of intent, he actually enjoyed some peace and quiet for the first time in what felt like days, or even weeks. He opened a big bottle of water with the intention of drinking the whole thing. His thoughts were scattered. He still had jetlag from his last flight across the world. He sat on the couch in a tee-shirt and boxer shorts with the TV on in the background.

Maddox had a steady stream of thoughts. Just running through his head. He told himself "The next step has to be finalizing the purchase of the training facility, like McCartney promised, and then attaching the Barcelona Academy program to it. Otherwise, there is no reason to continue all the travel and meetings and planning. I have to stop in New York and Venezuela for agency shit when all I really wanna do is go home. A lot of people are asking me what is gonna happen with TENACIOUS and all the projects," he continued thinking to himself. "It's such a stupid question. How the hell should I know what is going to happen with TENACIOUS? The answer is, something is going to happen. Something has to happen, right? How could nothing happen? Some days I think it's a legitimate project with great branding, like the day Paul McCartney submitted the bid for the two million dollar facility on behalf of TENACIOUS. I thought the train might start rolling down the track after that. But it's still a slow train. What kind of a real estate bid takes this long? Other days, I see how the Grasshopper behaves and I think the projects are one hundred percent fake. A total scam! But how do I know for sure? If you want to know the truth, I don't. I used to think I could tell what deals were good and which ones weren't. I thought I had a good crystal ball. But lately, I haven't been any good at predictions. I mean, who knew the Poobah and Party Wardy would go on a bender, culminating in a violent rape, in Saint Cortana? Who saw that train coming down the track? Who knew the Platform would start to crumble? Who knew that it would be this hard to get the promised funding for the TENACIOUS projects? I'm sorry I told so many people about TENACIOUS. TENACIOUS, if it doesn't happen, is going to be very hard to explain. It would be one thing if one or two of the projects fell off, but if the entire thing was a scam, it was going to be a huge mess. Is the facility real? Am I wasting my time and money in Spain? What if the whole thing was a mirage? A hoax? Hell, what would I tell the Spanish contingent from Sporting Barcelona? Many of them were looking forward to having a satellite program in America. What would I say to them if it's a hoax? Sorry? No, that would be absurd. No one would do a hoax like that. Why would anyone do a hoax like that? There's no way. TENACIOUS is real. TENACIOUS is definitely real!"

Maddox's mind was racing. If he didn't stop this, he was going to drive himself crazy worrying about TENACIOUS and his other Malone Agency imbroglios. He had to stop. So, he got dressed again and walked down to his hotel bar for half-a-dozen vodka and sodas, each with a lime.

Flush It

❋❋

After finalizing the letter of intent with Sporting Barcelona and flying out of Barcelona the following morning, Maddox was on his way to New York. At the airport in Spain, he had purchased a book called *Between the World and Me* by Ta-Nehisi Coates because he had seen some good reviews for it here and there and had read every other book in his travel bag. He started the book but stopped reading after covering enough pages to know that it was written in ridiculous, pompous prose by a low-IQ-semi-retard and was just an exercise in apportioning blame and guilt to entire groups of people for things that they didn't even do. It was strange that the shit-tier material was praised by establishment book culture. The publishing industry was bizarre!

"What a dog-shit book, I can't believe I bought that," thought Maddox as he threw the book in a trash can with a "thu-dunk" while walking out of the airport towards the car. He felt relieved as he rectified .

Maddox's smart phone buzzed and whirred, so he checked the display. There was an article, pushed right onto his smart phone screen. It was titled "How did public bathrooms get to be separated by sex in the first place?" The weird headline blared away on his shiny smart phone which both buzzed and beeped from the notification announcing the article.

"I hate this phone," thought Maddox as he deleted the notification. He locked his smart phone, the newest model made by Endless Content, the Super 6G, and put it in his jacket pocket.

Maddox got in the car that had just arrived to pick him up. In New York, during rush hour, as it was today, a line of cars sometimes comes to a rest, like a centipede that is walking along and suddenly sees a hungry chicken and freezes in its numerous tracks. Every foot, stopped like a broken clock. Today, the halt had already consumed fifteen minutes and it showed no sign of letting up. Maybe there was some obstruction up the road? Maddox couldn't be sure.

Maddox's smart phone buzzed yet again and Maddox saw a fresh e-mail from his friend Bart Odom, a buddy from Chicago that sold television advertisements. The e-mail contained only a link to a website. He clicked the link, which was to a short news article about the Platform Volleyball Tour.

"*Los Angeles* -- The Platform Volleyball Tour has filed for bankruptcy protection. According to papers filed in American Bankruptcy Court in Los Angeles on Friday, the Platform Volleyball Tour said it has less than $463,000 in assets and $7.46 million in liabilities. Among those owed money are Platform Volleyball champions Tomas Rawlings, Perry Dullfing and Lacy Stratton. The Platform Volleyball Tour had hoped to cash in on the popularity of the sport after the American sweep of most recent Volleyball Championships in Asia, even though those championships were played on a plastic platform made cheaply in Cambodia. But the troubled economy scared sponsors and investors away. The last remaining sponsor is Efficient-Pop, which is a wholly-owned subsidiary of the Platform Volleyball Tour. The tour shut down last week when it ran out of funding. It canceled the last five events on the schedule. The filing was first reported on Tuesday by The Block Street Telegram."

"Oh, shit!" thought Maddox. "This is not what I needed right now!"

Maddox immediately clicked his smart phone off of the internet browser and dialed the Platform Volleyball Tour's owner, Nathan Lawsin.

"Hey Maddox," said Nathan as he answered Maddox's call.

"Hey Nathan. You filed it?" asked Maddox.

"Yeah, had to. I had to flush it. Nobody was showing up and we couldn't get any sponsors. Efficient-Pop is losing money too — there's a snacking problem at the factory — and I can't foot the bill for the Platform Tour. It had to be done."

"Okay. Let me know if I can help."

Maddox had invested so much time, energy and political capital into the sport of Platform Volleyball. This bankruptcy meant that he would lose hundreds of thousands of dollars in future commissions that he would have received from Lacy Stratton and his other top Platform clients. Maddox felt queasy when he thought of all the money he just lost.

"Will do. I'm going to get it out of bankruptcy and sell it. Probably in the next sixty days."

Woooooonnnnnnkkkk!"

Maddox heard what sounded like a massive gas expulsion through his smart phone's speaker.

"Nathan, are you taking a shit?" asked Maddox, with disbelief in his tone.

"I was," said the eccentric owner of the Platform, who was certainly smiling broadly.

Maddox heard a toilet flush.

"That's so fucking rude, man," said Maddox.

Both Maddox and Nathan started laughing out loud.

"I flushed the Platform into bankruptcy. And now I flushed again. Not like I was gonna put it in a Thank You bag."

Maddox felt helpless. There was nothing that could be done. It felt like all the years he had spent working on Platform deals were wasted.

Maddox sent three short text messages to his clients. "The Platform Volleyball Tour filed for bankruptcy. Personal service contracts will be terminated."

On the message to Lacy, he added "I'll call you in an hour."

Of course, when Maddox tried to call Lacy in an hour, the call went into voice-mail, since Lacy had been overwhelmed with managing everything in her household while Carlton Duffer, the Bedbug, was relaxing in rehabilitation. Maddox left her a brief message saying that they should meet up to discuss the Platform bankruptcy.

Maddox kept dwelling on the But he knew, instinctively that he had to move on from dwelling on those contracts. They were gone and they weren't coming back, not anytime soon. With everything else going on, there wasn't time to dwell on the Platform Volleyball implosion. He had to bounce back, quickly, from this disappointment. The other problems he was facing weren't going to solve themselves.

He called Nathan back.

"Hey Maddox."

"Hey Nathan, I let the players know. Also, I just landed in New York. I'm in a car heading into the city. I was gonna see if Pepe could hang out tonight, he's in town to play the Metropolitans, but they are off tonight. They play tomorrow. Maybe you and I can get together too, hang out."

"Bring the Poobah to my place I'll get some food to barbeque. I'll buy something good. We can play ping-pong and watch television."

"Okay, let me check with Pepe."

Maddox hung up and sent a text message to Pepe's smart phone.

"You want to have dinner with my friend tonight? Ping-pong and television. He has an apartment in New York."

"Yes, Papi, I want that," came Pepe's response.

"Okay, I'll send you the address for your driver. I'll be there around six."

He told to Nathan, "we're in for dinner and ping-pong."

"Okay, I'm gonna get the food now," Nathan responded.

Nathan was always one to have tequila flowing at his apartment, and Maddox was trying to have a mellow night because he had a meeting with Maddox's PR guy Benjamin Cohen, who was helping Pepe and Maddox with a public relations strategy as it related to the rape. If April

Tilney ended up filing the civil claim for sexual battery, they needed to have a media strategy.

He sent a quick message to Benjamin Cohen. "I'm in New York and confirming our meeting for tomorrow morning about the Soliz matter."

"Yes, we're confirmed," came Benjamin's response.

"Okay, great, I'll see you in the morning," wrote Maddox.

Maddox eventually arrived at his hotel. Checked in, showered, shaved, and got dressed. Maddox quickly combed his hair and then took the elevator down into the lobby. He was overly-efficient in getting ready, and he was in the lobby about thirty minutes before he needed to leave for Nathan's apartment. So, he pulled up a chair at the lobby bar in the Intercontinental, which he frequented every time he stayed in New York.

Maddox knocked down two vodka and sodas, each with a lime and then he jumped in the car heading to Nathan's. Ten minutes later he knocked on the door and entered when Nathan opened it.

"Hello!" Maddox roared, barreling into the two bedroom, top floor apartment.

Maddox's voice echoed through the apartment. He figured he would bring high energy into the apartment to show that the bankruptcy of the Platform didn't have him down and out. Life would keep marching on, it always did. Always! The Platform Volleyball Tour sucked anyway! Why sit around and worry that it went bankrupt?

"What's happening, Maddox?" asked Nathan. He always had a little impish grin on his face. Some people said he was too mischievous, they said he was a douche bag, but Maddox viewed Nathan as a fun-loving, funny guy. A character. In fact, Maddox loved his sense of humor and his irreverent tone. He thought Nathan was funny, a hustler, a ham.

"I got a four-and-a-half pound porterhouse steak from Loebel's. You'll never believe this thing," said Nathan.

"Fuck yeah, you did. That's what's up. We're gonna crush that thing. Wait till you see Pepe eat! Pepe can eat like nobody's business!"

"We're gonna have a feast. When is the Poobah going to get here, so I can time the cooking? We're going to grill the steak on the roof."

"He'll be here in half an hour."

"Okay perfect. We can eat a little while after he arrives."

"Cool, he has curfew at the team hotel so everything should work out well."

"Sorry about the Platform Volleyball bankruptcy, I guess. Wasn't the way we envisioned it would turn out when you bought the property a year ago or whenever that was. I thought you had a lot of good ideas for the turnaround. I thought you guys did things the right way."

"Yeah, we had a good plan, but the sponsor dollars were too dry. Just too dry. It was like the Sahara desert out there. It was like a dried out old cunt. Not a sponsor dollar in sight," said Nathan.

"Yeah, I can see that. I go to a lot of the events," remarked Maddox.

"I wish it had worked out. God knows we tried. Some people think we were just fucking around but we really tried," said Nathan. "I'm just going to try to sell it when I can."

"Yeah, how long does that bankruptcy process take?"

"They told me I can probably sell it in sixty days. If you know anyone who wants to buy the Platform out of bankruptcy just let me know. I'll make a quick deal to get rid of the thing."

"I'll keep it in mind," said Maddox.

With Platform Volleyball, on the corporate side, it always sounded like the same old story. It was supposed to be a lifestyle sport, a marketing vehicle. Some of the events were on television. That was supposed to be a big deal for the companies that were sponsors of the events. They paid money for the sponsorship and promotional component of the events. People walked through the events and saw signage. They tested product. They milled around. They watched people play volleyball on a beautiful Platform built over the ocean. Someone won. Someone lost. This model had only worked for one short period in time, when Maddox Malone had leveraged Lacy Stratton's youthful winning streak — Lacy won over six hundred matches in a row — into national enthusiasm for the sport and huge ratings. Big brands were pushing product on the Platform, because people were watching.

That was when Lacy was young and single and fun. Now, she still won a lot, but would lose every so often. She was getting older too. She didn't have the magnetism of a young, cute single girl anymore — she had married the crooked-lipped Carlton Duffer, after all — ratings had just continued to decline.

Around this time, the sponsors started to catch on to the fact that the sport was a racket. The same few people milling around from event to event. No product was pushed.

The door opened and a twenty-five year old girl, named Amanda, walked in. It was Nathan's girlfriend. She was about five-foot-six, maybe one hundred and twenty pounds with brown hair and a cute face.

"Hey Maddox, we met in Miami that time when you stayed with Nathan at his family place. Right when he bought the Platform."

"Of course I remember. That was so fun. I remember that night well, even though it involved a lot of tequila. Good to see you, Amanda." They gave a quick hug and he kissed her cheek.

"No question about it. That night involved a lot of tequila, if I recall correctly."

"Yeah, I couldn't believe how much tequila Nathan drank that night. I felt like I was hanging out with Ernest Hemingway, except not as interesting. Not as much talent, not as many stories. Ha-ha!"

"Well, I have the genius of Hemingway, but that genius hasn't made its way onto paper yet. Someday," Nathan joked. Everyone chuckled, then laughed as the humor grew on them.

"What have you been up to, Amanda? Have you been hanging on any more chandeliers?"

Maddox decided not to make mention of the fact that, while Amanda was hanging on the chandelier that night, her left breast had popped out of her blouse, since she wasn't wearing a bra and a button had popped off her blouse. It was a very shapely C cup, which seemed, pleasantly, one size too big for the rest of her body. Her pink nipple had looked soft and supple. It looked as if it tasted of peach.

"Ha-ha, no-ooooo no-oo. No chandeliers, that's too dangerous! Really I've been going to a lot of parties. I party almost every day. Hanging out with this guy," she flashed her eyes in Nathan's direction. "I wish that wasn't the answer but I'm being honest," Amanda said with a giggle. "I guess I'm a party girl at this point. I'm just a party girl."

"Ha-ha! Nothing wrong with that," said Maddox with a smile.

Maddox received a text message on his smart phone from Pepe Soliz, the horny Poobah. "I'm here, Papi."

"Okay, I'm going to walk down and get you. Be there in a second."

Maddox walked out of the apartment and down the stairs. After greeting Pepe with a bro hug, he walked him back up the stairs into the apartment.

"Pepe, this is Nathan. This is Amanda."

"Hi Pepe."

"Hi everybody," mumbled the big Colombian Poobah. His belly was bursting out of his shirt!

"Are you hungry?" asked Nathan.

"Yes, Papi. I hungry. I really hungry."

Maddox could tell when Pepe's weight had been fluctuating by looking at him. He must have been binging on junk food and soda, because he looked very heavy. He was so plump! His face had blown up so much there was no meaningful hint of bone structure. It was as if he had been blown up like a balloon, expanding his face and head until it looked like a big brown Halloween pumpkin with some hair on top. His body-fat gushed and jiggled and flowed around. It exerted pressure on the belt strapped inside his jeans. How much could the belt withstand? It exerted pressure on the cotton in his tee-shirt. Gravity had a grip on him, pressing him down toward the floor. Despite everything, he smirked. He always stayed pretty happy-go-lucky.

Pepe looked over at Maddox with a face full of concentration.

"Hey Papi do you have dee mow-ney for dat girl yet?" asked the Poobah.

"What money?" asked Maddox.

"Dee lawyer helping me with dee rape say dat girl want mow-ney. She want one mee-lion dollars. Can you geev dat mow-ney to me?"

Maddox paused.

"Okay, Pepe, I'll figure it out," said Maddox with a gulp. "One million dollars!" thought Maddox.

"Thank you, Papi. Thank you for gee-ving me that mow-ney," said Pepe, with a look of peaceful satisfaction.

Pepe walked a couple steps deeper into the apartment. His momentum took him further into the room, where he spotted the ping-pong table in Nathan's apartment.

"Who gonna play me ping-pong?" asked the Poobah.

"I will," said Nathan with an impish grin. "Amanda is gonna go up on the roof and watch the grill. The steak will be ready in about twenty five or thirty minutes from now. It's a big piece of meat."

The ping-pong game was truly a battle of wills. Nathan Lawsin, with the home table advantage, played a crafty style of conservative shots, a defensive style, unless there was a high ball that he could smash. Pepe, the rapey Poobah, played a pressing top-spin style where he tried to cause Nathan to make errors under pressure.

It was a good game. It was hotly contested, in fact, it was never more than a two point differential. At fifteen to thirteen, Nathan held the advantage and felt like he was closing in on a victory. The heavy but nimble Poobah was able to fend off Lawson's defensive shots and then smash a ball to the deep left corner for the point. He played ping-pong with a quickness that belonged to a man a hundred and fifty pounds under the Poobah's actual weight, it seemed. In the world of ping-pong, he moved as if he was a spry, one hundred pound Chinese woman, or a little Japanese man who subsisted on only edamame, the humble soy bean.

The tension ran high, until it was finally game point, Lawson holding a twenty one to twenty lead. He served to Pepe's backhand, and Pepe hit a deep volley back, but it was high. Lawson circled the ball and hit a downward smash that ricocheted off the table and hit Pepe on the tee-shirt covering his fat, hairy belly. The game was over and Nathan had won.

"Boom Sha-ka-la-ka!" yelled Nathan, at the top of his lungs! "Boom boom, big boy!"

Pepe scowled. He just sat there, scowling.

"Don't take it too hard, big boy, it's my table. You'll have another chance someday! There's a home table advantage up in here!" Nathan yelled.

Nathan was fired up. Pepe's face became flushed with anger, but he didn't say anything. He lost, what could he say?

Nathan, Pepe and Maddox walked up to the roof. It was a nice night in New York. Amanda had turned the massive steak one last time after checking the internal temperature. It was about done. Nathan carved up the massive steak, which looked delicious. When the feast was over, Pepe took a car back to his team hotel, in time for the curfew, and Maddox took one to his hotel, where he night-capped at the bar with a couple vodka martinis, straight up with a twist.

Spreading the Pozz

❋❋

Maddox was up early. He couldn't sleep after four a.m. He laid there for another hour, in bed, dwelling on the Platform Volleyball bankruptcy and all the money that it would cost him. Maddox finally gave up and got out of bed around five-thirty. He made himself some coffee in the hotel room. It tasted like shit, but he forced that shit down because he wanted the physical effects of the caffeine to hit his body and mind. The caffeine buzz he got was minimal but it helped. He marshaled his energy. He felt good, all things considered. He took stock of himself. The most recent disappointment, the bankruptcy of the Platform Volleyball Tour, didn't seem to have crushed his will. His energy levels seemed fine. He was worried about the financial ramifications, but he felt energized and determined. He was just moving forward. He logged onto his laptop to review e-mail, then spent some time on digital media reviewing his feed. He had an appointment with a public relations firm to discuss any necessary media and community-related damage control for the Pepe Soliz rape aftermath.

When the time came, he took a car over to the public relations firm's office. The meeting commenced straight-away, and the discussion was back and forth with Maddox's long time PR guy, Benjamin Cohen, a vice president at the firm, taking the lead.

Benjamin made some introductory remarks and then said, "We just can't give the girl any oxygen. We have to cut the oxygen supply to any side of her story. It just needs to go away. We can't give the story any life."

"I know, but how?" asked Maddox.

"The answer from Pepe always needs to be: I already discussed that issue and I'm moving forward," said Benjamin.

"Hmm. Okay," said Maddox.

"I'm just moving forward, that's what Pepe needs to say," repeated Benjamin.

"But it's going to get a life of its own if the girl files a civil lawsuit for sexual battery," said Maddox.

"Only for one news cycle," said Benjamin. "That's a minor story."

There was a pause and then Benjamin continued, "We need to starve the story. Let it die on the vine. No oxygen, no water, no food. Just let the story die."

"Okay. I think I get it," said Maddox.

"Yeah, it's always, no comment or I already addressed that or that issue is being handled. If the reporters press too much, Pepe just needs to calmly walk away. He can't look upset, just walk away with a blank face or a slight smile. Not a big smile though, he's accused of rape. Nobody likes a smiling rapist," said Benjamin.

The conversation went on like this for a while. Same stuff. Standard stuff, for Benjamin.

At one point, Benjamin asked Maddox, "Hey Maddox, what's the story with the guy from your agency that was part of the gang-bang and rape? What on earth was he thinking? I saw that in one of the newspaper articles."

Maddox hated talking about Party Wardy but still offered, "Yeah, umm, yeah, well he's a guy named Ward Goldstein. He went to Harvard undergrad and Marquette law. So he's not stupid. But he failed the bar after Marquette. He's originally from Florida, he grew up there. His mom lives in Florida and his dad moved out to Montana. I think his dad was a business guy, a banker."

"Oh wow. Wow! I didn't know his name was Goldstein," said Benjamin.

"What does that have to do with anything?" asked Maddox.

"Nothing. I just have a client with that same name."

"Gotcha. A coincidence," said Maddox.

"Oy vey! Yep. Interesting. Another Goldstein spreading the

Pozz," said Benjamin.

"Yeah, I don't know much about that. Goldstein is a pretty worthless dude, that's all I know. He's pretty disgusting. I need to find some better client service staff. Add that to my list of shit to do," said Maddox with a resolved stare.

Party Wardy Goldstein, the Malone Agency recruiter, was reasonably well-spoken. He was mildly intelligent, at least on paper. He happened to be pretty good at taking standardized tests — that's what got him into Harvard. He was also lazy, opportunistic and possessing of poor character. He was parasitic, constantly trying to siphon money and opportunities from the Malone Agency. That's why he always lurked around the Poobah. That's why he had taken the Poobah out partying in Saint Cortana the night April Tilney ended up getting raped. He was a parasite, out latching onto people, trying to benefit himself. He had latched onto the Poobah and Maddox Malone, via his job at the Malone Agency. In fact, Party Wardy Goldstein was almost exactly like a Tick.

The Tick's lack of a soul manifested itself physically as well as behaviorally. Physiognomy was real! Goldstein had the most disgusting, nasty stench bubbling around inside of his guts. It was an extreme, strange case of colitis — not just a run-of-the-mill case. It didn't seem human.

"Yeah the other Goldstein, my client, is in a big PR nightmare right now. It's all public, so it's not like I'm sharing confidential information. He wrote a Pozz-ed children's book that got a heavy backlash," said Benjamin Cohen.

"That sucks for him. But it's good for you, I guess. Gives you something to work on," said Maddox with a grin. "Busy is good?"

"Yeah. It's good. My client, the other Goldstein, needs help. He got criticized for his book and, without talking to me, compared the criticism to the Holocaust. Now he's getting attacked for that — for diminishing the actual Holocaust. In fairness, it was a dumb comparison - criticism of a book is not anything like what Hitler did. I'm trying to get him to calm down and lay low. He won't do it. He's on social media all the time making it worse. He's drinking heavily. He's out of control."

"He compared the backlash to the Holocaust?"

"Yeah. For some people, everything is like the Holocaust. Every day there's a new one," said Benjamin. "It's overly dramatic and it makes the person look ridiculous. My Goldstein has tripled down on the comparison."

"Wow, yeah that's not smart. If every little thing is like the Holocaust then how could the real one have been that bad? That's dumb."

There was a break in the conversation for a moment.

"My job is really simple sometimes. My client, the other Goldstein, was spreading the Pozz. He got called out for it, and instead of just taking his lumps he played victim. If he just took it, the whole thing would have gone away in a day. Then he could have spread more Pozz instead of getting sidetracked by social media attacks."

Maddox's bright eyes flashed at Benjamin. He didn't recognize or know that term. He wasn't familiar with the Pozz. Hmmm.

"The Pozz?" said Maddox, quizzically.

"You don't know what the Pozz is?" asked Benjamin.

"No, I've never heard of it, not once," said Maddox.

"Oh boy. You have a lot to learn. The Pozz, the Pozz. You probably don't have time to talk about it," said Benjamin.

"Ha, ha. As long as we are all set on the plan for keeping the Poobah rape out of the newspapers. As long as we protect the Poobah from that girl! We can talk about what we want," said Maddox.

"Yeah, we covered it all on the Poobah. We will stick to the plan. I saw that you took notes. The only thing that will even register is if the girl files civilly for sexual assault. They will make that as flashy as they can and that will get coverage in maybe one news cycle. We just can't give her oxygen by responding. The Poobah will be unscathed!" said Benjamin.

Maddox was struck by how matter of fact Benjamin was. He gave no indication that he cared, not a single bit, about April Tilney. Maddox felt bad for what happened to April and her butt-hole. Both her body and her psyche had been damaged, badly. But this was just business for Benjamin, Maddox figured.

"Yeah, nobody is saying anything about it in Sunny Grove. No community groups ever really said anything. I told someone the other day, maybe the people in Sunny Grove just like sports more than they dislike rape. Or maybe they like Pepe's funny nickname — the Poobah."

"Perfect. So I can teach you about the Pozz?" joked Benjamin with a big laugh.

"Fine, I don't care. I just think it's a very odd topic," Maddox said. "You keep mentioning the Pozz. What is that, exactly?" asked Maddox.

"It's an attempt to spread degeneracy and filth, pushed through corporations and media. Pozz hates beauty and ignores truth. That's Pozz, Maddox."

"I know there's a lot of filth out there but you make it sound so bad," said Maddox.

"The Pozz is bad. It is-sss bad. My client, the guy I told you about — Goldstein — wrote a children's book about a gay African Santa Claus," said Benjamin.

"Wait, what?" asked Maddox.

"That happened. I call it Santa Pozz. Ha-ha. That's the Pozz, man," replied Benjamin.

"He did? No way. Fuck this conversation man. I don't need this," said Maddox.

"I'm serious," said Benjamin, pressing forward.

"I don't need to hear that, I love Santa Claus. I love Christmas," said Maddox.

"I swear it's true," said Benjamin.

"No way. Nobody tried to make Santa into an African that takes a dick. You're just messing with me. That can't be true, nobody would do something like that," said Maddox, with just a little flash of anger in his eyes. No angry twin emerged, his emotion was a combination of amusement and disbelief, with just a touch of anger, just a flash.

Benjamin grabbed his smart phone and pressed a few digital buttons. A screen came up that showed the cover of the book in question. A rendition of a gay African guy dressed as Santa Claus with a big fat ass peeking out of his red trousers was on the cover of the book, and that Pozz-ed version of Santa was smiling while kissing a bearded cartoon depiction of a white guy who was usurping the role of the real Mrs. Claus. Both the gay African Santa and the other guy had big puffy white beards. The African Santa had his hand on the other guy's crotch area. This thing was in a children's book format! It was real, the Pozz was right there on the screen! Benjamin looked angry. Maddox just thought it was stupid and gross. Maddox blew it off.

"Want to know the craziest thing about this story?" asked Benjamin.

"Not really," said Maddox.

Benjamin ignored Maddox and said "when people went on-line to criticize the book for being Pozz-ed, my client cried about the Holocaust and anti-Semitism. He compared the criticism of his book to the Holocaust because he's Jewish. You can't make this shit up! I stepped in and have everything mostly calmed down."

"I'd say I don't believe you again but..."

"My client played the victim instead of doing what he should have done — letting other people fight about his book," said Benjamin. "People mobbed him because he made himself the victim, never mind what he did to Santa Claus!"

"Mmm-hmm," Maddox nodded.

"Anyway, that's the Pozz—" said Benjamin, but he was suddenly interrupted by Maddox.

"I still can't believe that book that Pozz-ed Christmas. That's trash," said Maddox. "I guess we all have clients like that, though," said Maddox, thinking of the Poobah. "I wonder why your guy, Goldstein, couldn't come up with an original idea for his own character? Then he could just leave the real Santa Claus alone."

"That's the Pozz, man. It's not about actually promoting the things it promotes. I mean, I don't think he cares about promoting his gay African Santa. He just wanted to tear down the real, traditional Santa. Pozz like that is designed to tear down everything that is good. Everything we care about," said Benjamin.

It was a bit strange, because Maddox could tell that Benjamin Cohen really didn't like the book — but the book was written by his client. It made for an interesting conflict, one that Maddox could see on Benjamin's face.

"Mmmmhmm, I think I understand you," said Maddox.

Benjamin's face made clear that he was actually angry about, and disgusted by, the gay, African Santa book. He sat there, looking disgusted. Benjamin paused and took a deep breath.

"Here's another example of the Pozz. Third World immigration. A small but loud, subversive group is always present in this country trying to open American borders for all comers. This group, using the political process, pushed to change the United States in a fundamental way in nineteen sixty-five. Then, once the third world started flooding in, they screamed 'racist!' at anyone who said 'hey, maybe this immigration strategy isn't the greatest idea?'"

"Okay, but they are a small group of people, how can that be effective? How do they get the votes they need?" said Maddox.

"They're smart and persistent and they amplify their voice using propaganda. They're very good at that," said Benjamin.

"Okay, gimme and example," said Maddox.

"They Pozz-ed the Statue of Liberty with that disgusting poem — they're playing the long game. They put that poem up and act like it's the law of the land. For another example, that play, the *Melting Pot*. The author said there is only one way to world peace, and that is the absolute abolition of passports, visas, custom houses — including, in his mind, allowing the Third World into America. Essentially it's like that stupid song *Imagine*, by John Lennon. Guess what the *Melting Pot*'s real vision was?"

Maddox laughed to himself because that song was so ridiculous. But a whole generation of boomers heard the lyrics and had listened to that song countless times. They felt that song inside themselves. They absorbed that song. Some boomers made that song into their identity. Some boomers became that ridiculous song. Maddox was starting to think Benjamin was nuts. But, then again, Benjamin was smart and Maddox liked him.

"I have no idea about what the *Melting Pot*'s vision was," said Maddox.

"It was a way to create an over-class that rules over a demoralized working class with no identity."

"Oh Jesus, Benjamin. You're nuts!" said Maddox with an exaggerated smile. Maddox laughed. "A ruling class of overlords! You're nuts!"

"I'm not nuts!" yelled Benjamin.

"If you have to say you're not nuts, Benjamin, you're nuts!" Maddox said with a big smile.

"They want to rule over the nu-male! I'm telling you, Maddox! I'm right. They want to create a dumbed-down, de-racinated, soy-fed, fat working class of bug-like consumers. Led by people like that guy from the social network, you know the digital life guy. Everyone just lives digitally. Maybe to crush everyone's soul even more, they will strap a high resolution digital screen right on everyone's fucking face and call it virtual reality. Push crap all day every day until consumerism is the only thing left and until consumerism consumes humanity itself. There will just be a bunch of bugs left. Human bugs."

The conversation paused for a second while Benjamin's eyes blazed. They blazed! Maddox didn't agree with anything Benjamin said. In fact, he didn't understand anything Benjamin said. But, Maddox thought. Maddox considered. Maddox absorbed.

"Here's the thing, Benjamin. Why? Why would anyone do that? Why do people push the Pozz? Why not side with truth and beauty? That's the part I don't get," said Maddox.

"You're asking the right questions. It's impossible to be sure, but I think it's to create cultural chaos," said Benjamin.

"Cultural chaos? Why do that?" asked Maddox.

"Well if there's cultural chaos then there is really no culture at all. Right?" Benjamin replied.

"Yeah I guess a bunch of different people just living in the same place don't have a culture. Why do Pozz pushers want no culture?" asked Maddox.

"Because traditional culture is the most effective thing that can combat the Pozz," said Benjamin.

"I guess I can see that," said Maddox.

"The Pozz can't package its degenerate shit in a way that makes people interested in buying it directly," said Benjamin.

"So you're saying the strategy from the people behind this stuff is to break down traditional culture and then the Pozz can flow in freely through the cracks?"

Benjamin looked thoughtful for a few seconds.

"Yes. That's what I'm saying. You just made me think about Susan Sontag because she made a full frontal attack — rare for pushers of the Pozz. She openly called the white race and white culture the 'cancer of human history.' She said it with a straight face, and had no problem smearing whites with a broad brush, while enjoying the society that whites by-and-large had built in America. It was so fucking galling - even for me, and I'm a liberal Jewish guy from New York. That Susan Sontag is one brazen cunt with a capital 'C'. She's a dirty rutted-out cunt," said Benjamin, angrily.

Maddox just laughed. He had never heard of Susan Sontag. He loved the emotion that Benjamin was showing, though. Such an energetic attack — Benjamin looked pissed! Maddox didn't get all fired up because Susan Sontag called Maddox Malone, indirectly, a cancer. He had more important things to worry about than some mean and rotten old lady that lashed out against Maddox and his ancestors. "She can go fuck herself," thought Maddox, but he thought it casually, more dismissive than angry.

"So, I now understand the Pozz. What can be done to stop it?"

"People have to push back!" said Benjamin, excitedly. His face was excited, since he felt like he was spreading his anti-Pozz message.

"Who has time to run around fighting the Pozz?" asked Maddox.

"Anyone who doesn't want to live in a shitty, third-world-type country where Santa takes a fucking dick. That's who," replied Benjamin.

Maddox suddenly didn't think this whole debate was worth wading into. He agreed with Benjamin that Pozz was, very clearly, being pushed and spread. There was filth everywhere. But what could Maddox do? Could Maddox really make a difference? He didn't think so.

"It can be fixed. The country is Pozz-ed. But it can be reversed," said Benjamin.

"Hmm," Maddox intoned, while listening and looking at Benjamin. "That's gonna be hard. I don't think it can be done. Once you told me what Pozz is I immediately thought of a ton of examples. We're so Pozz-ed man. Now I can't stop noticing Pozz, everywhere."

"Just think about it, Maddox," said Benjamin.

"Alright, Benjamin. I have to get to the game soon then the airport, I'm heading to Venezuela for the XtraShoog Home Run Derby."

"How long are you staying in Venezuela?"

"Two nights."

"Okay, great, stay safe. I'm going to head over to the synagogue to meet my Rabbi. You grabbing a car out of here?" asked Benjamin.

"Enjoy it. Yep. Keep in touch on everything. Call me anytime."

Maddox and Benjamin shook hands and Maddox walked out of the office to grab his car to the Metropolitans game. Maddox sang along with some nineties rock and roll.

> Hangin' round downtown by myself
> And I had so much time
> To sit and think about myself

Maddox was only able to stay for three innings of the afternoon game. Over the right field wall, there was a huge advertisement showing a Chinese man dressed up as a woman, with a huge smile on his face. The man was holding a big black chocolate cookie — full of hydrogenated vegetable oil and processed sugars — with white frosting in the middle. The text on the advertisement read "Get inside me! Come to the party, people, we can do it!" Maddox laughed inside as he saw the sign. That was Pozz! It's right there! Benjamin nailed it!

In Pepe's first at bat he hit a ground ball to the second baseman and got out. Maddox had to head to the airport. He would see the Poobah soon enough in Venezuela. But for now, Maddox had to catch his plane down to Miami so he could connect through to Caracas. Maddox relaxed for a minute and listened as he checked his buzzing smart phone, which was practically jammed up with hundreds of notifications. Apps, e-mails, messages, calls, digital media, and a bunch of other stuff. In twenty-five minutes, after another car ride, he was at the airport.

After checking in and getting through security, he made his way to one of the airport bars and ordered a vodka and soda with a lime. The first sip went down easy as he thought of the rest of the trip to Venezuela and then back through Wyoming via Boise, Idaho. He logged on to an application on his smart phone to make sure everything looked good with his flight scheduling and departure. Everything was proceeding apace, and he was still thirsty, so he ordered another vodka and soda with a lime while the time ticked closer to his flight's departure.

After he finished that cocktail, he paid his tab and stepped into the bookstore. He saw a fresh, hardcover copy of George Orwell's *1984*. He had another copy at home, but couldn't resist the purchase after the conversation with Benjamin. Orwell would have been great to talk to about the Pozz! Orwell feared people who would deprive us of information through censorship and other forms of brainwashing. Maddox, in light of his conversation about the Pozz, wanted to understand Orwell's fears afresh. He bought the book and then headed back to the airport bar — he still had time for one more vodka and soda with a lime before he had to board. He ordered it and drank it. Like the others, it went down easy. Maddox Malone boarded his plane and slept all the way to Miami, without cracking *1984* or any other book that happened to be lurking in his bag.

Festival de Jonron

❋❋

When Maddox landed in Miami a couple hours later, he got off the plane and walked over to the airport bar and placed his order right away. Maddox's vodka and soda with lime was delivered with a smile from the cute young bartender. For no particular reason, Maddox felt a sharp worry about the pace of the TENACIOUS project. He took out his smart phone and called Paul McCartney. Surprisingly, the Grasshopper answered.

"Hello Maddox, let's do this!"

"Uhh, Hey Paul, I'm heading to Caracas for a Pepe Soliz event. Has the TENACIOUS facility purchase closed yet? We need to get this done," said Maddox.

"Yes, Maddox, TENACIOUS is a sure thing. Money is NOT the issue. Can you still come to Jackson Hole this weekend? I am bringing TENACIOUS wrestler LeSharrif Powell and his dad Kevin. Kevin is a little rough around the edges, though. But I'm hoping you can make it. Take no prisoners!"

Maddox responded, "Wait so it's closed? The facility purchase is closed?"

"Yes. Core Values! Can you make it to Jackson Hole?" asked the Grasshopper.

"Umm, okay, great. Okay, I will swing through on the way back from Venezuela. We can go over all things TENACIOUS. By the way, I didn't know LeSharrif Powell signed with TENACIOUS. Did he?"

"Oh yes, he signed with TENACIOUS sports. He is TENACIOUS!" said the 'Hopper.

"Oh, okay. I didn't realize that. Alright, I'm getting ready to board my flight. I'll catch up with you soon," said Maddox.

Maddox hung up and looked to his left and saw two sharp-dressed young men in suits. They were each drinking a cocktail of some sort. One of the men addressed Maddox.

"Hey, I saw your boarding pass on the bar. We've been here a couple hours because it was the only time our colleague could drop us off. Is the Caracas flight still on time?" asked the man.

"Yeah, I landed forty-five minutes ago coming from New York and it was showing on time."

"Okay, thanks. You heading down there for work?"

"Yeah, I'm connecting through here on my way to Caracas. I'm meeting a client for a Home Run Derby. Let me buy you a drink."

"Muh brotha? No shit, really? What do you do?"

"I'm a sports agent. I make deals."

"Oh that's cool. Like Jerry Maguire?"

"Ummm. Well, I guess," said Maddox.

"Which client is in the derby, if you don't mind me asking?"

"Pepe Soliz of the Sunny Grove Big Boys. The Colombian guy, but he lives in Venezuela now. Nickname is the Poobah. You heard of him?"

"Fuck yeah, I have. He's number thirteen on the Big Boys. I know him, of course. I'm a Dodgers fan."

"Haha. Where are you guys headed?"

"Also to Caracas. We work in the American Embassy down there. I'm Joe and that's Todd."

"Oh cool. I'm Maddox."

"Make sure you stay with Soliz and his security," Todd chimed in.

"Yeah, I've been down there a couple times with him. Will do."

"No, I mean it. Stay with them at all times or you will get killed. You hear?"

"Gotcha."

"I mean it, you will get killed," Todd said as he hammered the point home.

"Okay, I got you loud and clear. Always with Soliz and his security. I'm with you. I'll do it."

A scraggly boomer was having a loud conversation on the other side of Maddox.

The boomer said, "Well, I'm going down to help out because I think Venezuela can be a socialist paradise. Race blind, where all the people just live like brothers. Just living their lives, doing things. Eating in the sun. Chickens. Bananas. Pears. Apple Strudel. Imagine all the people living together in harmony. Imagine no countries. Imagine no possessions. It's like the Beatles guy, man, woo-hoo, ooh-ooh-ooh! Just imagine it," said the boomer. "We need that world. No bigotry, everyone living side by side, loving one another. Just living in harmony."

The guy was talking so loud. Maddox felt like telling him to quiet down, but instead Maddox scratched his head, clenched his teeth and ignored the guy — Maddox smirked because he had just talked about that stupid song the day before with Benjamin Cohen. The song was Pozz-ed. Maddox thought the boomer was delusional and Maddox, just by glancing at him, knew it was too late for the guy to course-correct.

"Sounds like we're boarding guys, I'm sure I'll see you on the plane," said Maddox. They exchanged good-byes and then parted ways.

Maddox settled into his seat at the front of the cabin. He put his headphones in his ear and pressed play on his music feed. He had some heavy rock on, but wasn't in the mood for that, so he flipped the feed over to some hillbilly music. He sang along.

> Girl you taught me how to hurt real bad and cry myself to sleep
> You showed me how this town can shatter dreams
> Another lesson about a naive fool that came to Babylon
> And found out that the pie don't taste so sweet

Now it's guitars, Cadillacs, hillbilly music
Lonely, lonely streets that I call home

Maddox reached into his computer bag, but he didn't pull out his new copy of *1984* as he had originally intended. Instead, he opened up his copy of *the Old Man and the Sea*. He felt like reading some Hemingway – just a little bit of Hemingway. He had read the book, this exact copy, several times, and, this time through, he was reaching the part where the marlin was starting to tire. Maddox Malone sympathized with that Marlin. A majestic creature, harpooned! Harpooned through his flesh! Maddox read for a while, but the early wake-up call started to catch up with him. The constant hum and buzz of the plane's engines were making him tired. He tilted his head toward the window and closed his eyes. He fell asleep right away.

While he slept, he had the strangest dream. It almost seemed like he was categorizing people that he knew into different groups. The consumers. The enlightened. The hybrids. The destroyers. The soy-men. The void. The parasites. The producers. The leaders. The intellectuals. In the dream, he was categorizing people he knew into these groups, understanding them better. In his dream, there were baskets that were based on the seven deadly sins. Pride, envy, lust, anger, gluttony, greed, sloth. He would see people he knew, people he knew well or casual acquaintances, and he had to determine which basket they would go in. An aggressive little gnome with a pitchfork would demand that Maddox pick a basket. Maddox would name the basket and the aggressive gnome would poke the person right in the ass until, properly coerced, the person would jump into their basket. It was strange! Understanding what moved them, what motivated them, what made them act. But the dream turned to a nightmare when that little gnome made Maddox pick a basket for himself. For himself! He quickly ruled out pride, envy, lust, gluttony and sloth. Maddox, being honest in his dream, was torn between the greed basket and the anger basket. Just the other day he was so angry at Garibaldi Vascoso, for example. But, when pressed, in the nightmare, Maddox told the gnome "greed" and that little mother fucker poked Maddox on the ass with his pitchfork until Maddox jumped in the greed basket. Maddox hated that nightmare! He woke with a start caused by both turbulence and the announcement over the plane's intercom that they would be descending into Caracas shortly.

After the plane landed, there was a frenzy of activity. Maddox rubbed his eyes, trying to make sure he was as alert as possible. Pepe's brother, Roberto Soliz, picked Maddox up at the airport. Because he was very round, Roberto looked like a ladybug — but one that was armed to the teeth. Maddox and the ladybug jumped into a black sports utility vehicle. Three motorcycle cops rode next to them, providing an armed escort. They were headed to Soliz's friend's house outside of Caracas. His friend was a guy named Raul Espinho, another Colombian who had moved to Venezuela to try to make money in the oil business. That's where they were going to meet up with Pepe Soliz. Then, they would travel by helicopter to the festival de jonron in Puerto la Cruz. In English, festival de jonron means home run derby.

They pulled into Raul's house. Pepe Soliz was sitting in the corner of the kitchen with a girl. She looked to be about fifteen years old. She had silver braces and wore a big smile. A huge smile! There were no statutory rape laws in Venezuela, at least none that Maddox knew about or that Pepe gave a fuck about. In fact, there really were no laws at all except whatever was convenient for the powerful people in the country. They just did what they did and laws were used as weapons of and for the powerful. Soliz, who didn't understand the concept of statutory rape anyway, had physically manhandled and then sexually obliterated the fifteen year old girl the night before and again that morning. He had completed the jigsaw puzzle. He had literally smashed himself inside her pussy until she was a sloppy mess down there. He was very aggressive with the little girl, he was unforgiving with her body. The second time he railed her it took him almost forty-five minutes to finish, and then he came inside her with a loud grunt and groan.

"Hey Pepe," said Maddox with a smile and a handshake.

"Hey Papi, Eet ees good to see you," said Pepe.

"It was fine. I felt safe with your brother and the security on the ride over, thank you."

"No problem, papi. He weel co-ome weeth us to dee derby tonight. I gonna hit some jonrons."

"Okay, cool, that a boy! Good boy," said Maddox.

"My brother ... he don't have no Eeen-glish but he good guy."

"Yes, we get along just fine."

"Hey, Papi, did you get that mow-ney for the girl?"

Maddox paused. Now Pepe the Poobah was bringing up the money every time he saw Maddox. Maddox breathed. He knew that the commission on Pepe's next contract would be somewhere in the neighborhood of five million dollars. So, it made a lot of financial sense to loan, or even give, Pepe Salcido, the horny Poobah, the money to settle April Tilney's sexual battery case. Doing that would result in big profits, big money, later.

"Yes, Pepe, I'm putting the money together. I'll have that money ready for you when we get back," said Maddox.

Maddox had, in fact, started putting it together. He listed a condo and sold some stocks — he had more than half of the money put together, in cash, and he was scrambling to get the rest.

"Okay, good, I need to geev dat mow-ney to dee girl. Thank you, Papi."

The conversation lulled. Pepe walked back into the bedroom with the little girl with braces. She walked tenderly but smiled. Maddox just sat in a chair in the kitchen and scrolled through some photos on his smart phone. He hated the topic of the rape hush money, and once it came up, again, it made him apprehensive. He just wanted to get through the home run derby and then head back to the United States.

The next twenty minutes went by quickly and then, all of a sudden, there was a frenzy of activity outside. A sports utility vehicle, a cop car, and two police motorcycles arrived. Pepe nodded his head to Maddox and they grabbed their bags and walked out the door, loading into the sports utility vehicle. The drivers all took off like a shot. They raced through side streets, and about twenty-five minutes later arrived at a small air strip that also had two helicopter landing pads.

Don Julio Santa-Rios, an executive from XtraShoog Venezuela, stood outside one of the helicopters. He greeted Pepe and Maddox with a handshake. A couple minutes later, a black sedan pulled up, with heavily-tinted windows, and Roman Castro, another professional baseball player down for the Home Run Derby got out. He walked slowly over to the helicopter and greeted Pepe with a hug and Maddox and Don Julio with a handshake. Everyone boarded the helicopter and strapped in for the flight. Pepe and Roman chatted in Spanish while Maddox looked out the window.

Having traveled just about everywhere in the world, Maddox was surprised that his first helicopter ride would take place in Venezuela. He was not letting himself think about the fact that Venezuela was an economic and political basket case. Were the helicopters down here even well-maintained? After Maddox, Soliz, Castro, and Castro's girl had loaded into the helicopter, the pilot commenced the flight. First, the pilot opened up the throttle to increase the speed of the rotor blade. Chooof. Chooof. Chooof. Chooof. The blade was producing a loud whirring sound. Chooof! The blade was turning at full speed and the pilot pulled up on the control, and the pitch of the rotor blade changed. Chwooof! Chwooof! Chwooof! The pilot pushed down the pedal and pulled up on the control. The lift-force produced by the blade finally exceeded the weight of the helicopter and its passengers, including the heavy-set Poobah, and the helicopter's skids lifted off of the ground. It lurched, then it glided. Everyone in the belly of the helicopter glanced around, enjoying the ride. No one looked fearful or apprehensive at all. The ride was smooth and uneventful. Maddox looked out over the lush green Venezuelan terrain for the entire flight. After landing, the group unloaded quickly and rode to the event in a black sports utility vehicle.

The crowd at the home run derby was raucous. They were consuming large quantities of beer, sometimes two at a time. With the suds flowing and the baseballs leaving the park in large numbers, the crowd was really enjoying themselves. Every time a home run was hit, the crowd roared! A major international soda company, XtraShoog, which was the main sponsor of the Home Run Derby, also had many young and nubile Venezuelan girls dressed up in form-fitting, XtraShoog-branded tank tops with yoga pants and tennis shoes. Their breasts were bulging through tight tee-shirts and tank tops. Asses swelled and ebbed inside tight, tight shorts. Sex was in the air, thanks to this squad of sexy soda girls bouncing around everywhere. They smiled and flirted through the entire night. It was a great time. Pepe finished twelfth in the contest, and Roman Castro looked like he was just screwing around, but he still finished third. There were other baseball players in the derby who also played in the United States, such as Miguel Cabrera of the Detroit Tigers, Pablo Sandoval of the San Francisco Giants, Elvis Andrus of the Texas Rangers and Bobby Abreu, formerly of the Philadelphia Phillies. Pepe Salcido did really well, and a good time was had by all. Most of the players all hit a ton of jonruns that night. It was a great event!

After the conclusion of the home run derby, the group went to the hotel in Puerto la Cruz. Maddox said his good-nights, and then went to his room and locked the door. Pepe and the Slug were heading back to Caracas, because they were returning immediately so Pepe could join the Big Boys on their road trip in San Diego. Needing a different flight, Maddox would have a private driver take him to the airport in Caracas the next morning, arranged by the hotel concierge. He felt relatively safe with that. Sometimes hotel staff coordinated with robbers to attack visitors, and rob them, at opportune and pre-planned locations. But this hotel seemed fine. Also, what else could he do? He took a breath, he was happy to have solitude.

Something didn't feel right, though. Maddox Malone was hot, then cold, then hot, then cold. He stripped off his clothes and got in the bed. He sipped on a bottle of water. He had the hotel television on. He fell asleep, briefly, on the couch. He stirred and walked over to the bed and then fell asleep, again.

Maddox awoke, late, at nine o'clock in the morning, but quickly realized that he had been sleeping in a pool of sweat. He had the chills.

He opened his eyes with tremendous effort. He looked at the clock. He rolled to the other, dry side of the Queen-sized bed and went back to sleep, almost immediately. He was so drained!

Two hours later, he awoke again. This time, because he felt someone looking at him. He forced his eyes open and looked up at a pretty face bending down over him, staring at him. Dayana Delgado, one of the hotel managers, a beautiful one, had been told by housekeeping that Maddox had not checked out and was lying in bed like a corpse. So, she came in to look him over. To make sure that he was actually alive. She stared at Maddox, who was naked in the queen sized bed, but, thankfully, for modesty's sake, his well-formed and nicely-colored penis was hidden under the bedsheet.

"Why don't you get up, Mister Maddox?" asked Dayana.

"I don't feel well. I have the chills. I feel really weak," Maddox responded.

"Ah, I see. I was worried when I heard from housekeeping. I know you are with the baseball group so I came to check on you myself."

"Thanks, I appreciate that. Sorry if I was supposed to be checked out already. I couldn't move."

"I'm going to go get a thermometer and come back. Maybe you can make it into the shower while I go? Then you can get dressed and we can see if we can get you feeling better. If not, you will need to go to the doctor, I'm afraid."

"Okay, I will try that. I feel really weak, but I will try to shower and get dressed," said Maddox, looking delirious.

"Have you been shivering and sweating all night?" asked Dayana.

"Yes, I did manage to sleep, but when I woke up I was shivering and laying in a puddle of sweat."

"Okay, I will be back with a thermometer and some fever reducer. I will be right back Mister Maddox Malone," said Dayana. Dayana walked out of the room, and Maddox watched her the entire way.

Maddox got up and tried to step toward the shower. But he felt dizzy and his nose started to bleed.

"Fuck!" he thought. "Did I catch malaria last night or something worse? What was going on?" he wondered. Maddox was worried. He often took his health for granted.

He didn't think it was safe to shower with the dizziness and the nosebleed. He didn't want to pass out and crack his fucking skull, so he got back in bed. He would tell Dayana when she got back, that he simply couldn't follow through on the original plan. He couldn't really stand up. When Dayana walked out, the whole room seemed to have darkened. Maddox took that as a signal that he should roll over and sleep, even if it was only for ten minutes. He felt bad about the blood in the bed, but what could he do?

Dayana came back and immediately became concerned. She shook Maddox awake.

"What happened to the shower?"

Maddox was in a daze, but responded, "I got up to do it but I got dizzy and my nose was bleeding. So I had to lay back down."

Dayana put the thermometer in Maddox's mouth and pressed the button. It beeped, she took it out. One-oh-four. One hundred four degrees! He was burning up. Dayana gave him four pills and some water. Maddox forced the fever reducing pills down and swallowed some water.

Maddox collected his thoughts for a second. He tried to smile, but he couldn't. He needed to rest, he told himself.

He said, "Dayana, can I extend the room for one night? I am supposed to check out now but I am not well enough to travel. Maybe I can sleep for a couple hours and then see if I feel better? I will change my travel to leave out of Caracas to tomorrow."

"Sure, Maddox. You are with the Pepecito Soliz group and this is not your fault, I will take care of the room for you. It is complementary. I know you will stay with us again next year. I hope you feel better soon."

"I really appreciate that."

"I will call your room in three hours to check on you," said Dayana with a pretty smile.

"Okay," said Maddox with a tired voice, "I'm going to get a little rest and see if I can kick this thing. Hopefully I don't die," Maddox said, mostly joking.

"You're going to be fine, we'll make sure of it. I'll talk to you in a bit." Dayana said.

Had Maddox been more lucid, he would have marveled at how good her English was. Way down here on the coast of Venezuela. In his fevered haze, Maddox imagined this very same coast in the sixteen hundreds. Teeming with natives, pirates, riches, malaria, humble wild burros and everything else in between. It was untapped territory! It was the open ocean, the overgrown green, lush, swollen landscape of South America. A territory with so much natural potential but so much limitation politically and due to the characteristics of the populace and the dysfunctional politics. Maddox put all those thoughts out of his feverish head. He looked at Dayana and that emptied his mind for a short time. He couldn't help but notice that she was very pretty. She was beautiful, physically. She had very European features, with a thin Spanish build, and was very reassuring, friendly, tender. Her face was expressive. Her breasts were likely c-cups. Her derriere was full and round, but firm. More importantly than her physical features, at the moment, was how tender and caring she was toward Maddox. It was very reassuring for him to have her help. "Thank God for Dayana," Maddox thought. Dayana walked out of the room and the door shut and locked behind her.

With Dayana out of the room, Maddox stripped himself naked. Despite the mega-dose of fever reducer, he was still hot to the touch and felt that he was burning up. The cool air conditioning felt good on his skin, and any clothing made him feel claustrophobic. Almost instantly, he was able to fall back asleep, although not before he had set his phone alarm for two and a half hours from the present time. He was out!

His alarm buzzed. He stayed in the bed. He still felt hot to the touch, but he didn't know what his temperature was. The phone rang, it was Dayana.

"How are you feeling?"

"I just woke up."

"You want me to come take your temperature?"

"Yes, please."

"Okay, I'll be there in a second."

Maddox put on some boxers but was too hot to put on anything else. Dayana would have to deal with the fact that he was in his underwear. She keyed herself in, said hello, and stuck the thermometer into Maddox's mouth. He mouthed it, letting it soak up his heat. One-oh-four, still. One hundred four degrees, even after the fever reducer. Maddox didn't know if he had food poisoning, flu or malaria. Or some other life-threatening illness unique to South America. Maddox worried that he was the outbreak monkey.

"Fuck this shit," he thought.

"I'm going to take you to the hospital," said Dayana. "You are too hot. Too hot."

"Thanks, I appreciate that," Maddox, in his feverish haze, misunderstood what Dayana was saying.

The fever was distorting his thoughts and making him crazed. He imagined Dayana naked. He imagined that they were husband and wife and they were living on a remote island off the coast of South America. They were part of an underground shipping line that transported rum, gin, and whiskey through underdeveloped areas, trading for much gold and silver in the process. He pictured himself sitting on a pile of gold and gold trinkets. He was delirious with fever! He imagined Dayana's conical breasts, her shapely ass, her smooth, waxed vagina. He looked at her mouth. He pictured it all. At least that pleasant thought helped pass a few minutes of the fevered haze. He became lucid for a second — "stop that, Maddox!" he thought. You're a married man, stop being a fucking pervy douche bag! He scolded himself. Then, he stopped being hard on himself. He was burning up! He was so ill, so delirious, he couldn't really blame himself for picturing Dayana like that. He wasn't in control of his mind!

"Okay, that sounds fine," he said, trying to give the appearance that he was still in control of his thoughts. Maddox didn't have the energy to argue.

Dayana went to his bag and grabbed him a cotton tee-shirt, some brushed cotton charcoal color pants, cotton socks and some flexible athletic shoes. He put everything on, requiring a major effort along the way. He was very apprehensive about going to a hospital in Venezuela. He wanted to get back to America as soon as he could. He made sure that he had his passport and his wallet - those two things, by themselves, could get Maddox out of the country when he was ready.

Dayana's connections, and the fact that Maddox had been at the hotel via Soliz, were able to get Maddox brought in through the back door of the hospital. There was no check-in procedure required for Maddox, thanks to Dayana's connections, and they put him into a bed in his own private room. They started him on some fluids via an IV. They took his temperature, and immediately gave him a mega-dose of acetaminophen, since he had previously taken ibuprofen, a different fever reducer. They applied a cold compress to his head, underarms and neck. He hated the feeling, but the doctors were determined to get his temperature under control. They told him to sleep if he could. He complied, as he was still incredibly fatigued. He rolled a little bit to the side and was able to fall asleep for two hours.

Maddox woke up when the doctor came back in to take his temperature. The doctor had a concerned look on his face. It was at this point, that despite his fevered incoherence, Maddox realized he was dangerously ill.

He panicked. Suddenly, Maddox was sure he would die. With

that thought, his senses became very acute. Time seemed to slow down. He felt strange, because the thought about death seemed removed and unemotional. Why? Just when he didn't think it was possible for things to move slower, time seemed to slow down again. He noticed every little thing, every little noise, every detail. Sometimes details that seem trivial can be ignored, or at least glossed over. This was not the case for Maddox, not at this moment. He felt like he was having ten thoughts at once but they were all crystal clear. He could hear everything. The analog clock hand ticking. The bed creaking or rustling with every motion. Footsteps in the hallway. Paper rustling under the breeze generated by the air vent. He heard every little thing. His mind buzzed with thoughts. How could he get home? How were his kids doing? He thought of Thomas and Chester and their little faces. "What was Felicia up to, right this minute?" thought Maddox. Then, he thought of how far behind he would be on his e-mail responses.

That last thought really irritated him. He was in a hospital in Venezuela and he was worried about e-mail responses? Why was he living his life this way? If he died in this hospital, what had been the meaning of his life? Transactions? Representing the horny and rapey Poobah? Selling Pogo Backs? Selling XtraShoog? Working on Volleyball deals? Listening to Carlton Duffer's stupid ideas and watching his crooked lip? Longing for a TENACIOUS training facility? Of course he had his family, but the boys, and Felicia too, were young and he hadn't even spoken to his wife Laura in a couple of days. She didn't even know he was in the hospital in Venezuela. Maddox's smart phone wasn't equipped dial out of Venezuela, and the burner phone with a Venezuelan phone card he purchased was out of minutes. Part of him didn't want Laura to know how sick he was, anyway. He just had to power through this, she couldn't help him. Not here, not now.

He figured that his family would be devastated if he died in Venezuela. But how devastated? Life might just go on!

That was a terrible thought. That thought alone sent Maddox into a spiral of disappointment and despair. He stared ahead, miserable. "Fuck this!" he thought. He was so upset, his thoughts didn't go any deeper than that, not at the moment.

There was simply so much strain on Maddox that his body had finally given in to a virus. He had flown so much, traveled so much. Poor quality rest. Missing nutrition. Too much vodka. Maddox was working himself to death. It had all caught up with him, here in Venezuela with some mysterious virus causing a dangerous fever to spike.

Suddenly, by drawing courage from deep within himself, Maddox simply decided he was not going to die in Venezuela. He started to will it! He convinced himself of it! He began to breathe easier and he started to cool down. It seemed to take forever for each minute to go by. With his positive outlook, plus all the medication and the IV taking hold, Maddox Malone's health started improving.

The doctor told him that the fever reduction tactics were working, they had him down below one hundred degrees. That was good, he said. Then he told Maddox to go back to sleep and walked out of the room. In two more hours, the doctor came back in. Maddox's temperature had stabilized! It was holding steady, under one hundred degrees. Maddox said he wanted a driver to the airport, via the hotel, to get his bag. The doctor told him that was fine with him, since Maddox was there unofficially anyhow, having been brought through the back door by Dayana. He still felt miserable, tired, weak and delirious, but he wanted to get on a plane to America. Thirty minutes later Maddox dragged himself out the same back door that he came in, and into a black sedan driven by Tito, a little squat indigenous South American fellow with a pot belly and long black hair. Tito wore lots of turquoise jewelry and he had six tattoos that looked like they were done at home. Tito was missing the pinky finger on his left hand. Maddox wondered what had gotten it! Tito drove fast. Tito and the gas pedal worked well together. They were flying down the road!

Soon, Maddox Malone was on the first available flight out. He was still feverish and delirious, and still worried about his illness, but at least he was headed to Miami. Physically, with each hour that passed, he felt like he was getting better. Just a little bit at a time, but it helped. His morale improved as he was pretty sure he had beaten the nasty virus that caused the fever. He knew that he was beating the virus, or whatever it was — he felt like he had just won his own private home run derby.

Boomer Barbeque

❋❋

Full of medication, groggy, disoriented, dehydrated, slightly feverish and shaken from the illness he experienced in Venezuela, Maddox Malone still managed to make his connection out of Chicago. He desperately wanted a vodka and soda with a lime. But Maddox but did not purchase one. No alcohol until the fever was totally gone, he told himself. Instead, he bought a large iced Americano. It wasn't the best for hydration but he craved, he needed, the caffeine. Maddox went straight through security. No bar, for once, no bookstore. He boarded a flight to Idaho. Boise to be exact. Despite the caffeine from the coffee, he slept for the whole flight and when he landed he grabbed a rental car and another large iced Americano.

Hour-by-hour, Maddox Malone was starting to feel a little more like himself. He felt like he would have his energy back fully in another day or so. Mentally, he was completely over the illness he experienced in Venezuela — physically, he just needed a little more time; he still felt fatigued, worn-out. Another rush of caffeine would really help, he thought. He plugged his smart phone into the rental car's auxiliary jack and sang along to the music.

> Everyday it's something
> Hits me all so cold
> Find me sittin' by myself
> No excuses, then I know

Maddox was driving from Boise to Jackson Hole, Wyoming, doing seventy-eight miles per hour in a sixty-five mile per hour zone. He was very tired, but his temperature was basically normal, just above ninety-nine degrees. Maddox was now, finally, on the tail end of his trip. He was heading to Jackson Hole in order to meet up with Paul McCartney regarding the ongoing TENACIOUS projects. There were so many of them that needed the pledged financing from the 'Hopper.

Maddox continued driving and before long he arrived in Jackson

Hole. Going out to the big field to eat barbeque and drink alcohol became routine at the ritzy private subdivision. In fact, the activity center encouraged residents and visitors to go to these gatherings every day.

Paul McCartney, the Grasshopper, had obtained the keys for a family property his grandfather had purchased forty years before and invited LeSharrif Powell and LeSharrif's father, Kevin, to visit. LeSharrif was an excellent wrestler. Then, McCartney had hounded Maddox Malone to come up to Jackson Hole as well, even though Maddox was traveling all the way from Venezuela. McCartney was hopping around out at the barbeque, drinking Grey Goose with pineapple juice and live-action-role-playing, acting – pretending – he was LeSharrif's manager even though there was no such managerial relationship in place.

The Grasshopper was showing off LeSharrif Powell like he was his pet - "He's going to be a champion," McCartney was telling anyone who would listen. "He might look little but he's got an incredible take-down! He's going straight to the top."

LeSharrif's dad, Kevin, was from the 'hood in Philly. There's no way that Kevin Powell knew that Paul McCartney would consistently use racial slurs to describe him when he wasn't around. If Kevin knew this, he would have beat the shit out of Paul McCartney, for sure. It was a bit circular, because McCartney slurred him since he was violent and rough around the edges, and the slurs, if found out, would have certainly brought Kevin to violence.

The racial slurs were spoken by Paul McCartney once he had downed several Grey Goose cocktails. The vodka loosened up the Grasshopper – he started to share more of his real thoughts! The Grasshopper pulled more than one person aside, while pointing to the Powells and complimented LeSharrif while slurring Kevin in the nastiest and most disgusting sort of way.

"LeSharrif Powell is a really nice kid. Kevin Powell? He's a God-damned nigger. You know, there's a difference. There's a difference. He's a violent nigger. He's always talking about fighting and violence and talking about his bitches. I don't trust him," said Paul McCartney, the

'Hopper.

Twice, Maddox overheard Paul McCartney's slurs. Maddox just shook his head. He found the whole situation to be ridiculous and obnoxious, not to mention outright racist and unacceptable because of the slurs. It was so degrading, so shallow!

This was the ridiculous scene that Maddox had flown thousands of miles to walk into! Two African-Americans being paraded around by Paul McCartney like zoo animals for the other rich whites. Many a dapper white boomer was out at the barbeque taking a gander at the blacks! They were the only African-Americans on the whole property. Something about the whole situation seemed wrong to Maddox. It was stupid. Maddox was tired, bored, and growing angry. He was angry with the Grasshopper.

To Paul McCartney, though, with his pet, LeSharrif, out on the field, this was heaven! He was standing there, sipping his Grey Goose, and waiting for passers-by to say hello so he could humbly introduce them to the wrestler and drop hints that he was LeSharrif Powell's manager. The residents that engaged with McCartney and the Powells were, by and large, visibly uneasy around the black Powells. Of course, they tried hard to mask it. Their eyes froze and their faces were dominated by big shit-eating grins – McCartney loved this because he thought it made him look edgy. He thought it made him look cool. It was such a novelty to Paul!

This scene, right here in Jackson Hole, helped Maddox Malone put his finger on one of the things that had been bothering him about Paul McCartney for quite some time. It made him incredibly uneasy. It was this: if McCartney could easily mislead people into thinking that he was LeSharrif Powell's wrestling manager, but he wasn't, what did that tell Maddox about the rest of the TENACIOUS-branded projects? What did it tell Maddox about McCartney himself? Maddox Malone didn't want to think about that right now. He had been through so much, just in the past few days. He didn't want to become inundated with negative thoughts about McCartney and TENACIOUS. He didn't need more negativity in his life.

Instead, he enjoyed the weather and the beautiful view. The yellows, oranges, blues, greens and browns were stunning. The sunlight, so soft! The wind, easy and comfortable! Jackson Hole was truly spectacular. It was, Maddox figured, one of the nicest places in the world!

McCartney was hitting the Goose hard, he was several cocktails in already. He was getting on a roll, talking to everyone he could. McCartney cornered a chubby, middle-aged man named Dave, a boomer-cuckold. Maddox didn't catch Dave's last name. McCartney was practically hopping up and down when he spoke, he was buzzed, and he was excited. He was in his element. He simply couldn't brag enough about TENACIOUS, all while his skunk-stripe shimmered and his scar sparkled and glinted.

"Now don't you forget it, Dave. Dave! TENACIOUS is the brand. TENACIOUS! We're going to have training facilities, sporting academies, a golf tour, a wrestling division, you name it. Maybe we'll eventually do space exploration like that one South African guy. We already have an agreement with Sporting Barcelona to run our Tennis Academy in Phoenix. We just got back from Spain with that deal signed, sealed, and delivered. We took no prisoners!"

Maddox's face went blank. He showed no emotion as Paul spoke. Maddox was thinking that, well, it's certainly true that the letter of intent was signed, but the TENACIOUS facility purchase was not finished — and there would be no place to put the Sporting Barcelona Tennis Academy until that happened. Maddox had just pushed his questions and negative thoughts out of his head, but they came flooding back in. He felt a rush of bad energy. He suppressed anger. He kept looking at the Grasshopper with a blank stare.

The Grasshopper continued, speaking loud and fast, while almost, but not quite, hopping. "When you think of sports you're going to think of TENACIOUS! We will never be satisfied! Core Values!"

"That sounds fantastic," Dave responded. Dave was seven cocktails in and, despite what he said, his face suggested that he didn't really give a fuck what the Grasshopper said about TENACIOUS.

McCartney kept talking, wildly, to Dave, despite Dave's lukewarm expression of interest. McCartney's billowing haunches popped as he bragged! His majestic skunk-stripe glistened!

"The reason we can do all of this with the TENACIOUS Sports plays is, honestly, because of the success my Grandfather had with his company, PartDok. Oh what a company that is!" said McCartney. "My grandfather built that company based on certain values. He called them core values. Product Focus, Aim for Perfection, Honor, Respect for Everyone, Ingenuity, and Continuous Effort & Improvement."

Maddox's face turned to stone as he heard McCartney talk about Core Values. His eyes burned. Maddox was thinking, but strangely no actual thoughts came to his mind. The closest expression of Maddox's thoughts, right at that time, would just be the sound hmmm. Hmmm.

McCartney continued, "I think of PartDok's products as precision instruments because they are so specialized and so precise. That's why no one can compete with us over at PartDok. Core Values! I love you, grandpa."

Dave kept powering through his cocktail, with about thirty percent of it remaining, and McCartney continued his monologue.

"We're starting TENACIOUS Golf in Philadelphia, Dave. You know, that's originally where I'm from? That's where my Grandfather started PartDok. I've got a guy working for me, his name is George Korpine. Great guy. Great guy! He runs a small golf tour right now. But we're going to make it huge. Maddox here is going to help with sponsorship and media. I've invested a few million, you know, uh, you know just a few million dollars into the Golf tour to get it going. That's pocket change for me. Take no prisoners!"

Maddox's face stayed unmoved, like it was set in stone. Maddox knew that when McCartney claimed that he had invested money in George Korpine's golf tour, he was lying. He had certainly promised to invest, but no money had been transferred to Philly Hole Fanatics. Maddux gulped. Maddox became lost in his own thoughts, the same ones as before. Why would McCartney lie about the TENACIOUS golf division, so casually? Maddox was aggravated. He tried not to show any emotion on his face. Maddox snapped out of his own thoughts when he heard McCartney's high-pitched laugh.

"Ha-ha-ha-ha-ha," McCartney laughed and chortled. His face suggested that he was so exhilarated with the stories that he was telling about TENACIOUS. He looked so proud to be associated with the Powells, and with Maddox. His face suggested a smug satisfaction with the barbeque — it was the face of accomplishment.

Maddox hadn't heard the comment that inspired the laughter but, because of the loud laughter, he tuned back in to the conversation. During the minute that Maddox was lost in thought, McCartney had, Grey Goose in hand, struck up a conversation with a different boomer-cuckold, Mark, and the cuck's young wife, Alexandra. Dave, the prior boomer-cuckold interlocutor, had stumbled off in his drunken stupor. Mark's wife, Alexandra, was a solid eight. She was a nine with extensive hair, nails and makeup work. Her old boomer-cuckold husband thought she was a ten.

"Hi Paul, good to see you," said the cuckold. "Do you remember my wife, Alexandra?" Alexandra was checking out her smart phone, which throbbed and pulsed and glowed with a bright white light. She barely looked up.

"Hi Mark! Of course I remember Alexandra. It's a wonderful day in Jackson Hole. Isn't this the best place? I brought some wrestlers, you know, great entertainers, and a top young sports agent out here today. That's Kevin and LeSharrif Powell over there and this here is Maddox Malone, one of the top young sports agents in the country. Maddox is amazing! Boston College and Berkeley Law. Take no prisoners!"

Maddox was incredibly frustrated by these remarks. He was here to follow up on the TENACIOUS projects, not to be used as a status prop for the Grasshopper at this stupid-fucking-God-damned-boomer-barbeque. Fatigued from his illness and travel and frustrated with the Malone Agency's mounting issues, Maddox, for just a second, felt like socking the Grasshopper right in his mouth. He remembered the sound from the punch that was landed in the fight he and Major O watched in New Orleans. He thought about McCartney's face making the same noise. Like a wet rag thrown into a barrel of oil! Instead of punching McCartney, though, Maddox gritted his teeth and kept his mouth shut.

"That's fantastic. What an exciting business! It must be fun. What's that movie? Jerry Maguire?" said Mark.

Maddox winced inside. He hated that movie. Fuck Jerry Maguire!

"Ummm, yeah, Jerry Maguire," said Maddox with a forced smile that looked more like an angry smirk.

Mark had made some money selling insurance. Quite a bit, in fact. Enough to get Alexandra to marry him, at least. She tapped into Mark's pile of cash and funneled it out for her pleasure. For her pleasure!

"Yeah, it's a great time to be alive. Ha-ha-ha-ha-ha! I'm going to be the Chairman of a company called **TENACIOUS** Global Sports. The goal is to have a diversified sports company. My wife's company is going to be doing physical therapy in the training facility, too. She's around here, Emma's here, somewhere. Core values!" said the Grasshopper.

"That sounds great. You know Alexandra here played tennis in college. Over at, uh, the University of Virginia. So she's a big sports person," said Mark, timidly.

Alexandra, who was about thirty years younger than her rich husband, looked to Maddox to be disinterested in the conversation. Maddox noticed that she was pounding citrus-flavored vodka drinks, three sips at a time. The vodka was going down like water. She looked, to Maddox, like she wanted to be on her smart phone sending messages to one of her boyfriends, not listening to her old husband Mark Cucault talk to some other boomer — especially a curly-headed boomer with a skunk-stripe and exaggerated haunches.

"Yes, I played at Virginia," said Alexandra with obvious

disinterest. Her short shorts showed the bottom left quarter of her left butt cheek. The right cheek peeked out, but not quite as much as the left.

"That's great," said Paul. "My nephew, Derrick McCartney, plays baseball at Virginia right now."

"Oh wow, small world!" said Mark with one of those forced, awkward laughs meant to fill space and time and project comfortability. Alexandra was looking off to the west, holding her vibrating smart phone as if she wanted to access it, but couldn't.

"You're never gonna believe what TENACIOUS does! TENACIOUS is gonna to take over the sports world! Take no prisoners! Ha-ha-ha-ha," said McCartney with another drunken, high-pitched cackle.

"I can't wait to see it!" said Mark.

Alexandra walked off briskly to get a refill of her citrus-flavored vodka drink. Mark rocked back and forth. His eyes followed Alexandra and he had a nervous look on his face. Maddox had no idea that Mark had gone through Alexandra's smart phone the night before and he had seen a number of messages from phone numbers he didn't recognize. The texts weren't explicit, but there were enough of them for Mark to suspect that he was getting cuckolded on a consistent basis. Maddox had no way of knowing that Mark suspected Alexandra was getting lit up. But Maddox knew something was up, just by looking at the Mark and Alexandra.

Mark shook his head very slightly and drew a breath. Maddox couldn't help but stare at Mark. Even though Maddox didn't know the back-story, Mark looked, to Maddox, like he hated his life, this barbeque, being married to Alexandra. Maddox was fascinated. He thought for a minute about Mark and Alexandra. Maddox imagined that Mark, in marrying the younger Alexandra, with her perky, watermelon-flavored chooch and tiny little wa-wa, realized, too late, that he had run the risk of being made a cuckold. It is a risk that, to a greater or lesser degree, applies to every married man. For cuckoldry naturally comes with the nature of marriage. Peanut butter goes with chocolate. The shadow goes with the body. The horns of the cuckold fit nicely on the husband's head. Because, you see, any married man either is, has been, will be or may be a cuckold. Maddox shook his head, slightly, still looking at Mark.

Maddox had no way to be certain that the suspicion and ill-feeling from Mark was extremely warranted. Alexandra, who was very nice to look at, had her own inclinations hidden just under the surface. Maddox just watched her pout and skulk. Sometimes she chatted and forced a smile. Maddox noticed something about Alexandra's face. Something naughty! Very naughty! Maddox imagined Alexandra's secret life. He imagined that as soon as Mark was on a business trip, or even sitting in his office, a cunning side of Alexandra emerged. Maddox guessed that she would go shop — drinking champagne and vodka. Then, she would head to the gym and yoga. And, at various times and in various locations around town, she would get pinned to the wall, spanked, thrown into an aggressive and active sixty-nine, bent over, or simply taken in missionary by her boyfriends. Phillipe, her svelte personal trainer. Ramon, the guy who clipped the hedges and then cleaned the chimney. Maddox snapped back into the conversation, and out of the world he imagined, rightly or wrongly, for Alexandra, when Paul McCartney spoke again.

"You see the Powells over there?" said McCartney, which snapped Mark back into the conversation. "LeSharrif is going to be the wrestling champion of the world someday. A real superstar! I am going to promote his matches. We already have a deal in place, don't we Maddox?"

"Uh, yeah? We do?" said Maddox, unconvincingly and unconvinced. "We do?"

There was no deal in place. Maddox's stone face came back.

"Wow, that's incredible, Paul. You have that McCartney touch what with your main company and all. The one from your grandpa," said Mark.

"PartDok. Core Values!" bellowed the 'Hopper.

"Yeah, PartDok. Now sports? Now sports! Amazing, man. Congratulations. You are the man!" said Mark. Mark glanced sideways, in the direction of the Powells, then quickly averted his eyes and gave a plastic grin to no one in particular. He just plastered a stupid grin on his face.

Maddox saw Mark lurch, as if he were startled by the Powells. Maddox wondered what was going on in Mark's head. When Mark saw the big black Powells, in his mind it was as if he had been instantly transported to sub-Saharan Africa. After the lurch, Mark took a big step back. Then to the left. It looked as if he had been startled by his thoughts alone. Was that fear? Was that intrigue?

Mark kept staring at the Powells. "What is he thinking?" wondered Maddox. Maddox guessed that Mark was picturing the Powells as African tribesman, without the worry of modern life and modern amenities.

Maddox, bored with the boomer barbeque, decided to mess with Mark a little bit.

"Mark, you look a little concerned. You ever seen a black person out here in Jackson Hole?" asked Maddox.

"Ummm, yeah, of course. One of the bus boys at the golf club is black. Looks like Evander," said Mark.

"No shit? So you're down with the brothers, then?" said Maddox.

"Yes, I guess you could say that!" said Mark with no hint of irony.

"You ever been to the 'hood in Baltimore?" Maddox asked, teasing Mark.

"Hell no," Mark said with a sheepish grin. "But I've seen The Wire on TV. I know how it is, I've seen it."

Maddox was bored of the barbeque — bored of all the privileged boomers — so he kept constructing his own imaginary world of Mark and

Alexandra to pass the time. Maddox imagined that Mark secretly admired the terror that some blacks, especially inner-city blacks, were able to inspire in members of the white community. Would he, Mark Cucault of California and Wyoming, ever consider going to a black section of Baltimore or Detroit and walking around? Hell no! Not in a million years. Maddox imagined that Mark felt powerless and he knew that he inspired fear in precisely no one. Especially not his wife Alexandra! Maddox could tell.

Oh Alexandra, thought Maddox. The world of Alexandra — such intrigue!

Alexandra had walked off to get more vodka, and Maddox imagined that she was on her smart phone sending nudes to her boyfriends. Maddox thought Alexandra looked at him, Maddox Malone, a bit suggestively. Could he be imagining that? Maddox looked over at Mark whose face, very clearly, showed that lingering doubt and insecurity was eating him up. Maddox figured that it was eating him up, slowly, starting with his balls.

The conversation with Mark waned, and so Paul McCartney hopped off to refill his Grey Goose and pineapple juice. Once filled, the Grasshopper immediately started to pluck the Goose. He walked back over towards Maddox. In the meantime, he had bumped into his wife, Emma, who walked back over with him.

"Hey Maddox, look who I brought back, it's my sweetie! My sweetie and my life partner!" said McCartney with a disgusting, sappy tone. To Maddox, he sounded so ridiculous, so fake. But he persisted.

"Oh, hi Maddox, how are you?"

Maddox couldn't believe he was enduring this. Why was he even here?

"I'm good, Emma. Good to see you," Maddox lied. They gave each other a little kiss on the cheek.

Grasshoppers usually mate with other grasshoppers. In the case of Paul McCartney, however, he had married a desert phasmid —

commonly referred to as a stickbug. The Stickbug was rail thin and fully emaciated from constant exercise and a strict caloric intake limit. The Stickbug constantly fed on leaves! In fact, she used her salads as a status symbol. It was a source of pride. She would even customize the salad everywhere she went to show her awareness of different ingredients. For example, she might substitute zucchini for potato chunks to show, to signal, to the waiter and anyone and everyone else who noticed, her preference for green vegetables over simple starches. Hell would freeze over before the Stickbug would bite into a lowly potato! She viewed her salad orders as a badge of honor, as a badge of discipline, as a tribute to her ability to maintain a stick figure. Of course, there was nothing feminine or attractive about her wrinkly rail-thin body. She looked like a weak high school boy who consumed too much soy. McCartney preferred big-breasted voluptuous vixens like Chanel — he had no attraction to his wife Emma and her grisly flesh piles attached to her crusty-looking brown nipples that tasted like batteries.

McCartney's smart phone rang and buzzed. He eyed the screen and his face lit up.

"Maddox, this is convenient," McCartney said, and he motioned Maddox over. "I've got Roland Stanton, you know, the lawyer, on the phone, he's following up on the TENACIOUS projects. Can you talk to him and make sure everything is moving forward?"

Maddox had met Roland Stanton (with Paul McCartney present) one time in Philadelphia, when the TENACIOUS companies were formed. Stanton was remarkably similar to a silverfish. Silverfish are primitive looking insects which are a common sight in homes, especially when they scurry across the floor or up a wall. The speed of the silverfish may be frightening to some people, but they are genuinely harmless bugs. Roland Stanton, similarly, couldn't really be considered harmful. He just sort of existed, lawyering away. Doing lawyer stuff. Silverfish have very tough and durable stomachs, and they are able to subsist on things like book bindings, wallpaper glue, photos, sugar, coffee, hair, dead insects, shedded skins and even leather. Roland liked potato chips and macro brew. Silverfish are always wingless, have silvery scales covering their body and have distinct tails. Roland Stanton had silvery hair on his boomer head and two tails on his boring blazer.

Maddox took McCartney's nine hundred and thirty dollar smart phone and held it to his ear. The Silverfish launched into his spiel. This call is unnecessary, thought Maddox.

Why were they doing it again?

When is McCartney going to provide the funding required for the TENACIOUS projects?

When is the purchase of the TENACIOUS training facility scheduled to close?

Discussion of any other topics is a waste of time. A distraction.

But for Roland, this was what he did. He scurried around the floor like the silverfish bug, talking about bullshit and performing meaningless activity involving e-mail and paper. Spend time on the phone, accumulate the billable hour. Maddox talked to the Silverfish for thirty-five or forty minutes, although Roland would follow up the call by marking fifty-five minutes into his billing sheet. Roland, as always, seemed nice enough, but they only covered old information.

After what seemed like hours to Maddox, they were wrapping up their general conversation about TENACIOUS.

"This sounds fantastic," Roland said, "TENACIOUS Performance and TENACIOUS Crowd Sports. McCartney will provide the funding for the companies and you will pull together plans and use your network to assemble a team and develop the projects."

Maddox couldn't believe that the Silverfish was just sitting on the phone stating the obvious. No shit, Maddox thought. No shit!

"That's the plan," said Maddox. "That's been the plan all along. What is the timing on this? We've had this same conversation before."

"Hurr durr, I don't know the answer to that but I'll find out."

This exercise, the phone call between Maddox and the Silverfish, ended up as yet another source of frustration for Maddox, for one simple reason. No firm answer given to the question, which Maddox asked directly, of when the training facility purchase would be finalized and when the rest of the funding would be delivered. Roland just dodged the question.

"Ummm, okay," said Maddox. "This is just an endless loop."

"Herr Durr, McCartney is very real, ha ha err," says the shit-eating Silverfish.

"That's great, Roland. We put in the bid, but what about the closing? We have to lock this stuff down, we're losing time and credibility. Yesterday, I sent a detailed e-mail regarding all of the projects while I was traveling back from Venezuela. He needs to answer that with specific timelines. Obviously, tomorrow, since I'm with him right now in Jackson Hole and he's drunk."

"Oh hurr durr, I see, I see, hurr durr," said Stanton. "He'll get it done, Maddox," said Roland. "I've spoken to him about it and he's going to do it all. He'll do it all. Don't worry, Maddox. Hey, by the way, I have to ask, have you been receiving my bills for the legal work I've been doing for TENACIOUS Performance and TENACIOUS Crowd Sports?"

"Yes, Roland. I've been receiving them. TENACIOUS has way more commitments and obligations than it has money, but I'll make sure that we get your bills paid next week. Let's get this going like it's supposed to be. We need to get this facility purchased and built out."

"Hurr durr, u-huh. Mmmm-hmmm."

"Well, thanks for your representation of TENACIOUS and help get Paul McCartney to follow through on his financing commitments. I appreciate it." said Maddox. He was incredibly frustrated. But Maddox Malone kept a diplomatic tone. He suppressed his frustration. His face was flushed and he was talking more loudly than usual.

"Ah, herr durr, fantastic, fantastic, Maddox, thanks for sending me that money for my bills. It's what I do. So, thanks. U-huh. Thanks, we'll talk soon," said the Silverfish, smiling and chewing his cud as he clicked off the line.

Right when the call concluded, Maddox was fine for a moment. But a few moments later, Maddox felt rage bubbling up. It kept growing. His angry twin emerged, and he walked over to Paul McCartney, the Grasshopper. McCartney was circling around the boomer barbeque still making small-talk about the Powells and TENACIOUS. Maddox walked up to the Grasshopper and looked him right in the eyes.

"Hey, Paul. I spoke with Roland Stanton. He gave me the run-around with non-committal lawyer-speak! These are major projects, they can't move forward without the financing you promised. We need to get the funding in and get TENACIOUS moving. We need to close on the purchase of the facility. A lot of people are waiting on this. What in the hell is going on here?"

"I know, Maddox. I know. You are doing a great job building up the brand. TENACIOUS will be the biggest brand in sports. Let's do this! Money is not the problem! Core values! Ha-ha-ha-ha." said McCartney.

The Grasshopper was hammered. He was lit. He staggered off, with the Jackson Hole horizon setting an impressive backdrop that accentuated his prominent, billowing haunches, which were extended with exertion. He headed back in the direction of the boomer-cuckold Mark and his wife Alexandra, who had resurfaced. The Grasshopper was almost spinning, but he still was able to scroll through his phone, on tunnel patrol! The 'Hopper looked back at Maddox and almost stumbled. Maddox started to walk off, angrily thinking about what a waste of time this Jackson Hole stop was. Maddox had decided, right then, to leave early.

Maddox Malone jumped into his rental car fifteen minutes later and was headed back to Boise, Idaho, to fly home. He decided to leave a day early, since the Grasshopper was just hanging around at the boomer barbeque bullshitting and getting drunk. When he arrived at the airport, Maddox, for the first time in weeks, didn't want to drink vodka and soda with a lime. He was coming off a scary illness. He just sat in a corner and cracked open one of the books in his computer bag.

Flashman at the Charge, by George McDonald Fraser, had been lurking, waiting to be enjoyed, in his computer bag and Maddox was at the part where Flashman caught Lord Cardigan in his wife Elspeth's bedroom, and Flashman surmised that the pair wasn't intending on comparing birthmarks. Maddox laughed out loud a couple times as he read the book. In fact, the book provided a great escape — it was hilarious. Travel went smoothly, and hours later he landed in Phoenix and finally was headed home.

Football Sunday

**

Maddox arrived home late and snuck back into his home office and went to sleep. It was football Sunday. Denver was playing Oakland. Maddox represented one player on each team. He went over to the neighborhood bar to watch the games. Elsewhere on this Sunday, energy was buzzing in the air. Feet were pounding the dirt and the cement. Things were moving, all over. Everyone could feel it. All across the country, they were out in full force. In addition to the workers there were also the non-workers, the viewers, the scavengers, the consumers, the eaters, the managers of the reproductive cycle, the leader of each house or group. Everyone played a role. The work and the energy was effusive. It was football Sunday and life seemed good!

On this particular Sunday, as was usually the case during football season, and almost every day to be completely honest, the males were filling no productive role in society. All around the country. The males had a complete lack of critical thought. They were content to receive food from their sisters and, in many cases, had not yet taken any nuptial vow or flight. Many didn't do any work and many were in-cel, meaning involuntarily celibate. If they were not in-cel, they were vol-cel, meaning voluntarily celibate, because they had sex available to them but they didn't take the sex. In these types of cases many felt, for some reason, that if they took a nuptial flight they would end up, figuratively or literally speaking, dead. It was not immediately known why they felt this way. Either way, they did not engage in sex but instead waited for food from the females and tried to find other entertainment or distraction.

The principal female reproductive type was differentiated from a sexual female that might not be functionally reproductive. Females might be virgin or inseminated, pregnant or infertile. They took different roles on this particular day based on their characteristics. The principal female had reproduction on her mind all the time. Some spent all day every day searching for mates – and this particular Sunday was no exception. It caused a clear and particular look to take hold of her face, many called it the breeding face, and the reproductive females had many ways of trussing themselves up to increase their chances of the lay.

There were minor workers, performing tasks. Cleaning the floor. Taking out trash or other rubble. Eliminating waste from the system. Preserving the system! Keeping things moving, efficiently. They filled a role and they plugged away. A particularly efficient worker could move seven times her bodyweight in trash and other refuse, all before noon.

There were major workers, performing herculean tasks. Finding food. Bringing it home to the males. Looking for processed sugar, carbohydrates, soy. They didn't care what they brought back to the males, they wanted to bring something. On this particular Sunday, it seemed that the major workers reached a new peak of efficiency and productivity. It was almost as if they were on auto pilot. They didn't even have to think! Grab the carbs, deliver the carbs. Find the liquids, deliver the liquids. See refuse, remove refuse. Find a task, do a task. Finish a task, do another. The energy was contagious.

There were mothers, enjoying the day. Strutting around. Making themselves heard. Exerting themselves. In some cases, dominating. Some of them would bathe their young. They might rub them down. They might rub their tummy. They might touch and rub and kiss them. They might be feeding the young. Carbohydrates, processed sugars, soy. Doesn't really matter.

Sadly, some who imbibed too much of the carbohydrate sludge would vomit. Dizzy headed. Barfing everywhere! Disgusting, they also regurgitated food along with the carbohydrate slush. They made noise and watched the battle on the field when they could. Back and forth they went.

The sisters went out and foraged for the males. They looked high. They looked low. They looked for processed sugar. They looked for simple carbohydrates. They foraged for soy. These things are readily available and they are produced by a shadowy presence that neither the males nor females fully understand. But they are out there producing, because the materials are there. When they find food sources, they sometimes lay out a trail to guide the gatherers to the cache. Sometimes they qualitatively rate the cache, but using weak criteria that doesn't tie to quality. As electronic trails become more common, the efficiency of the search rises over time. They learned from each other. They emulated each other. New routes. Same food. New approach. Old approach.

The females carry food particles inside the home and deliver them to the lazy males. The males have no self-awareness. The males have no strength. The males have no pride. The males have no motivation. The males have no role models. The males have no drive. The males have no confidence. The males have no support structure.

But neither do the females, who carry on, busy-like. The women are props, devoid of meaning and with no connection to the worthless males. Delivering processed sugar. Delivering carbohydrates. Delivering soy. Delivering misery over and over.

But if no one realizes they are miserable, are they really miserable?

They are programmed by something else. They are programmed, partly, by biology. They are also programmed by something that they can't quite understand. But everyone is programmed so it all seems so normal. Life carries on, it's Sunday after all. There is no time to think about anything meaningful. There's too much activity for that. There's no way to get out of line. There's no way to think about doing something different, much less do it. In fact, there may not be the capacity to think about anything meaningful, anyway. Its all hum and buzz and hustle. Get the materials, imbibe, dream about sex, watch the battle play out on the battlefield, like it did the week and month and year before. The differences are immaterial from day to day and week to week. It's the same motion, the same movement, the same outcome, over and over and over. The programming holds the day and no one takes an interest in change or any serious topics. Nobody can look past the next taste of simple carbohydrates, or the next buzz of electronic communication.

The communication streams are imperative to both the males and the females because it is important that everyone be on the same page. Everyone needs to pull in the same direction. If anyone strays from what they are told, they become outcasts. Everyone needs to make a push for the group. It is important that there is uniformity for the mindless worker and the useless male. They need to be controlled to accomplish the goals of the group. With uniform communication towards uniform viewpoints, there can be a push toward uniform behavior and control at the top of the society.

It is important that the males and females both make a trail so that their actions can be copied. Eat this sugary food. Consume soy. Imbibe carbohydrates. Watch this. Do that. Stay on course. Consume what you are supposed to. Learn from the tube and the group. Do what everybody else does, because everybody else does it. Fit in. Don't communicate anything that isn't accepted by the group at large. That would be a disaster. Never go your own way. Don't question anything that is widely disseminated among the group. Use the right products, eat the right simple sugars, carry the right bags. And don't notice anything. Never notice!

The warrior class, those who actually played in the game, was at risk for harm. But, the general population was achieving bodily pleasure on that day. The carbs! The gluttony! There was no need for cares, for hopes, for fears, for worry. There was only the present joys! Drink the sludge, eat whatever comes your way. Oh look, over here! Now look, over there! There was no need for allowing feelings into the mix, no hopes, no cares, no worries, no fears. The thought employed was surface only. Nothing meditative, nothing deep. Nothing profound. Nothing long term. Oh, I want this. Oh, I hope I can find that. Oh, I hope someone brings me this. Oh look, that's new, what is that? Can I have some?

Some pop music was playing in the background:

We used to play pretend, give each other different names
We would build a rocket ship and then we'd fly it far away
Used to dream of outer space but now they're laughing in our face
Saying, "Wake up, you need to make money"

The music just kind of droned on in the background. On football Sunday, no one is ever bored because there is always something happening next. And, on the rare occasion that nothing is happening, there are readily available carbs. Swallow them. There are always, seemingly, more activities and amusements. Football Sunday droned on. Maddox's players did fine.

As night fell, Maddox, in his familiar routine, climbed under the covers and onto his full-sized mattress resting on the ground of his home office. He sipped on a soda water with a splash of cranberry juice and grabbed his book from his desk. He opened it up and started reading. It was Ray Bradbury's *Fahrenheit 451*. He was at the part where Guy Montag engaged his wife and her friends in a debate about family and politics. Then, Guy read to them from a book of poetry. Guy's wife, Mildred, and her friends react emotionally to Montag's reading because books are illegal. The wife takes some sleeping pills and goes to bed. Guy Montag then hides his books in the yard and listens to Mildred screech emotionally charged rhetoric at him. When that marital episode is over, he heads to work. The firemen are called to an alarm, and Guy is dismayed to discover that it is his own house that is to be burned because he possessed books.

Guy's wife Millie had reported him!

When Maddox reached that part, he shook his head, disgusted with Millie and her actions. Overall, he found the book to be stilted, forced, formulaic, predictable and therefore quite boring. But that part intrigued him, the betrayal. He hoped that Guy could recover and rebuild! Fatigue set in and he put his book up on his desk, rolled over, and went to sleep.

Marla's Wage-cuck

❋❋

After Football Sunday, Maddox spent Monday in his office and Tuesday he flew to Chicago for meetings. When he landed, he was dismayed to learn that his bag never arrived, because it was lost by the airline. Maddox needed to check in to the hotel and get a fresh shirt to wear as he was meeting Bart Odom, a friend of Maddox's who worked in television advertising sales, for drinks and didn't want to wear the tee-shirt he had on. Several times before he had used the department store across the street from the hotel for emergency clothing - jackets, jeans, other clothing. Walking in this time, through the mall, he was, for the first time, put off by all the stores and the crap in the stores.

Displays of trinkets, clothing, stationery, scents, stuff, jewelry, candy. Each store and separate counter was a show place of a bunch of stuff for the masses to observe, long for, purchase. Besides the shirt that was on his mind because of the bag issue, there was nothing there, he thought, which he even cared to own. It was stuff that would be put somewhere and other stuff might even have to be purchased to put the stuff in. So much to consume! The mall was well-lit and buzzing with people but it felt totally empty to Maddox. Why bother? How much stuff did he really need? Truth be told, Maddox was still bothered by his nightmare, the one where the gnome pushed him into the basket for being greedy. That galled Maddox! Was he greedy? Was he materialistic?

He found a comfortable looking golf shirt in the department store, purchased it, changed at the hotel quickly and then went next door to the restaurant to meet Bart. Bart was at the bar and stood up when he saw Maddox walk in.

"Maddox!" Bart hollered. "Listen to me, Maddox!"

"Oh no, here it comes," said Maddox with a laugh.

Bart and Maddox made some small talk for a while.

Eventually, Bart zeroed in on his goal, "Hey, I know the

Platform Volleyball Tour went bankrupt. If it comes back can you make sure I get the advertising sales gig?"

Maddox noticed that Bart's facial features seemed smallish, almost compressed, as he spoke.

"Yep. You got it. That works for me. I know what you can do," Maddox replied.

Bart just stared at Maddox, who kept speaking.

"Sell away, man. You got the job. You're fine."

Maddox didn't feel like going into the fact that the relaunch of the tour was not going well. He didn't voice his real thoughts about the sport, not right then.

"Great because I need to find a new wife and that's not cheap," said Bart. When he said this joke, he still seemed like he had a tight affect. He needed to loosen up! This was early in the conversation for Bart to bring up his divorce – they hadn't even finished a single cocktail – but Maddox rolled with it.

"You should try the Ukraine or the Dominican or maybe Asia," Maddox needled him. "You can order a bride right there on your Endless Content smart phone - they have a button for ordering - and she'll be on the next flight out here. You should try one of those," Maddox said. Maddox was joking, but he held in his laugh and kept everything deadpan. He looked at Bart and could tell he envied the way Maddox could loosely joke about things that violated basic social norms – without seeming too weird. It was, in the colloquial, known as talking shit. Maddox was good at it and Bart just couldn't figure it out. Bart had no knack for talking shit.

"What do you mean try one?" asked Bart. Bart was smiling.

"Like a chew toy. Chew on her. Come on, man, get with it. Haha. I'm kidding. I'm trying to lighten the mood, man. You seem so down. But really, think about it, man. Go somewhere, Bart. Go to Russia, Ukraine, the Czech Republic, Korea. Go find a nice girl," Maddox said with a big smile. "Get off your fucking knees, Bart."

Convention had always defined Bart — inwardly and outwardly! Still, they both chuckled at Maddox's invocation.

Bart was looking across the bar at two young women, one tanned brown with dark brown eyes and dark brown hair with yellow streaks in it from the sun. The other girl had black hair but blonde roots, sort of a reverse version of the usual dye job. The dark girl was an eight and the dyed black girl was a six or seven only because she was out of shape. She had very pretty features, though. If she were more fit, she would have been pretty enough to be a model, except she was around five-foot-seven so she was a too short to be a serious fashion model. So, her ceiling was nudey magazines or porn. She could have thrived in those.

"So, realistically, do you think the Platform relaunch is going to happen?" Bart said, wistfully. "Nothing seems to be moving at all, in fact."

"It's a coin flip," Maddox said. "Platform Volleyball is just gone. Here today, gone tomorrow. The old owner, Nathan, still holds all the rights but he says he's trying to sell the Platform and also Efficient-Pop. He says he should be able to sell it in about sixty days, after the bankruptcy stuff goes through."

"Got it."

"Hey, what are you drinking?" asked Bart.

"Vodka and soda with a lime."

"That sounds good right now."

"Yeah, it's a crisp, decent buzz without a big commitment. I only drink them when I travel, but that's what I usually get."

Maddox, who wasn't counting, was on his eighth vodka of the day. Airport bar, lunch, plane and now the restaurant. It added up — he was buzzed, but since he had drink them over the course of the entire day, the buzz was dull and not sharp.

"So what's up with the Pepe Soliz shit that was in the news? What happened? What was the Poobah doing?" asked Bart.

"Oh man, Bart, everyone asks me about Pepe Soliz. Pepe. Pepe. Pepe. Pepe Soliz. That's my life. Can't anybody ask me about anything else?"

Bart stared at Maddox, trying to prompt an answer.

"He went out with his brother and a recruiter from my agency, a guy named Ward," Maddox told Bart. "They brought a girl back to the house and Pepe and Ward both lit her up. She called the police for rape. It was a really bad story, Bart. It's getting sorted out. I'm putting some money together for him to give to the girl to make the whole thing go away."

"Woah," said Bart. Silence followed for a few seconds. "How much money?"

"A million bucks," said Maddox with wide eyes.

Maddox quickly ran the numbers in his head. He had sold a condo and a large chunk of his stock portfolio. He already had six hundred seventy five thousand in readily available cash pulled together. He still needed to come up with a few hundred grand. It was hard because he was spending money getting TENACIOUS started. And Zaine was giving stacks and stacks of cash to seemingly every football player in the country. Zaine just gave twenty stacks to Major O and Big Elk two days before. Maddox Malone had to figure out how to get the rest of the money, or he would lose the Poobah as a client. He knew it.

Bart spoke, bringing Maddox back to the conversation. "Sports creates a weird environment for some of these guys. If he couldn't hit a baseball he'd be shoveling shit or selling drugs. Now, he's got fans instead of a shovel. He probably feels entitled to do stuff like that. Entitled to sex. It's nuts," Bart said.

"That's true," Maddox confirmed.

"Well we're not going to solve all the world's problems but we can have a couple drinks and chill," Bart said. "Let's go talk to those girls across the bar."

"Okay, I will wingman as the married friend. That will definitely help you meet someone. You can thank me later."

They grabbed their drinks and walked across the bar.

"How are you ladies doing tonight?" Bart asked.

Maddox looked at the two girls and knew they didn't have interest in Bart. Clear as day. But like a politician, Bart persisted.

"We're good," said the brown-haired girl.

"I'm Bart and this here is my friend Maddox. Maddox Malone."

"I'm Jamie and that's Tori," said the girl.

"You guys are hanging out?"

"Yeah, we are friends from college catching up for a drink."

"That sounds fun. I'm from Chicago and Maddox is in town for a couple days," said Bart.

"Oh, that sounds good - Maddox what do you do?" Jamie asked.

"I'm a fortune teller," Maddox said.

"Nice!" said Jamie. "Do mine?"

"To read your fortune, I have to be in the right mindset. And unfortunately I'm not because the airline lost my bag. So I don't think I could get an accurate read. Sorry, I'm just being honest," said Maddox as he gently grabbed her hand. "But let me see what we've got going on here."

Maddox stared at her palm intently. Jamie melted. Bart looked jealous but only for a split second. Tori sat there.

"Yeah, let's do it another time when my mind is right," said Maddox.

"I'm dying to take you up on that," Jamie said. "I want to do it as soon as you get your bag and get settled. Are you busy tomorrow?"

"I don't know yet it sort of depends how things play out," said

Maddox as he looked across the bar. Maddox seemed disinterested.

Maddox was quite casual with his response, while Bart's face, staring intensely at Jamie, made him look like he was undressing Jamie in his mind. Was she fully shaved? Or waxed? What color were her panties?

"I'll send you a text," Jamie said and she pulled a pen out of her bag and glanced at a napkin where Maddox took the cue and jotted down his phone number. She took her glistening smart phone out and immediately sent Maddox a text message. His smart phone buzzed and whirred to life. Maddox was trying to figure out how he might pass her off to Bart but didn't have a plan yet. Maddox wasn't trying to get Jamie's number. Maddox seemed to be was having a difficult stretch in his marriage, communication-wise, but he wasn't going that route with Jamie. No, no, no. He looked down the bar but his mind was elsewhere.

Bart gracefully wrapped up the conversation so the women could eat their food which was about to arrive and Maddox and Bart walked back to their prior spot across the bar.

"You closed her number on your first line," Bart said. "Shooting fish in a barrel."

"I was trying to wingman, honestly. I didn't want the number and I was being goofy with my fortune teller thing. I just hate saying sports agent because I immediately have to deal with fucking Jerry Maguire," said Maddox.

Maddox was telling the truth but he admitted to himself that it did feel good watching Jamie swoon. It just felt good, even though he had no desire to take her upstairs and give it to her. Maddox and Bart sipped on their vodkas and made some small talk about sports. Bart joked that since he had the commercial sales deal wrapped up for the Platform they could talk shit and chase tail. Maddox laughed at the line, which was marred only by Bart's wimpy delivery.

"You gonna start dating again? Jumping back in with two feet?" Maddox said.

"Yeah, I figure I have to at some point. I was married for eleven years," Bart said. "Until Marla asset-cucked me and left me for dead."

"What does that even mean?" asked Maddox.

"Well, let me tell you. Marla selected me based on the fact that I had a decent salary when you factor in my commissions. My bosses loved me!" said Bart.

"Mmmm-hmmm," Maddox made a noise as he pictured Bart kissing the asses of his bosses while he slaved away to get good-boy points in his sales job. Maddox cringed.

"I was into sports and comic books to pass my time. She had no interest in these things, but when we were around people we knew, she pretended to."

Maddox just sat there while Bart went on about Marla.

"Marla has a degree in Inter-Sectional Dance Theory. I shit you not."

"I don't even know what that is," said Maddox with a dismissive look.

"Yeah, no one knows what that is — even the people with the degree. It's crap. Apparently they dance away -isms and the -phobias."

"Wait, what?"

"Yeah, man, they do dances to drive away sexism and xenophobia and shit like that. Technically it's a theory degree but, get this, these bitches actually get out on the dance floor and put it into practice. It's hard to believe. Something's wrong."

"No way?"

"It's true."

They paused.

"Anyway, Marla worked full time in human resources for a hotel chain, and all of her money went to paying off her loans for her dance degree. All of it, every penny. She spent her days pretending to be slammed at work while she was really goofing around on social media."

"You gotta be kidding me!" said Maddox.

"Nope. She was always taking titty pictures in the bathroom and messaging them to boyfriends privately."

"Woah, man, ha-ha what the fuck? Really?"

"Publicly, her social media accounts always posted shit that she got from me to make it look like she really did, have it all. Purses, trips, plates of food, wine, jewelry, my car and my sports utility vehicle."

"What a nightmare!" said Maddox.

"Yeah. So get this. I caught her messaging a guy from her work, a guy named Jaxson. But not just the trendy name Jackson — even hipper than that. Jaxson with an 'x'. Younger than me, of course. He worked in the cubicle next to hers and they used to take bathroom breaks together, if you know what I mean. When I called her out on it for cucking me, since the messages on her phone made clear that they had an affair, she left."

Maddox Malone's eyes went wide.

Bart continued, "She just walked out the door. Oh, by the way, when she left, she took half my shit. Now I live in a one bedroom condo surrounded by a bunch of hood rats. And I'm still paying her, every month. So, I wage-cucked myself for years and then Marla asset-cucked me after she cucked me for real. I'm fucked, man. Just kill me."

"Holy shit, man. That sucks. Why do you have to give her anything? You should just go off the grid and get into crypto-currency. Then, tell her to pay for her own bullshit dance degree, that fuckin' thing. Let her dance away all her bullshit -isms and -phobias with Jaxson. And hopefully Jaxson goes bald and gets fat. Fuck Jaxson. Fuck her, man. Fuck Marla."

"Well, ahem, Jaxson is six two and wiry with a ton of hair and, apparently, an insatiable sex drive. I saw on her texts that they do all the positions. All the fucking positions!" said Bart.

"Oof. Man. That's shitty," said Maddox, with commiseration-face.

"But thanks for the thought. She just sucks. That lady sucks."

"Man, that's fucked."

"Yeah, well, after all of that, it's kind of crazy getting back into dating. Things have changed."

"In what way?" asked Maddox.

"Well the technology involved in dating is way different than it was. That's one thing. Also, to be honest people are different than they were just ten or fifteen years ago."

"Yeah, I hadn't thought of that. Texting, social media, dating apps, meetup apps, whatever. All that stuff must make things way different."

"Yep, all that shit is pretty wild," Bart said. "Just stay off that shit, man. Even if you're ever single again. It ain't worth it."

"I bet. Drill down for me. I mean, fuck? Specifically. Exactly, what is a wage-cuck? I never heard of that."

"Well, that's what I was and to be honest I still am," said Bart. "You heard me selling you earlier, trying to make a buck on that ad deal for a new Platform Volleyball Tour," Bart said as they both chuckled regretfully. "That's a wage-cuck. I sell my time and my soul for some money. I'm dead inside but I still go after commissions."

Bart laughed as they both paused for a second. Gallows humor! Maddox was thinking.

"Okay, so it means that you work? A lot of people do that," Maddox said, trying to understand Bart's perspective.

"Well, yes in a sense but the difference is the type of work. I don't mind working hard. I like it. But selling ads for shitty products wears on you after a while. Fuck, I worked on advertising for Pogo Back. A bunch of kids ended up dead and paralyzed from those fucking things. I mean, Pogo Backs were impossible to control. People were careening everywhere."

"Whoa, you sold ads for Pogo Back?" asked Maddox with a surprised look on his face.

"Yeah, man. We pushed the hell out of Pogo Back. Sold a million of 'em or more," answered Bart.

"I put their snowboarder deal together with their outside marketing agency. Remember the commercial where the snowboarder strapped his Pogo Back on and jumped off of Mount Everest? It was CGI but still. That helped put Pogo Back on the map."

"No way! I didn't know you did that," said Bart.

"Swear to God."

"Pogo Back killed a lot of people but at least it was fun to work on. The owner of that company was so wild he was always getting up to something."

"Isn't he the guy that married the porn star?"

"Two, at the same time. He's on the run in East Asia, somewhere. Running away from questions, running from shadows, running from life. But it wasn't dull. Whenever I went into their offices I saw the craziest shit."

"Yeah, you can say that again."

"Here's the thing. I forget who wrote it, but I read once where someone wrote, 'If you are immune to boredom, there is literally nothing you cannot accomplish in the corporate world.' That's true. That's the key to the corporate world. I kind of miss working for Pogo Back - that wasn't boring," said Bart.

For Bart, he had, for many years, conquered the boredom and drudgery of the tedious bureaucratic work world. He'd been selling television ads for eleven years, for fuck's sake. What Bart had just started to realize — just in the last couple months — was that he conquered the tedium by dulling himself, his character, his mind, his body, using distractions like television, comic books, sports fandom, macro brew, heavy carbohydrates, popular music, video games and other forced hobbies that deep down, he didn't really care about. He didn't even like drinking beer. But he drank a couple beers every day, anyway. It's just something that he did. If someone asked him why, he wouldn't have a good answer. It happened. Then it happened again. Then it was the next day.

"So what do you want to do?" asked Maddox.

They paused.

Music played in the background at the restaurant.

> When I'm ridin' round the world
> And I'm doin' this and I'm signin' that
> And I'm tryin' to make some girl, who tells me
> Baby, better come back maybe next week
> Can't you see I'm on a losing streak

"I don't fucking know," said Bart. "I don't know what I can do."

They paused again. The conversation was relaxed and intense at the same time. Both guys were engaged.

"That's the thing. I know you're mad about Marla, but ... Look at it this way. After she left you still kept doing the same thing. So you can't really slam her for that. You kept doing the same thing after she left. So, maybe you got wage-cucked but maybe you did it to yourself?"

"Well that's the thing about it, man. That's exactly it!"

Bart's eyes flashed wildly with excitement.

"You lost me. What's it?" asked Maddox.

"I used to do this job because I wanted a family. All that went away with Marla and Jaxson's, uhh, thing. Now, the reason I do this work is different than it was. I'm not technically wage-cucking for a family or a woman because I don't have those, but now I'm doing this because it's what I do. It's me, now. And that's the worst part about it. A fucking wage-cuck! The horror!" said Bart.

"Okay, I think I understood that. Still, if you don't work, what are you gonna do, just wander the land?" Maddox said with a laugh.

"I don't mind working, I just don't want to be a soul-less econo-bot. I actually don't even mind selling television ads. I just don't want to do it for products like Pogo Back. Not trying to be a puss. I'd just like to push decent products. Nothing degenerate. Nothing that kills people fast like Pogo Back or slow like soda."

"It's hard. In a sense, no one is a slave. No one has to go work for an employer. No one has to live in a city. No one has to live in a high-rise apartment. But most people don't have the ability to work for themselves. Most can only survive as wage slaves," said Maddox, generally agreeing with Bart's thrust. "Or wage-cucks as you call them."

"I think that's probably true."

"It's a long way out of there, I think," Maddox said. "It's hard because you will second guess yourself."

"It's always a long way to anywhere good," Bart agreed.

"So what are you gonna do?" Maddox asked.

They both thought for a second, then Bart spoke again.

"With everything we talked about, I'm just gonna try to re-make myself. I still have to work, I can't afford to quit. But I've been thinking about cutting down on my tech, eating better, and exercising more. Then I'm gonna go from there. I have a long way to go."

Maddox listened to Bart's simple answer. Maddox suddenly felt so damn sorry for Bart. Bart suddenly seemed so mediocre, so common. Chubby. Alone. Bored. Helpless. So trapped! Marla siphoned his economic value and left behind a fat, burned-out shell of a man. Maddox would rather have adventure, even outrageous misfortune, even his current disappointments, failures and problems, than a static, tranquilized normal American existence in a corporate cubicle. Watching sports on television, drinking microbrew and waiting to die? No thanks.

But Maddox felt uneasy. A string of questions streamed through his mind.

"What if Maddox was also mediocre and he didn't know it? What if his commissions were meaningless for his future, for establishing anything meaningful and permanent? Yes, he could use the money to buy shit? But so what? He already had a lot of shit. No, don't think like that!"

So what? He hated that last question and tried to banish the thought. But he couldn't and Maddox thought he felt the ground shift underneath him. He knew that wasn't real, it was just a sensation in his mind. It wasn't real — even if it was real to Maddox. Wait, but if it was real to Maddox was it real?

Maddox and Bart sat in the bar, silent for a couple minutes. At that point they were half-way finished with their fifth vodka and it had been a good conversation. They were both buzzed, but they had been there for quite a while so they were not stumble-drunk.

"I don't want to do the same thing I've been doing. I don't mind selling ads or pushing product somehow, but I want to work with one product that is decent. It doesn't have to be perfect, just a fundamentally decent product," said Bart.

"That sounds practical. In fact, that's a really thoughtful thing to say," said Maddox with an earnest face suggesting that he really meant it.

Bart looked over at Maddox. His eyes flashed.

"By the way, Maddox, you realize that all the sport deals you do, you're a lot like me? The sports are just media delivery mechanisms for the stuff people like me push in there. We download that shit right into people's heads. So, you're also playing a role in pushing all the meaningless shit. You're part of the machine. You're just cool because of that Jerry Maguire bullshit you do... You're not in a cubicle."

"Man, fuck Jerry Maguire — I'm so sick of hearing about that movie," interrupted Maddox.

"You, Maddox Malone, you might be a handsome guy and a sports agent and all that. But you still work for the machine, Maddox. It only grows, it never shrinks," said Bart.

Maddox thought about that Pogo Back promotion deal. He thought of the XtraShoog Soda promotion he did for Lacy Stratton and her babies. Soda for her babies! He did so many shitty deals like that. He thought of all his transactional work. His Malone Agency. He thought about the Pozz that he discussed with Benjamin. Fuck, he thought, maybe Bart was right?

"Well, fuck everything, man," Maddox said with a laugh meant to lighten the mood and clear his own mind by dismissing all the unsettling thoughts once and for all. "I know we came here to talk about the Platform and to make sure you got that gig if it happens. Ended up somewhere else."

"No man, we came here to chew bubble gum and bang bitches," said Bart, awkwardly and unconvincingly. "And I'm all out of bubble gum."

Three seconds of awkward silence ensued. Maddox widened his eyes.

"I really enjoyed it, Bart. Perhaps, somewhere, some day, at a less miserable time, we will see each other again. Ha-ha," said Maddox with a laugh.

It was a light-hearted reference to a book Maddox had read sometime before. Bart took it as irony, and it worked. They both laughed, shook hands, and parted ways.

Maddox walked back to his hotel. A thought hit him. He recalled, ever so slightly, the sense of awe he felt as a little boy, when he was camping with his parents in Northern California, outside of Sunny Grove. Maddox would stare up at the sky and look at the stars and the moon. He would look specifically for a comet, a shooting star or clusters of stars. He would stare at the moon. He would reflect on, and imagine, the history of the area. He would sit there and soak in the beauty and mystery of the Earth. Maddox could remember those times very well. They seemed somewhat distant now, but they were not gone. Maddox thought of all the useless shit that he saw when he walked over to the department store to buy the shirt and something gnawed at him. None of that inspired awe or wonder. None of those items meant a God-damned thing to Maddox, not anymore. Why was he feeling so negative, so disappointed lately? Was it self-deprecation? Was it doubt? Was it failure? Was it overwhelming regret? Was it the Malone Agency issues and problems? What was going on? Maddox couldn't tell. He walked on, back to his hotel on Michigan Avenue. He sat down at the bar at the hotel restaurant. Suddenly he locked back in on all the problems he was facing with his agency. Poobah rape hush money. TENACIOUS delays. Illegal payments to Obadiah Ballard. Platform Collapse. "Fuck man, I need to catch a break," Maddox thought.

Maddox was starting to worry, deeply. And that was something very, very different, because Maddox Malone had never worried much before.

Baggage Free

✤✤

Kalli woke up feeling very energized. She was looking forward to seeing Ashleigh later that morning. She was excited for the sea-change coming in her life — excited to leave Michael for good. After Billy and Tanish had played their game of rumpy-rumpy for an hour in the cheap motel, Ashleigh had, for her part, made the final decision to leave Billy. They would both be leaving Oregon for good. Kalli had been able to scrounge around the apartment, in pockets, and elsewhere and she found an extra thirty dollars in ones and fives. She also worked a double shift the day before and made an extra one hundred and forty bucks on tips from bartending. When combined with the other amounts that she had been able to squirrel away, she was up to three hundred and ninety dollars. That was more than nothing!

Ashleigh, as promised, called Kalli the next day. Billy had left the house, so Ashleigh could speak freely.

"Hey Kalli."

"Hi Ashleigh. I'm so excited that we can go. But what happened?"

Ashleigh's face was saturated with a heavy anger mixed with sadness. A heavy reflection of disappointment. Her face, and particularly her lips, were indecently compressed. Her eyes were wide and wild, with a noticeable redness and a watery consistency.

"Well, you'll never believe this, but I caught Billy fucking around with some weird hairy guy at the motel ten minutes from our house. A guy, haha! A man. I saw a text message, then I followed him over there. I got a picture of him doing foreplay. Doing foreplay! I shit you not, there was cock everywhere. It was unreal! Ha-ha-ha," Ashleigh laughed, but she looked like she wanted to cry and puke, again. She was over it. She needed to rebuild, not bottom out further.

"Seriously?" asked Kalli. "Are you lying?"

"Not lying," Ashleigh responded, as she thought of the picture on her phone of Billy tenderly and longingly fondling Tanish's penis. "And that fucking faggot hasn't touched me in months. I put my little shaved pussy right in front of his face a couple times a week and he never does a God-damned thing. Now I know why. What a fag!"

"Wow, I've only met Billy a few times, but I didn't see that one coming. They are so religious in his family. I never thought he might be gay," Kalli said a bit sheepishly. She was shocked at Ashleigh's crass language, but then again, she was understanding of it because of the drastic nature of the breakup.

"Yeah, I didn't see it coming either and I've been married to Billy for years. I'm still in shock," Ashleigh shook her head, slowly, as she spoke.

"So, what are we gonna do?" asked Kalli.

"I have that new car, it's really nice. I don't have a lot of money, but I'm going to drive it to Arizona. Can you help with gas?" Ashleigh asked, with a hopeful tone.

"Yeah, I've set aside almost four hundred bucks. What's mine is yours. I'm gonna pack a bag or two and get the hell out of here. Michael punched me the other day again. This time at home. You know how you said you're done? Well, I'm done too. I hate that fucker."

"You have got to be kidding me. Are you serious? I didn't like how he grabbed you the last time we hung out, but obviously, that is ridiculous. He punched you again? Fuck that guy. We're both getting out of here, like Thelma and Louise. Okay, so what time should we go?"

"Michael is going to be gone by nine so any time after that. I'm gonna send him a text to break up with him. I wasted a lot of time on that guy and this is where I end up? I'm fat and broke, stuck in Oregon. I'd rather be a Rajneeshee. I'm done."

They both paused their commentary for a moment.

"Works for me. Let's meet at nine thirty. I'm going to send the sex picture of Billy and his boyfriend to Billy's mom. She's the only one I care about in that family, anyway. I actually like her. She's gonna kill him for cheating on me and then she's gonna be crazy since it was with a man. It's the only funny thing about this whole mess. It's the only thing that makes me laugh a little. They are so religious. Not my problem, though. Not anymore."

When nine-thirty rolled around the following day, Monday, Ashleigh picked up Kalli at Kalli's apartment. She pulled up in her white sedan. Kalli was already waiting in the driveway. She couldn't wait to leave Oregon and Michael. Kalli had a backpack, a duffel bag and a small hard case full of a few valuables. Other than some things that her parents were storing for her in their house in Phoenix, these were all of her possessions! She had nothing to show for spending time in a relationship with Michael. No new skills, no assets, no good feelings. She hadn't saved any money beyond what she would use for gas to get out of there. She didn't feel healthy or fit. Time had passed, with no avail. She was upset with herself, upset with life. She felt low. She felt worthless. She felt stupid. She was disappointed with this whole relationship and her entire stay in Oregon and Seattle. But, she had a hop in her step. She felt horrible, but she hadn't lost hope for her future.

When Kalli threw her bags into Ashleigh's car, she jumped in the passenger seat with a pretty carefree look.

"Hey girl, thanks for picking me up," Kalli said.

"Of course! I'm so excited to have you ride with me," Ashleigh said with a warm smile.

"I brought everything I own, haha. Pretty pathetic! I feel like such a loser."

"Well, life is crazy. I don't have shit either and to top it off I just realized I was married to a gay guy for five years. Five years, Kalli! I have this car but all our money and stuff is under Billy's control. I want to get out of town and deal with that later."

"Hey, look at the bright side — he could have been into bestiality," said Kalli, smiling broadly.

They both looked like they might die laughing. It really lightened the mood. Ashleigh laughed for an entire minute and she wiped a couple of tears, tears of laughter, from her eyes.

Finally, Ashleigh responded, "Well, I have to be honest the other dude looked like a goat so it's kinda the same thing. Oh, that reminds me, I gotta send that picture to Billy's momma."

Ashleigh fiddled with her smart phone for a minute, pulling up the X-rated picture of Billy and Tanish getting ready to pound it out. She sent it to Mary, Billy's mother, without a note. She thought it might cause Mary to faint, but Ashleigh sent it anyway. It had to be done.

"Alright, that's taken care of," said Ashleigh with a devilish grin.

The young women laughed as they raced down the road. At least it was a nice car, fast enough and equipped with leather seats. Ashleigh had the car doing a brisk eighty-five miles an hour in a sixty-five mile an hour zone. Billy and Michael were out of the picture. Billy and Michael were single men, they just didn't know it yet.

"Let's text them at the same time? Once we're just out of town?" said Ashleigh with another devilish smile.

"Okay, that sounds good."

Half an hour later, they pulled over to get some gasoline. Kalli went and paid thirty dollars at the register and that was enough to almost fill up the car. They were set for a few more hours of driving. But, after an hour, they were both getting hungry. They pulled over and each bought a turkey sandwich from a roadside deli. They also took a few minutes to type out text messages on their smart phones, with Kalli writing one for Michael and Ashleigh composing her break-up message to Billy.

"Michael, I wish you the best things in life and I enjoyed my time with you," Kalli lied. "But I'm moving on with my life. I left Oregon today. Without you. I hope you can do everything you want to do, it's just not going to be with me anymore. Take care."

Kalli showed the message to Ashleigh and then hit send. She felt relief and disappointment at the same time. She felt loss, not because she cared about Michael anymore, but because she had spent valuable time pursuing a relationship that failed miserably. Between Alaska, Washington and Oregon, those were several years that she couldn't have back! Kalli and Michael had entered into the relationship with high hopes for themselves, for the future. The relationship ended with Kalli battered and bruised, feeling weak and fat, with no trust in or hope for Michael. She had no trust in herself and her decisions. But, happily, she hadn't lost hope. This was just another of life's disappointments. That's what the disappointments do, they accumulate with time. A series!

When Michael received the message, he was at lunch at the restaurant he cooked for. He read the message twice and didn't immediately respond. His face showed acceptance that Kalli was gone. Then it started to show anger. Michael put his wide-screened smart phone down, grimaced, shook his head slightly. He kept breathing, of course. His face showed more anger. He turned red. Anger was soon smeared all over his face. He pounded his fist on the table. He looked like he wanted to threaten Kalli physically. He looked angry enough to firebomb Kalli's house. But she was gone — she didn't have a house anymore. He couldn't hit her. And she left the apartment for him to deal with. Powerless to hurt Kalli, Michael just sat there looking angry.

After she reviewed Kalli's text message, Ashleigh mustered up the courage to send a message to Billy to let him know that she was leaving him.

"Billy, thank you for the good times. I appreciate you and will always love you. But I know that you met up with a man at the motel the other day and enjoyed each other's company. I know what you did. I can't live with that. I am leaving you and I'm leaving Oregon. You'll hear from my lawyer. Take care, Billy."

Ashleigh showed the message to Kalli, who nodded with a half-grimace, half-smirk. Kalli had her eyes gazing, though, at Ashleigh to give her some warmth, some strength, some unspoken encouragement. Ashleigh thumbed the send button and the smart phone did the rest.

Ding!

Billy heard his smart phone notification a few seconds later. That happened often. But, when he opened the text message, his face immediately showed panic. Leaving him? Another man? Tanish? Tannnnnissshhhh! No-o-o-o. What now?

Billy immediately called Ashleigh, who declined the call. He called again. She declined the call again.

Billy sent Ashleigh a text message from his smart phone.

"Baby, you can't leave me. You can't do this to me. I love you."

"You didn't love me when you grabbed that guy's weird penis. By the way, I saw that thing close up, on your phone. I know what you did," Ashleigh responded, showing Kalli the text after she sent it.

"You keep saying that. What are you talking about?" Billy's face was white. It was stretched. It warped! His mouth twisted and curved. The twists and curves waxed and waned, waxed and waned.

"I'm talking about what you did with that guy at the motel last week. You either fucked him or he fucked you, or both. I know what you did," Ashleigh wrote. Her disgust started to bubble up. She spent five years with this guy and now all she could think was that he was a closeted, but sexually active, homosexual. And she was a cuck-queen. She couldn't believe it. She almost gagged. She almost vomited. She managed to hold it together.

"Baby, I swear on the bible that I never did that. I didn't do that. I don't know what you are talking about." Billy replied.

Ashleigh glanced at Kalli and forced a smile. She selected the image of Billy and Tanish engaging in their foreplay. She attached it to the text thread with Billy and hit send on her smart phone. When it arrived, Billy's fingers raced to open it. He saw the image was of him, through the motel window, partially obscured by the curtain, with his hand grasping, desperately at Tanish's body. He shook his head, slightly. Then, Billy hung his head. Then, Billy put down his smart phone.

He didn't respond further, and Ashleigh didn't send anything else to Billy. What else could either of them say? She gunned the

Volkswagen onto the freeway on-ramp.

Ashleigh and Kalli were back on the road. They were baggage free, with the abusive boyfriend and the homosexual husband not even visible in the rear view mirror. The girls took comfort from the fact that they had each other for the duration of the trip.

Ashleigh turned up the music, which was playing country music radio. Both girls sang, with Kalli singing loudly.

> I'm hell on heels
> Say what you will
> I've done made the devil a deal
> He made me pretty
> He made me smart
> And I'm going to break me a million hearts

An hour later, Kalli was on the phone with her mom. Kalli's mom, from her previous visit, had known that Kalli wasn't happy. Her mom had been the one that told her she was too heavy, that she didn't look like herself. She had said "you look like shit," in those exact words. It was some honest, motherly advice. Tough love, even.

"What are you going to do?" her mom asked at one point during the conversation.

"Can I stay with you for a month? I'll need some time to get a job and save my money for an apartment."

"Of course. You think you're going to want to live in Phoenix?"

"Well, I'm finished in Oregon, finished in Washington, I'm finished in Alaska, and I'm not going back to Los Angeles. So yeah."

"Okay, well, we love you and we will help in any way you need. Drive safe."

Kalli hung up her smart phone, grateful that her parents were in her corner. She looked forward and enjoyed the open road. She let Ashleigh know that she was more than happy to drive for a shift. Ashleigh said that she would take her up on that the second that she started to feel fatigued.

They kept pressing forward. The road seemed to flow smoothly in front of them. It bent. The car ripped along. They drove, they passed cars, they stayed on track, lurching toward Phoenix at an average speed of seventy five miles per hour.

Kalli felt pretty good. She felt like she had lost a huge albatross in the shape of an abusive, alcoholic boyfriend. She felt younger and lighter already, even though she still wanted to trim back down to a healthier weight. She was one-sixty, and, while she didn't feel any urge to get back to her modeling weight of one-thirty, she felt like one-forty was about right for her five-foot-eleven frame these days. Along with the weight loss goal, she felt like she could re-gain her personality, re-gain her edge. She wanted to be active again. Maybe get herself a new horse. She hadn't even ridden in a couple of years. And, that was one of her favorite things to do.

Stay on course, she told herself! Keep your eyes open! Keep your ears open! She knew she lacked formal education but she didn't lack energy and initiative. She was still funny and talented and pretty. She just had to get her mojo back. But, a tiny bit of confidence was starting to bubble up. She could feel it. She thought about positive aspects of her life. She wasn't burdened with student debt or the seeming obligation to use some shitty degree or other — like a lot of her friends from grade school. She had plenty of common sense — if someone offered Kalli and Inter-Sectional Dance Theory degree for one hundred and fifty thousand dollars she would have just given them a confused or sarcastic look while walking away.

Kalli wasn't stuck working as a nurse or something just because she had spent money to study it. She was thankful she didn't have some marketing degree that would plant her in a cubicle for the foreseeable future. She could do whatever she wanted, whatever she could figure out, whatever she could create for herself. Whatever she could manage, she could do. Maybe that would be nothing? But that was the risk in life. She could have taken no risk, not a single one, and been, right now, in a cubicle somewhere drinking coffee, going through papers, and listening to some fucking orbiting dork talk to her about meaningless shit. But where was the joy in never taking a risk?

Suddenly, a positive thought hit Kalli out of the blue. She knew that she would be successful. She knew that she could do it, she could make it in life. She felt better on her own than she had with Michael already. And she hadn't even been gone for a full day. She couldn't get that time back, so she just told herself to learn from it. That time was gone. So she stayed positive and kept it moving.

Ashleigh and Kalli were ripping down the highway, making good time!

While Ashleigh was driving, Kalli took a few minutes to scan some social media on her smart phone. She wanted to keep Ashleigh company, but fifteen or twenty minutes of silence would be great. A little escape, then she would get back to the music and chatting with Ashleigh for the next few hours of the drive.

She was shocked, though, as she logged on to her social media feed to see that a sexual abuse and rape epidemic had been exposed in her old home, Hollywood. Her whole, entire digital media feed was covered with stories about girls coming forward to point out that they had been attacked, abused, even raped, by a disgusting old, fat Hollywood movie producer and pusher of the Pozz.

Kalli kept scrolling on her smart phone, growing more and more horrified. Kalli had been in Hollywood, inside the belly of the beast. But she had left without feeling fulfilled by the Hollywood lifestyle. She had worked there, but only managed to get by. Barely! She might have filmed some commercials and advertisements, but never had a major breakthrough with acting, she never became famous or rich. She hadn't even set those things as specific goals for herself. She had no knowledge of the conversation that Maddox had with Benjamin Cohen regarding the Pozz. She didn't know what it meant to be Pozz-ed. But she had lived in that culture out there in Hollywood. She was surrounded by those movies, those videos, the modeling world, the party scene.

Kalli was keenly aware of not feeling safe as a woman in

America. She didn't feel safe in Oregon, around Michael. He had punched her right in the face, after all. She didn't feel safe when she was in Alaska, watching how some of the tribal men eyed her. She had actually worried a time or two, in Alaska, about being raped — although it didn't happen. And, years before, she felt uncomfortable around certain men in Hollywood as well. Certain predators just seemed handsy and pervy. She, luckily, had never met the disgusting, corpulent pervert who was in the news today. But she had lived among the same people that were subjected to his scorched earth reign of penis-wielding terror.

What kind of degenerate society was this? Why should she always live under the threat of physical violence or sexual assault? She had, very recently, had her face bashed in by a man. Punched right in the face and called a fat bitch. How did she get here? A pretty girl, punched in the face by an angry, threatening guy. This was not acceptable. It was insane. How was this happening? What was wrong with that guy, with this society?

Kalli kept scrolling, and the details of the Hollywood-based producer scandal kept flooding her feed. Hotel assaults. Unwanted massages. Sex for career boosts. Grabbing breasts and vag. Masturbation displays. Persistent requests for oral sex during business meetings. More unwanted massages. More wild erection displays. Sex for movie roles. Aggressive, rapey chasing. Acting roles offered for sex.

One of the victims said, "I had to defend myself. He's big and fat, so I had to be forceful to resist him."

Wait, What? He masturbated in a flower pot? Okay, that's enough, thought Kalli, as she closed her digital media feed and clicked off her smart phone. That's enough.

The digital media feed upset Kalli. It made her sad! It made her think about her own circumstances, even though she had been victimized by domestic violence and not by sexual assault. She didn't belong in Alaska or Oregon. And the news about the rapey producer reminded her that she didn't belong in Hollywood, either. But where did she belong?

She liked outdoor activities, horses. She loved to sing. She wanted to be in a real relationship, even if she struggled to find something that worked for her. She knew Pozz when she saw it, but not because it had been formally explained to her, like it had to Maddox. She knew that she didn't like it. She instinctively felt that she wanted something much more traditional than what she had experienced thus far in her life. But what was that? What would it look like? It seemed like when she really thought about what she wanted, it was something from a bygone era. A ranch? A farm? A husband — do they still make those, or was it too late for her with the wasted time? Some stability. Something meaningful! Something she could be proud of and really committed to. Ties to the community. She loved to socialize, and she was funny and charismatic, so people liked to be around her. She liked to go out dancing, karaoke, drinking, listening to music. Whatever! She was reaching, grasping for something that she couldn't get a hold of. She still wanted to sing, but that possibility sounded so remote, so far away. She thought it might be impossible. How could she even get started again? Was this stuff even possible? Could she get there or was she going to be a punching bag in her next relationship, if she even started another one, too?

Kalli sunk into a state of despair. She put her smart phone down, put all that stuff out of her head, and started chatting with Ashleigh again. They turned the music back up, and enjoyed the ride. Small talk was okay, she didn't need any more heavy thoughts.

Those would have to wait.

Kalli had always been a free spirit. She was always impulsive. She made decisions and then she lived with them. Her plans constantly changed. Sometimes her plans would change before she ever set out on the plan in the first place. It made her fun, but it made her life a wild ride. Now, she sensed something new about herself, on this ride home. She sensed that time was slipping by and that she worried. She worried that she would never get it right. She hated to admit it, but she was scared! Was she really going to go from place to place like this — bouncing around and hoping that something clicked? This was something different for Kalli — no matter what had happened before, in

Hollywood, Alaska, Washington, Oregon, wherever — she had never worried like this before.

Trifecta of Misery

❋❋

Major O was sitting in his usual bar in New Orleans, telling stories. On this particular day, he was about seven vodkas into the night and he was getting to the part of his favorite story where the crowd did that chant during the huge intramural game with Air Force.

> Hey Ho! Hey Ho! You can't stop fuckin' Major O.
> You got the planes but we got the Mo', you can't stop fuckin' Major O.

Major O was telling his stories to a guy he had met about an hour before. The guy was about six-foot-two, brown hair, wearing slacks and a white button down with a tie. Sleeves rolled up. The guy laughed at the stories. He liked Major O. The cocktails were flowing steadily for Major O, while the other man nursed one drink the entire time.

"Yeah, man those were the days!" said Major O. He was drunk, as usual, but of course quite coherent and charming. It was just another day at the neighborhood bar.

The other man was listening intently.

"That's incredible. You must have been a really good football player," said the man.

"Yeah, I could play a little ball. Taught everything I know to my son. He's gonna be kuhhhmff."

"Kuhhhmff?" asked the man.

"Comfortable," said Major O.

"Aha. Does he play ball?" asked the man.

"Yeah, he plays college ball in Louisiana right now," said Major O.

"No shit?" said the man.

"Name's Obadiah Ballard."

"Oh, I know who he is. He's special! He's gonna be a high draft pick," said the man, with excited eyes.

"You're damn right about that! That's why Zaine and the Malone Agency been givin' him stacks of cash for months now. He's gonna be a high draft pick and get that big contract."

"Wait, what? Who?" asked the man.

"Oh yeah, Zaine Fuller and the Malone Agency been givin' O-Bad and a bunch of other players stacks of cash — for months now. He's gonna sign with them for the draft," said Major O, a bit drunkenly. "They even been givin' cash to me, good old Major O."

A few minutes later, the man said his good-bye to Major O. He walked out the door of the bar — one that Mark Twain, coincidentally, had frequented back in the day — and pulled out his shiny gold smart phone. He pressed a few digital buttons on the shiny big screen.

"Hi Barrett," said the woman that answered the phone.

"Hi Phyllis," said Barrett. "I need you to come into the office early tomorrow morning. I just got some information presented to me and we need to open an investigation first thing in the morning. It will be me working on it personally, and can you please get a message to Special Agent Fredrickson in financial crimes. I need him on the team as well. I'd like to have the investigation formally opened before noon tomorrow."

"Will do. Have a great night," said Phyllis.

"Thanks," said Barrett Harmon, a Special Agent in the FBI, as he hung up the phone.

ii

Halfway across the country from Major O and the FBI Agent, Maddox was looking at the screen on his glowing smart phone, still in Chicago, when the bartender, a beautiful young Japanese girl in a white tank top and denim shorts, came over and took Maddox's order. Unsurprisingly, the order was a vodka and soda with a lime. Maddox dialed the Grasshopper on his phone, and, once again, the Grasshopper did not answer his call. Maddox gripped his smart phone in his left hand and entered some text into the messaging application. He had not been able to reach Paul McCartney for more than a week. More than a week! What was going on? Where was the Grasshopper?

"Paul, I really need to talk to you. All of the TENACIOUS projects are overdue. The facility purchase has not closed, I spoke to the real estate agent. The wrestling and golf people are calling me every day. Where are you? Nobody can reach you. Maddox," he messaged the Grasshopper. He had a pit in his stomach. A sinking feeling. This wasn't good.

Maddox thought to himself, "at what point do I try to make a contingency plan?" He also was thinking that it would be really hard to even contemplate a contingency plan. What would he do? With his thoughts snowballing, he sent another message to the Grasshopper. He was writing in all caps. Desperate times!

"PAUL, CALL ME AS SOON AS POSSIBLE. THE WHEELS ARE FALLING OFF THE TENACIOUS PROJECTS THAT WE HAVE BEEN WORKING ON FOREVER. WHERE ARE YOU?"

Even if the Grasshopper wasn't going to answer, sending the message was helping Maddox. Now that he sent two text messages from his smart phone, he felt that he could put TENACIOUS out of his mind, hopefully for the rest of the night. Maddox took a sip of his vodka and soda with lime. He was alone at the bar, and he was kind of hoping for some conversation – he felt a bit isolated. He was down on himself! He would have to wake up at five in the morning to get to the airport.

The upside was that there was a breakfast place at the Chicago airport that made a ridiculously good egg sandwich. That, a breakfast sandwich, was the only positive thing Maddox could think of. The egg sandwich contained egg and cheese and also had precisely the right amount of flavor and spices. That would be enough to get him up and over there. If that egg sandwich didn't exist there would have been no guarantee that Maddox would have gotten out of bed – that's how frustrated Maddox Malone had become.

Force of habit caused him to check the digital media feeds on his smart phone, for what he hoped would be, what he considered at least, a mental break. He accidentally clicked on a video that was on his digital media feed. He watched it for a few seconds — it was really weird, it was a degenerate lady on a television show singing a song about her pussy and anal sex and multiple genders. Claiming that gender was a construct, whatever that means. It seemed to Maddox, paradoxically, that it mean something and nothing at the same time. Maddox reflexively thought back to his conversation with Lacy Stratton about Danielle Duffer and her transition, but forced himself to stop. The whole thing was silly! That wasn't Carlton Duffer's sister, he thought – a man is not a woman and a boy is not a girl. He didn't know what Danielle Duffer was, but he knew with certainty that Danielle was not Carlton Duffer's sister. Oh well! Maddox watched the video for another minute — this was a youth-oriented show, it seemed. It claimed to be about science. "This was more Pozz!" thought Maddox. Pozz-ed garbage! Benjamin Cohen was right!

He decided that he would play one song, then put his phone away and either chat with the bartender or another patron if one walked in. He wanted some human contact, he was finished with his digital smart phone for the day. He sang along.

> Such a mess, well I don't wanna watch you
> Disconnect and self-destruct one
> Bullet at a time

He was almost finished with the song when his smart phone rang and buzzed and lit up. It was his wife Laura. He picked it up on the first ring.

"Hey," said Maddox with a nice, enthusiastic tone – even though he was overly tired.

"I just can't do this anymore! Thomas is not listening to me. I'm tired Maddox. I'm just so tired. This is so hard. This is so difficult. I just can't do this anymore. I can't. I just can't! Fire Station! Fire Station! Where are you?"

As she spoke, she was making hysterical crying noises. Maddox rolled his eyes because she did this to him all the time. All the time! He was taking gut punches all day trying to get money for Pepe Soliz to pay April Tilney. Trying to find the Grasshopper and get the TENACIOUS projects moving. Trying to resurrect the Platform, again. Dealing with Lacy Stratton and Carlton Duffer. Trying to continue to grow the Malone Agency. Now, after gut punches all day, here came the kick to the balls. Thwumpp! He hated this exact conversation — it repeated itself quite often — and wanted to be off the phone.

"I'm in Chicago, like I said. Sorry to hear that. It's eleven here and I'm on an early flight tomorrow."

"I'm just so tired Maddox. This is so hard. He doesn't listen to me. He just doesn't respect me. I can't do this anymore. Fire Station. I just can't do it! It's too hard," said Laura.

Maddox took a sip of his vodka and soda with a lime. When he picked up the phone, he had every intention, every conscious intention, of being completely friendly, being positive, maybe having a fun conversation. He wasn't going to burden her with all the wild shit he was dealing with. He had every intention of being light-hearted and friendly, but he couldn't muster that anymore after the crying and complaining started. This happened all the time, and it was a huge energy drain. The negativity, on top of all the other negativity Maddox was already dealing with, was overwhelming and smothering. It sapped his energy and almost destroyed his spirit. There was no positive spin to put on this call. He hunched his shoulders. There was a scowl on his face. He paused. Then, he started to get angry.

"Laura, I want you to get a grip on yourself. Take a breath and deal with Thomas. Calm down. You need to calm down."

"Get a grip on myself? Get a grip on myself? Calm down? Oh that's just great! Calm down?" Laura cried and screamed at the same time. She was making noises that Maddox could not describe, that he didn't think were possible.

"Well, yeah. I don't know what else to say. What the fuck do you want me to do?" said Maddox, losing his composure.

"Hooh. Maddox!"

"Well, Laura, it's eleven o'clock here, I have to be up and heading to the airport in five hours. I already told you that. I'm beat. I have been in meetings all day. I haven't even gotten on e-mail yet, and that's going to take me some time. I'm trying to unwind for an hour before I do that. I wish I could help. I really do. He does the same thing to me and I deal with it as best I can."

"It's just so hard. And I never know where you are. I never know what you are doing. I am all alone. We have nothing that we ever talk about. We have nothing in common anymore. You never pay attention to me. I am just so lonely. This is just so hard," Laura said.

It was true, Maddox was always gone. But what could he do? Quit the Malone Agency? He didn't have a choice in the matter — not one that he saw, anyway.

"Ummmm. Saying that we never talk is not a great conversation point. Why don't you bring something up that we can talk about? I get berated and hammered on every time I talk to you. Why don't you say something funny or interesting? Maybe that will help us talk. You know, after you say something interesting I'll say something back - that's how this works."

Maddox, on some level, knew that firing back like that would make things worse, not better. He had lost his temper. He lost sight of the Chill Factor — Omar Matish would be so upset with him. But Maddox had become angry! He couldn't take it, anymore. He felt compelled to say what he said. Maddox was tired. He was finishing a fourteen hour day on a stretch of months and months of travel. He wouldn't be the dumping ground for problems and bad feelings.

"You're so mean to me. I'm so lonely. I'm lonely, Maddox! I thought I would call because you never call. I'm having such a hard time with Thomas tonight I wanted to talk to you. Or someone," said Laura.

"Okay, I get that. But I can't have problems dumped on me that I can't solve from here. I'm happy to talk about them or give encouragement but I can't just have bad things dumped on me when I can't do anything about them. If there's a way for me to actually help, or talk about it normally, I'm happy to do that," said Maddox.

Maddox was still angry. He had reached a full boil. He was abusing his body, his health, flying all over the country. Working his ass off to support his family.

Maddox already had a bunch of problems that he was having difficulty solving. And, a few times a week, especially when he was traveling, Laura would burden him with these awful phone calls. When he was out of town, there was nothing he could do to help with Thomas. Thomas was a very difficult child and he was very stubborn. Thomas just didn't want to go to bed at night and it was very hard to deal with. It was hard to handle, for Laura, for Maddox. It would have been hard for any mere mortal. Maddox had a difficult time getting Thomas to go to bed when he was home. When he was home, he always tried to help. But, from here, from far away, there wasn't really anything he could do. He tried to regain his composure. He tried not to be a hateful husband. He didn't want to devastate his wife. But this conversation was a recurring nightmare, and it always started end ended the same way. What a chasm! What a gap! What a divide!

Maddox's face went blank. He took another sip of vodka and soda with a lime. Then another. He felt like he was in a daze. Best to get the call over with and get back to drinking before he crashed for a few hours. It was always the same, and he had no enthusiasm for the call. No investment in it. He hated the call. He wished the battery in his smart phone was low. Shit, he wished his battery was dead. But it wasn't - so he was forced to plunge on, through the rest of the call.

"Okay, try to stay patient with him. If you want me to talk to him I'm happy to do it. Its eleven o'clock here and I have to finish my emails and be up in a few hours. But whatever you want."

Maddox halted his response and took stock of the conversation. Now she had gone silent. Laura had now achieved the trifecta of misery. The trifecta of misery! First, crying. Second, accusations. Third, awkward or aggressive silence.

Crying, accusations and silence.

This was pure, unfiltered misery. Nothing could be worse on the phone after a long work day. For a moment, he felt compelled to break the silence. Then he reconsidered. Fuck it, he thought. Who cares? I'll think about something else, and Laura can sit there in silence.

And sit in silence she did! A minute went by. Then another. It almost felt like a psy-op.

Why was she doing this? Did she secretly hate him and want him to feel horrible? Did it unburden her somehow to dump problems on him? Problems that he couldn't solve from fifteen hundred miles away. What was the point of this call? His mind wandered to the flight he had tomorrow. He was headed to Miami. He thought about the recruitment of Obadiah and Elk for representation by the Malone Agency. Two great prospects! He tried to keep things positive. He made a quick mental checklist of the things that he had to finish on the flight. If she was going to try to break him down, he was just going to think of other things

"Maddox, Maddox, Maddox."

"What? What do you want? That's my name. What the fuck do you want from me, Laura?"

There was silence. Maddox heard Laura gasp. "Oh fuck," thought Maddox. I just f-bombed my wife over the phone and I'm on the road pounding vodka drinks – two or three at a time. What is wrong with me? He knew he was wrong to talk like that but he couldn't control his speech any more. His anger got the best of him. That angry twin, again!

"You can't talk to me like that. You can't swear at me," said Laura.

"You can't bait me like that. I'm in Chicago and you're calling me to tell me that you can't get Thomas to bed? I've been there. I've been there a lot. I've been there a thousand times. We never talk about anything? Okay, I'll converse for both of us. It's weird - I don't have a problem talking with anybody else. But I'm sure it's me. I'm sure this is all my fault. Maybe if you complain about it more it will get better."

Now, Maddox heard Laura crying on the other end of the line. He cringed. Now he felt guilty. Now he felt like a jerk. An asshole. He hated this situation. It kept replaying itself, as much as two or three times a week. The call came in. Maddox answered, upbeat. The trifecta of misery occurred. The call finished. The chasm widened. The gap, the abyss, the fissure, the gulf. Call it anything, it was wide! He felt a deep dread. He felt a deep distaste. Deep down, Maddox didn't feel like it could change. He felt helpless. He felt a sense of inevitability. He almost felt sick to his stomach. But then he took a breath and forced himself to calm down.

"I'm sorry I swore at you, I'm just frustrated. I'll call you tomorrow." Maddox said, as evenly as he could, and hung up.

He tried to shake it off. The trifecta was such a downer. When the kicker, the silence, came in to the call, it was always the worst part. But even worse than the silence itself was the fact that he knew it would happen again, within a night or two. He grimaced and sipped his vodka and soda deeply, twice. Now a third sip. Fuck this! Fuck everything!

"You want another one?" asked the cute little Japanese bartender.

"Yeah, definitely. No question," said Maddox, trying not to grimace.

She poured him a vodka and soda and squeezed a lime into the glass.

"I'm Akari by the way."

"Hi, I'm Maddox. I used to play Atari with my cousin Colby. Like a retro thing."

"No, I said Akari," she said with a huge smile. She was in.

"Haha. Oops. Oh well either way, nice to meet you," he said. Maddox knew her name but was just messing with Akari.

"How long are you in town?"

"Only tonight. I go to Miami in the morning. Gotta get up at five."

"No shit?"

"No shit. That's the life that I've chosen," Maddox said with a hint of sarcasm.

"Well, it's good to have you here."

"Yeah, I always stay here when I'm in Chicago. It's good to be here."

Akari walked off to serve another patron. Maddox looked at his social media feed. As he scrolled, he was seeing a lot of digital Pozz, just degenerate shit everywhere, so he shut it off without looking any further. A wave of angst came over him. Pepe Soliz rape money. TENACIOUS stagnation. Absent Grasshopper. Platform Volleyball bankruptcy. Nonstop travel. Marital chasm. His life was wild. His life was out of control. He felt like leaving. Escaping. For a minute, he envisioned himself single. In Italy, drinking Chianti. In Greece, enjoying the sun and the view and eating octopus. In Japan, visiting, and more, with a round-titted geisha. In Zimbabwe, running for his life from a bloodthirsty mob!

He kept picturing himself, far away from here. He snapped back to reality because he knew he would miss his kids too much in any of those other places — so the fantasy wasn't even a good mental escape. It just made him feel worse. But, he knew that the trifecta of misery was taking a harsh toll on him, on his personal stability. He felt out of control of his emotions and his thoughts. The trifecta of misery, combined with every other disappointment he was experiencing currently, seemed as if it were slowly breaking down his spirit.

Akari walked back over.

"You want another one?"

"Honestly, I don't care. Yeah, I'll take another one. Rough day," said Maddox.

Akari laughed but in a way meant to encourage Maddox, not mock him.

"How often do you come to Chicago?" asked Akari.

"Like once a month."

"I'm pouring you one more, on the house. But then you're cut off," she said with a friendly smile, jokingly. "Take it up to your room and get some sleep for your flight. Get going! I'll see you next time you're in town, I'm sure. You always stay here."

"Okay, Atari. That sounds good. I'll catch you later, girl. I'll see you back here in a month," said Maddox. They both smiled at the intentional mispronunciation of her name.

Maddox took the vodka and soda with a lime and went up to his room on the thirty-second floor. His fatigue hit him. He climbed right into bed and fell asleep without even taking a sip of the cocktail.

Rise of the Bugmen

✺✺

Maddox spent the day recruiting in Miami, meeting Elk Fearghus for about ten cocktails. Might have been nine, might have been eleven. No matter the number, it was standard fare recruiting. The booze and the stories, they both flowed. When the day was finally over, Maddox took a cab to the airport. He got dropped off at the curb and walked, making his way from ticketing through security, all the way to his gate. On the way, he bought a large iced Americano from a local coffee vendor. It tasted great. But something else was off! Maddox sat at the airport bar, and drank a vodka and soda with a lime. When he finished that one, he drank another one.

Eventually, a woman at the bar struck up a conversation with Maddox. She was a federal prosecutor, originally from Russia, working in South Florida and now living in the United States permanently. She took to Maddox immediately and bought him a vodka shot with a splash of lemonade. They spoke freely about Russian literature and American society. It was a fun and free-ranging conversation. When they drank their shots of vodka — following a toast to the Russian giants of literature — they clinked their glasses together and smiled. Then Maddox bought a round of the same shots and another vodka and soda with a lime. With their boarding times approaching, Maddox and the woman, whose name was Irina, exchanged phone numbers to keep in touch for the purpose of sharing literary tips and recommendations, and parted ways with a handshake. Maddox boarded his plane, heading to Phoenix, and took twenty minutes to start the process of sobering up. He had drank a lot with Irina, just like he had with Elk. Once he started to feel less buzzed, he cracked open one of the books he brought on the trip. *The Oak and the Calf*, by Solzheintsyn.

He was at the part in the memoir where Solzheintsyn was recounting Alexsandr Tvardovsky's pathetic end at the hand of the vicious Bolsheviks. Tvardovsky was removed as editor of the publication Novy Mir and the magazine shut down. That was soon followed by a stroke and death, and it was over for Tvardovsky. It was over for

Tvardovsky so suddenly! The title of the memoir comes from the old story of a calf that butts it's head into an oak tree, over and over. In fact, the calf will keep going until he breaks his neck butting the oak, or until the oak cracks and comes crashing down. Maddox loved the story. At times, he thought he was the calf.

He finally landed in Phoenix and made his way to his car. He jumped in, fired up the engine and rolled up the one-oh-one towards his office. He had so much to do at the office. He grabbed an iced Americano at a drive through and kept moving. He parked at his office. He hustled in and started getting his work done. E-mails, phone calls, text messages, planning travel for the rest of the week. He was getting things off of his plate, one after the other. It felt good.

He saw, out of his peripheral vision, someone approaching his office door. He looked up.

Marcel Valstencher, the Slug's cousin and a client service representative at the Malone Agency, looked almost exactly like a Dung Beetle. The Dung Beetle's odd chin gave him a direct resemblance to the dark bug that loved to eat shit. He was a dead ringer for the bug. Marcel loved to eat shit, too, in the sense that he followed Pepe Soliz around and just kissed his ass. He would do anything Pepe asked — if he had to eat shit, he would. For the service, he got some crumbs. The Malone Agency paid him to follow Pepe around and kiss Pepe's ass. He got paid for that by the Agency and sometimes Pepe would give him some crumbs as well.

Maddox was torn when it came to identifying the worst thing about the Dung Beetle.

His cologne and personal stank.

His face was ugly.

His breath was disgusting.

His bitch tits sat there, sweltering and sagging.

His girlfriend was a two hundred and thirty pound white trash stank-cunt.

Maddox, instead of debating the topic with himself, focused on his odor, a mix of body stench and overpowering cologne, because it was so oppressive. His stench envelopes entire areas, like a dust cloud.

Maddox looked at the Dung Beetle with complete disgust. Maddox was so disgusted his face turned rectangular, and his eyes beamed. Ticks. Grasshoppers. Caterpillars. Stickbugs. Bedbugs. "What is this gross creature and why does it exist?" thought Maddox. Was this the rise of the bugmen?

Maddox pulled the hammer out of his desk drawer and held it tight against his hip at an angle such that Valstencher, the Dung Beetle, couldn't see it. He circled around his Italian glass desk to get himself in striking distance, continuing to make small talk with the Dung Beetle while it shuffled through the papers it had brought into the office. Suddenly, Maddox swung the hammer with his right arm, wind milling his shoulder in one sweeping, graceful, beautiful, but violent motion. Maddox brought the business end of the hammer down on Valstencher's head. The blow thudded into his ugly skull. His dull face looked even more confused than usual. The Dung Beetle cried out and then collapsed onto the rug. Maddox smashed his head again and again on the same spot. Blood gushed. The Dung Beetle was dead.

The hammer attack was only a brief fantasy for Maddox. It didn't actually happen. Instead of being dead, the Dung Beetle was standing in Maddox's office with his big, dumb face right in front of Maddox.

Still, even though it wasn't quite a murderous level of hatred, Maddox felt a deep visceral hatred for the Dung Beetle.

Maddox told himself to breathe. He told himself that he couldn't let everything get to him. He told himself to relax. "Relax, Maddox," he said, almost loud enough for the Dung Beetle to hear him.

"Boss, Pepe Soliz, he really worry about dee money for dat girl," said Valstencher.

"I'm putting the money together, Marcel. I just told Pepe that in New York. I just told him that. What's the issue?"

"Yes, but do you have dee mow-ney?" said the Dung Beetle.

"It's close. I'll have the rest in a couple days."

"Okay, I going to tell Pepe dat everything is okay," said the Dung Beetle.

"Good. I have everything coming together. I'll be able to give Pepe the money in a few days."

"Okay, boss," said the Dung Beetle.

Maddox knew that with a limited intelligence quotient and only basic English skills the Dung Beetle could only grasp key points from what Maddox said. That was okay. It had to be good enough. He didn't want to speak the Dung Beetle's language.

"I'll catch you later, Marcel," said Maddox.

The big, dumb Dung Beetle, arms at his sides, his shoulders rounded, shuffled his feet across the office to walk out the door. The toxic-smelling cloud of body odor and cologne enveloped him, a six or seven foot bubble of shitty-smelling and moist nastiness. While Dung beetles live in many habitats, including farmland, forest, and grasslands, this particular Dung Beetle was of the desert variety. Those that eat dung do not need to eat or drink anything else, because the dung provides all the necessary nutrients for them to grow and thrive. This Dung Beetle really zeroed in on the Pepe Soliz's dung. It gave him sustenance! The Dung Beetle moseyed off to call Pepe, the horny Caterpillar-like Poobah, to tell him that Maddox would have the million dollars soon.

I Hate That Fucking Guy

❋❋

It had been almost two weeks, at this point, since Maddox had heard from the Grasshopper. The Grasshopper had hopped away! In full pursuit of information about the Grasshopper, Maddox landed in Philadelphia and jumped a cab to the hotel. He would have taken a car service, but his smart phone battery was dead. As a result, he couldn't use his ride-hailing app and the ride was more expensive than it should have been and the cab was not as clean as it should have been. Once he got into the cab, he plugged in his smart phone which immediately started to take an electric charge into its battery – the Endless Content device was powering up and resuming operation. The digital device started buzzing and whirring and beeping and glowing as it came back to life to deliver messages, information and, of course, the flow of Pozz. He put his earbuds in and was playing his own music stream on his smart phone once the battery hit three percent charged. He didn't feel like engaging in small talk with the driver, not today. Maddox sang along, but only in his head.

> Yeah, Johnny Cash helped me get out of prison
> Long before Rodriguez stole that goat
> I've been the Rhinestone Cowboy for so long, I can't remember
> And I can do you every song, Hank Williams ever wrote

The cabbie dropped him at the hotel out by the old Italian section of Philadelphia. Maddox grabbed a quick ice tea on the way in the door, and also guzzled down a bottle of water. He was thirsty after the flight and felt dehydrated. Quick shower, change and another cab to a classic Italian restaurant where he met up with George Korpine and Steve McCartney, the father of Paul McCartney, the soul-less Grasshopper.

The TENACIOUS projects had reached a crisis point.

For over a week, Maddox called and sent messages to the Grasshopper every day. He got no response. He got no acknowledgment. Maddox could not reach the 'Hopper, not at all. A few more days went by with no sign of the Grasshopper, whatsoever. After numerous phone calls and text messages, Maddox decided that it wasn't productive to call the Grasshopper anymore. He had hopped off, apparently!

Maddox called TENACIOUS' lawyer a few times as well. Roland Stanton, the same old boomer lawyer that Maddox had spoken with on the phone while he was at the boomer barbeque in Jackson Hole. The guy that was supposed to be doing the paperwork for all of the TENACIOUS companies and projects. The Silverfish!

The Silverfish, like any shit-tier lawyer would, fielded a couple of Maddox's calls, and billed TENACIOUS for the time, but he was only able to muster comments such as "hurr durr, Maddox, errr hurr durr, I don't know I can't reach Paul McCartney either. Hurr durr, errr, I'm not sure what's going on."

"Roland, can I get the TENACIOUS files sent to me so I can have another lawyer look at options for pursuing McCartney for his unfulfilled promises?" asked Maddox.

"Errr, hurr, durr, I don't know about that Maddox, Paul McCartney is my client too, err hurr durr."

"Wait, what?" asked Maddox.

"Yeah, err, Paul McCartney is my client too and those files are privileged."

Maddox saw where that was going and ended the conversation.

Maddox alternated between rage and worry. He woke up for at least an hour in the middle of every night – the hour of failure. Maddox had called this meeting in Philadelphia a week before with George Korpine, who had been promised an executive-level employment role as chief operating officer of TENACIOUS golf. In turn, George, called Steve McCartney. Steve had been very friendly with George Korpine over the years and was a supportive sponsor of Korpine's small golf tour, Philly Hole Fanatics.

The lunch was ready to begin. Everyone settled into their chair. Maddox had a stunned look of disbelief on his face. George Korpine had a look of amazement. Steve McCartney, who was usually a nice guy, today had a disdainful demeanor – anger mixed with some embarrassment for his drug-addled, fucked up son. He looked like he was about eighty years old. Steve was wearing a one hundred thousand dollar watch and dressed in a sharp Italian suit. His father's company, PartDok, was a powerhouse and Steve, like Paul, projected the image that he had all the money in the world.

After everyone greeted each other with the standard hellos and how are yous, they kind of looked around the table. Maddox put his smart phone in his jacket pocket. McCartney put a pen and notepad on the table.

George cut the silence, this wasn't the kind of lunch where there would be a lot of small talk.

"I can't believe this whole thing turned out to be bullshit. I can't believe it's taken all this time and Paul hasn't come through on one thing. Not a damn thing," said George.

"You don't know my son," said Steve McCartney. "He's a God-damned liar. He's a liar."

After Steve said this, the statement hung in the air. Everyone soaked it in. Saint Augustine argued that there is a difference between someone who tells a lie and someone who is a liar. A liar takes delight in lying, rejoicing in the falsehood itself. Paul McCartney, according to his father, was a liar.

"I don't know how this happened? Why would anyone do that? What was the purpose of lying to all of us?" Maddox asked. Maddox was asking rhetorically, but holding out just a little bit of hope that someone would have an answer.

"I lost a ton of time and my reputation is fucked. I went to bat for TENACIOUS. I was out there promoting it like it was real," said George.

"What did he promise you guys for TENACIOUS?" Steve McCartney asked.

"Three million in funding, just for expanding the golf event series," said George.

"That's only one part of it. Also, the TENACIOUS Training facility, wrestling, tennis academy, and other things," said Maddox. "It was a bunch of projects. Every week, sometimes every day, there's a new excuse for why the funding doesn't arrive."

"Yep. He's a God-damned liar," added Steve.

"So is the lawyer for TENACIOUS. Roland Stanton. He's covering for Paul and he won't turn over the TENACIOUS files. He says he didn't document any of the pledges Paul made."

"I remember when you went out to meet with them about TENACIOUS," said Korpine. "Obviously I was involved in the golf side. He offered me a job as the chief operating officer. Then, he totally fucked me. He strung me along for almost two years. It has to be bullshit. He's not all of a sudden going to start coming through now."

"Yeah, I guess the golf division turned out to be total bullshit. Just like the other parts like the training facility. And a tennis academy. We just went to Spain to do that deal. I'm not sure how I'm going to tell Sporting Barcelona it was fake," said Maddox.

"When was the meeting with the lawyer?" asked Steve McCartney. "I can't believe this shit. I can't believe it."

"It was well over a year ago. That's how long this has been going on. I can get you the exact dates and all the paperwork. Your son attended the meeting and promised he would provide the funding for all of the TENACIOUS projects. He said that he inherited PartDok and that's where he was going to get the money. He always said that money was not the issue, then he would yell 'let's do this.' He had all these little catch phrases," said Maddox.

"He's such a God-damned liar. He didn't inherit my dad's company, PartDok. He didn't inherit that company. My brother in law,

Marty, inherited it and runs it. I get cash allowances from it because my dad didn't think I was business-like enough to inherit it and run it. It pissed me off at the time, but I have to admit that my dad was right. He knew I liked to drink too much and chase women too much to be the guy," said Steve.

"Take Mr. McCartney through the detail, would ya? Maddox, what were the companies called?" asked George.

"The companies were TENACIOUS Performance and TENACIOUS Crowd Sports. TENACIOUS Crowd Sports was to promote various specific sporting events throughout the country. TENACIOUS Performance was a company that was set up to develop an athletic training facility in Phoenix. A separate company was also created for wrestling," said Maddox.

"That's consistent with what he told me," added George Korpine.

"It doesn't surprise me at all," said Steve as he angrily shook his head. The corners of his mouth curled up with anger as he continued speaking. "He's such a liar. Everything he says is a God-damned lie. I am so embarrassed that he's my son."

"Didn't you start a ton of work on that training facility, Maddox?" asked George "Obviously, I was focused on the golf project."

"We hired architects and consultants. We wrote up all the plans and worked on the location. Paul even submitted a formal bid of almost two million dollars for land and a building for the facility. But, after the owner of the location made a counter offer, Paul disappeared. He never responded to the counter."

"He was probably in rehab," said Steve McCartney.

"Wait, what? Rehab?" said Maddox.

"Oh, yeah. Paul has been to rehab like five times. At the Pinkerton Facility, they give discounts for return customers, ten percent," said the Grasshopper's father, Steve McCartney.

"Oh, that's cool," said George, nodding his head.

"Five times?" said Maddox. "So does he get fifty percent off or does the discount stay steady at ten percent?"

"I don't know, but it's a good question," said Steve.

There was a ten second pause in the conversation. Maddox suddenly floated above the trees, not worrying about the details of the Pinkerton Facility discount any longer. He floated above the trees and he could see the TENACIOUS forest for the first time. A wave of stunning realization came over him. He was sure he had been hoaxed by the Grasshopper.

Maddox sat there in stunned silence.

"Anyway, he always goes to the Pinkerton Facility — it's one of the best rehab places in the world. Rudy Pinkerton's an old buddy of mine here in Philly. We used to bet on the ponies together when we were kids."

"Oh, great! I'm screwed," said Maddox, finally.

"Yeah, when he goes there he just disappears for a few weeks. It's nuts."

It all registered with Maddox. It all clicked. The delays, the erratic behavior, the excuses, the promises, the catch phrases, the big talk. Now, rehab. Taken together, it hit Maddox. Maddox gulped. He winced, shook his head slightly. He breathed. He blinked. He soaked it in. Maddox had, every so often, feared that the entire TENACIOUS project might be an elaborate hoax. A fake. Now, he was certain that it was.

"Holy shit! Wait, what? Are you serious?" Maddox asked, with a stunned look.

"I hate to tell you, but this whole time and all this shit was fake? All the TENACIOUS projects," said George.

"It has to be. It's gone on too long."

"He's such a God-damned liar," said Steve.

"I also see his computer browser open to a site that has a bunch of hookers on it. It's like he doesn't even know that other people can see what's on his screen," said George.

"I overheard him talking to one while I was on the phone with him one time. He had told me to tell his wife he was with me if she asked. Then, he asked the girl he was with if the doctor was in. I heard her say, yeah, I'm the head doctor then the line clicked off," Maddox said.

"No shit?" said George.

"Yeah, he said, hey baby is the doctor in?" said Maddox.

"He did?"

"Yeah, and I don't think that bitch was a doctor at all," said Maddox.

Everyone paused. Disbelief engulfed the table.

"Back up. I have to understand this. So, you two were working on all this shit for months and months, or years, and he never came through on what he was supposed to do?" asked Steve McCartney.

"Not only us. There were five other people, at least, working on the TENACIOUS facility concept, including meeting with potential vendors, sponsors, strategic partners and employees, as well as scouting numerous possible locations for the site of the training facility. That's just one other example of how people were affected by this guy."

"He did the same thing to Tony Capote."

"We can get Tony on the phone right now if we want."

"Okay."

Maddox dialed Tony on his smart phone and put the call on the phone's loudspeaker, real quick. The restaurant was buzzing loud enough that it wasn't out of place or disturbing for Maddox to place the call.

"Hey, Tony."

"What's up my man?" said Tony Capote.

"Quick question, how much did Paul McCartney claim he was going to fund into the TENACIOUS Wrestling program?"

"Two million dollars to get the series started. To be honest, most series start with a lot more than that but that's what was said," replied Tony.

"Yep that's consistent with what I was just saying. That's all I needed to hear. Thanks for picking up, man."

"I'll catch you later, brother."

Maddox hung up the call with Tony Capote.

"So he lied to that guy too?" asked Steve.

"Guess so," said George.

"So maybe this whole thing was a hoax? I can't figure it out. Why would he do that?" said Maddox.

"Something's wrong with him," said Steve.

"I feel stupid for believing the offer he made to me was real," added George. "I feel stupid for spending that much time on this project. TENACIOUS Golf. What a joke!"

"Well, he fooled a lot of people, including me. It wasn't only you. I spent a lot of time on the projects and am still dealing with the fallout from all the projects still sitting there, doing nothing. It wasn't only me, either. A lot of people were fooled. I guess they are fake projects. What other conclusion can I draw? This is so fucked up," Maddox said, looking stunned and downtrodden.

There was a full ten second pause at the lunch. No one made a sound.

"I'm so embarrassed he's my son," said Steve McCartney.

The conversation wore on.

"Why would he do that?" George asked at one point.

"Who knows," volunteered Maddox with a shrug. "That's the thing about this whole TENACIOUS thing. Why did he do that? Why did he fake all this shit? He didn't have to do that. I don't know why someone would do that."

Steve McCartney chimed in, "he's a liar, that's why. He doesn't care about anyone else. This is what you have to realize about that guy. He doesn't care how this makes anyone else feel. He doesn't care what happens as a result of his lies. He doesn't care about you, Maddox, or you, George and he never will. He doesn't care about anyone. Not you guys, not his wife. Not me. Not his mom. Nobody."

"This whole thing is insane," said George.

"This is a huge problem," said Maddox. "Everyone knows about TENACIOUS and they are going to think I'm full of shit."

"I wish he wasn't my son. I hate that fucking guy," said the Grasshopper's father.

"Why would he do that? Why make this whole thing up?" asked Maddox, again.

"I hate that fucking guy!" repeated Steve McCartney.

The lunch wore on for another hour. More conversation was had by all. More disbelief. Maddox participated in the conversation, but he had basically checked out at this point. He just sat there, thinking about the damage done by the 'Hopper. He had spent a lot of time on the TENACIOUS projects. And a lot of money. Maddox was reeling. The only rational takeaway now, looking objectively at everything the 'Hopper did, was that the projects were fake. The Grasshopper was never going to do these projects. He just used TENACIOUS to status signal in places like Jackson Hole. So he could claim he was involved in sports — a sexy industry. That was the only explanation that Maddox could come up with, and it floored him.

TENACIOUS was fake. A scam. A hoax. A joke. A prank. A racket. A swindle. A run-around. A trick. Maddox couldn't believe it, but here he was. He would have plenty more time and reason to agonize over TENACIOUS and its aftermath, but for now his thoughts turned another huge problem.

Maddox Malone still needed to find over three hundred thousand dollars more to give to Pepe to make his rape victim, April Tilney, go away.

Mattress King

❖❖

The lunch with Steve McCartney and George Korpine had the same effect as a bucket of cold water poured on Maddox's face. A steaming dump taken right on his doorstep, noxious and discouraging. It was piss right in his face, the piss of a diseased and decrepit raggedy old bum. Instead of the lingering doubt, he now had certainty that the Grasshopper had hopped off and wouldn't be doing what he promised. Maddox was totally fucked on TENACIOUS. How could it be otherwise?

His smart phone buzzed and whirred. A bit of good news! Grover Giles, the father of the Malone Agency intern Niko, had been able to locate a private lender for Maddox for the last three hundred twenty thousand dollars he needed, so Maddox could give Pepe Soliz a million bucks and he could pay off April Tilney. Grover had confirmed that the wire would be going out that same day. Maddox, after selling a condo and some stocks, together with this loan, would have over a million dollars in readily available cash for the Poobah. Okay, that's a relief, Maddox thought.

With the Pepe Soliz money in hand, Maddox had to get back to working on things with a chance of productive output. So, he decided to review the status of the post-bankruptcy Platform scene. He knew that his old contracts weren't coming back. Nathan Lawsin had flushed everything and the Platform was not operating.

Maddox decided that he would hustle to catch the next flight out of Philadelphia and head out to Manhattan Beach. He had been there so many times when he was building the sport of Platform Volleyball the first time around. It certainly wouldn't feel the same after the Platform Volleyball bankruptcy. With no active contracts and no meaningful events taking place on the Platform, it was left for dead. It had flatlined! There was no buzz. No revenue. There was nothing going on. That said, Maddox decided that he would survey the ruins of the Platform, as if it were a modern day Roman Coliseum.

He got in a cab and told the driver to head to Philly International Airport. The sky was a dusty blue with a smattering of clouds. A little breeze blew. It was a nice afternoon. He arrived at the airport, made his way quickly through ticketing and the expedited security line. He checked his bag to Los Angeles and headed for one of the airport bars. He sat down and ordered a vodka and soda with a lime. There was a man two stools away, watching a tennis match. Maddox shook his head since the match made him think of Sporting Barcelona and the disappointment of the TENACIOUS projects. On a whim, and on his third vodka and soda, he decided to send a text message to the Grasshopper, one more time.

"PAUL, WHERE ARE YOU? I MET WITH YOUR DAD, STEVE, AND HE TOLD ME ABOUT YOUR STAYS IN DRUG REHAB. WHAT THE FUCK IS GOING ON? WHERE THE FUCK IS THE MONEY FOR TENACIOUS? IS TENACIOUS FAKE? IS TENACIOUS A HOAX? SAY SOMETHING YOU FAGGOT! MADDOX."

Maddox's flight was uneventful. He woke up in the Los Angeles. Everything screeched to a halt while he regained his bearings and woke himself out of his sleepy haze. After a few minutes, his senses, thankful for the extra rest, were very sharp. He put the book he had been reading, the *Moviegoer* by Walker Percy, back into his shoulder bag — He was fascinated by Binx and Kate and had read about fifty pages of the book before he fell asleep. He put his earbuds in his ears and sang along as he walked out of the terminal.

> Someone's gonna tell you lies
> Cut you down to size
> Don't do me like that

Maddox made it out to the curb and jumped in the car that was waiting for him. He made a quick stop to drop off his bag at his hotel, leaving it with the bellman so he could check in later in the day, and then he made his way out to Manhattan Beach's Fourteenth Street volleyball courts in the same car. After he was dropped off, he walked briskly down to the sand courts where Lacy Stratton usually practiced. With the

Platform closed down, she practiced on the regular sand. He watched for a while, the balls going back and forth, the sand blurring into the Pacific. Volleyball may have been okay to play, thought Maddox, but it was really boring to watch. Bored with the volleyball itself, he glanced around and saw a gaggle of surfers paddling out to catch waves. It was a hazy day. It was a good day, a beautiful day, despite everything! He looked a little further in the distance, and saw the Platform. It was still there, looking deserted. Maddox shook his head as he was flooded with memories of his past deals.

ii

A few miles away, a wild scene was playing out with the Bedbug. Lacy had been hurt financially by the Platform bankruptcy which erased a lot of her income. She also had started a clothing line, called Platform Vibe, which failed miserably. She wasted about six hundred thousand dollars on Platform Vibe. Also, there was additional stress in the family because Danny Duffer's transition wasn't going well. In fact, the transition was going very poorly.

You see, Danny had become a girl, Danielle, two years ago, but she had also become depressed and suicidal. Since Danielle had become a girl, she had really been hit hard by all of the institutional sexism and discrimination in the country. The sexism and discrimination was prevalent in all areas of life, Danielle thought. In addition to those things, Danielle also perceived misogyny everywhere — and, following her transition, her wages at the grocery store had instantly been reduced by almost thirty percent, without negotiation. They told her it was a performance-based adjustment, but Danielle was convinced otherwise. Danielle was in a bad place, mentally - and she was extra confused because, although she had become a girl, she still had a penis as if she were a boy - and she was having a hard time with that thing. It was always there and she often felt threatened and menaced by it. Todd and Barb had divorced by this time, so they were not really any help to Danielle. Danielle asked her brother Carlton Duffer for help — she needed money to eat and to buy drugs — and when Danielle asked Carlton for money, naturally, the Bedbug asked his wife Lacy Stratton. These factors, combined with the birth of several offspring, extra mouths to feed, conceived with the Bedbug, led to intense feelings of financial stress for Lacy.

So, a few weeks after the Bedbug had been released from rehabilitation, Lacy had asked the Bedbug to get a real job. Previously, Carlton Duffer, the Bedbug, had masqueraded around, for years, as a Platform Volleyball player, but the reality was that his travel and training expenses in connection with the sport outweighed his modest semi-professional earnings. Lacy couldn't afford to pay for the roughly forty year old Carlton Duffer to play around on the Platform any longer. The Bedbug, fresh out of rehab, feared that he would be rooted out of his infestation if he did not comply with Lacy's request, interviewed for a number of sales jobs in the Los Angeles. The Bedbug received employment interest from a large mattress store chain, Mattress Kings, which called him back for an interview. His interview went poorly — because Carlton Duffer was a fucking idiot — but Mattress Kings desperately needed to increase its sales force. They were in a pinch. The manager hemmed and hawed a bit, but ultimately offered Carlton Duffer a job in the sales department. All the Bedbug had to do was pass a drug test and he could start selling mattresses.

But the drug test, that was the catch! That was the rub! The Bedbug had been getting high on the Dragon and the Moose almost every day since he got out of rehab. His face showed just a bit of panic when the manager told him about his drug test. Lacy had just spent forty thousand dollars for his rehabilitation stay. He couldn't admit to her that he was hitting the Dragon and the Moose every chance he got. He was in a bind!

After a couple hours of panic, he gathered himself. He called his friend, a stoner named Tanner, and told him about his predicament.

"Hey man, I got an issue that I need help with, yo," he said with his twang. "Ner, ner, ner."

"Oh, hey bro, what can I do you for, he-he," said his friend, Tanner. Tanner was a skinny, soy-fed pothead with a concave chest and a scraggly, punchable face.

"Well I got to go get the old job going and I got an offer from a mattress store — you know Mattress Kings ner ner they got that ad on the teee-veeee — but I have to pass a drug test. I can't pass it, bro. I can't. I've been hitting the dragon and the moose. And I can't tell the wifey because, ner ner, because well dude the wifey just paid for my rehab from the last time I got caught hitting the dragon, the moose and the yoga instructor. Ner ner ner! Ner ner ner!" the Bedbug said as he laughed uncontrollably.

"Oh shit, I got you bro! I got your back, I'm on the attack."

"What can I do?" asked the Bedbug. "Ner, ner."

"Just go to the smoke shop on Twelfth Street. You know Julio? I'll call them and have them set aside some stuff for you. We're gonna beat that test using fake piss, brosie. That's what we're gonna do. I'll call them and they will have all the instructions for you. This shit is easy, man. I got it booked, just watch."

"Okay, thanks man. I love you bro. Ner, ner. Can't wait to hang with you at Coachella, broseph. Ner, ner, ner. Ner!"

Carlton Duffer was laughing hysterically at the end, with his distinctive laugh. His face shined and he smiled broadly. His lip crooked out.

The Bedbug scrambled over to the smoke shop, while Tanner called in the order. When he arrived, they had what he needed. A plastic packet of fake piss attached to a long, winding leg strap. The guy working at the shop, who went by the nickname of Rory, showed him how to administer the pack, attach it to his leg, and ultimately wizz the piss right out of the main tube. Pissss! Pissss! A big smile crossed the Bedbug's face and he rubbed his hands together. He crooked his bottom lip out as much as he could.

"So that's all I have to do?" asked the Bedbug.

"That's exactly it, except one more thing," said Rory.

"What's that, broseph?"

"You have to microwave the piss. Don't boil it though. Just get it to a hundred degrees. Don't burn yourself."

"Okay, how hard can that be? I got you bro. Ner, ner, ner."

"What do you need this for, anyway?" asked Rory.

"I got to pass a drug test to work over at Mattress Kings. I just need to work there for a little bit until my wife Lacy gets off my back. But I've been getting wacked out and busted up every day since I got out of rehab so I can't pass without your help. So here I am, ner, ner, ner."

It was the early afternoon, and the Bedbug, a nocturnal creature, was groggy, so he drank some coffee to get himself moving. He also hit the Moose, just once, real quick.

While the Bedbug was procuring the piss, Maddox and Lacy were talking some business. She took a five minute break from her practice to go over everything with Maddox. They hadn't connected with each other to talk about the Platform, other than by text messages, in weeks. Maybe even a couple of months. Five minutes was incredibly short, but it is what they had — and Maddox had flown all the way in for this conversation and also to have a brainstorm about the Platform. To see if he could come up with a magical idea for a Platform resurrection. Given the sad state of affairs in the sport, the conversation was rapid.

"Hey, yeah, that bankruptcy was really shitty news, but there's nothing we can do about it. We have to move forward. Obviously, Nathan was free to file and we don't really get a say in the matter. We just have to see what happens."

"Yeah, I lost a lot of cash based on the termination of my personal services agreement. It sucks because I just closed down Platform Vibe and I lost a ton of money on that too. And Carlton isn't working, yet. You know he was just in rehab. Jeez, Maddy. This sucks."

"I know, Lacy. It's just tough right now. I know what you lost because I lost your contract and also the ones I did for the other guys, and that will not be matched any time soon. There's no money in

Platform any more. I've got to be honest, I think if it comes back at all it will take a few years. That's just what I think."

"My husband, you know, Carlton, was saying something about minivan deals? What do you think about that?"

Maddox was confused.

"Like a sale on a minivan? I would just look on-line."

"No, no, no. Carlton was saying that he felt like, since I'm a mom, that a minivan company might pay met to be in a commercial for them?"

"Fuck Carlton Duffer!" thought Maddox. "That guy is a fucking idiot."

"Oh, oh. Umm, err, well, I don't know. I know most of the marketing people at the car companies and I don't think there's a minivan endorsement out there. Not for you, not since the Platform collapsed. I just don't think that's out there. They use actors and models for their ads, every time."

Lacy stared at Maddox and Maddox could see what he thought was disagreement in her eyes.

Maddox continued, "I don't agree with Carlton. I've tried with car companies and they just aren't interested. Sorry Lacy."

"Oh, that's not what my hubby Carlton says. He says we can get a seven-figure minivan endorsement deal, with a commercial. He says it's a great fit for me and the kids. He wants to be in the commercial too."

Maddox thought of the crook in Carlton Duffer's bottom lip. Maddox let a few seconds of silence pass and he took a breath.

"Okay cool. I'm sure Carlton Duffer knows what he's talking about. Why don't you have him make some phone calls?"

"Yes. Carlton is also talking to Brett Favre's agency and they are offering to work for me. They did so much for Favre and others. They say maybe we have overlooked some opportunities?"

Maddox paused. He pictured the Bedbug's ugly face and crooked lip. Maddox laughed, inside only, he didn't make a sound outwardly.

"Listen, I say go for it. We had a good run! More than ten years. If Favre's people can find something I can't then you guys should go for it. Give it a shot," said Maddox.

There was a pause and the conversation became tense.

"You don't seem hopeful anymore. You have no enthusiasm for the Platform, not like you used to. We need to grow our sport of Platform Volleyball."

"Well, I'm not hopeful — not at the moment. Not for Platform Volleyball. Nobody wants to watch it and that's a fundamental problem. The only thing that's worse than losing hope is hiding it from yourself — I have to be honest with myself and with you. I just don't know if Platform Volleyball can make it back."

Maddox paused. He wasn't trying to be mean. He was trying to come across as matter-of-fact. Maddox loved and respected Lacy. She had always been good to Maddox and he liked her. For that reason, he didn't want his anger to shine through. There just wasn't room for Lacy, Carlton Duffer and Maddox Malone on the Platform. Maddox had decided he would move on and not work on Platform Volleyball deals any more.

He continued, "There is no respect for the sport in the marketplace. The bottom feeders are out. People like Favre's group — no offense — have never worked on the Platform but they say they are gonna do this, gonna do that. They're not gonna to do shit. Pardon my French."

More of a pause, more tension. Maddox hoped he hadn't been too blunt. He wanted to be honest, but he didn't want to hurt Lacy's feelings.

"Forget all of that. Look, we took a swing for the fence. We had some big successes. With the time-frame of a rebuild from this bankruptcy, things don't look great. I'm not saying you can't rebuild and do your thing. You can! I know your hubby Carlton Duffer wants to get involved in your management — your dad told me. And he wants to use Favre's group, he wants to work with them. That's fine with me."

"Okay, then this is goodbye, for now?"

"It's goodbye, for now, Lacy. But you can always call me with questions or whatever."

"Okay, Madd. I'm going to get back out there for some more exciting bump, set, spike action. We've got to take our sport of Platform Volleyball to the next level. This sport has so much potential. We just need to grow it. I'll catch up with you later. Love you, Maddy. Thanks for the chat."

"Thanks Lacy. I'll catch you later," said Maddox.

iii

Maddox walked off the sand at precisely the same moment that the Bedbug, eyes darting, was making his way into the office area of the drug testing company that handled such matters for Mattress Kings. My how the Bedbug wanted this job! Carlton Duffer wanted to be a Mattress King! The Bedbug had the piss bag that Rory had arranged for him stashed in his windbreaker pocket. He asked the lady at the front desk if he could go wash his hands in the kitchen area. She pointed the way. He was sweating, feeling heavy nerves. Breathe! He breathed in and out. He breathed in and out. He walked steadily, stiffly, straight ahead.

The Bedbug made his way to the kitchen, balancing on his little insect feet and looking around surreptitiously. He pulled the fake piss out of his jacket pocket and put it in the microwave. He entered one minute on the timer and hit the button marked "Cook". He licked his lips. He rubbed his brow. His bottom lip crooked out. It jutted! The piss was heating up. Before long, he would be selling mattresses, maybe even two at a time. He knew it! Fifteen seconds went by as the microwave heated up the piss. Then fifteen more. Then fifteen more. The Bedbug was rocking back and forth, looking excited and nervous.

Luckily for the Bedbug, the receptionist had not suspected anything when he walked in. Like most people, she never imagined that the Bedbug might be in the kitchen heating up fake piss. But he sure was. He was! And the microwave was in its final stretch. Ten. Nine. Eight. Seven. Six. Five. Four. Three. Two. One. The Bedbug was ecstatic. His plan was working perfectly. He quickly grabbed the bag of piss and scurried from the kitchen to the bathroom. He hustled out of the kitchen. He quickly strapped the package onto his leg. With that process complete, he immediately walked back into the lobby.

There was a problem. A big problem! As the liquid sloshed around in the bag, the temperature evened out. For some reason, one portion of the liquid, just more than half of it, had become incredibly hot in the microwave. Scalding to the touch. Liquid magma! And as he arrived in the waiting room, the Bedbug felt the micro-waved piss was burning his leg. It was burning him badly!

"Yowee, mother fucker. Yowee! Oh that's hot. Oh that's hot! Oh that's ho-o-o-t!" said the Bedbug intensely, but also as quietly as he could.

The Bedbug locked his face down, making no outward expression indicating pain. He locked his face down tighter than Fort Knox. He crooked his lip to about thirty seven degrees and he stayed silent and steadfast. That didn't work, so he crooked it a little more. It jutted out at the strongest angle he had ever made — almost forty five degrees. Somehow, maybe thanks to the crook in his lip, the Bedbug didn't scream!

Suddenly, Carlton Duffer couldn't take it anymore, so he finally winced. He started to sweat even more. The bag felt like it was searing into his leg. Burning the flesh off the bone. He tried to grit his teeth and ignore the burn but quickly he was all done with ignoring. He imagined that the bag was melting his flesh like butter. He thought there would be permanent damage to that specific portion of his flesh. It was as hot as lava and it would not stop burning him until it had gone through his entire leg, even the bone, even the more stringy tendons and muscles. He was going to have a gaping hole in his leg! With a look of panic, he took his left hand and pulled the bag away from his leg to get some relief from the scalding liquid.

The searing stopped and Carlton Duffer's panicked face relaxed. But there was another problem now!

When he pulled the bag away from his leg, the pressure exerted by his hand squeezed the fake piss with enough force that a couple big squirts shot out of the tube. The fake piss was trickling down his leg, down his knee, down his calf. And that fake piss smelled exactly like fresh vinegar! His pants were getting wet. "Oh no, oh no, not this, not now!" said the Bedbug under his breath. He released the bag with his left hand and, once again, embraced the burn on his leg. He winced, then masked the wince with a smile. His lip crooked to forty degrees. Then it jutted to fifty degrees — the strongest angle he had ever created. There was nothing else he could do. Two minutes later, with the temperature in the piss bag calming down, settling down to bearable levels, his name was called.

"Carlton Duffer, please report to the front desk."

The liquid on his pants was noticeable, but the piss technician didn't happen to see the splotch. So, he was able to waltz into the room, squeeze the fake pee into the cup, and hand it to the technician. The piss technician put it into the instant reader. Bzzzzz. The piss came back clean!

The Bedbug said thank you, and walked out of the room. He walked out into the cool beach breeze, under the warm California sunshine, secure in the knowledge that the mattress sales job was his. He laughed. "Ner. Ner. Ner." He called Lacy, who didn't answer because she was practicing volleyball.

Carlton Duffer left her a voice mail.

"Hey baby, I got the job. I'm a fucking Mattress King! Ner, ner, ner."

Toxicity

❖❖

Carlton Duffer's incredible victory over the Mattress Kings' drug testing system contrasted sharply with Maddox's losing streak. The Bedbug had celebrated his new job by hitting the Dragon and the Moose. He was exhilarated! Maddox, in contrast, was finding new lows! Nothing was going right for Maddox! Maddox's smart phone rang and buzzed, and then it whirred and beeped as he stepped off the plane. He had flown back to watch Obadiah play a football game in New York. What could go wrong with that?

Well, it was Laura calling. Maddox grimaced and breathed in before answering. The last five phone conversations, maybe ten, between Maddox and Laura had been horrible, and when he was home they had barely been speaking to one another. They could hardly look at each other. In fact, he couldn't remember the last enjoyable, civil conversation that they had. This wasn't Omar's Chill Factor — this was the Ice Factor!

"Hey!" said Maddox.

Laura stayed silent on the other end of the line.

"Hello?"

Silence.

"Hello?"

More silence.

"Can you hear me?" Maddox asked. "Hello?"

"Hey," said Laura, sadly.

"Oh I didn't think you could hear me. I kept saying hello."

Laura didn't say anything back to Maddox. She sat on the other end of the phone in silence. What was this, a psy-op? Like last time? Maddox was walking through the airport in New York, going to get his checked bag. This was ridiculous. At this point, he thought she was trying to inflict pain on him. Make him miserable. Make him crack. To get to the trifecta of misery, she wasn't even going through stage one and stage two anymore. She went straight to aggressive silence!

"Are you there? Hello?"

Silence. Maddox couldn't take it anymore. He hung up the smart phone which made a dull beep.

Even though he knew the connection was fine, he composed a text message on his smart phone that said, "I think we have a bad connection. I couldn't hear anything. Grabbing my bag and heading to Obadiah's game. I'll call you later."

He added his name, sent the message and kept moving. As he walked toward baggage claim he was lost in his thoughts. He tried to block out all of his unpleasant and depressing thoughts. He wanted to view his situation in an advantageous and honorable light. He wanted to stay positive. He knew he was putting Laura in a tough position — everything was going haywire and he wasn't communicating. But he didn't see another way. He didn't see any way out except staying the course, going further in. With Maddox enduring everything

He hated the communication in his marriage. It was unbearable. It was ridiculous how awful it was. The silence was the worst, but when she spoke to him it was bad too. The edginess in her voice. The contentiousness of every comment. The derogatory tone. The monotone harping and lecturing. How was this sustainable? How had he gotten himself into this mess? He didn't know what to do about it. He was already neck deep in this mess.

Maddox grabbed his bag from the spinning luggage rack and walked out to his ride. He popped his earbuds in and sang along.

> The toxicity of our city, of our city
> New, what do you own the world?
> How do you own disorder, disorder?

He enjoyed that song and felt energized from it, but after if ended, almost on cue, the melancholy came back over him. He had good reason for these feelings, as everything seemed to be coming down on him all at once. He needed a positive situation, a positive development, a victory. He needed a win! He had been pushing for one for months now, and everything still seemed to be hurtling towards more disappointment. His mind rapidly reviewed everything again, for the one thousandth time. He was in a box. Everything was so painful. He had put the Grasshopper out of his mind for a couple days now. But he still had to deal with the TENACIOUS hoax. Why would anyone do that? It seemed impossible months before, but after the lunch in Philadelphia the illusions were breaking down. The building and land for the training facility was still not purchased. These projects were stagnant, a total standstill. The Grasshopper was still missing — three weeks with no contact. TENACIOUS was obviously a hoax.

Maddox's driver continued toward his hotel. Maddox was still deep in his gloomy thoughts as he approached the hotel. But everything changed in an instant. A sudden thought came to him, like a bolt of electricity, and it changed his entire mindset immediately. He remembered that he was sitting in the XtraShoog luxury suite for the Monday Night Football game that evening. At this thought, his mind cleared up, he realized that he could use some of the vodka and soda that would be in the suite to relax himself and gain some distance from all of his problems. Maddox realized that it was sad and alarming that this thought, the thought of drinking vodka at the football game, relaxed him, but there it was. He went with it. What choice did he have?

This thought put some hop into his step as he exited the car, thanked the driver and walked into the hotel. He wanted to take a quick shower and drop off his stuff and then head out to the Stadium. As he walked in to the hotel, he decided to stop for a vodka martini, straight up with a twist, at the hotel bar. This familiar place provided him with so much comfort! His heart beat with joy as he sat down and placed his order. The bartender delivered the drink with a friendly smile and the first sip hit his lips and it awakened his soul. He felt relaxed, he pushed the problems out of his mind as he took a deep breath. Another sip. Then another. He checked his smart phone. No call back or text from his wife. On the one hand, he felt apprehension about that since he had hung up on her and then sent a message to her from his smart phone and she simply hadn't responded. On the other hand, there was nothing to say, and he didn't want any more aggressive silence over the phone. Silence on messaging was one thing, and it was better than active silence during a call. He didn't want to endure the trifecta of misery. Not today.

Maddox sipped his martini and immediately his thoughts moved off of his main problems. With his mind off of the Caterpillar, the Grasshopper and the Platform and its Bedbug, Maddox felt a wave of relief come over his mind. Possibilities felt like they were opening back up. His imagination was firing back up. He loved that feeling, the feeling of openness and possibility spread out before him. He finished the martini in the next few minutes and then ordered and drank another one. It went down easy and his body and mind relaxed. A wave of euphoria came over him.

When he finished his second martini, Maddox paid his tab in cash since he had not checked in yet. Then he walked to the front desk, got his room key and went up to his room.

Immediately upon entering his room, he put his bags on the luggage stand and stripped off his clothes. He felt free, and wanted to be out of the clothes that he had traveled in. It always felt so good to take off airplane clothes. He pictured the little bugs — lice, gnats, whipper willows, that burrowed their way into his fabric on the plane. He wanted those clothes off! He walked around naked for a minute.

Maddox grabbed a pear out of the fruit basket that the hotel had placed in his room due to his status as a frequent guest. He ate it in five bites. Chew. Savor. Swallow. Chew. Savor. Swallow. Chew. Savor. Swallow. Chew. Savor. Swallow. Chew. Savor. Swallow. The pear was juicy and delicious. In fact, he couldn't believe the level of taste that came out of the fruit. He asked himself if the taste was real. It was bursting with flavor. Bursting! He shook his head in disbelief.

He thought about Pepe Soliz and how he was multiplying himself with any woman who would let him inside her. What if, due to overpopulation and unrestrained Third World reproduction, the planet could not keep up production on wonders like this fabulous, natural, yellowish-green pear? What if that happened? He turned the air conditioner lower, as the room felt stuffy and oppressive. Minutes later, he was in the shower scrubbing down to get cleaned up to head to the Hive Stadium for O-Bad's game. He soaped his armpits, he soaped his nicely-shaped pink, shaved balls, his ass, his stomach, his shoulders. He soaped everywhere, because it had to be done! He felt clean, he felt good.

The martinis had relaxed him quite a bit, but soon enough restless and fitful thoughts started to creep back into his mind. He realized that in spite of all the thoughts he directed toward his current set of circumstances, the problems that the circumstances entailed could not be unilaterally solved by Maddox. He simply could not solve these problems alone. This was difficult for him to accept. He had a hard time admitting that he couldn't fix, or handle, anything that happened. He was not in control of his own destiny, not on the matters that were bothering him and occupying his time and thoughts. Some of the decision-making capacity belonged to others. This was unsettling. He decided that he didn't like to be at the mercy of these people. He resolved that he would do something to change these circumstances.

But the resolution to do something was extremely frustrating, because he didn't know what he would do. "What can I do?" he thought. He wanted to resolve things, and fast. He was tired of everything being so touch and go. Everything had gone haywire.

His marriage? That was another question, entirely. He sat on his hotel couch and thought deeply, as deeply as he could, about his marriage. Inside the cell of his marital life, it was impossible to complete an innocuous conversation without anger and rancor. Therefore, it was impossible to get to the root of the matter and fix what was wrong. Since everything about it was wrong, it was impossible to have some sort of a foothold, or an angle, to approach and fix what was wrong. There was no place to put the wrench, the hammer or the screwdriver. There was no place to apply some duct tape or some glue since everything was in disrepair. With every day and every argument, with every angry conversation, the marital bonds weakened and the gap widened. They stopped thinking about each other, except when they had to. The thoughts, when they came, were all negative. The second negative thought was more negative than the first. And the third was more negative than the second. And so on. Whenever either of them thought of the other, energy was sapped, since negativity saps energy.

He and Laura were not on the same plane, not at all. Connection seemed impossible. The thought gnawed at Maddox deeply and it made him feel incredibly uncertain and unsettled. He had put so much time and emotional energy into being married, especially at first, and the feeling that his marriage was breaking down, day by day, was exasperating. Being married was such a large part of his identity, of his appearance and persona — even though he had to admit to himself, when he thought deeply about it, that the marriage was flagging. The breakdown felt bad and Maddox didn't see a solution. He was frustrated; he didn't know what to do. As more time went by, Maddox realized he had things to do and couldn't sit there thinking any longer.

So, he put on a tee-shirt, jeans and some tennis shoes. He was almost ready to head out to the Hive Stadium. He looked in the mirror to make sure everything was up to par. He had a quick thought. He needed to get himself to tone down his vodka and soda habit. He knew that. He knew, deep down, that he needed to consume fewer cocktails. But, he allowed himself to accept the notion that, as long as he could dial it back later, the vodka could help him get through this stretch of disappointment. Just a few more weeks, he told himself. He felt a surge of energy and good feeling. But tonight, Sunday night, it was going to be a football game and several more vodka drinks. What a combination! Reforging himself would have to start on another day. It would have to wait, again. Tranquilizers!

Maddox headed down to the lobby. Rather than head straight out to catch his ride, which he had ordered on his smart phone. He stopped off, again, at the hotel bar. He ordered another vodka martini straight up with a twist.

After he finished his third martini of the afternoon, he stepped outside to jump in a car. He put his ear-buds in his ears and waited.

Soon, he hopped in the black sedan and relaxed and listened to some music while the driver took him to the Hive Stadium. He sang along with Kurt Cobain.

> I'm so happy because today
> I've found my friends
> They're in my head

Maddox was excited for the game! O-Bad had been playing very well, and it would be fun to see him play in person. He felt a sense of serenity as he told himself that during the game, he would not allow himself to think about Pepe Soliz, Paul McCartney, Lacy Stratton, Laura Malone — or anything that was weighing on him heavily. He would enjoy the game — there was plenty of time to worry about that other stuff later.

It was in this mindset that he walked into the stadium for O-Bad's game. Maddox went in the gate. Up some stairs. Around a bend. Up an elevator. He entered the XtraShoog luxury suite, said hello to all the folks inside that he knew. He looked out on the stadium. There was a buzz. An energy. The vast mass of men and women in the stadium below the suite blurred in his eyes. The number seemed endless. The individual blended out of view. The Hive Stadium was appropriately named since it seemed to work like an ant colony. Everyone was seemingly buzzing around doing something. Drinking beer. Eating processed food. Urinating. Buying souvenirs. Checking and participating in social media on their smart phones. Smart phones were everywhere, of course — they were held out in front of almost everyone's face. It was almost as if the smart phone was a magnet, pulling its person behind it. Maddox though, wow, it's hard to tell if the person owns the smart phone or the smart phone owns the person.

Maddox went over to the bar area in the XtraShoog luxury suite. He mixed himself a vodka and soda. He made it crisp but not so strong that it would taste like rocket fuel — they had good flavor. The vodka brand in the suite wasn't good, but it was passable for a cocktail or two. It would serve the purpose that Maddox had in mind - escape by getting drunk, at least a bit drunk.

He sat down in his seat and watched the game. His smart phone kept buzzing and took a few minutes to respond to a few text messages. After thirty minutes or so, he got up and poured another vodka and soda. He sat down and took a sip. Then another. It went down easy, so he finished it and made another. The buzz felt good to Maddox.

Maddox, a bit drunk, focused back on the game as the second quarter started. On the first snap of the second quarter, the quarterback took the ball and rolled out to the right. The stadium, the hive, hummed with anticipation as the play started to develop. O-Bad was running a go route straight up the right sideline. The quarterback heaved the ball in O-Bad's direction. As O-Bad was crossing the ten yard line, he didn't have any separation from the defensive back. It looked like it would be a tough chance for a completion. But O-Bad was tracking the ball better than the defender and from the ten yard line to the five, his acceleration was causing him to break away from the defender. The defender, sensing that he was beat, grabbed O-Bad. It was an illegal grab, and the referees immediately started the process of pulling and throwing their yellow flags to call a pass interference penalty. That would have been a nice result and a big gain for the New York Ogres.

Right then, however, something magical happened. Magical! Something incredible. Something that caused almost every little bug, every super fan, many of whom had dedicated a large portion of their life to being an Ogres fan, to erupt in cheers. Many of the little bugs spent as much as thirty or forty hours a week consuming sports content. This was their moment! This was their time! This was what they lived for! As the yellow flags were flying, and as the defender was hurtling out of bounds, the ball was completing its downward arc. O-Bad stuck his right hand up and speared the ball as if it was a fish speared on a harpoon. The ball stuck in his gloved hand and both feet came down inside the boundary. The stadium hive erupted with cheers. Thousands of people sipped their beer while others screamed. Hundreds of preservative-laden hot dogs were bitten into, in celebration of the catch and the resulting touchdown. Beers were chugged. French Fries were stuffed down throats, sometimes ten at a time. Popcorn, in the form of Efficient-Pop, was stuffed and chomped. No one seemed to notice the taste of the vegetable oil. High fives were given and received. Everyone went wild, yelling, cheering, drinking and eating! The bugs were in an actual frenzy! The announcer could be heard on the television in the suite saying "that could be the greatest catch I've ever seen."

The XtraShoog luxury suite, which was filled with corporate types — econo-drones, econo-bots — was usually immune to the rattle and hum of the cheering and typical noise of the Hive Stadium. But not this time. The XtraShoog suite also went wild with cheering and high fives. Maddox's smart phone buzzed as it received dozens of text messages from people who saw the spectacular catch at home, on TV. Maddox shook his head with amazement. It was wild! It was the most incredible catch that Maddox had ever seen! He was thrilled for Obadiah. Maddox answered a few of the texts, including one from Major O.

Everyone was buzzing with excitement for a solid twenty minutes after the catch.

The big screen flashed to the owner's suite. A haggard, gray-skinned old man and a bloodless, drained old woman celebrated the catch with an awkward, stiff handshake. They tried to smile but the smiles looked like death stares. They looked so old, like skeletons with grayish skin hanging off of them. The owners' box looked like a crypt. When they noticed they were being shown on the large screen in the Hive Stadium, they tried to increase the size and enthusiasm of their smiles. Big, exaggerated plastic smiles covered their faces. They had reached maximum smile capacity — their smiles could not, physically, get any bigger. They looked almost ninety. Maddox, for a second, wondered why those two even care about something like a football catch. Their faces looked really happy, unless you looked at them carefully. Maddox thought "they are so old, do they even know what happened on the field?" It was strange to Maddox. When he looked carefully, their faces looked very empty. The smiles looked fake. Their faces looked sad. They looked like they were trying to mask their sadness and emptiness by smiling and celebrating a football catch.

That said, it might have been the greatest catch ever made in the sport. Maddox was happy for O-Bad. Heck, he was happy for himself and the Malone Agency. Catches like that would create tremendous opportunities to make money.

Maddox poured one more vodka and soda, but made this one a double — he drank it. By then, he was pretty hammered — and turned back to the game. He was getting on a seven a.m. flight the next day to go to a technology conference on the west coast — it was a place to mingle with potential sponsors and generally network. He wasn't looking forward to the long flight, but he hadn't seen his friend, Kiowa, in almost a year and was looking forward to that. The rest of the half of the football game went along without much fanfare. Maddox left at the conclusion of the half.

When he left, he sent a message to his recruit, O-Bad, from his smart phone.

"Great game, O-Bad. What an incredible catch. I'm on the early flight tomorrow so I'm gonna watch the second half from the hotel and I'll get in touch after my flight tomorrow."

Maddox hit send on the message so that it would be waiting on O-Bad's phone when he reached the locker room. He would talk to O-Bad and Major O some more tomorrow.

Maddox went back to his hotel. He ordered himself another vodka martini straight up with a twist, his fourth martini of the day, to go along with the four vodka sodas he drank at the XtraShoog luxury suite. It all added up, a little at a time, and Maddox was hammered.

After half an hour, he felt like retreating to his suite to relax. Buzzing, drunk, he decided he was done drinking. He had too much and he finally cut himself off! He signed off on his tab and walked to his room. Once inside, he opened a bottle of water and immediately drank half of it, starting the process of sobering up and hydrating. He shook his head at himself for getting drunk. But, he told himself, at least he wasn't worrying about everything. Not anymore.

He changed into an over-sized tee-shirt and a pair of gym shorts and laid down on his bed, sobering up. After half an hour, his mind was starting to sharpen. He was still buzzed, but he didn't feel drunk anymore. He opened the book he was reading, *A Brave New World*, by Aldous Huxley. He was at the part where the Director shows the boys hundreds of naked children engaged in sexual play and games like Centrifugal Bumble-puppy. One of the World Controllers introduces himself to the boys and begins to explain the history of the World State, focusing on the State's successful efforts to remove strong emotions, desires, and human relationships from society. Huxley feared that people would develop a brainless, empty culture, preoccupied with crap. Huxley realized that man had an almost infinite appetite for distractions. It was an ambitious book, and Maddox found it at least slightly interesting but found some of it cumbersome and annoying.

Maddox Malone thought about *A Brave New World* and the Pozz in the context of the game and the great catch by Obadiah. He was so happy for O-Bad. That was one of the best catches ever! Then, all of a sudden, he felt a wave of travel and alcohol induced fatigue come over him and he fell asleep.

Digital Facial

❋❋

It only took Kalli a few months to get back on her feet in Phoenix. She started saving money immediately, and she was living with her parents at first. She took a job as an assistant to a veterinarian — a vet tech. The vet was a guy named Dominic, who did mostly equine work. He was a Mormon and one of those painful-looking blonde guys with a flat, smashed face that looked like a dinner plate with some features painted on it. Kalli started hiking and walking, and riding horses again. She kept trimming down from her Oregon weight. She felt so much better. She was exercising and riding horses every day. She was visiting with her parents, regularly. Michael was in the rear-view mirror!

About this time, she decided that she wanted to move onto a ranch, where she could keep the two horses she bought and also board other peoples' horses. After searching for a couple of months, she found a ranch in North Phoenix and put some money down on it. She worked out a rent-to-own deal with the current owner. Before long, she was in there and things were looking up. She was excited!

On this particular morning, she trudged outside of her house at five thirty in the morning. She mucked a couple of stalls and then started the process of grooming her horse, Bistro, for a morning ride. She had kept her smart phone in her arm strap and it was streaming music through her earbuds and she sang along.

> Ain't gotta be alone to feel lonely
> I'm gonna turn off my phone, start catching up with the old me

She brushed Bistro, her big beautiful Argentinian gray thoroughbred, picked his hooves, put on his boots, strapped on his saddle and his bridle, and minutes later she mounted Bistro and took him out into the arena for a nice ride. He was overly energetic, and he kept trying to break into his cantor instead of holding a trot. He snorted and guffawed. But Kalli stayed alert and kept him in line. The early

Phoenix sun was glowing a soft yellow and the temperature was comfortable, something in the mid-sixties or upper-sixties, fahrenheit.

When Kalli had finished her ride, she had a nice rush from the exercise. Her body felt good!

But, soon thereafter, she fell into a state of despair. She was usually an optimist, she had always made the most of tough circumstances. But some things were nagging at her. Her life wasn't going how she wanted it to go in some important ways. Since she had returned to Phoenix after leaving Michael in Oregon, she had been focused on getting some money put away and getting situated in her own place. That was going well, because she was working with the veterinarian, boarding horses at her new place (her barn was filled even more quickly than she had hoped), and she was picking up bartending gigs once or twice a week to supplement everything and give herself some cushion, monetarily. Financially, she was doing fine. But she felt lonely. She felt empty. Also, she was drinking a lot. Somewhat out of habit and somewhat out of boredom. A vodka here and a margarita there. Beer too. Almost every day, a few drinks here and there at the local bars in Phoenix. She couldn't put a finger on what was missing.

She did know that she wanted something else and it was coming into better focus for her. She wanted to sing! She loved music and wanted to make some of her own. Even when she had been pursuing modeling and acting opportunities in Hollywood, in the back of her mind she had always preferred singing. She hadn't seen a path to be able to pursue music. She couldn't seem to break through. She would meet people here and there and try to form a band or a project. Or just jam. But the other musicians were unreliable and she couldn't seem to get a rhythm where she could get original music on paper and ultimately recorded.

There was a problem that Kalli seemed to encounter when she tried to put together a band. The guitar players were too horny to focus on music, they were always off chasing after some girl or other, even Kalli sometimes. The guitar players were not reliable. They would usually gig around playing cover tunes so they had money to buy whiskey and marijuana. Or coke or meth. After they gigged around for a while, usually with very limited success, they would usually burn out of the music scene and into a drug-induced stupor. Rather than wanting to make country or rock music, they were always trying to make music of another kind. This was frustrating for Kalli, who never had trouble getting attention from men in that regard. She didn't want that kind of attention, though, not now. Not from just any guy. Not from some scraggly guitarist — you're not Jimmy Page dude, she thought. She wanted to make an album. She wanted to sing. She wanted to be in a band.

Kalli's budget, after her move to the ranch, was tight but she was not overly stressed by it. She was getting by. The ranch was nice and, to her, having lived in various places and having gotten by, at times, it felt like a luxury to Kalli.

"You're over-thinking this," Kalli told herself when she thought, carefully about her future in music. "You need to get some things on paper and the rest will come together. You need to put yourself in a position to sing. The rest will take care of itself. Trust me. Trust me. It's going to happen."

She gave herself a full pep-talk in her mind. She was staying positive. She tried to maintain her confidence in connection with her hopes of recording. She wrote in her journals so that she had material for her music. She worked hard on her ranch, and also as a vet tech, and with the bartending shifts here and there. Things were going fine. She needed to get to the next level.

"You're never going to be happy if your only definition of success is to create a best-selling album. Maybe it will happen and maybe it won't," Kalli thought to herself. She wanted it to happen but she didn't want to have any bouts with disappointment based on the timing and the windy road that would lead to recording the album. She had many fits and starts before and she didn't want her goal of making music to become a negative force in her life. She didn't want the concept of the album to become a source of dismay. She had to give it oxygen but also she had to let it happen when it happened.

So, Kalli felt herself moving between two worlds. There was her physical world, centered around her little ranch. A nice, practical way of life. Physical work. Enjoyment of her animals. Her parents and friends, and occasionally a guy that she went on a date or two with, would come over to the ranch to see the horses, play with the dogs, and see her ducks, who she called Thelma and Louis. Things felt free and easy. Things felt open. This morning had been peaceful, tranquil. She had a great ride on her horse! The chores around the ranch were done and she was had time to go run some errands before heading east into Phoenix to do a four hour shift as a bartender. She figured that would net her about an extra hundred and fifty bucks. She was getting better in terms of her approach conserving her resources. Physically, she was strong from all the outside work she was doing.

The other world was the idealized world of music. Concerts, records, albums, karaoke even. This was her free time. She would go into a record store and pick out a few albums at random. To see if there was a world of music that she was missing out on. She loved country and rock but wanted to know about what people were recording in other genres. She still had an old transistor radio that her dad had given her many years before. She played it often, because it brought back good memories. She knew that she wanted to do music, always. She was enchanted with music. Her music would take her where it chose to take her, that's the bottom line. She didn't know where that would be!

ii

Five hundred miles away from Kalli and her horse and music thought-fest, Maddox was walking into a tech marketing summit. He had been invited by Kiowa Wilmenton. Kiowa was a consultant who worked for himself, but was also an alumnus of a big microchip corporation. Maddox and Kiowa had worked out a large sponsorship deal several years before for one of Maddox's clients. It was a win-win where the microchip company had received some nice publicity and Maddox and his clients had received a nice amount of cash. Everyone had enjoyed the deal and Maddox and Kiowa had become friends. This morning, Maddox had made the early flight from New York to Los Angeles. After he arrived, he jumped in a waiting car which he rode out to the convention center.

He walked into the convention center and he was amazed by the environment. Thousands and thousands of people moving around, checking out devices, smart phones, computers, checking out technology. Something was off! He walked into the main room and there was a man, a Bug Wrangler, who took the stage and started into his presentation. He was showing how the newest model smart phone, which Endless Content was calling the Super Duper Terminal 6 Double G, would unlock by scanning its user's face. The phone was being released to the mass market that day - and it was being introduced to the world at this conference! Facial recognition!

This particular Bug Wrangler was named Tim, and he was on the stage to push a new smart phone, to push it hard to a very receptive audience. In fact, he was the chief executive officer of Endless Content, the largest smart phone company in the world. Just before he went out on the stage, he checked his professional networking account, where he had twenty-seven thousand, five hundred and sixty-two connections. He was so proud of his network! He hoped they all shared his views. He didn't want anyone who disagreed with him to be on his network. Endless Content users should all agree with him, and with each other - that was his mantra! Anything else was wrong, and constituted hate - maybe even a crime. He quickly sent personal messages to fifty of his connections with pithy platitudes about tolerance and avoiding all -phobias and -isms. Then, Tim posted a picture of his breakfast to his digital media feed. He was short and dumpy. He was stout, with stubby legs that looked like small barrels. He had a unreadable, almost blank face that surrounded two beady, small little eyes that darted around a lot. His eyes, besides the motion, were empty.

The Bug Wrangler spoke loudly into his microphone, standing in his large-waisted, short-legged, heavily-branded jeans, a button-down shirt and two thousand dollar brown loafers. He hollered, "We love you! We love you!"

The crowd exploded with cheering and applause. The patchy-bearded weirdos were making noise in support of the bug wrangler's pending announcement. Outside the conference hall, a few heteronormative birds chirped and sang. Inside, the techno-corporate hive buzzed and buzzed!

The Bug Wrangler continued, "We've got a lot of very savvy, very forward-thinking people here in this conference. In the next week and the next month and the next year, you guys are going to be doing something that is incredible. You guys are taking things seriously. World peace! Ending poverty! Changing the climate! Sexual freedom! Equality for Furries!"

Everyone laughed and roared with applause. The Bug Wrangler continued.

"Also, you guys are devoted to your technology. Your technology is everything to you, it's everything. Everything! It's what puts the butter on the bread. It puts the motor in the boat! It makes you so efficient. You key off each other. You take cues from each other. It helps you progress! No-phobias, my friends! None of those! We love the pixels, don't we? We love 'em! And when they ask us what we're doing, you can say, we're evolving. EVOLVING, I SAY!"

The crowd went wild again. Applause! Cheering! Screaming!

After pausing for a few seconds to swig some water out of his plastic bottle the Bug Wrangler kept driving his speech forward, "That's how we're going to do better in the long run. We're gonna evolve. And someday soon we're going to evolve so much – we will find world peace, full tolerance, eliminate hatred, we will all agree – and everything you do will be done with one thing. Your face. YOUR FACE! We're going to build the best facial recognition system in the history of the world and nobody can stop where we are going! Endless Content is going to scan your face. Let's leverage the data. Let's leverage the technology! Let's reformulate!"

The crowd was cheering and buzzing, in a frenzy, so the Bug Wrangler became even more excited and elevated his energy level and his volume. The Bug Wrangler was yelling into the microphone.

"Nobody can stop the growth of Endless Content thanks to you, our customers! Post your content! Work those jobs! Consume! I love you so much! Show me your face! Let it scan all over your face! We're going to do it to your faaaaa-aaaaace! Thank you, love you!"

Roaaaarrrrr. Roaaaarrrrrr. Roaaaarrrrrr!

The crowd had gone from frenzy to pure madness, unfiltered excitement and maximum enthusiasm. The buzz had turned into a roar, and it just kept growing louder. Everyone's faces lit up with excitement. Almost everyone screamed and exclaimed their enthusiasm for having their face blasted, over and over, with the new scanning technology. They wanted the Super Duper 6G to scan every nook and cranny of their face. Every curve, every imperfection.

"Facial!" yelled a little ant. "We're gonna get a digital facial!"

"Facial fucking recognition! We got facial recognition! I can just feel it hitting my face!" bellowed a stocky beetle.

"We're going to the next level! Scan my fuckin' face! Say it again mother fucker!" hollered a little roach.

"I'm gonna do everything with muh face! Muh face!" yelled a yellow-bellied spittlebug. His face suggested that this, this Endless Content Super Duper smart phone, was even more exciting to him than his masturbation session the night before. That session was the one where he had jerked off into a white sock with red stripes while looking at a picture of a little goth chick that he almost hooked up with at a party six or seven months back.

"Track me. Track my motions! Track my face! Digitize me!" screamed a funny little rhinoceros beetle.

Every single bug in the audience exploded with applause. The ants, the beetles, the roaches. They all loved the announcement from Endless Content! They roared. They pumped their fists! Their little bug feet shuffled and their antennae waved wildly. Their smart phone cameras snapped pictures of the new smart phone that their leader, the Bug Wrangler from Endless Content, was holding up above his head.

Smart phones snapped pictures of smart phones snapping pictures of the new smart phone – the Super Duper 6G. They couldn't imagine a day where the world's final phone was created. Perhaps one day the smart phone could be built inside their bodies? They hoped! They couldn't contain their excitement.

It occurred to Maddox at the time, as he was holding his own smart phone, that facial recognition was unnecessary to unlock a stupid-fucking-smart-phone. It occurred to him that, over the riotous din of the Bug-men, he couldn't hear himself think. Scan my face to unlock my phone?

"Wait, what?" said Maddox, under his breath. Then, one second later, he said, in a low voice, "fuck that, I would never do that. What a clown world."

Maddox's distaste for his smart phone and its petty little stash of efficient and expedient technology grew exponentially in that split second. Fuck smart phones. Fuck that Bug Wrangler. Fuck Endless Content. Fuck 'em all. Maddox was tired of Endless Content and their Bug Phones.

In fact, it occurred to Maddox that most of the features of the smart phone, even the one he had, were wildly over the top. Maddox used it as a communication tool, for calling and sending text messages, and for personal navigation. It was very useful for those things. The navigation, to be fair, really helped when he was traveling for the Malone Agency in an area he was not familiar with. But when he found himself overdoing it on digital media – which, if he was honest, was quite often, sometimes a few hours at a time – he questioned himself. He hated it, but did it anyway. Wouldn't his time be better spent reading or in a conversation with someone interesting? Or lifting weights? Camping? Hiking? Hunting? Fighting practice? Shooting practice? Working? Making something? Doing something? Writing? Also, why did the Bug Wrangler want an impression of all of his users' faces? What was the Bug Wrangler really up to?

Maddox walked out of the conference hall. He just stood there, waiting for Kiowa. Maddox had decided that he would take off after he chatted with Kiowa a little longer. He didn't want or need any new tech and, suddenly, didn't feel like networking.

His smart phone buzzed. It had received a text message from Pepe Soliz, the rapey and horny Poobah.

"Hey Papi, can you meet me tomorrow in Phoenix? Wee are playing dee Snakes."

"Sure Pepe. What time is good?" responded Maddox.

"Around one. Dinner after dee game please."

"Okay, man I'll see you then."

Maddox was fine with meeting up with the Poobah. He had the hush money ready to give to Pepe so that Pepe could pass it along to April Tilney. Maddox would just write the Poobah a check for a million dollars. Maddox breathed out, thinking how nice it would be to have that over and done with.

Just then, Maddox's friend Kiowa walked out.

"Madd-man, you gave up on the speech early!"

"Yeah, I started feeling weird about the speaker and some thoughts started piling up on me. I guess I'm not as enthusiastic about technology as maybe I thought I was. I used to get all the new gadgets and now I don't care when new tech comes out. I'm not trying to be a downer. I'm sure it's a neat smart phone – the one I have is the Super and now the new model is the Super Duper. So there it is. Fuckin' facial recognition, man."

"Wow! All I do is shop for, buy and use my tech. I love tech. God, I love tech!" said Kiowa.

"I was like that. I haven't been as much lately. I'm not feeling it. Too many screens. Too much digital. It's all Pozz-ed," said Maddox.

Maddox said the last two sentences with an intentional, choppy cadence and a playful smirk. He couldn't articulate all his thoughts, but he really was thinking that tech and his smart phone were a negative force in his life. That specific thought had been popping into Maddox's head, here and there, for the last few months. But today, after the scene with the Bug Wrangler pushing his Super Duper Bug Phone on the crowd of bug-like consumers, the thought rushed in, fully, and took residence in Maddox's mind.

"That thought hits me sometimes. But I power through it and it never seems like the thought fully takes hold. Then, before you know it, I'm on to a new gadget," Kiowa said with a funny look on his face.

"Yeah, man. I was like that. I don't like it anymore. Too much digital. That facial recognition shit made me want to ditch my smart phone entirely. The Super. The Duper. The Super Duper. Fuck all of that shit. Maybe I'll just get a flip phone, old school. I wish."

"I sort of agree but I feel trapped by my screens. I have so much time and efficiency invested in them. They have all my shit stored in them. My whole life. All my pictures. All my accounts. All my content. All my passwords. All my apps, I check them all the time. All my social media. How can I be social without social media?"

"I don't know man," said Maddox. "I don't know. You can't get rid of tech, that's for sure. It keeps pressing forward, gaining more ground. Who's gonna roll this stuff back?"

"The solution is clearly not to condemn all technology because then you just become a wack-job. But what is the solution, though?" asked Kiowa.

Maddox was surprised that Kiowa was engaging this much. He was a techy! There was a pause and both men thought.

"Well, we have to identify the problem clearly so we know what we are solving. That's the issue, right now it's a chaotic discussion. A free for all. We can't solve a problem when we don't know what it is."

"Okay," said Maddox. "Let me take a stab at expressing what I'm thinking. First, technology is useful and can advance the quality of human life. There are many examples of that."

"I'm with you so far."

"Second, because it is so useful in a lot of ways, it is possible that we are enslaved by the same tech that we are trying to use for our benefit. Just look at all these people staring at their screens. They look like they haven't been outside in weeks."

"Still with you," said Kiowa.

"Third, with useful, helpful technology comes other technology that is not helpful and is really just a delivery system for the Pozz. I learned that from my friend Benjamin."

"What is the Pozz?"

"Well, think of it as propaganda that pushes outright degeneracy. Shitty stuff, shitty behavior, shitty products, shitty lifestyles. Consumerism. Pure consumerism. It's just a riff on the word poison. It gets unleashed into society in a bunch of ways like through corporate media and entertainment. Tech gets the assist. A computer constantly in your hand pushing products and media and other stuff, whatever else they want to push? That's why the Bug Wrangler was so happy. That's why Endless Content is the richest company in the world."

"Okay, okay. Pozz. I have to remember that one. So, for the tech stuff, I think I see. Basically all we are talking about here is limits. How do we use and limit our use of technology at the same time?"

"Yeah, that's it. It's a really hard question. Look around this conference, everyone might as well have a smart phone strapped to their fucking face."

They both looked around the room, scanning bug after bug. There was a beetle. An ant. A spittle-bug. A fly. Another beetle. And so on. They all had Endless Content branded smart phones less than one arm's length from their face.

"It's true, man."

Holy shit, they both thought, judging by their faces. Faces, antennae, little feet. Scurry. Buzz. Scan your screen.

"I was thinking about it this way. We often are so enamored with the tech itself that we forget to think about its significance. What about its meaning for us?"

"It's a hard question because even while we think about it we're inundated with tech. It's hard to carve out some time to just think. You can't think with your fuckin' smart phone buzzin' and beepin' all the time. Messages, phone calls, e-mails, apps, games, digital media, sexy chicks postin' semi-nudes, thirsty dudes blowing up their mentions."

"Yeah, I'm trying to work through my thoughts on this. People have been thinking about this issue for a long time, but lately I don't feel like people really are thinking about it. I feel like the smart phone changed that. People love their smart phone so much they don't want to consider the possibility that they are living badly. If the thought crosses their mind they get angry because their smart phone is more important to them than their life. If a friend or a loved one tries to come between them and their smart phone they lash out."

When he overheard the conference attendees conversing amongst themselves, he thought the conversations were hilarious, and sad, at the same time. One attendee would excitedly cite a feature of the new bug-phone and another attendee would instantly exclaim his or her enthusiasm for some other feature on the device. The other bug would nod and agree and the conversation would go on. They would cover feature after feature in a state of suppressed sexual frenzy. The devices were superior to the bugs themselves. In many ways, the devices controlled the bugs. The devices subsumed the bugs.

"I had a thought. Technology makes people so captivated, so dazzled by the tech itself that it takes away the ability to think more deeply about things. Why think about purpose or meaning when I have some flashy distraction going on this screen or whatever? Also, for some the question is how, not why, can you even think about purpose or meaning when you've never thought deeply about anything? People become thoughtless and that's bad. I say this because I know it happens to me sometimes," said Kiowa.

"Yeah, that's what I was thinking. Thoughtless! You know what is already thoughtless? Insects. Bugs. That's what's been worrying me," said Maddox.

"Ha-ha, what?" Kiowa was shocked at Maddox's comparison.

"Well, if you take away deep thought, if you take away thought and meaning, are we even really human anymore?"

"Technically."

"Good word."

Maddox's mind raced. He thought about his own Endless Content phone – the Super 6G – and also Football Sunday. He realized that the pro-technocracy propaganda was too powerful and too pervasive to be modified. He was certain it would just keep growing until everything was digital. "Humanity will soon be eclipsed by the technology created by humans," thought Maddox. He kept thinking, staring forward. When the technocracy is fully realized, the enslavement to technology will not even be felt any more. It will be so ingrained that it will be impossible to notice. People will take all their cues from their tech, all behavior will be derived and controlled by it. Men and women will finally be uniform. The problem of free will, achievement, and individuality will have been solved once and for all. Maddox concluded his thoughts by confirming, in his own mind, that tech is going to destroy humanity, the only question is when the light of humanity will be extinguished once and for all. Maddox felt defeated. Maddox snapped back into the conversation with Kiowa.

"I heard one little guy holler that he wanted a digital facial."

"What?"

"Yeah, he said he wanted a digital facial. And the Bug Wrangler was standing right there, over him, ready to splash his face," said Maddox.

As he said this, Maddox felt hopeless, again.

Old society, traditional society, was dead, he thought. But, in a strange way, this gave Maddox comfort. Once Maddox realized that and accepted it, he stopped feeling unsettled about the rise of the bug-men. He felt less burdened. The hopelessness Maddox Malone had felt was replaced by a feeling of freedom and determination. The end game wasn't necessarily to roll back technology or defeat the bugs — there was too much, there were too many.

But the point was to fight, to resist — when possible, when it made sense. Just do what you can, he thought — even if it's only a little bit. Be yourself! Subvert!

Go down fighting against them!

The Hoax Has Run Its Course

✢✢

The Grasshopper was, on this particular night, in a drug-induced haze — yet again. In fact, he was having a hard time keeping it together. He had struggled to even check in to his hotel room in Las Vegas, because he was so drunk and high. When he arrived, he was so high that he practically skipped into the check-in line. He buzzed past a couple arguing about something, it was either a political issue or something about a debt collection. McCartney wasn't sure.

"Why can't we use a helicopter?" the woman had said to her boyfriend, fiancé, or husband.

"Caroline, you can't just throw people out of helicopters. You can't do that. What are you thinking?"

"See, that's where you're wrong, Steve. That's where you are wrong. Stop acting like such a little pussy," the woman had replied.

The Grasshopper, in his drug-induced haze, jumped out of fear. Were they trying to throw him out of a helicopter? He panicked, but a moment later he realized they were paying no attention to him. He was fine. He kept walking through the hotel, haunches billowing, towards the casino area. His haunches flexed and brimmed! His square jeans, propelled by the same haunches, kept moving.

Paul McCartney, who hadn't spoken to Maddox Malone in almost a month, was all in on the substances. He had seven Grey Goose drinks, and he had snorted several lines of coke and done a dab of speed. He had also eaten a hallucinogenic mushroom that he had mixed into a chocolate concoction. He was seeing things! He was flying higher than a blimp. The Grasshopper was fucked up!

He was not entirely at ease navigating through the hotel while he was that high. In fact, he was paranoid! At one point, he imagined that hotel security was after him. He hopped over a railing, jumped over a fake rock display and ducked behind a designer purse rack in a store featuring mostly fine leather goods. But when he peeked his bulbous, bug eyes out over the purse he realized that they were, in fact, after a kid who had mistakenly walked out of an ice cream store without paying. Judging by the look of terror on the kid's face and by the speed with which he coughed up the three dollars and twenty seven cents, it was definitely not an intentional act on the part of the kid. The chubby little kid just wanted to lick on some ice cream and pass some time.

Everyone in the area seemed excited. It was Las Vegas after all. McCartney was no different. His mind was racing, his nose was dripping, causing him to sniffle every thirty seconds or so.

He yelled "let's do this!" when he walked out from behind the purse rack. There was a Chinese couple, actually from China, who saw him yell. It startled them. They were Chinese, not Chinese-American or what not. McCartney's outburst made the Chinese uncomfortable, but the fact that McCartney was in the single most boring Roman Laredo blazer and set of dad jeans ever created gave them comfort that he wasn't any kind of a threat. They shook their head and said something, but it was in Chinese so who really cared? Who could understand what they said, besides them? What was that curly brown-haired, skunk-striped boomer going to do to them? Nothing, they figured. There was nothing that he could do. McCartney glanced over at them and wondered if they were Chinese Supremacists. McCartney thought Chinese people were cool. But Supreme? Jesus! No! That's an insult to everyone else. In his head he heard a voice say Too Wong Foo. Too Wong Foo. Over and over. He shook his head to try to stop the voice and walked on. Too Wong Foo. Too Wong Foo.

The Grasshopper's eyes darted left, then they darted right, then they straightened out and focused for a second right down the middle. Then they glanced up and finally they scanned the ground, distracted by the complicated pattern on the carpet. He clenched his sprat tight, savoring the clench.

As the 'Hopper kept walking a skirmish broke out. People were hollering and screaming. Las Vegas, with all its money and consumerism, didn't tolerate that type of shit for very long, rest assured. It was bad for business. Two bald white guys wearing military-style overcoats were looming in the middle of the mall, doing something that attracted the attention of the police. McCartney just kept hopping along.

Paul's phone rang. It was Maddox Malone calling him, for the first time in over a week. Maddox had given up on TENACIOUS. He had given up on Paul. But he called at that moment, for whatever reason. The Grasshopper didn't answer.

"Forget Maddox Malone," Paul muttered, drunkenly, under his breath. He started talking to himself. "I'm in Las Vegas. I'm going to party. I don't care about TENACIOUS. Training facility? Never-mind that. Core values! TENACIOUS Tennis Academy? I don't even like tennis that much. And screw my dad, he's an asshole anyway — he told Maddox Malone I went to Rudy Pinkerton's facility? That's none of Maddox's business. Let's do this!"

Paul walked into the men's bathroom at the Venetian. He took out a sack of white powder from his Roman Laredo jacket pocket. He balanced a bump of the coke on the knuckle of his thumb and then "phhhwwwwwttt" sucked it into his nose. He walked back out of the bathroom and went straight towards the blackjack table at the Venetian. Along the way, he misjudged his distance from an octogenarian who was sitting at a slot machine, pumping in nickels. The Grasshopper's right haunch caught the old man in the middle of his back and the old man tipped over. The old man just didn't have enough strength in his left leg to stop the momentum. McCartney pretended like it didn't happen. He didn't say sorry, he didn't help the old fella up. He just walked the rest of the way to the blackjack table. He placed a thousand dollars, in hundreds, on the table to get some chips.

The cocktail waitress walked over to the Grasshopper right away.

"Can I get you a drink?" she asked.

"Goose and cran," he responded. "I only drink Goose. Top of the line! Let's do this, ha-ha-ha-ha-ha!"

"Coming right up."

The dealer started the hand, as McCartney was the only one at the table. It was a hundred dollar minimum, which is what McCartney bet. He was dealt a Queen and a six, against the dealer showing a two.

"I'll stay," said McCartney, waving off the dealer. "Grandpa always liked me to be careful with his money. I'm going to stay and watch you bust. Let's do this!"

The dealer flipped his ten, which made twelve, and then dealt himself a seven. He swept up McCartney's chip.

"Oh, what the fuck!" exclaimed McCartney.

This time, McCartney put down two hundred in chips. The dealer handed McCartney a pair of eights. The dealer was showing a five.

"There's a split! Take no prisoners!" exclaimed McCartney. The dealer split the eights and McCartney put another two hundred dollars on the table. He dealt a three.

"There's a double. Grandpa, thanks for the chips! Core Values!" McCartney put another two hundred in chips on the double. He had six hundred dollars on the table, all of a sudden. He couldn't believe it!

The dealer gave him a five. Sixteen. Not what he wanted, but it would have to do. The card sat there. They moved to the other eight and the dealer flipped a two.

"Lord alive, another double. Bring the thunder, I say! Ha-ha-ha-ha-ha!" said McCartney.

McCartney moved two more hundred dollar chips onto the table to back the second double. The Grasshopper had eight hundred of his grandpa's dollars on the table. The dealer flipped a seven. Seventeen. Shit! McCartney gulped hard. He wanted some of the white powder he had in his jacket, but obviously he couldn't hop over to the bathroom. Not right now.

Right then, the cocktail waitress brought him his drink. The skinny curly brown-and-gray-haired boomer gave a gesture with his hand and said "thanks honey!" He grabbed his Goose and immediately plucked it.

The dealer flipped his other card. It was an eight, so together with the five he had a thirteen. He dealt himself another card, a six. He won both of the hands and swept up McCartney's eight hundred dollars.

"Fuck this!" McCartney exclaimed. He jumped up and practically hopped away from the table. He sprung back into the bathroom and took another snort of the white powder. Straight up his nose.

"Phhhwwwwwttt!"

He walked back out of the bathroom.

"Okay, blackjack didn't work out. But at least I have more of my grandpa's money!" he thought.

What now? He was a frenzy of activity — because he was so high — he had energy spilling over everywhere. He sidled up to the bar and ordered a double Goose with cranberry juice and tonic this time. It arrived and he took a big sip. He was buzzing from coke and vodka, and still hallucinating from the mushrooms — he felt great!

Right at that moment, Maddox called Paul McCartney again. Maddox was killing time at the airport in Los Angeles and wanted closure on the TENACIOUS hoax. So he called. He would have bet thousands of dollars that McCartney would not answer the call — McCartney hadn't answered for weeks. And he would have lost! McCartney picked up on the second ring.

"I have the package!" McCartney said into the smart phone's microphone. "It's central. Central to me."

"Wait, what? What are you talking about? Paul, this is Maddox calling again. It's been almost a month. I had lunch with your dad. I know TENACIOUS was fake. I know it was a scam. I know about rehab. I was just calling to tell you to go fuck yourself. Fuck you and all your bullshit. Why would you do that? Why would you fake TENACIOUS?"

"Look over there, it's two women riding tall with their stomachs outstretched on a half-dressed Ogre. They are riding on the Ogre, taking him."

"Paul, Are you drunk?"

"I fear that Ogre. I fear what he can do. Stop complaining about TENACIOUS. I'm sorry to have bullshitted you, but that's how life is. Uncle Marty got PartDok, not me! Ha-ha-ha-ha-ha! Time to drive! Be driven for success! Core Values!"

After this exclamation, Paul McCartney, the Grasshopper, hung up the phone.

Maddox looked down at his shiny smart phone with resignation showing clearly on his face. TENACIOUS was never real, it was just a diversion for the Grasshopper. TENACIOUS was bullshit, a distraction from his boring trust fund and the disgusting Stickbug. It was an excuse to travel. It was just a story to tell to the boomer-cuckolds in Jackson Hole and wherever else. It was always bullshit — Maddox knew that now, very clearly. The Grasshopper walked off and laughed. Already, Maddox was sure that the drunk and drugged Grasshopper could barely could remember the phone call with Maddox. Maddox shook his head and started to think about how to pick up the pieces.

ii

At the same time, a few hundred miles away, one of McCartney's prostitutes — the young one named Chanel with the big tits, pencil eraser nipples and nice lithe body — decided that she had enough. She had enough of people like Paul McCartney. She had enough of spreading her legs and opening her mouth — and taking cock — in exchange for money from people like McCartney. She had enough of Xanax, crystal meth, wine, and citrus-flavored vodka. She didn't want to be strung out anymore. She didn't want to feel empty anymore. In the last three months, she had visits from two hundred and seventeen people like Paul McCartney. She hated her life. She had no help, no way out that she could find, and she was done.

Chanel had spent the last couple of hours driving her sedan from Phoenix north to Flagstaff. Her wheels kept turning and she kept her eyes on the road. She made her way towards a brewery that she had been to, several times, with an old boyfriend a couple of years ago — before she had become a prostitute. Each time she had been here before, she had a couple of wheat beers — she loved that place. She thought about that, and she wanted to smile but she couldn't muster one up. She had really liked the guy, the boyfriend, whose name was Vaughn, but Vaughn had knocked her up — refused to pay for her abortion and then he left her for a different girl. On this night, instead of turning into the brewery parking lot, she went straight. She pulled over to the left on the street and waited.

Chanel had a song by the famous rapper Cray-Cray — a hood rat that fancied himself as a pimp — playing in her car, via her smart phone. The track was called Gotta Pay the Cray, and she was half-listening. She was on a heavy dose of Percocet and she was zoned out.

> Gotta pay the Cray
> Gotta do it all day (do me, do me)
> Look at me get high
> Look at me get low
> Just pay the Cray every day
> Pay the Cray, Pay the Cray (pay me so much)

A few moments later, as if on cue, she saw a train's light in the distance. She waited another two minutes, then put her car back into drive and maneuvered it about seventy-five feet forward, then under the railroad crossing barrier. The barrier jarred a bit and then bent out of the way and snapped back over the car. At that moment, the train was barreling down the track towards Chanel's car. It was a massive combination of metal and speed. The train was only a few seconds away. Chanel drew her head back and her eyes grew wide. Her face looked like she was still in a stupor, but suddenly it looked less so. So quickly the train was on the car! The train had no time to stop. The train's impact on the car created a loud burst of a variety of noises. Crashing, screeching, grinding, scraping. Chanel screamed right as she was about to die. Her face, right as the train hit, seemed to indicate that she was thinking 'Where am I? What am I doing? What for? Can I get out of this?' But that was impossible. It was too late. The train's impact demolished the car, crushed her head and her body. Her brain and heart ceased to function due to the catastrophic impact. Chanel, whose real name was Allison Grace Taylor, was dead almost instantly. It was all over for Allison.

iii

Back in Los Angeles, when Paul McCartney hung up on him, Maddox felt many different emotions all at the same time. Anger. Disgust. Resentment. Fear. Relief. Resolve. Bitterness. Maddox had believed McCartney about TENACIOUS because he wanted to — not because McCartney was overly believable. Now, Maddox finally gave himself over to the place that he had not wanted to go for months, for over a year. He finally gave himself over — fully and completely — to admitting that the TENACIOUS projects were all fake.

He let himself absorb the fact that Paul McCartney was a phony and a fraud.

There would be no TENACIOUS training facility. There would be no TENACIOUS tennis academy and wrestling and golf events. McCartney would go back to his McMansion where the Grasshopper and the Stickbug would wallow in their silent hatred of one another. McCartney would count his allowance dollars from his grandfather. He would drink his Geese, snort his coke, take his 'shrooms, and use his hookers. He would probably find someone else to bullshit, another Maddox Malone. He would create another TENACIOUS-like project so he could brag about the phony project to his boomer acquaintances. Maddox was almost sure of it.

Maddox boarded his plane in Los Angeles. He was heading back to Phoenix, where he would, at least, get to see his family — and also he had agreed to meet Pepe Soliz the following day to hand him a check for one million dollars so Pepe could pay off his rape victim. Maddox was exhausted, and after the plane took off, he fell asleep and had a vivid dream.

He dreamed about a story that he read long ago. Maddox Malone had read it in the original Ancient Greek, in fact. He had taken some time to translate it to English, as an exercise in his study of the language. The Island of Crete was inhabited by Cretins, but before that term became a pejorative, there was a man named Daedalus and his young son Icarus living in Crete. Daedalus was a gifted inventor.

He made all sorts of things that were useful, including a motorized vibrator for her, the first of its kind. The King of Crete approached Daedalus to see if he could create something for the King. Daedalus did not disappoint, as he created a labyrinth to contain the King's Minotaur. The King was pleased. But the King wanted more. He had his private army capture Daedalus and his son and lock them in a cave above the sea. The only entrance was through the labyrinth that Daedalus had invented. The cave was above a cliff overlooking the sea.

It was a lavish imprisonment. The King provided for whatever Daedalus and his son needed. His son was sometimes bored but Daedalus was able to occupy him by creating toys and other things for him. But time drove on and eventually the son complained that he had no hope for a life of his own. How could he develop his talents in an isolated cave? The son began to have sexual desires — how could he meet a girl when he was stuck in this cave.

"Your Majesty, surely you must see that my son is becoming a young man. He is stuck in this cave. How can he develop? How can he grow? He may have a vibrator, but he doesn't have a girl!"

The King squinted his eyes and thought. The King decided that Daedalus' son needed to stay with him to keep him company. Without him, who knows what his productivity would be. Daedalus' son explained to him one day how he envied the baby birds that he saw flying free off the cliff. Daedalus, the inventor, went to work. He made two long light metal frames with hinges. He made straps with leather that could attach to arms. He gathered feathers that fell off of birds who flew overhead and landed nearby. He created mechanisms that allowed the frames to steer and pull. When he had enough feathers, he used candle wax to attach them to both of the frames. His son was overjoyed. He had two frames, so he realized that his dad would be coming with him.

The inventor reminded his son one last time: "Now son,

remember, if you fly too close to the ocean your wings will become too heavy with spray from the waves. If you fly too close to the sun your wing-wax will melt and you will lose your feathers and your ability to fly. Follow me and you will be fine."

The inventor and his son spread their wings as wide as they would go and leaped, one after the other, off the cliff and out over the ocean. They soared up and down and side to side. They flew back and forth. Such Freedom! Such adventure! Blazing a trail. Doing new things. But the son started to get too aggressive, too comfortable, too wild.

"Stop!" shouted Daedalus, "The wax will melt if it gets too warm. Not so high. Not so high you little shit! Cut it out!"

But the boy wasn't listening. He kept flying higher and higher. Maddox also felt a flying sensation, as if he was right there with the boy. It was exhilarating. The boy flew closer and closer to the sun until the wax started to melt. At first, he lost his feathers slowly, then he lost them all at once. He flapped his mechanisms, but no longer were they working like wings. They were metal poles with no feathers. He could no longer fly. As Daedalus watched in horror, the boy plunged toward the sea frantically flapping the pulleys with his arms. When the boy finally hit the water, there wasn't a feather left attached.

The boy's name was Icarus.

Maddox woke up with during some significant turbulence on the flight, which to him seemed fitting. The dream had been very vivid. That fall hurt, the fake projects hurt. Maddox let himself absorb the disappointment. He had to.

Suddenly, Maddox felt like he was running. Running free, with a gate in front of him. The gate led to an open area. Once he got through the gate, he would close it. But, there was a problem. It was as if he felt a tremendous pain in his leg from a dog biting him. A big, snarling mouth with rows of teeth gripping and re-gripping Maddox's leg. Digging, clamping, tearing, gripping. Digging again. Clamping again. Tearing flesh! Oh the misery! Oh, the pain! But then all of a sudden, as if helped by an angel, the dog's teeth were released and Maddox was able to bolt through the field, unabated. His calf muscle was mangled, it was torn. But his leg still worked! He ran, he sprinted, he strode, he fled. Is there a greater pain than a dog's teeth sunk into your calf?

Is there a greater freedom than the release and full escape from the jaw of the same canine? Maddox was going to find out.

Maddox needed to figure out what the hell he was going to do!

It Ain't a Little Problem Anymore

✳✳

It was the hour of failure. Maddox woke up with a start, instantly awake with his energy buzzing. This exact thing, the hour of failure, had been happening to Maddox Malone around three in the morning, most nights, for months now. The hour of failure had initially started to insert itself, once in a while, into Maddox's sleep schedule after the Pepe Soliz rape. But the hour of failure really established itself once the TENACIOUS projects began to flounder and stall. On any given night, the hour of failure might last more than an hour. It might last two hours. Sometimes, it would even last four hours. But, for the last few months, it always came, every single night. When it did Maddox's eyes would spring open and sometimes he couldn't go back to sleep, no matter what he tried. It was the hour of failure, and on this particular night it happened at three twenty two a.m. He wasn't planning on getting up until six.

Maddox didn't want to look at the digital, red-numbered alarm clock he had on his nightstand next to his bed. He didn't want to know how many hours of restless sleep he might have left before it was time to head into the office. It was a cool night, and he had the window cracked, even though his wife Laura told him he wasn't supposed to do that because, she said, snakes or dirt could get into the room. Or dust. Snakes? Dust?

All through the cool, dark room he could feel pressing doom, pressing gloom. He thought about the meeting he had with Soliz at eleven a.m. — a million dollars of easy come and easy go. He worried about how he would tell all the other people affected by the TENACIOUS hoax that the gig was up. He couldn't believe it, and he sat there, zoning out, punishing himself for ever getting involved with the TENACIOUS plan. How stupid was he? How could he fall for that bullshit? He dwelt on TENACIOUS for at least forty minutes, and it seemed like hours. Then, his mind darted to the play of Obadiah Ballard. That catch! Little O-Bad was doing so well. That was a positive! But, he hadn't heard from Major O for a while, and he felt a dull sense of alarm regarding that. Not a blaring alarm, just a dull alarm. Also, he had not resolved anything one way or another with the illegal payments Zaine had made to all the players and their families. He had been so busy with other things, and, besides, he didn't know what to do.

He heard an engine rev in the distance, probably a biker riding his motorcycle in the middle of the night. The engine ripped and roared in far in the distance, but it was still quite audible. The noise carried through the Phoenix desert. He heard a pack of coyotes making a kill on a rabbit in the north Phoenix desert. A fuzzy rabbit. Loud shrieks, persistent, loud, for a couple minutes.

Most nights, almost every night, Maddox slept in his home office. But tonight, for some reason, he and his wife Laura slept three feet away from one another, in the same bed. When that happened, they used wholly separate sets of blankets and sheets. Maddox liked to sleep in the cool and Laura liked to sleep warm. Over time, this resulted in a mismatch of blankets and sheets littering the bed. Laura bitched at Maddox about it. She didn't care if Maddox could sleep or not, Maddox thought, she just wanted pretty looking blankets and sheets that she liked. She wanted them to look pretty and fancy. Maddox just wanted to sleep and be comfortable. He didn't care what the blankets looked like. To Maddox it was more important to be able to get a bit of sleep than it was to make Laura happy about the decor. Tonight, there was no sleeping for Maddox, not because of any blankets, but because of the sense of alarm relating to his business.

Maddox hadn't said anything to Laura about the meeting with Pepecito "Pepe" Soliz. Since the trip to LegoLand, Maddox had really tried to avoid talking about the Poobah and the rape of April Tilney. Laura didn't know anything about the million dollars for April Tilney. They were having a hard time communicating about anything. How would he tell her he was going to pay a million dollars in rape hush money? To top it off, Laura didn't know that TENACIOUS was a hoax yet. That had cost Maddox so much time and money. Heck, Maddox wasn't even sure if Laura knew about the Platform bankruptcy. Never mind the blankets, there might as well have been a Chinese wall between Maddox and Laura.

Maddox's reasoning, to the extent he had any, for not sharing was that he felt he was best positioned to handle the stress of the situation. With his two young boys — and Felicia — in her primary care, he didn't want Laura to worry about all that stuff. Maddox Malone, for what seemed like the first time in his life, was worried enough. He gritted his teeth and just lay there in bed, working toward the morning.

So, rightly or wrongly, Laura was mostly oblivious to Maddox's stress — other than whatever she could pick up on his face from time to time. In terms of the bed, she was facing the other way, on her back, head tilted to the side. Wearing sweatpants and a sweatshirt, under the blankets as well.

Once, they were able to communicate freely and clearly. They even said wedding vows together! They were happy for a while after that. But things had been very tough, very strained, for years. So strained! Maddox, while worried about the situation with Soliz, was still, perhaps unreasonably, confident that the issues surrounding the rape payment and the TENACIOUS hoax would not affect his marriage and his family relationship with his two boys, Thomas and Chester, and his little girl, Felicia. It was an unreasonable confidence, though. There was no communication and the only bond, the only reason to stay in the marriage, was the children. That was something but often times, for other people, thought Maddox, that was not enough. Maddox had been protecting them and shielding them from this fallout for a long time, now. He felt protected in the desert, in North Phoenix, removed from the big centers of business. More of a connection to the earth and to nature. He could see the stars in the sky vividly because of less ground light up here. He breathed and relaxed, at least a bit. He just sat there, thinking about all this stuff. After all, it was the hour of failure!

His boys slept peacefully on the other side of the house. Two great kids, Thomas and Chester. Happy little boys. Smart boys. Felicia, his cute little daughter, slept in her little bed as well. He rubbed his right triceps due to a momentary itch. Once he rubbed it, it went away and everything felt fine again. For some reason, Maddox didn't know why, he thought of the Columbus Day celebration in the Dominican Republic from a few months ago. It was fun, with great weather, great food and some sangria — celebrating a brave explorer that helped find the continent that would eventually, after years and years of yeoman's work, seemingly impossible work, be transformed by brave settlers and pioneers into the United States of America. He had no idea why that scene popped into his head during this particular hour of failure. But he remembered the beautiful day vividly.

Then his mind really started revving up. It started going full speed. April Tilney's little butt-hole, Pepe Soliz in the bathroom, the Potato Bug at the Big Boy's game, Football Sunday, the Dung Beetle and his cologne, Paul McCartney hollering "Let's do this!" at the Boomer Barbeque — and his dad, Steve McCartney saying "I hate that fucking guy," Carlton Duffer and his aspirations to be an agent, Danielle Duffer hitting a triple, Bart Odom and wage-cucking, Omar and the Puddle Bear, Vegetable Oil Kills, the Platform, the stench of the Tick, Dayana Delgado helping him make it out of Venezuela alive, the scurrying Silverfish and his lawyer-dodges, the Digital Facial ... and on and on and on. Thoughts, scenes, events, plans — they all buzzed through his head. These thoughts, the hour of failure, kept spinning!

His eyes were wide open, staring at air. "Wait, can you even stare at air?" thought Maddox. Staring at the cracked window, thankful that there was no light of dawn, yet. It was the hour of failure, after all, and it always seemed to last forever.

Maddox couldn't take his thoughts anymore. He was tired of the hour of failure. So, he got up and went into his home office. Instead of laying down in there, he grabbed a book off his desktop. Cormac McCarthy's *No Country for Old Men*. He was at the part where Chigurh kills Llewelyn's wife, Carla Jean. Llewelyn, of course, was already dead, but Chigurh went and killed Carla Jean, a cute young girl because, well, because he said he was gonna. Carla Jean had made Maddox laugh when she responded earlier in the book to Llewelyn goading her to "just keep it up" by replying "that's what she said." Maddox had enjoyed that line and found Carla Jean to be endearing. A funny country girl. Maddox thought back to the part where Llewelyn said something like sometimes you have a little problem ... and you don't fix it ... and then all of a sudden it ain't a little problem anymore. Hmmm. Maddox sat there for a moment. *Sometimes you have a little problem and you don't fix it then all of a sudden it ain't a little problem anymore.* Llewelyn was God-damned right about that, thought Maddox. He read and thought. Read and thought. His body felt fatigued and twitchy. His body was tired but his mind was wide awake, running full speed.

ii

A couple hours later, Maddox showered, drove Thomas, Chester and Felicia to school, grabbed a large iced Americano from a local chain coffee shop, moved some weights around for thirty-five minutes and was in the the Malone Agency office in North Phoenix by nine twenty two a.m. Despite lifting, Maddox felt weak. He felt soft.

As usual, there were no Pepe Soliz rape articles in the Sunny Grove newspapers. Nothing at all was bubbling up on-line. There was no buzz about the rape, none at all. No outrage directed at Pepe, whatsoever. On the one hand, Maddox breathed a sigh of relief — when he thought about his large commissions — but it also nagged at him. Why didn't anyone care about the girl, April Tilney? *Rolling Stone Magazine*, a Pozz-ed old boomer pop culture rag, had taken the time to publish an article about a rape hoax at the University of Virginia — but they never got around to saying anything about Pepe. Why? Maddox wondered why — he thought it had something to do with the Pozz, but he wasn't sure exactly what that was. People always focused so much on perceived slights or their agenda to tear something down that they didn't like — perhaps a University of Virginia fraternity — but here was an actual violent rape that no one bothered talking about! The rapist just kept running around, eating bacon pizza and doing destructive shit.

On a business level he was fine with the rape not receiving due attention — hell, he was paying Benjamin Cohen to keep a lid on it. On a personal level, he wondered how sick the society really was. Why wasn't April a priority, for anyone?

It was a busy hour for Maddox. He made his routine calls, to clients, sponsors, advertisers, recruiters, teams, and journalists. His hour was up and he had to start to drive south to meet with Pepe Soliz, who was in town for a baseball game against the Snakes. The time had arrived. Maddox confirmed that he had the check for a million dollars in his shirt pocket. He touched it with his right hand. Pepe, as a professional athlete, made more money than Maddox Malone, but the Poobah spent all his money on family, friends, baby mommas, potato bugs, night clubs and other things. He had some assets, cars, jewelry, electronics, but no meaningful cash at the moment. And, one of his Venezuelan accounts had been seized — that country was a financial basket-case — and he lost almost a quarter million dollars. Maddox strode out of the office. Out of habit, Maddox looked left then right before he jumped into his sports car. He buzzed with anticipation — he was excited to move on from the rape incident.

He took the first sip of his second iced Americano of the day and felt good. He felt energized by the caffeine - a stimulant bringing energy to him from without — although he knew he was a bit over-caffeinated already. After he parked at the South Phoenix hotel where the Big Boys were staying on this road trip, he walked straight into the hotel lobby. Maddox Malone closed his eyes and took a breath. He saw Pepe Soliz, sitting over in a corner. Pepe Soliz had a tight, double XL, blue tee-shirt on with an ornate tiger printed on the front. His belly was flowing. His chins were bursting, swelling, flush. Puffy. Ornate. Diamond earrings. A neatly trimmed leprechaun-style beard and a fresh, short haircut. Jeans and brown loafers. There, next to him was a liter of XtraShoog and some orange cheese-flavored chips. Maddox could usually peg Soliz's weight, which always fluctuated dramatically, within five pounds by eyeballing him. Today, Maddox figured Soliz for two hundred sixty-five pounds. In actuality, that moment, Soliz weighed two hundred and sixty-nine.

For a brief second Maddox's mind stopped working. He went blank. Then everything came back together. Everything cleared and he became focused. He clasped hands with Soliz and they patted each other on the back. A bro hug from the Caterpillar-like Poobah.

"Hey, Pepe. How are you my man?"

"Do-eeng good, do-eeng good. I'm tired annn hunnngry. How you do-eeng Papi?" said the Poobah.

"Good, real good," said Maddox.

Maddox sat down in the chair next to Pepe. Time seemed to be ticking, moving, rolling, slowly, very slowly. Maddox swore that time almost stood still. He looked at Pepe. Pepe looked at him. Pepe sat there. So Maddox sat there. Pepe seemed to want to project a casual air about himself. But then again he always did that. Pepe looked down at his smart phone and started playing around on it. Maybe he was sending a text message. Maybe he was looking at social media. Maddox didn't know and didn't really care. Maddox pushed his head back and took a minute to think. For some reason, Maddox Malone didn't hand Pepe the million dollar check immediately as he had planned.

Maddox looked at Soliz while Soliz fiddled on his smart phone. Soliz had incredible hands and hand eye coordination which allowed him to hit a baseball with excellent acumen and force. Besides that? An empty smile, an empty head, and a full belly. Probably a dozen random offspring running around. They had nothing to talk about except small talk and baseball. Maddox breathed again.

"When do you guys leave for San Diego?"

"To-morrow morning, Papi."

"Got it. That will be a good road trip."

Maddox thought back to the time in San Diego that he had to go to one of Pepe Soliz's baby mamma's place to get his smart phone and some other stuff back. Soliz had been staying with the baby mamma and she kicked him out. While Soliz was taking a nap, she had gone through his text messages, she threw the phone against the wall and slapped him awake while yelling "¿Por qué estás enviando mensajes de texto a esas otras perras?" Soliz had left the house in his Escalade and then called Maddox for help. The babysitting was the worst part of the job.

"Yeah, it will be good. We are playing good right now."

It was all so strange. Two men, from different parts of the planet, brought together by a sport which was quintessentially American but was played religiously in some third-world places as a means to escape failed, broken societies.

Maddox looked at Pepe again. He knew it before, deep down, but this scene served to crystallized things for Maddox. The scene froze and he had a moment of pure realization. He had perfect clarity, in exactly these words: We have nothing in common.

Nothing, not a single thing, in common.

While Maddox thought this, he felt as if the million dollar check was burning a hole in his shirt, in his chest. It was just sitting there, nestled into his pocket. "What am I doing?" thought Maddox. Just give this fat-ass the check. "You'll get five times this amount back on his next contract commission," he told himself. But Maddox didn't give him the check. Instead, he looked straight ahead.

"What time are you going to the park today, Pepe?"

"Early, prolly aroun' three, Papi. I goeeng early."

There was a pause and Soliz looked on his smart phone again.

"Papi, I have to ask you some-teeng" said Soliz.

Here it was. Drumroll. Bring the thunder!

"Okay."

"I need your help weeth dat thing, weeth dat mow-ney for dee girl. Remember i tell you dat in New York. Valstencher say you have dee money."

Maddox didn't reach for the check. Maddox, unexpectedly, felt himself freeze. He looked at the Poobah and suddenly, almost strangely, he felt anger. Anger bubbled up into his chest and his mind. But there was something different about this anger. This wasn't Maddox Malone's angry twin surfacing. This felt more like Maddox Malone's immune system, working.

Maddox didn't say or do anything, so Pepe spoke again.

"I don't have dee moww-ney to geev to that girl. I need you to help me Papi, in dees moment. Can you geev me dee mow-ney?" asked Pepe.

Maddox pictured the Jerry Maguire character in the movie yelling about money — then he pictured that same character, dancing like a monkey on an ocean pier with a tin cup in hand begging for change. Maddox sat there, thinking. He felt alone. The room was full of nothing but his thoughts. For a brief second he felt that he could do anything. He could yell, jump, punch, run, spit, fall, fly, whatever. He was alone. Everything stopped. It felt like each second took a week to pass. He felt everything at once. Anger, outrage. He felt nothing. Emptiness, detachment. Each second sat on him like a sumo wrestler. Maddox Malone was drowning and flying at the same time.

"Will I give you a million dollars to pay off April Tilney? No, I'm not going to do that, Pepe. I'm never gonna do that. I won't show you that kind of money," said Maddox with a look of solid determination.

The determination quickly faded, and Maddox squinted and sat there, trying to process what he had just done. That wasn't the plan! Pepe grimaced like he had been kicked in the balls. Some anger showed through on Maddox's face even though he tried to mask it. Pepe breathed. Pepe still looked angry. He looked furious, in fact. And confused.

"Okay, Papi, thank you for coming to see me. I going to take a nap before I go to the park."

"Hey, one more thing, Pepe," said Maddox.

"What's dat, Papi?"

"My commission for the current year of your contract with the Big Boys is due. You need to save some money so you can pay that to me. I'll have my assistant Eleanor get in touch."

Maddox, without giving Pepe the usual bro-hug, walked out to the hotel valet and got his sports car back. Maddox drove onto the one-oh-one and headed north. He floored it, driving as fast as he could.

iii

He pulled up to the house after a thirty minute cruise. He walked in. Laura, Thomas, Chester and Felicia were all home.

"Maddox," said Laura, looking concerned, "is something wrong?" She had, yet again, picked up the stress on his face.

Should he tell her about Pepe Soliz immediately? Maddox needed to tell Laura, now. He needed to tell her about Pepe, the Grasshopper, the Platform. He should tell her about Zaine paying Obadiah too. He knew it. But Maddox Malone swallowed his tongue. He froze. Maddox stood there, thinking, but he didn't say a God-damned thing to his wife.

He snapped back to reality as he heard Chester approaching.

"Daddy!" said Chester, walking toward him. "See these cards?"

Chester held up an Aaron Rodgers football card and also a Tom Brady. Under those was a Steph Curry rookie. Maddox had bought them all for Chester's birthday and they had them graded together for Chester's collection.

"What are they?" said Chester.

What are they?

"Football cards."

"Of who?"

"Looks like Aaron Rodgers and Tom Brady. I don't know about the third one."

"Daddy! You got it."

"I'm going to clean up and run to the office for a couple hours," Maddox said, addressing Laura.

"Do you know what time it is? We have dinner tonight with my parents."

"I don't know, Laura."

"They really are looking forward to it. We were going to that Indian place. Thomas loves it."

"Laura, I have to, I'm busy as you know what."

"Daddy, I want to get a Gronk autograph card."

"Oh yeah? Sounds good buddy."

"Can we go to the card shop on Saturday? Can we go?" asked Chester.

"If we have a good park session, yes."

"Do you think you can finish your work if we push dinner back an hour to seven thirty? Everyone would really love to see you?" Laura persisted.

"Well, yes. I'm gonna jam I'll be back in a couple hours. I'm just dealing with a bunch of shit at work."

"Everything okay?"

"Yeah, sure. Everything's fine," Maddox lied.

He hopped into the sports car and headed north. Music was pumping out of his speakers.

> 'Cause I fell on black days
> I fell on black days

Maddox sang along. Seven minutes later he parked and strolled into his office.

He took a breath. Two men and a woman walked by his office window, heading to their suite next door. They were about Maddox's age. They were talking, laughing, telling stories. The men both had khakis and loafers with a polo on top. The woman had a skirt, blouse and heels. They looked like they had sneaked out for happy hour and were having a great time coming back to finish the day. They looked like wage-cucks, and each of them clung to a smart phone, of course, but for a moment, for at least that one moment, the smart phone screens weren't the focus of their day. They left their smart phones alone for a moment

— they didn't stare into the screens. They were having fun, just socializing and shooting the shit. They looked happy. The rest of the world was still marching on. Nobody cared about Maddox's problems and dealings other than Maddox. Nobody cared.

Maddox knew that a man had to have trials to achieve true greatness. But this couldn't go on. Something had to give! Something had to finally go Maddox Malone's way. Right?

The Ebb and the Flow

❋❋

Maddox drove back to the office and logged back onto his computer. By the time he got back, he had already received an email with a digitized document attached to it. The e-mail was from the Dung Beetle, Marcel Valstencher. It was a scan of a letter from Pepecito "Pepe" Soliz terminating his representation contract with Maddox's agency. His new agency, whoever had given him the million dollars, obviously helped him with the letter, which was written in English.

"Dear Maddox: I appreciate your work over the years but after our recent meeting now I feel you no longer fully support me and I need to terminate our representation agreement. Thanks again. Respectfully, Pepecito "Pepe" Soliz."

Maddox caught his breath. He shook his head, then he grimaced. He tried to shake it off. He had to be honest, this one stung. The commission on Pepe Soliz's next contract would be somewhere around five million dollars, Maddox thought. But Pepe was a rapist! Who needs that in their life? Yet still, the angst!

His office telephone rang. He picked it up.

"Hello?"

"Hey, Mr. Malone, it's Chrissy Franken from *the Business Journal of Sports*. I hope this isn't a bad time."

Maddox stayed silent.

"I heard a report that Pepecito "Pepe" Soliz terminated your representation. You know, with the Malone Agency. I wanted to see if I could get a comment."

As she spoke, he remembered her face from meeting at a sports conference a couple of years prior. She had a dreadful, gaunt face that was overrun with tension. She was rail thin, with no feminine styling and certainly no sex appeal. She was a cubicle-dweller, probably almost forty-five years old, childless – no connection to the land or the future of the country – and simply calling to get Maddox's quote on an event that, to all outsiders, would appear to be a business setback for him. To her, she didn't care about how this might or might not affect Maddox. She wanted to get a quote to put in her journal so that her journal could continue its cycle of circulating and selling advertisements and advertorials.

"Oh, yes. Yes, I got the termination on an e-mail."

"How do you feel about that?" asked Chrissy, the Flatworm.

"Honestly, it's fine. The relationship ran its course. I wish Pepe the best. Go Poobah! What else can I say?" said Maddox.

"Well how damaging will this be to your business?"

This was galling. Maddox smiled, but it was one of those angry smiles that he did every so often. He pictured the Flatworm sitting there, rubbing her hands. This woman had no regard for Maddox, for the Malone Agency, for anything. Maddox figured she just wanted to get her quote so she could file her article and then go home to the cats in her apartment. So, he told himself to take it easy.

"Ummm, well, Pepe is just another guy. It's just another commission. He's a good player. I'm sure he'll have a lot of success with his new agency. Good luck to the Poobah."

"Are you disappointed?"

"Life involves disappointment. Sure, I'm disappointed. But that's fine."

"Do you think he made the move because some other agency has a connection with a particular team?"

"No."

"Oh. Why then?"

"It was time. It was the right time."

Maddox tried to block the mental image of the Poobah raping April. He didn't say anything about the million dollars, about the hush money for April Tilney.

"Was this building up for a while, then?" asked the Flatworm.

"Sure. Things always ebb and flow. Things ebbed a while ago. This was the flow," said Maddox.

"Well, thanks for taking my call," said the Flatworm.

"Take care," said Maddox.

When Maddox hung up the phone, he thought back on that day at LegoLand in the soft, golden-yellow California sun. He remembered when little Chester had asked him to go to the park to play ball. He could picture the exact look on Chester's face. That made him smile, for a second. Then Maddox thought back to the call that he had received that day, when Pepe had been arrested.

"Sooome-teeeng ees wrongg, Madd-ox! Sooome-teeeng ees ver-ry ver-ry wrong," Garibaldi had said.

Yes, something was very, very wrong. He thought about the brutal rape of April Tilney. But, he felt the tug of money on his soul — he thought about the money, the commissions, from Pepe Soliz. Just like he always used to.

But this time, when he felt that tug, that disappointment over losing Pepe Soliz's money, something different happened. Something that had never happened to Maddox before. Maddox Malone felt something push back on the tug of Pepe's money. He couldn't quite figure out what it was. Something was pushing back, this time. He was certain of it. But what was it? Was it relief? Was it rejection? Was it something else? Maddox didn't know.

ii

A few minutes later, Maddox heard a knock on his door. "That's strange," thought Maddox. "I'm not expecting anyone."

Maddox opened the door and two men were standing there. One flashed a badge and said, "Hi Maddox, I'm Special Agent Barrett Harmon and this is my partner Special Agent Fredrickson. We're here to talk to you about Zaine Fuller, the Malone Agency, and Obadiah and

Otis Ballard. Can we come in?"

Time stopped.

A moment later, Maddox, without saying anything and with a stunned look on his face, motioned the men into his office.

They sat down on the couch. Special Agent Harmon explained to Maddox that he didn't have to speak to them without an attorney. Maddox, tired of everything, said that he would rather just speak to them now. Agent Harmon said he thought that was for the best.

Agent Harmon continued, "We already know everything from Major O. Great guy by the way. We know about the payments to Major O, to Obadiah, to Elk Fearghus and to E-Fear. We know about the payments to Jeremiah Raspico."

Maddox just stared at the agent.

Agent Harmon continued, "so, Maddox Malone, you have a decision to make. You can call a lawyer and fight this —"

"No, I'll just tell you what I know. I should have done that earlier but I was dealing with a couple things. I had some stuff go haywire on me. Where do you want me to start?" asked Maddox Malone.

"Just start at the beginning. Tell us everything you know about the payments Zaine Fuller made to the Ballards, the Fearghuses and anyone else."

Maddox sat there for a second. He felt a tinge of fear. A tinge of regret. Then, for the next fifteen minutes, he told the Agents everything he knew about the payments. He just told the truth and figured he would let the chips fall where they may.

At the end of the story, Agent Harmon said, "Thanks Maddox. That's consistent with what we talked to Major O and Elk Fearghus about. I appreciate you being open with us and not using deflection tactics. While you should have reported the payments right away, we understand that life is not always perfect. You were put in a tough situation — next time, you need to act quickly to nip things like this in the-

"

"Yeah, there won't be a next time on that type of thing," said Maddox bluntly, interrupting the agent.

"We're not focusing on you for this investigation — we're focusing the investigation and the charges on Zaine Fuller. But you should know that the league may also take action against Zaine and the Malone Agency. This would have happened no matter what you did today, whether or not you cooperated. We have all the evidence."

Maddox didn't say anything further. During the whole conversation, he resisted the urge to deflect and excuse the payments. They were rampant in the industry, but they were still illegal and corrupt. They were wrong. Maddox had plenty of other things on his mind. Maddox just admitted what happened and moved on from there. At this point, they were over and done with. They were the least of his worries.

The agents left and Maddox went about his day. He sat at his desk for a good chunk of the day. He thought. Then he moved to the office couch. When he moved over there, he sat and thought as well. Finally, the day was done.

Rivers of Blood

❋❋

Almost at the same time that Maddox hung up the call from the Flatworm asking about the Poobah's termination of the Malone Agency, Kalli received a frantic call from her mother, Patty. She was crying hysterically.

"Your brother Remy is dead. He's dead," Kalli's mom was crying.

"Mom, what happened?"

"He was having trouble with those damn pain pills. The kickers. The police said he shot himself."

The kickers came from a four foot tall, beautiful, hardy flower, Papaver somniferum. The poppy. The flower blooms in a wide array of gorgeous colors. It thrives in moderate climates, does not need tending, attracts few destructive pests, and is tougher to kill than most weeds. When the bloom of the flower fades, what is left behind is a grayish pod fringed with tube-like flutes. Thousands of years ago, it is believed that a man named Tumultuo learned to crush the flower's bulb-like pod and mix it with water. The resulting mixture, Tumultuo found, had an oddly euphoric effect on the human brain. His brother, Martirio, first found out that if you cut the pod with a sharp instrument, capture its flowing white sap, and leave that to harden in the air, you'll get a smokable nugget that provides an even more intense experience of euphoria.

Even the venerable Homer called it a substance characterized by wonder. Those who consumed these substances, Homer said, could not be affected by anything. They could not be moved. Every attempt to banish the poppy, destroy the poppy, or prohibit the poppy — has failed.

In present day, opioids from the poppy poured across the United States' porous, unprotected border with Mexico, and more than six million Americans, like Remy, were facing some form of opioid addiction or other. Remy had battled opioid addiction for years and then, one day, today, he lost.

"Oh, shit. Jesus. Mom, I'll come over to you."

Kalli rushed to her car and drove fifteen minutes to her mom's house.

She turned up the music to try to drown out her thoughts. Ruby Haze, a new country artist, was singing on the radio. Kalli sang along, she really liked this song and that helped calm her down, at least momentarily.

> It's such a cryin' shame
> I kind of liked you in that hat
> But when you do me dirty, boy
> You got the wrong country girl for that
> When you do me dirty boy
> You got the wrong .... country girl for that

Kalli drove as fast as she could. When she got there, her mom was still crying. So was her dad. She took turns hugging them both. She cried as well. Two hours went by in this fashion.

Kalli's older brother had left a note before he shot himself in the head behind his house. The note read "To my family: I feel trapped. I can't go on like this. I am stuck in same cycle over and over. I can't recover. I can't concentrate. So I am doing the best thing I can do. You have given me everything you could, more than you could. You have been in every way all that anyone could be. I can't fight any longer. I know that I am letting everyone down. I owe all the happiness of my life to you, even though it was only here and there. That was my fault. You have been entirely patient with me and incredibly good to me. You have given me everything. I need to say that – everybody knows it. If anybody could have saved me it would have been you, my family. I have nothing left. I must go on. Love Remy."

Kalli read the note twice. She started crying, again. Her mom was crying. Everyone was a mess. Emotions flowed, rolled, splashed, and bounced around wildly. She couldn't take it. Her parents were hysterical. After another thirty minutes went by, Kalli realized she was out of time.

"Mom, I need to go to work," said Kalli.

"Can't you call in?"

"Not with this short of notice, they will fire me no matter what the reason. I work in thirty minutes. I'll call you later tonight."

"Okay, honey, I understand, I understand."

Everyone was still crying.

"I will call you during my breaks at work."

"I love you."

"I love you too."

She hugged them both and got in her small sports utility vehicle to drive back home to change and then head over to work. Kalli was in a daze. Her brother was dead. It made her think about her own life. The more she thought about her circumstances, the more a new sense of fatality weighed on her.

Kalli felt the uselessness of struggling against her circumstances. She had always tried to adapt herself to circumstances. Hollywood, Alaska, Washington, Oregon, now Phoenix. She had always tried to make the best of her situation, whatever it was. But, when push came to shove, when it came time to accomplish something big or to cross-over from just-getting-by into the realm of success and that oh-so-elusive concept of happiness, she always found a way to miss out. She might sabotage herself. Some event might distract her. Her plans changed. Her attention waned. Whatever, it always happened. Or, find a way to blame someone or something for sabotage. Ultimately, she could only break things down. She could not build herself up, not long term. She could tear things and other people down, including herself. Herself most of all, to be honest! And she could destroy her environment, her path to success, any given relationship, ultimately her life. She always felt herself too over-matched by outside events, by powerful forces, by fate. Sometimes, by near-term desires or ill-considered plans that took her off of a better path. Why had she moved to Oregon in the first place? Why Alaska? Why Los Angeles at fifteen? Suddenly, she regretted everything.

This was a terrible feeling! Why was she not doing better?

Kalli took out her notepad that she wrote in from time to time. She opened it to a blank page and wrote herself a very short note.

She wrote, "The less I need the better I feel."

Kalli put her pen down, and for a few hours her spirit felt at ease. Then she began to have creeping doubts about her cute little saying. She still needed certain things. It might have been nice to think that she needed less of them, or whatever, but that didn't change the fact that she had to head to the bar and grill in a few minutes to push drinks around for tips so she could pay her bills. She wondered why the euphoria from the little saying was so short-lived. As she changed into her work clothing, she kept pondering these things. Her room began to spin around her, and her tile floor started to roll and ebb under her feet. The dizziness was followed by a wave of nausea like she had felt after Michael, her ex-boyfriend from Oregon, had punched her in her face. Her room felt hot, suddenly. Ten minutes before she had felt at peace, thanks to her journal. Now, it seemed as if she were going to die. Maybe she wanted to die? Little by little, her nausea and dizziness subsided. She stood up, put some lotion on her face and hands, groped for her baseball hat that she sometimes wore while bartending and then stumbled outside towards her vehicle. The sunlight hit her face as she kept dragging herself towards the car. As she reached it, she saw a sports car drive by. She was sure that the driver was looking at her intently. As he drove by, she realized that he wasn't looking at her at all. She thought she was losing her mind.

Her thoughts jarred back to her brother's suicide and to her mom and dad. A heavy, brooding faintness came over her. She actually leaned her head against an outside wall. She didn't know if she was going to cry or not. She wasn't in control of herself. Seconds went by, maybe even minutes. Finally, she opened her eyes. She had to get to work so she didn't get fired by her short, stocky little boss. Maybe it would be a good thing for her, to work an eight hour shift, from four 'till midnight. She could get her mind off of things. Like her brother's death and her parents' (and her own) incredible sadness. She was melancholy for the rest of the day and the rest of the night. She felt anxious. She thought she would never be a successful singer, and her acting and modeling days were long gone at this point. She liked tending her horses, but she didn't want to be a bartender forever. The whole thing weighed on her. She felt sad for her parents, who had put so much into her brother. Trying to help him, trying to make him successful. She felt the heavy weight of disappointment as much as she had in years and years.

ii

Maddox had just arrived at his office, and not because he had a lot of busy-work. He was there because he wanted to think strategically, deeply, meditatively about his business and anything else that came to mind. He needed a re-set, and he had to think.

Maddox Malone was bust.

Pepe Soliz's commissions — gone.

TENACIOUS hopes — gone.

Platform Volleyball contract revenue — gone.

Obadiah Ballard future commissions — those certainly would be gone now that the FBI was investigating the emerging bribery scandal.

Maddox Malone was bust. He just sat there, in his office, trying to create a spark. He needed a light bulb to go off. He needed something to click! He had done this every day, ever since his final meeting with Pepe. Trying to focus in on a plan. Trying to figure out what to do. Thinking. Wondering. Imagining.

iii

Across the country in Minnesota, life's disappointments had finally caught up with Party Wardy Goldstein, the Tick. Not only had the disappointments of his life caught up with the soul-less parasite, but they had overtaken him entirely. The Tick had been in Minneapolis, Minnesota, on a football recruiting trip for his new agency — Superior Sports — where he was really working on behalf of a scam charity trying to get clients of the firm to donate money to his friend's fake charity, so they could split the proceeds. The Party's his health had taken a turn for the worse. He didn't feel right. His intestine had released, via the Tick's valve, a stench so noxious, so putrid, so revolting, that the Tick himself gagged. Hisss! Hisssss! Hisssss! The rank gas seeped out of his release valve and became an overwhelming presence in his hotel room.

His face showed only withdrawal and remorse. He just sat there in the middle of the fumes. Ward Goldstein was an old-ish man at this point. He was approaching forty and he had never done anything worthwhile or meaningful in his life. He was a degenerate, a scoundrel. A piece of shit. He had no prospect for a decent girlfriend or wife. He had no apparent skills. He was shallow. When he spoke, it was always a jumble of bullshit and clichés. The Tick took out his smart phone and sent a text message to his mom, Nancy. It read, "I have to go now. Thanks for everything."

Then, Party Wardy walked out of his room and took the elevator down into the lobby of his hotel. He strolled out the front door and was soon on Washington Avenue. It was cold out! He kept walking, west, towards the Washington Avenue Bridge. When he was about thirty feet away from the bridge, he rubbed his stomach. He stopped rubbing his stomach and both his hands clenched into fists. The Party kept walking. He reached the bridge and saw a happy couple walking on the other side of the bridge. A man and a woman, in their thirties, walking fast to try to reach their destination and get out of the freezing cold, joking with each other and smiling along the way. The Party trudged on, through the ice and the snow, alone. He released his valve. Hiss. Hisss. Hissss.

Ward Goldstein turned and waved to the couple, with a forced, rigid smile. His lips were stiff with what looked like apprehension and white from cold-chapping. The wind was whipping and howling and it wasn't going to settle down. Not today. He concluded the stiff smile, and turned slightly to his left. Then he took two short steps and jumped off of the bridge, hurling himself toward the frozen west bank of the Mississippi River, landing with a loud pudddd-ddddd sound — the body hit first then his head — ninety feet below. On the way down, his only thoughts were of his rotten insides and his foul stench. When he landed, blood seeped out of his broken body and onto the Mississippi River's icy embankment. The noxious gasses in his middle oozed out of his newly-unclenched valve. Just like that, it was all over for the Tick.

Maddox had not been in touch with the Tick for months. Maddox had fired Party Wardy the day after Maddox refused to give rape bailout money to Pepe Soliz — the same day the Poobah had fired the Malone Agency. Maddox had no idea what the Tick was doing, and never thought about it.

Nonetheless, one of Maddox's acquaintances, a guy named Kyle Drury, had heard the news about Party Wardy from his younger brother's social media feed, and he called Maddox on his smart phone.

"Ward Goldstein just jumped off a bridge in Minneapolis. He's dead," said Kyle.

"Really?"

"Yeah."

"Well, thanks for letting me know, Kyle," Maddox said and they hung up a moment later. Maddox thought briefly about LegoLand and the parasitic Tick's role in the rape of April Tilney — but he didn't have time for that. Not now. He lost enough time dealing with the rape and its aftermath. "Turn out the lights," thought Maddox, "the Party is over." With that, any further thought about Ward Goldstein and his suicide left Maddox's head, he hoped, for good.

Maddox moved himself over to his office couch — and just sat there, deep in thought — he didn't have a single thought about the Tick. He just sat there and thought about life and whatever else crossed his mind. The agency, his kids, the gym, recent news, and books he had recently read. He thought about his circumstances with the Malone Agency, yes, but he also thought about possibilities separate from that. He left his smart phone at his desk, where it sat, whirring, beeping, buzzing, pushing notifications and the Pozz. Maddox Malone ignored his smart phone, and he became lost in thought.

Suddenly Maddox Malone received a jarring, almost unbelievable, text message from his wife, Laura. It read, "Maddox, I'm filing for divorce. We have no connection anymore. Can you please come to the house at three to discuss?"

Maddox read the text twice. His eyes went wide! Holy shit, he thought. Holy shit! When the clock approached three p.m., he got in his sports car and drove home. He walked into his kitchen.

"Wow, Maddox. We really are a pair," Laura said. Her jet black hair didn't move, not a bit. She just stared at him.

"Not no more, we ain't," Maddox thought, echoing his client Chris Black's comments on that fateful day at LegoLand. But Maddox didn't say anything.

He glanced over at Laura and glanced around the kitchen.

Maddox looked around the large, adjoined kitchen and living room at his house and at his wife. The dog, Kingsley, was over on his dog-bed chewing on a toy. Maddox felt sick. He wasn't nervous or jumpy, but he was in a daze. He felt drowsy. Kind of like a waking dream. He hated the feeling he was experiencing. He wanted to get this over with and feel his normal energy. So the best thing was to just get it over as fast as possible. He would get back to normal, right? He never expected his marriage to fail. He never really expected to fail at anything, but here he was, a failure. So many failures in a row!

The thing that gnawed at him, really chewed him up was not the discord with Laura. They were grown adults and they talked to each other with such disdain and disrespect, what did they think was going to happen? Maddox didn't want to be away from his kids half the time, and he had been willing to stay, for years, in a failed marriage due to that fact. It had all been difficult for Maddox, too — not just for Laura. A wife who hadn't shown any personal regard or genuine affection for him in what he figured must have been ten years. The marriage was hopeless. It was over. He had, for a long time, viewed his family as his final bunker, where he could retreat and rebuild his life after he sorted through the rubble of Pepe Soliz, TENACIOUS, the Platform, the FBI visit and everything else. In the end, Maddox realized, that didn't work. Things had just gone too haywire. It was over.

"Come on," she said, "sit down. I'll get you a drink. You want some water?"

"I'm good. I just had a big iced Americano at the office."

She went into the kitchen, and he looked down at his hand. He took stock of his marriage in his mind. Maddox was sleeping in his home office ninety-nine out of one hundred nights (as he had for years) — avoiding Laura as much as possible. He hated how she spoke to him in person, even more than the phone calls. His yardstick for measuring people was always how they treated him. And no one that he knew treated him, and spoke to him, worse than she did. How does that happen? The tone, the lack of respect, the disdain, the negative energy, the misery. But in a strange way he didn't want to end the marriage before today, before he received that text message on his smart phone. Primarily, because of the kids. Secondarily, because he hated - hated - to fail at anything. So, thought Maddox, this was the next in a long series of disappointments. Life!

Presently, Laura returned with a water. She sat down in the other kitchen dining chair, with a forced smile. She took a sip of water.

"So here we are, Maddox. I got your card and I wasn't able to talk about it sooner because I was with my friend Kristen. After she left, I was busy with work and then the stuff came up with school. I just wanted to send you that message this morning to let you know that I didn't need any more time to think about what you said in your card."

"Umm, okay."

Maddox had left a short note on a rather ridiculous greeting card, with a drawing of a bear on the front. He bought the card at a department store for a couple bucks — and he wrote a note on it offering to try to keep the family together and give his best efforts to salvage the marriage. It wasn't overly deferential. He wasn't going to kiss her ass. He may have been a horrible husband in many ways - absent and brooding to name two - but she had been a horrible wife and a negative, depressing partner. They were in this together and both of them were responsible for the toxic marriage, thought Maddox. She hadn't made him feel any happiness in years. And she hadn't tried. And he was sure she felt the exact same thing about him. So the note wasn't apologetic at all. It just offered, once more, to try.

"Yeah, I got the card, but I still want to get a divorce. Things change, Maddox."

"Okay, Laura. I wanted to at least offer that up. I don't want to be with you either, but I feel bad for the kids. I love those kids and I remember how shitty it was when my parents got divorced. After a couple of days went by and I didn't hear from you about my note I figured it wasn't gonna happen anyway."

"I don't want to hurt you but I don't want to be married to you anymore. Things change," Laura said.

Maddox sat there.

"You, you were always so far away," said Laura.

"I get that. Our marriage was the worst. I can't remember the last time I enjoyed talking to you. Still, I felt like a dog that had been run over by a truck when you texted me about getting divorced."

"You don't know what a dog that has been run over feels like," Laura challenged.

"Wait, what?" said Maddox.

"You heard me," said Laura.

"I said that's what I felt like. I don't care about the dog. That's what I felt like," said Maddox.

"But you don't know what that dog would feel like."

"Holy shit. I felt like a dog that got run over by a truck. It's an expression. And even if it isn't an actual expression it's easy to understand. Maybe I'm the first to say it. But don't tell me it doesn't make sense. It makes sense."

"How would you know what that dog would feel like, Maddox?"

"What the fuck are you talking about, Laura?"

"I said, how would you know what that dog would feel like?"

"It's not a specific dog, Laura. And I've been hit by things so I would have to imagine that except on a bigger scale. And being a dog. I just imagine it. It would really suck to be that dog. You know, if he got hit."

"Never-mind the dog. It just doesn't seem realistic."

"It does to me."

"You've changed, Maddox Malone. I just want to be inspired by someone. You don't do that for me anymore. People get divorced. People get divorced all the time. It's time to move on."

Maddox's mind wandered for a second. "Fuck it, then," he thought. He suddenly wanted to leave. He couldn't believe he logged so many years in this marriage. Let's get it over with, then.

"Right, so I have to move on. It's over. I want the kids half the time, like we talked about. Like we agreed upon. Okay?"

"Yes, of course. Half and half. That's what we agreed to," said Laura.

"Good luck to you, I wish it was a better marriage."

"Me too."

All those thoughts buzzed through his mind in just a minute. He snapped back into the present conversation with Laura.

"So, we'll just get everything worked out as soon as we can. I have an attorney helping me. It should be really simple since the custody will be fifty-fifty and I'm not looking to loot all your assets from your hard work at the Malone Agency and the law firm before that."

"Okay, whatever. I'm not even going to get an attorney. I can't stand that shit. It's all fine. I'm over it now, I was just fixated on the kids," Maddox said.

The thought of losing his kids part of the time was still gnawing at his soul. It was eating him up, even now that he had accepted everything and moved on from the marriage mentally.

"Even if I wasn't, I don't have a choice. Things change. Like you said, people get divorced. It happens all the time. There's nothing I can do except move on. I'm gonna go rebuild my life. Since all that shit happened with Pepe, TENACIOUS, the Platform and O-Bad, there's a lot of work to do."

He looked at Laura's face and felt precisely nothing. She looked at him with what he viewed as disdain. Maybe he imagined that but he saw it. He didn't care. His thoughts, even though repetitive, kept swirling around in his mind. He was the one who took all the risk in a crazy business. Not Laura.

He was asked for a million dollars after Pepe raped April Tilney. Not Laura.

The Platform bankruptcy cost Maddox hundreds of thousands of dollars. Not Laura.

The Grasshopper hoaxed Maddox with TENACIOUS. Not Laura.

Maddox endured a major scandal when Zaine was caught paying Obadiah. Not Laura.

Maddox had to endure Carlton Duffer, his crooked-out lip, and his stupid ideas. Not Laura. That guy was a fucking idiot!

"It didn't have to be this way, Maddox. I don't understand why you didn't tell me about what was going on. I mean, I had to hear about you suing Pepe for unpaid fees from my friends and family. They saw it on television."

Maddox's temper boiled. The conversation had seemed like it was wrapping up, now they were starting in again.

"We've been over this. I don't give a fuck what you heard and from whom. I'm not the bad guy because I had to sue that fat piece of shit for my fees. I'm so God-damned tired of hearing about it. I'm so tired of the fucking Poobah and the fucking Big Boys."

"I felt stupid and left out. I didn't feel like you worked at our marriage."

"Well, maybe I didn't think marriage was supposed to be so much work. So much misery. When was the last time you told a joke?"

Laura gasped.

"Well I don't think you love me anymore," she said.

"Why would you say that? You texted me this morning for a divorce. What am I supposed to say? You complete me?" Maddox laughed to himself and thought of the Puddle Bear - who actually said that to his ex-wife. His face stayed blank, though.

There was a long pause. So much angst in the room.

"You're a great dad and you love your kids. But you don't love me and I can't do that anymore. You wouldn't even go to a marriage counselor."

"Fuck no, I wouldn't. Marriage counseling is a setup for a man. I'm not gonna say shit and then have it used against me by you and some hand-rubbing psychologist later. That's how that shit works."

"See, Maddox, that's how you are about everything."

"I am how I am. I should have walked away from Pepe Soliz the day he did the rape. It was all over when he tore up April's little butt-hole."

Laura gasped again, louder this time.

Maddox tilted his head and sneered involuntarily, he was feeling a decent amount of rage but wanted to bottle that up instead of show it here. He understood that she was feeling the way she was feeling. But he felt the way he felt, too, and he wasn't moving. Nobody was gonna move an inch to even try to cross the chasm that had developed over the years — and that meant that the marriage was over.

Laura cringed.

"Maddox. Okay! Enough! Well I feel like you take it out on me. I feel like you never loved me."

"Oh great, this again. None of this shit has anything to do with love. I represented a rapist, and that cost me money and business. TENACIOUS was fake and that really hurt my business. You just can't handle it. You cut bait. You don't think I can be successful again after TENACIOUS and the Soliz stuff. You don't think I can recover. You think I'm burned out. Hell, I am burned out — at least on how I used to do things. This isn't about fucking love. You're just bailing out."

"You bailed too, Maddox. You bailed too. You were supposed to tell me if you were having problems. That is what marriage is supposed to be. You should have come to me. You should have talked to me. I could have helped. My parents would have helped you," said Laura.

She looked sad. That made Maddox sad.

"Well, I just thought I could handle everything. I always did before."

"People need help, Maddox," said Laura.

"That's probably true. Still, why bring that up now, after everything is over?"

"It could have been different," said Laura.

"I can't go back and change things. Everything went to shit but watch what I come back with, I'm going to be better than I ever was. I'm going back to what made me who I am, and that's not a bunch of stuff. I've been thinking about things. I'm just starting to think about things."

"Oh Maddox..."

"I'm going to tell my story too, when I'm back on my feet. I'm gonna tell what I learned."

"You're not going to tell your story, Maddox. Just move on from your Malone Agency, just go get a normal job. You're a lawyer. That's what you are. The Jerry Maguire thing just didn't work."

"Oh fuck," thought Maddox. "It was that God-damned movie again!" He couldn't escape that movie!

"I'll tell my story if I want, watch me do it," said Maddox with resolve showing on his face.

"No, you're not going to."

"I will if I want. I'm gonna," said Maddox.

"No, you're not," said Laura, stubbornly.

There was a pause.

"Come on, Maddox. Be realistic. You're getting all worked up again. You're not going to tell any story. There is no story. Just move on."

Laura sat there for a second, just looking at Maddox. Maddox knew that she had changed — and she could see that he had changed as well, and was letting out bottled up thoughts now that the marriage was finished. He wasn't holding back. Maddox could see Laura's change in her eyes. She was not going to be with him anymore, he could see it. It was over. It's over, man. Time to move on. He just stared ahead. There was nothing he could do about Laura, but losing his kids half the time really gnawed at him.

He kept coming back to it! Otherwise, he would have just shut up and walked out the door and moved on with his life as best he could. The thought felt like it was killing him.

Over time, Maddox's world had morphed, it had almost vanished; after this conversation with Laura, after the finality of it, he felt utterly alone, at least in Phoenix. Actually, he felt alone throughout the whole country, the whole world. He felt sad, bitter, miserable, yearning, and regretful. He felt the sting of failure, disappointment over wasted effort, sadness brought about by lost time. Embarrassed for having a failed marriage, since he always felt sorry for divorced people and kids with divorced parents when he was growing up - since he was now sorry for himself for his failure.

Importantly, and from the sum of all his activity, he learned that where there is a chance of success, a chance of gain, there is a corresponding chance of failure, loss, and disappointment. Of all the things he learned lately, this may have been the most prominent. He hadn't experienced that part of life before — and now he experienced it time and time again.

"Okay, Maddox," said Laura. Her face was dismissive. Removed. Blank.

"Okay, Laura. I'm going to my office for a while. I'll sleep here in the home office until I can get everything moved out into a new place. You can have the house. I'll move out as fast as I can. I'll just figure it all out. I'll catch you later. Thanks for everything."

"Okay, Bye."

Maddox got in his car and went for a drive. He drove all the way out of Phoenix and went west on Carefree Highway so he could take the long way to the office. He wanted to drive for a while, and drive fast. He turned up the music.

> I know the pieces fit 'cause I watched them tumble down
>
> No fault, none to blame, it doesn't mean I don't desire to
>
> Point the finger, blame the other, watch the temple topple over.

Maddox took his sports car up to about eighty-five miles per hour in the fifty-five mile per hour zone. He turned to the right, heading north on Twenty Fourth street. He took the backroads and then headed back to the east to get to his office. He parked and walked in. He sat down. His office was small but nice. He sat in his desk chair for a few minutes but quickly moved to his comfortable gold leather couch. He thought back on his broken relationship with Laura. He thought about a lot of the good times. Mostly, he thought about his kids. He felt like a failure as a person, as a dad.

All those thoughts were buzzing through Maddox's head at the same time. He had a vacant look on his face. He sat on his office couch. He had some music playing through his office sound system.

> She hurt my eyes open, that's no lie
> Tables turn and now her turn to cry
> Because I used to love her, but it's all over now

At least it was comfortable! And now, it was Maddox, sitting on his office couch alone. Night was falling. Everything was growing dark, with a large vacant parking lot outside. Maddox's mind flooded with thoughts and frustration. He felt angry. He was also feeling a tinge of hatred, if he was honest. But that bothered him too, because, while he felt that Laura was a bad wife who often spoke to him in an unacceptable manner, he didn't think she was a bad person. In fact, she was a decent and good person. And she was the mother of his children, a loving mother. So, now Maddox felt hatred for himself for hating Laura, even just a little bit. He had to admit, he was a brooding, non-communicative withdrawn husband with a wild business that required constant travel.

Maddox breathed.

He calmed himself down, reminding himself there is a difference between anger and hatred. He had to be comfortable with anger, which was going to happen, but he didn't want to embrace hatred. He felt disgusted. There was an ocean between them, and there had been for a number of years. Cold silence. Fundamental difference. Finger pointing. Doubt. Suspicion. The pieces used to fit, but then they fell apart.

He sat in his God-damned office. He could hardly see straight. Still operating inside the waking dream! He still felt like a dog that had been hit by a car. He walked out of the office holding his smart phone which was buzzing with digital media notifications, pushing the Pozz. Probably another article about bathroom access for trannies! He ignored the notifications but went to the phone application and called his sister Angela, but she didn't answer.

"Hey Gel, it's me Maddox. Just calling to say hello. Love ya'.

Bye."

He started driving to his house. His smart phone buzzed, and it was his sister calling back.

"Hey, Laura threw me out."

"Seriously?" Angela said, then there was stunned silence from Angela.

"Yeah."

"Ooooh," Angela groaned. "That's shitty."

"I know. Sort of is what it is at this point. I'm just leaving my office."

"You mean right now? That's where you are?"

"Yes."

"You need a hotel? You want to come here? You're welcome with me and Steve, obviously. I can get you a plane ticket."

"I'll keep sleeping in the home office until I can move out. I'm disappointed."

"Yes, of course you are."

"I'm just gonna try to do what I can to get back on my feet. I'm just freaked out about moving out of the house because I'm dealing with a bunch of bullshit from my agency. Had some stuff go nuts on me."

"Yeah, I get that. That's all you can do. Disappointment is okay, try to stay positive. Everything is going to be all right."

Maddox paused.

"How do you know?"

"I just know," she said.

"I like that. Say it again for me."

"Everything is going to be all right."

When he got home, he went straight into his home office. He

grabbed the book he was currently reading, *the American* by Henry James. He was at the part where there was a conversation around the Tristrams' Parisian dinner table. Newman, the American, openly admits that he is out in Europe looking for a wife. He admits this to Tom and Lizzie Tristram, an unhappily married American couple. Maddox was absorbed and kept reading the book for the next hour. Maddox thought that it was so interesting that Newman would do that. Newman wanted to go find a woman. He admitted it, openly. It was like he was shopping for a pair of shoes. And Newman wanted nice shoes! This part of the story was so incredibly interesting to Maddox. Maddox had always been much more subtle than that. He thought Newman was setting himself up - but what did Maddox know?

He read for a while and put down the book. He lay there, again, in a sort of a daze, a waking dream, thinking about loss, damage, destruction, deep disappointment. He missed his kids already and he hadn't even moved out of the house yet. All of the same thoughts were cycling through his head over and over and he hated the repetition! He thought of something else that Henry James had written.

Be not afraid of life.

Maddox tried to rally himself. He was nodding off to sleep, and he told himself to not be afraid of what was coming. He had to accept the change, accept the new challenge. Embrace it. Use the lessons, use his past to grow. He had to live. He couldn't let these events consume him, eat him alive. Lately, he felt like he was letting that happen. He wondered how he could stop dwelling on the past. The only way to do that was to believe that life was worth living. Search for meaning. Work on himself. Develop himself. Develop his thoughts. Find joy. Have fun. Embrace kindness. Maddox wanted to work hard again, just as he had in the past. But this time, he wanted to work on something worthwhile — no rapists, no volleyball, no fake training facilities and fake funding from Grasshoppers with billowing haunches, no bribes for football players and their families. He told himself that all of this stuff, all of the Malone Agency stuff, just filled his life. It filled the space. But deep down inside he knew that all that shit wasn't right. He didn't want to give up hope. He told himself there was something out there and that he just needed to hold on and believe. He had to find something to do that was decent — maybe even fun — and rewarding. He surprised himself, because when he thought of ideas for things he wanted to do, he wasn't always thinking of money first. But he still couldn't think of anything to do next. That was the problem!

Non Fregit Eum Sed Erexit

✤✤

More weeks went by, just like this, and Maddox gave over to irritation. The disappointments had mounted! Maddox' whole framework for life had been shaken by the fact that TENACIOUS was a hoax. He had been through so much with everything else as well. Pepe, Laura, Lacy, Obadiah, everything. But it was TENACIOUS that really changed Maddox. It changed him! In fact, it was irritation from TENACIOUS that tore down Maddox's framework. His entire framework for life tumbled down!

Maddox had always lived a certain way. He had certain characteristics and specific understandings over time. He had a way that he expected to go about his life. He had done it for a long time. In some ways it seemed like this framework served him well. He was successful and people looked up to him. He was a successful agent at the Malone Agency. He was a successful lawyer at Decker & Formenter. His old framework and outlook was compatible with corporate success. It was compatible with hobbies and pastimes. It was compatible with fun and even pain. Anger and even hatred. He wasn't letting himself give over to hatred much, anymore, but when he did, he made it through. It didn't break him down. He was managing his hatred and his anger quite well.

But, Maddox had become irritated. Irritation like this, for some reason, was not compatible with Maddox's world view and, in a sense, it was irritation, more than anything else, that finally, completely tore down Maddox's old world view. His old framework, his old views on life – they broke down.

Irritation.

When this irritation set in, for the next month or so, Maddox went here and there feeling like a solitary figure, even though he would interact with people in a normal manner. He thought a lot. He replayed everything in his head. He would sometimes think about what might have gone differently for the Malone Agency, for TENACIOUS, and in his family life, had he taken different courses of action. Could he have taken a different approach in general? Was he made for something better than transactions? Why had he become an agent, anyway? These thoughts gave him a certain enthusiasm for himself and his abilities. He had worked so hard to create the Malone Agency. But the Malone Agency had, at least in the end, brought him personal and professional turmoil, disagreement, distrust, disappointment, disaster, damage.

At times, during this period, he was gloomy and not completely irritated. Sometimes his mental solitude, even while he walked in crowds, lost in his thoughts, made him feel relaxed. Sometimes, just thinking deeply gave him comfort. Maddox believed that he had paid too big a penalty for everything that happened. He felt pride in himself and his achievements. He had worked hard, he had done so much! So many deals. He knew that there were not many people who could have done what he did. He was never scared to do anything, to try anything. He was invincible, at times. He did deals that no one else could have done. He took risk.

Now, though, in some ways, his senses sharpened. His vision seemed better. His balance seemed better. He still noticed everything. He was sharp, he was on edge. He began to fast intermittently. Some days he would spend without eating anything and kept himself going with iced coffee and psyllium husks all day. The first day he did this the following morning, his hunger was so intense he ate fourteen scrambled eggs in one sitting, with French toast, all while practically raging with intense emotion that he couldn't categorize. He felt alive!

Sometimes, his thoughts were very positive, and other times Maddox felt like he was being consumed by madness. His enthusiasm for himself and his abilities and accomplishments at times inexplicably changed into hatred and bitterness. He thought about all the problems and disappointments that he had faced over time. And there were many! But it was something specifically about the end of the TENACIOUS hoax had thrown him off — it irritated him and took him out of his life's framework entirely. He kept coming back to the TENACIOUS hoax, he couldn't shake it. The hoax seemed to constantly chase his mind and overtake his thoughts.

Why had Paul McCartney faked the funding of the TENACIOUS projects?

Why spend time that way?

Why?

This specific topic vexed Maddox immensely. Maddox Malone couldn't move on from the topic.

"What motivated Paul McCartney?" Maddox asked himself, again and again.

Paul McCartney's actions didn't fit into any system of thought, any framework for life, which Maddox recognized. Because McCartney's actions didn't fit anywhere in Maddox's views on life, Maddox had to change those views.

In a strange twist, it was the soul-less Grasshopper that changed Maddox Malone's views on life more than any other person ever had.

Even weeks after their dramatic exchange in Las Vegas — when the TENACIOUS hoax finally ran its course and Maddox told the 'Hopper to go fuck himself — Maddox still couldn't believe that there was a person with the same value, the same characteristics, as a simple grasshopper.

Stuck in this irritated state, Maddox became obstinate in re-evaluating everything. He was obsessed. He thought about his experience with the Grasshopper, who always seemed to yell "Let's do this!" when he was talking about the TENACIOUS projects. But he never actually did anything, other than get drunk and high and use hookers.

One day, Maddox thought of a question, a single question, which would, eventually, helped him emerge from the rubble, rebuild and re-fashion himself and his entire outlook on life.

"Why try to figure out Paul McCartney?" is the question that Maddox asked himself. Why bother with that guy? Maddox couldn't read minds. Trying to figure out what motivated Paul McCartney was impossible, for Maddox. He resolved to close that line of questioning down, permanently.

And once Maddox Malone had Paul McCartney, the degenerate Grasshopper, blocked out of his mind — he thought of the question, a paramount question, that marked another turning point in Maddox's life. The first turning point had been when he told the Poobah that he wouldn't give him the hush money for April Tilney. He had, at that moment, rejected the very thing he was about to learn about. It was the first step towards driving it out of his life.

And then he thought, very simply, why? Why did Maddox — Maddox Malone — want to do the TENACIOUS project? Why had the project been so important to him?

Once he thought about that exact question in that specific context, the floodgates opened. He thought about modern capitalism. He thought about subversion. He thought about materialism. He thought about the Pozz. He thought about advertising. He thought about corporatism. He thought about technology, like Endless Content and their Super Duper digital facial blast. He thought about cultural and familial bonds. He remembered the feeling like a dog that had been hit by a truck. He thought about traditions. History. Then, focusing sharply, he thought about greed. He thought about Pogo Back, XtraShoog, Efficient-Pop and Pepe Soliz. Maddox Malone realized that he had wanted to believe Paul McCartney's lies about TENACIOUS because Maddox wanted more. More money! More notoriety. More action. That's really what it boiled down to. Good, old-fashioned greed. If Maddox had his own priorities straight, he would have been immune to the Grasshopper and his strange brand of bullshit.

Maddox didn't realize that what he had was so great. So great! Three beautiful children. A wife, Laura, who was a good and decent person. He was careful not to idealize the vision of his horribly flawed marriage — Maddox and Laura had a fundamental inability to communicate which may have, in fact, proved impossible to overcome even without all of the disastrous events. But, like Laura, Maddox did not do a good job of nurturing the marriage. He didn't know how. Like his own parents' marriage, once there was a gap — Maddox and Laura could not figure out how to close that gap. Neither could, independently, and they certainly couldn't do it together. If Maddox had prioritized things better, rather than putting work above everything, there may have been a chance for a miracle. A chance to find common ground. But with the way Maddox was obsessed with deals, with work, with growth, with money? There was simply no chance that they could put the pieces back together.

For several weeks Maddox ate only every other day, and he mostly fasted the other days with the exception of psyllium husks, some almonds, black coffee and water. Plus a boiled egg here and there. Months went by, with no vodka. On the days he ate, he went and lifted heavy weights at his gym. He watched his body transform, again, from a corporate-type body back to a muscular, rangy physique – like he had when he was younger. Maddox was being re-forged by iron, working off the effects of the Malone Agency and the cast of characters involved. He stopped cutting his hair and rarely shaved his face. He wore athletic clothes and tennis shoes, tee-shirts inside out and bandannas to push back his thick, brown hair. Sometimes he even tied his hair back to keep it out of his face.

He was starting to put the pieces of his life's framework, a new framework, in place. He felt like he was beginning again. Many things, he dropped outright. Some he kept. Some he modified. Some he added fresh. He continued to think for hours on end.

He received new motivation, he regained his appetite and started fasting for blocks of hours instead of blocks of days.

He continued having intense, physical sessions at the gym, often for longer than two hours. He opened up his library again. Biographies, classics, philosophy, history, comedies. He read books he had read before, and also books he had never heard of. He flew threw them, voraciously! Maddox Malone began to breathe again and his once-vibrant spirit drew nourishment again. He went through many days like this, cheerfully and freely, as if nothing in the world had ever irritated, vexed or depressed him. There was no physical or behavioral sign of distress from all the events. Sometimes, he would just sit and think.

During this time, he generally felt his courage revive. It had waned, and he had withdrawn into himself. Because of Paul McCartney, Pepe Soliz, Zaine Fuller and others, even Laura Malone, he just didn't trust anybody. Now, he was starting to feel more emboldened. Stronger. Not fragile, not anymore. He was coming back. But, it was not a perfect process. Sometimes, this flickering flame of courage would wane or go out entirely. To save himself from that irritation and malaise he would go to the gym, the shooting range, the driving range, fighting practice, a long hike, drive to the lake, read his books, work on a home improvement project — which was something he never did in his old McMansion — or when he had his kids after school or on the weekends he would take refuge at the park for long games of football, baseball or basketball.

These activities saved him - for without them - there would likely have been nothing but fixation on his recent disappointments. Maddox was learning about himself, and he knew that he would have dwelt on these things, brooded on them, for as long as he let himself. He wouldn't have survived if he spent all his time thinking about the Grasshopper, the rapey Poobah, the Tick, the Platform, his failed marriage. With activities helping him to forget these things for hours and days at a time, his state of mind seemed to become strong again.

The only real joy he had found, involving other people, over the last few months was from spending time with his kids. And, since he had moved out of the home that he had raised them in, at times those relationships - so fundamental to Maddox - felt strained. So, even foundational relationships weren't all joyful. They were flawed, too. The broken flower pot of life! Of course, Maddox understood, the kids wanted to be in their comfortable surroundings that they had lived in their whole life. And, unfortunately for Maddox, that was Laura's house now. He had just moved on after their last conversation after taking a few weeks to make some plans. Even though he had to, at times, he didn't want to speak with her again. Speaking with her generated too much negative energy. He didn't take any time to haggle over assets - he felt above that fray and he believed he could make money again if he wanted to.

He didn't hire a divorce attorney, he thought that idea was distasteful and gross. He felt like that process would have damaged him, even further. He couldn't picture talking to one. He pictured Laura's team of attorneys, rubbing their hands, grasping, enjoying the moment of Laura's acquisitions - and earning fees for their time. Maddox just left, because she demanded an end to the horrible marriage. He left. Other than those few social activities mentioned here, he spent time dwelling on his solitude, he turned back to full days of eating only a couple handfuls of almonds, a boiled egg, black coffee and water.

And so, as that process played out without Maddox attending the court proceedings, the marriage ended, not like it began, with enormous hopes and gallant dreams, but rather with a whimper, a few miserable groans and plenty of hard feelings — bitterness and, for hours or days at a time, contempt. Given the levels of misery that it entailed at the end, Maddox was, he guessed, thankful to be out of it. There was no alternative.

But it wasn't a great time for Maddox. It wasn't even a good time. He felt lonely quite a lot. He felt angry at times. He felt disgusted. He felt disappointed. He felt broken. He tried not to get consumed by hatred — he still didn't like his angry twin. It happened, to be sure, but only once in a long while. He knew that anger, hatred and disgust could break him if he allowed it. All of the events changed him. They damaged him, for now. But he had to move forward anyway. He had to take lessons away from the failed marriage and everything else. He had to learn from it. He was determined to do that.

One day, after reading Seneca and Hoppe for several hours in the morning, Maddox was hiking near the Boulders resort, south of Phoenix, before heading to his Krav Maga fighting class with Geoff Packard. Geoff was a badass fighter and instructor and he trained Maddox once a week for hand-to-hand. Maddox's smart phone rang and buzzed. Calling was a guy named Eric who was a venture capital investor in Sunny Grove. Maddox took the call without too much excitement, but did agree to fly out the following day to meet Eric and catch up. They had known each other for years. He set the flight schedule so he would have time to visit some spots in Sunny Grove that he always loved.

After he landed, he couldn't resist taking the rental car and heading toward the Golden Gate Bridge. Maddox sang along to the music.

> Let's head on down the road
> There's somewhere I gotta go
> And you don't know how it feels
> You don't know how it feels to be me

He cruised north and soon parked at the Golden Gate Bridge observatory. He got out of the rental car and started walking. As he parked, he looked to his left and saw a couple buildings. One of the buildings was a bar. The weathered sign outside the bar said the Flying Horseshoe. Maddox, who had given up his old vodka and soda habit for several months at this point, didn't go in to the Flying Horseshoe. But it reminded him of something. He couldn't place what his thought was, though. He got out and started walking.

With him he had a large iced black Americano, unsweetened. The coffee, like the wind, was sharp and bitter. The Golden Gate Bridge, forty miles northwest of Maddox's childhood home of Sunny Grove, was such an inviting sight that he breathed in deeply and started walking towards it, soaking in every bit of the scenery. Birds flew gracefully overhead. The wind slowed down and showed its gentle side, a nice breeze. The sun shone. The clouds moved. The bay ebbed and flowed. Then it ebbed and flowed again.

It so happened that a bike race was crossing the bridge at the same time that Maddox was walking towards the bridge. He re-routed himself to take the walk down below the bridge. The sand ladder and other scenery was amazing. The weather, was perfect, about seventy-three degrees and the gentle breeze that had, at least for the time being, replaced the more aggressive wind. Maddox Malone had found himself well-disposed for this expedition, he was in great physical shape and moved easily and gracefully across the terrain. He was muscular again at six-foot-one and two hundred pounds, but moved really well because he maintained his flexibility in addition to his lifting and fighting routine. He was strong but prized his agility and range of motion as much as his brute strength.

After enjoying the area for an hour and a half he returned to the rental car, saw the Flying Horseshoe once again, and went to meet Eric. The meeting was fine, albeit uneventful. After taking time off to get settled in his condo after his divorce, and to work on his physical fitness – he had successfully re-forged himself using iron – it was necessary for Maddox to think about work again, about re-building his income streams. He was still figuring out his outlook and his plan. His outlook on work was entirely different, but at the same time it was not fully-formed, not yet. More clearly, he simply didn't know what he wanted to do.

As he got ready for bed at his hotel, he thought back to the beauty of the day's walk. He had enjoyed the beauty of nature, the water and the sky, combined with man-made excellence in the form of the Golden Gate Bridge. It was away from all the degeneracy of the once physically-beautiful city of San Francisco that had been destroyed by its feckless politicians - some of the worst grifters the world had ever seen – it had become one of the most Pozz-ed places on earth. San Francisco was steeping in human shit, literally, which sat there, in the streets, steaming and stinking. There were intravenous needles in the streets. AIDS-ridden needles which presented a deadly physical manifestation of the Pozz, which usually took a metaphysical form. The politicians were virtue-signaling weirdos that had dedicated their lives to the government kleptocracy, milking a cow that never ran out of milk, while pretending to perform public service, finger-wagging and lecturing good, normal people - using nasty buzzwords - all day. They claimed tolerance but, for those who paid attention to what they actually said, they just sounded weird and very intolerant of people who dared to disagree with them. And what they said was stupid, it made no sense - because they had no respect for truth.

Maddox was out on all of that. Maddox felt happy and content. With his books and his thoughts, he had been contemplating virtue and a return to virtue for man generally and himself in particular. To start this process, he checked his habits and made sure that he maintained good ones. An Ancient Greek guy had taught him that virtue is habit – so he figured that vice must be, too. With the passing time, his vantage point improved and he couldn't believe he had been tied up with the Poobah, the Grasshopper, the illegal payments, the Platform. Carlton Duffer via Lacy Stratton. He just couldn't believe that he, Maddox Malone, had ended up here. That wasn't what he envisioned when he started the Malone Agency years ago. He wasn't full of regret, necessarily. He wouldn't have endured all of his recent disappointments on purpose, for sure, but once he did, he was strangely happy that he experienced failure – now he knew what it was. He had touched it, felt it, and tasted it. He wanted to do better from now on. To be better! He made a vow to become more virtuous. The commitment felt great and profound. Maddox felt warm and relaxed. He felt so good he didn't think the feeling would ever go away.

After returning to his room, Maddox fell asleep. He slept well for several hours. But when he woke, he felt his old despair. He didn't want to get out of bed. He missed his kids, he felt badly about his failed marriage, he was disgusted and irritated with the Malone Agency and everything that happened in his business. Everything had gone so haywire, everything was a mess! The broken flower pot!

It seemed that his whole life was disappointment. A series of disappointments. His outlook became gloomy and desolate again. His circumstances seemed so irrevocably ruined, so destroyed, that an invincible disgust for life overtook him. He tried to defeat this feeling by hitting the hotel gym, hard. Five sets of twenty hamstring curls. Five sets of twenty leg extensions. Five sets of fifteen pull downs. Five sets of twenty rows, followed by eight with a high grip. Air squats. Dumbbell curls. This was the best, the only, return to virtue that he could manage while isolated in the hotel.

After he lifted, Maddox realized that he had to take his disappointments more lightly. He had to let them glance off, somehow. He didn't need to allow disappointments to arouse a level of irritation that led to destructive thoughts, destructive behavior, vodka, soda, bad energy, fatigue, paralysis.

Maddox had a great moment of realization as he walked out of the hotel gym. Maddox Malone realized, while he was walking out of the gym with his muscles pumped up, that he needed to live again. He realized that life was a composite of many trivial things. He realized he had made the mistake of discarding too many things in life because they were, by themselves, trivial. He remembered that he knew this from his study, at Berkeley, of the classics written in Ancient Greek and other writers as well, mostly Brits from the seventeenth or eighteenth century. Great conversations written about by those men were, in fact, often about trivial matters. The discussion of trivial matters revealed a glimpse of important truths.

Why hadn't he locked this stuff down years ago? Why wasn't his thought process more secure, more regimented, more thorough, more developed? Why had this taken him so long? Years! And he still wasn't there. He grew frustrated. Because of his feeling of disappointment, he dropped all his thoughts regarding virtue from the night before. His life had become too tumultuous to focus on the big picture. He had to grind out the little stuff. It was the inscription that he had, very purposefully, included in his wedding invitation when he married Laura years before.

The inscription read:

> KEEP YOUR HEART WITH ALL
> VIGILANCE, FOR FROM IT FLOW
> THE SPRINGS OF LIFE.

It wasn't so much that he had forgotten the saying, but he had ignored it while he got down in the dirt and fought the Bug-men. He had allowed circumstances to change him, to guide him. When he thought about fighting, though, he suddenly felt battered and bruised by events. These same old thoughts brought his mood down somewhere close to despair and withdrawal. He indulged his melancholy thoughts as he trudged to his rental car. Something made him want to head north to the Golden Gate Bridge, one more time, before flying back to Phoenix. His mind was running wild again, jumping from topic to topic. He was reliving the events with Pepe Soliz, Garibaldi Vascoso, Paul McCartney,

Zaine the recruiter, Lacy, and everything else. Grasshoppers, Bedbugs, Ticks, Beetles and Ants — Soul-less hybrid people. Bug-men and Bug-women. He parked the car again in the bridge's observatory deck. His disgust with life had become extreme, increasing every minute of the drive. He was often put in a bad mood by an impending trip to the airport. Rental Car. Shuttle. Security. Coffee. Wait. Board Plane. Fly. Dodge conversation with bugs on the plane. Land. Take shuttle. Pay parking. Drive home. Everything was mundane, everything was a trap.

But this feeling was different than the normal apprehension of tedious travel. This was different than life's normal disappointments, which Maddox had been able to absorb, lately.

This was what despair felt like! Maddox Malone was not in control of his mind, he felt low. He felt bad.

He headed up to the bridge and started walking across. "What is wrong with me?" thought Maddox. Somewhere close to the midpoint, he leaned out toward the railing of the Golden Gate Bridge, over the rocks and water in the bay far below, while the mysterious desire for life struggled with an intense feeling of despair and extreme frustration.

He lingered at the rail, above it. The emptiness, the dirtiness, the corruption, the evil, the dishonesty, the loss, the failings, the degeneracy. The Pozz. He felt it all. The rail was firm and solid. He leaned further. A gloomy light pitched down from the bridge itself, from the lights overhead. Time slowed down. Maddox noticed everything. He noticed where paint was peeling. He noticed every chink in the metal on the bridge. He noticed uneven cement. He heard the wind whip by him, the aggressive San Francisco wind had come back! He heard the werrrp, werrrp, werrrp of tires crossing over grooved pavement when cars drove by. Werrrp! Werrrp! Werrrp! He groped at the rail, a dull fear of heights gripping him. Still, Maddox Malone thought about it. He smelled a strange, foreign stench, briefly, then it was gone. His hand slid along the rail. He felt a hand grab the back of his jacket. Or thought he did. He glanced back and no-one was there, nothing was there. Not a person, nothing at all. The light from the bridge glared down, pushed down on him. He thought he could feel eyes looking at him, even though there was no one walking on the bridge and the vehicle traffic was light. He looked at the glaring lights again and noticed that they had become softer, or seemed to.

He lingered and thought. Then suddenly, out of nowhere, Maddox drew back from the rail with great force and resolve.

Before he walked away from the rail, on a whim, Maddox tossed his smart phone off the Golden Gate Bridge. He just plucked it out of his pocket and with a smooth, graceful upward motion, fluidly extending his arm to a thirty-seven or thirty-eight degree angle, he threw it into the San Francisco Bay, hundreds of feet below. He was so high up, he couldn't even hear the Endless Content make a splash — but it was gone. It whirred and buzzed and beeped and glowed, and screamed, all the way down - until it hit the water, then it just kind of disappeared. Maybe the content wasn't endless, after all? Maddox Malone breathed in, then out.

Lucky Horseshoe

✸✸

"Once more unto the breach, dear friends, once more;"

~ William Shakespeare, *Henry V*

Most things that are good are forged out of difficulty. Good things are created despite hardship. Good things are brought about amidst tragedy. Good things are pushed through, overcoming fear. Good things are surrounded by, and triumph over, disappointment. They triumph over life's series of disappointments.

Maddox had let his old life be ruined, not entirely, but in very large part, by his greed. He had no filter and he didn't set limits and boundaries for himself. He worked all the fucking time and lost sight of important things, beautiful things. And, ironically, Maddox Malone wasn't even any good at being greedy. He had come to realize that he didn't even love money, not that much. He just sort of loved *chasing* money, so he did it. For the fuck of it. He finally figured all that out because he never ended up holding onto much of the money he made. So, it must have been the chase. What else could it be? Regardless — it was still his greed that had brought him to the edge. It brought him to the rail of the Golden Gate Bridge. But something happened when he was up there. Something finally clicked for Maddox Malone. Maddox had stayed on land, and it was his Endless Content Super 6G smart phone that ended up in the water.

He woke up the following day feeling good energy. Like he used to — like the years when he started the Malone Agency, like law school, like a teenager, when he was so full of hope — except his energy was even better, more positive. It was a great day to be alive! Maddox felt good in his own skin. He was in shape, he was as smart as ever, and, anyone could say anything about all the shit that went down with Pepe, TENACIOUS, the Platform, O-Bad and everything else — but Maddox

Malone had tons of experience for his age. Maddox Malone knew how to make deals. Maddox Malone knew how to make things happen. He had made so many deals — and now his experience was better-rounded because he had also touched the bottom. He finally got some experience with bad decisions and epic failures — the wheels fell off while he was rolling along at full speed and Maddox Malone had to figure it out.

Suddenly, the thing, it happened. An image - a glorious image - sparked in his imagination. He pictured the Flying Horseshoe, the bar that he saw the night before near the Golden Gate Bridge. His mind raced. Hmmmm. He still had over a million dollars set aside in his Malone Agency account!

He needed to make a phone call. He reflexively patted his pockets. Oh shit! Maddox had thrown his smart phone - his Endless Content Super Terminal 6G - into the San Francisco Bay the night before. Hmmmm. He scratched his head and drove to his cell phone service provider's store, which was about twelve minutes away.

"How can we help you?"

"I got rid of my smart phone," said Maddox, leaving out the fact that he had tossed it off the Golden Gate Bridge. "I need to get a new phone."

"Okay, what model are you looking at?" asked the store staffer, a worker bee, while waving his hand at a bunch of smart phones. The smart phones glistened. They beckoned. They called out to Maddox with their shiny screens and their digital buttons. They whirred. They hummed. They beeped. They gleamed!

Maddox looked at the phone and a brief flash of desire showed on his face. But it went away quickly with a slight shake of Maddox's head.

"I don't want a smart phone," said Maddox, with a steady, resolved look on his face.

"Ha-ha, wait what?" said the worker bee. "You don't want a smart phone? Why?"

"I just want to be able to make phone calls and send text messages. That's all I want. Do you have a basic phone that can do calling and texting? Like a flip phone or something. Not a smart phone. I don't need an Endless Content phone in my hand."

"Wait, what?" asked the worker bee.

"I don't want a smart phone," repeated Maddox.

"Well, how are you gonna use your data?"

"What data?" said Maddox.

"You have to get data with your phone plan."

"I don't think so," said Maddox.

"Says right here you do," said the worker bee, pointing at the plan description.

"No I don't," said Maddox.

"Yeah, you do. We don't have a phone plan without data."

Maddox paused. He stared at the worker bee.

"Okay, just give me the least data you have. I'm not gonna use it, but whatever. I need to make a phone call, right now."

Maddox spoke slowly. He was frustrated but he stayed calm. The angry twin kept napping, or at least doing something else.

"Why are you doing this, man? It says here on your account that you had the Endless Content Super Terminal 6G — that's a great smart phone! How can you make this change?" asked the worker bee, incredulously.

"Yeah, I had that phone, man. That's the one I got rid of," said Maddox.

The worker bee seemed distracted.

"Hey man, have you seen the Endless Content Super Duper Terminal 6 Double G? It's the latest model and you can even unlock it with your face," said the worker bee.

"Yeah, man. I've seen it. I don't want that. I'm not going to take a digital facial, man," said Maddox. "Just grab me that flip phone."

The staffer gave Maddox a funny look, walked away, and came back with a forty-five dollar flip phone. Maddox bought it and walked out after the service was activated. The worker bee buzzed back behind the counter and picked up his own smart phone — he had purchased the Endless Content Super Duper Terminal 6 Double G using debt financing that the worker bee would pay over the next two years by spending his time working at the Endless Content retail store, pushing Pozz indirectly. He got Thursdays and Fridays off, though. The guy's Super Duper had two protective cases on it and a shiny gold color underneath. After the worker bee picked up his phone, he immediately checked six different social media feeds, watched a twenty second clip of free pornography — featuring not only a triple penetration but also a wild-eyed roving midget doing the unmentionable — and then he responded to several text messages. He did all of that with a blank look on his face.

Maddox left the store with his new phone. He flipped it open like it was nineteen-ninety-nine and then Maddox dialed his retired football client Chris Black.

"Yo, Madd-man!" said Chris as he answered.

"Put down the whiskey and the pain pills mother fucker! We gotta talk," said Maddox.

"What about?" asked Chris.

"What was that idea we had a couple years back? That contest idea."

There was a full five seconds of silence.

"You talkin' about Horseshoe Bonanza?" asked Chris. Maddox couldn't see, but on the other end of the line, Chris' eyes were wide and his mouth involuntarily formed a huge smile!

"Horseshoe Bonanza! That's it. That's it," said Maddox, with a look somewhere between resolve and excitement.

"H to the B, baby — the Madd-man is back!"

"That's right Cee-Bee. I saw a bar last night called the Flying Horeseshoe. That's what reminded me. What did we have in there, in the contest?"

"Million dollar prize to the winner. Team sponsors and mascots. Pay-per-view streaming. I was gonna have the alpaca on my team. You had a peacock."

"Okay, now I remember everything."

"We haven't talked about that in like two years. What happened?"

"Let's just say I have a million dollars burnin' a hole in my pocket and I want to try out our idea."

"Absolute Madd-man!" yelled Chris Black.

"You have time to come out and work on it with me?" asked Maddox.

"Does a bear shit in the woods?"

"I'll call you back."

Maddox hung up with Chris and called Nathan Lawsin.

"Hey Maddox."

"Nathan, what's up?"

"Nothin' how are you doing?"

"I'm good."

"You want to sell the Platform?"

"Yes," said Nathan. "Yes I do."

"How much you want?"

"A million bucks. I paid two million, by the way," said Nathan. Maddox imagined the impish little grin on Nathan's face. He couldn't see him, but he was certain that it was there.

"Does that include Efficient-Pop?"

"Yes, but I have to tell you Efficient-Pop is losing money. The product is popped in Vietnam and, this is not common knowledge, but those little fuckers have a big appetite for popcorn. They eat half our popcorn supply before it makes it out the door."

"No shit?" said Maddox.

"No shit. There's nothing we can do about it. When we go out there and try to stop the snacking and they just give us the run-around and its business as usual when we leave. They're just too shifty and quick."

After a brief pause, Maddox said, "alright, I'll do the deal as long as I can give you the million in ninety days but I can start using the Platform as soon as I want. I take title to the Platform immediately."

"Done and done."

Maddox hung up the phone with Nathan and called Grover Giles.

"Maddox Malone!" said Grover.

"How's Niko doing in school?"

"Great. And I have a book recommendation, a guy that wrote a massive demographic st–," Grover was saying, before he was interrupted by Maddox.

"Grover, I don't have time to talk to you about your race and IQ shit right now. Those are ideas. This is life. I just have one question."

"Shoot," said Grover.

"That money, the money I borrowed to give to Pepe to pay off his rape victim, April Tilney?" said Maddox.

"Yeah?"

"I didn't give it to Pepe Soliz. In fact, fuck Pepe Soliz. My question is this... Can I use it for anything I want, as long as I make the pay-back date of one hundred twenty days?"

"Yes, you can. What do you have in mind?"

"An event. That's all I needed to know."

Maddox hung up the flip phone call with Grover and called Bart Odom.

"Maddox Fuckin' Malone," said Bart.

"Sup Bart."

"Nothin."

"Bart, Did you do the shit you said you were gonna do last time we talked in Chicago?"

"Hell no, man. I've just been watching porn and playing video games on my phone," said Bart.

"Wait, what? What the fuck?" asked Maddox.

"Ha-ha, I'm just messing with you Maddy. I'm starting on it, yes. Started working out. Long way to go."

"Okay, fuck all of that. We can talk about all that later. I bought the Platform. Can you come out to Los Angeles and help me sell ads for an event?"

"Why did you do that? Nobody watches volleyball. Volleyball sucks, Maddox," said Bart.

"I know Volleyball sucks," said Maddox.

"So why did you buy the Platform, Maddox?"

"Hey Bart, who said the event was Volleyball?" said Maddox, his eyes blazing as he spoke intensely into his sturdy little flip phone. They blazed!

"That's what I'm talkin' about! I'll be there tomorrow."

Maddox hung up with Bart and called Omar Matish.

"What's happenin' Big Dog?" asked Omar.

"Nothin' how you been?" asked Maddox.

"Good, I found this cute little cherry down in Hollywoo—"

"I don't have time to hear any of your stories about women, Omar," Maddox interrupted. "Hey, I bought the Platform and Efficient-Pop."

"The fuck? You serious?" asked Omar.

"Yeah. Can you and the Puddle Bear help me move some product?" Maddox said.

"Wow, you had to Puddle-Bear him? He's gonna kill you," said Omar, laughing.

"Omar, focus. Can you guys move some product for me? We have to move fast."

"You want us to sell Efficient-Pop? That shit is terrible! But, if we can sell the Pogo Back, we can sell anything," said Omar.

"Not exactly, Omar. We're overhauling Efficient-Pop. They make that shit in Vietnam and it's swimming in vegetable oil and nasty preservatives. Vegetable Oil Kills! We're gonna change everything and re-brand it as GoodPop. Locally sourced, natural corn topped with fresh, wholesome, old-fashioned butter and iodized salt. Only the best ingredients."

"Absolute Madd-man!" hollered Omar.

"We may not be saving the world, but we're going to make a good, honest popcorn. Traditional popcorn. We're going to make the world a little bit better."

"I'm in. When do we start?" said Omar.

"Now. You get your usual fee."

Maddox hung up with Omar. He had to catch his flight back up to Phoenix. He was thinking rapidly and also listening to some music as he headed back to the airport. He sang along.

> Just about a year ago
> I set out on the road

Seekin' my fame and fortune
Lookin' for a pot of gold
Things got bad, things got worse

With those phone calls and a few more not recounted here, Maddox Malone made deal after deal. Maddox had pulled the entire structure together for his Platform event by the end of that afternoon, after flying back and spending the rest of it in his little office in northern Phoenix. His sturdy little flip phone was up to the task. Each call was carried out and concluded with perfect audio clarity and, when he hung up, the calls were ended with precision.

So everything was set for the big day!

The Horseshoe Bonanza's Platform Challenge would be a one-on-one Horseshoe match, between two event attendees, selected at random based on their section and seat number. The winner would receive the prize of a million dollars. The loser would jump off the platform after yelling "Vegetable Oil Kills!"

Tickets were priced at five hundred dollars each, and everyone who attended, of course, had to commit to the terms of the contest — acknowledging both the prize money and the leap. The platform could hold, at maximum capacity, five thousand fans. Fans were not allowed to bring smart phones onto the Platform.

This was an outright ban!

If they wanted to smash their face into a screen they would have to do it elsewhere. Too much digital content. Too much Pozz everywhere. But not on the Platform - the Platform had become a beautiful and majestic safe space, a bunker, difficult for the Pozz to gain entry.

There was only one sponsor allowed onto the platform. GoodPop, the re-fashioned popcorn company that Maddox had bought, along with the Platform, from Nathan Lawsin. Maddox had immediately shut down production of the popcorn in Vietnam, and brought the entire operation back to the United States. It's true that GoodPop was now operating inside occupied California, run by the corrupt kleptocrats who were still squatting in that once-beautiful state — but Maddox was okay with incremental change at this point. He had to be. It doesn't require an Aristotelian scholar to know that when a country degenerates to the point that one major political party imports illiterate voters by dangling state handouts - and the other major political party allows it because it wants the cheap labor for its corporate masters - that particular democracy has run its course. At that point, it's all over except for the fighting, the crying and gnashing of teeth - that will come later. Maddox had to be okay with incremental change, at least for now. He had to start somewhere.

Maddox put Omar and the Puddle Bear in charge of pushing GoodPop, with its new ButterFresh deployment system. They immediately put the revamped product into their sales channels. Even as production started, Maddox had his attorneys writing a patent for GoodPop, since he came up with the idea of having a little packet of fresh, wholesome butter included in the bag — and Maddox had an conceived of a device that, with a twist and a pop, instantly heated the butter so that it was scalding hot, but not boiling. Drizzled on the fresh, locally-sourced popped-corn it tasted absolutely delicious! It was the best popcorn the world had seen in at least sixty or seventy years. A tasty treat! Popcorn was suddenly really fucking good, again.

The event would not be televised. Maddox did not want degenerate, Pozz-ed television ads attaching to the Horseshoe Bonanza. Maddox had canceled his cable television subscription long ago — but if he was in a restaurant or somewhere with a television on he always noticed that the advertisements were disgusting, pushing outright Pozz and horrible products. By banning television, Maddox knew that he was also banning big food, big tech, soda, empty carbohydrates, and any other harmful product that would try to attach itself to the Platform's Horseshoe Bonanza. It's true, Maddox thought, that popcorn may not have been chock full of nutrition, but Maddox had created a locally-sourced, wholesome product with minimal processing and no vegetable seed oils. It was an incremental win! A starting point for the long journey back from a shit-tier product like Efficient-Pop. A starting point for the long journey back from big food's government-enabled obliteration of everything nutritious and good.

Instead of television, people could stream the platform event on a website that Maddox purchased that afternoon, HB dot TV. The charge for the event was twenty-nine dollars and ninety-nine cents. Bart Odom was placed in charge of pushing the streaming sales — cryptocurrency was the preferred payment method, but Maddox instructed Bart that the Platform would, for now, still accept the dollar. Bart was off and running — selling away. Bart had all the contacts and plenty of people that owed him favors. For each viewer, Maddox had instructed Bart that five dollars would be donated to charities helping people with tech addiction. It was Maddox's little push back against the vile, degenerate Bug Wrangler and the Digital Facial that Endless Content was splashing on the country. The rest of the money would remain with Maddox's company.

The event was scheduled for sixty days out. Maddox, Omar, the Puddle Bear, Chris Black and Bart went to work. They also added a few support staff to their team. They were ready to roll!

In the meantime, Maddox had a crew of volunteers from the University of Southern California, led by Niko Giles, Grover's son, clean up the platform. With a few days of cleaning and filling in chinks and potholes and applying a fresh glossy varnish — the platform was ready to go. It looked beautiful!

A few weeks went by. Maddox felt great about the event, but he called a team meeting because sales were slow. Everyone showed up on the platform. There were clouds overhead and the day was very gloomy.

"Guys. Guys, listen. You know I don't call bullshit meetings," said Maddox.

Everyone nodded in agreement.

"We're scuffling, though. We're scuffling. We're putting up a million bucks for this fuckin' contest. We gotta sell some tickets. We gotta sell some GoodPop. We gotta sell some advance live streams. What's going on? What's our problem?

Omar replied first, "I think this thing is going to catch. I think it's going to work. We just need a trigger."

"I agree with that," said Bart. "Everyone is so used to the old way of doing things. This is so different, so original. I agree with Omar that this thing is gonna catch on. I believe. We just need a little bit of luck."

"Okay but how do you know?" said Maddox, with a bit of hope shining through on his face, which seconds before had shown signs of outright frustration and disappointment.

"Sometimes you just gotta have faith — like when you're a little kid and you just know Santa Claus is gonna show up on Christmas," said the Puddle Bear. "It's gonna work out."

When Maddox heard the Puddle Bear say the words "Santa Claus" he almost staggered back with anger. Some hatred bubbled up in Maddox, but he quashed that down, elbowed it back down to anger. His immune system! The cause of his angst was the fact that Maddox remembered Benjamin Cohen telling him about that Pozz-ed book — the one in the children's book format where the author made Santa Claus an African that was constantly on the creep, taking a dick up his ass and also dishing one out. Maddox Malone flashed with anger for a second, because he loved the traditional Santa Claus. The real Santa Claus. He loved Christmas! But, he didn't have time to get angry about that Pozz-ed book. Not right now.

That disgusting book was drop-kicked out of his mind as something else clicked. Maddox's eyes went wide, and then he immediately called Benjamin Cohen.

"Maddox Malone!" said Benjamin.

"How you been, Ben?"

"I'm okay. You got another rape crisis going on?" asked Benjamin.

"No, I'm through with all of that."

"What's up?" asked Benjamin.

"I need your help with PR for my event. 'Member that guy, your client, you told me about that one time? Not the guy that tried to make a new Santa that takes a dick. The other guy you mentioned a while back, the Swedish video guy. He streams video."

They spoke for another minute, and when they hung up, Benjamin Cohen called in a favor for Maddox. One of his PR clients was a blonde guy with a beard who posted online videos, one a day - he had a funny name and was a great online personality. The guy was fucking hilarious - and also really popular. Maddox had gotten into the habit of watching his videos - and he thought the guy was an outright genius. The streamer was from Sweden but lived in the UK. He also had tens of millions of subscribers to his online videos. He was a long-time client of Benjamin's — and, after hanging up with Maddox, when Benjamin called his client, he agreed without question to Benjamin's request that he would do a quick promotion of the Horseshoe Bonanza in a couple of his upcoming videos.

Maddox received a text message from Benjamin that read "Pull up your big boy pants, this thing is gonna go off. Hope you're ready."

And that was all it took! The buzz, the excitement started immediately after the first video was posted. The remaining tickets sold out in one hour after the video was posted, and the streaming sales spiked globally.

ii

Soon enough, the event day was here. The day of the Horseshoe Bonanza had arrived! It was a picture perfect day. Seventy-six degrees on the Platform, and the soft and easy golden sun just showered down on the Platform, everyone just basked in the beauty of nature, the light, the ocean while standing on some man-made excellence, in the form of the once-decrepit but now-renovated Platform. The crowd snacked on GoodPop, often two handfuls at a time. People conversed with one another. People laughed and told stories. They made jokes. Nobody had a smart phone, so nobody could reflexively stare at a screen - nobody took a digital facial, not here, not now.

Then, the event, the Horseshoe Bonanza, began! "Everyone get ready for the event of a lifetime!" hollered the oval-headed Master of

Ceremonies. "We're here today for the Horseshoe Bonanza! It's a simple, traditional game of skill. Two contestants will be selected at random, here, now. One will stand on this side," he said, gesturing to his left where the peacock mascot pranced around mightily, very light on its feet, "and one will stand on this side."

After gesturing toward the peacock, the Master of Ceremonies gestured to his right toward the alpaca mascot, as the majestic alpaca neighed and whinnied and bucked!

"Standard Horseshoe Rules are in effect, two points for a ringer and one point for a six-incher! The winner will walk out with a One Million Dollar Prize!"

The crowd roared!

"And the loser will plunge themselves off the Platform and into the Paaaaaaa-ci-fffffff-ic Oooohhhh-cean!"

It was impossible to tell if the Master of Ceremonies was serious or joking about jumping in the ocean. Jumping off the platform was insane! That had killed Harry Oswald! The crowd roared seemingly twice as loud! They all continued snacking on GoodPop, many still stuffing two handfuls into their mouth and some going for three! The hot, fresh butter tasted so good on top! They couldn't get enough.

"Now, for the first selection! Will whoever has ticket 34B please ... head ... toward ... the ... center ... of ... the ... platform!"

Everyone checked their tickets, and, suddenly, Rudolph Pinkerton showed a wave of excitement and amazement — right on his face. The owner of the Pinkerton Clinic, the inveterate gambler, was about to make his biggest bet of his life! Rudy Pinkerton didn't know how to swim! He waved to the roaring crowd and walked down by the peacock, smiling. The crowd hooted and hollered with excitement!

"Well, I owe six hundred thousand dollars to my bookie anyway, what does it matter?" Mister Pinkerton muttered as he walked down the stairs.

The announcer continued, "If you have ticket 69C please ...

head ... toward ... the ... center ... of ... the ... platform!"

The holder of that ticket knew right away that it was hers. She had checked her ticket number when Rudy Pinkerton was called and laughed to herself because of the number 69 it contained. She knew that anyone sixty-nining with this particular girl would get a five-inch long surprise, right in their face. It was Danielle Duffer!

Carlton Duffer had used Lacy Stratton's shiny red credit card to pay the twenty-nine dollars and ninety-nine cents and he was streaming the Horseshoe Bonanza on his smart phone from his room at the Beach Comber Motel.

When the camera panned in on Danielle Duffer, Carlton Duffer screamed, "Hey Summy, that's my son — err — brother — err — sister! Ner ner ner! I got her that ticket Summy! Ner ner ner!"

Summer, the yoga instructor, just lay there with her open hand resting seven inches to the right of her wonderful, ripe, little apricot.

The California sun shone down on the beautiful, rebuilt Platform. The yellows, the oranges, the blues, the golds — how they shone!

Maddox Malone stood and looked out over the platform and felt a rush of warmth, of beauty, of love, of hope. No smart phones. No television. No junk food and XtraShoog. No Pozz. Just a beautiful day out over the ocean, on the Platform.

The Horseshoe Bonanza contest began and it was a hard-fought.

Rudy Pinkerton jumped out to an early lead, but Duffer fought back. Soon the match was tied at nineteen a piece. The game was being played to twenty-one.

Pinkerton threw a six-incher! Twenty to nineteen!

"NOOOTTTT TOO-DAYYYY!" he yelled with his chin tilted back. "Not today Miss Duffer!"

However, Danielle Duffer, after taking a deep breath and taking one and a half steps forward as if on a high-wire, extended her arm so gracefully it was as if she was throwing her last horseshoe with the Hand of God itself. And maybe she was, because she tossed a ringer! The horseshoe had just hung in the air, defying gravity, gleaming, glistening, even glowing. Sparkling, shining, coasting and gliding. When it finally came down, the crowd was so silent that the metal-on-metal sound of the ringer carried all the way out over the ocean. Even the birds and the fish seemed to celebrate.

Danielle Duffer had won the million dollars!

"How ya' like me now! There's a new Caitlin up in this bitch!" yelled Danielle with her deep voice.

"Golly gee wiz," said Rudy Pinkerton, the fine-looking gentleman, to himself. "Oh well, my bookie was gonna kill me anyway!"

With that, Rudy Pinkerton bellowed "Vegetable Oil Kills!" and then plunged himself off the platform and into the water.

Danielle Duffer basked in the glow of victory, smiling and blinking wildly! It is quite possible that no-one had ever blinked tht rapidly before. The Horseshoe Bonanza was complete! It was a smashing success! Maddox Malone just stood there, on the Platform, enjoying the event, enjoying the day. He snacked on a little bit of GoodPop, after he drizzled some scalding hot butter on top. Maddox smiled, just a little, and nodded his head.

Courage

✸✸

Γηράσκω δ' αιει πολλά διδασκόμενος

- Solon

At the moment Rudolph Pinkerton belly-flopped into the Pacific Ocean, he didn't know that Maddox Malone and the Horseshoe Bonanza staff had arranged with the United States Coast Guard for the jumper, no matter whether it was Rudy Pinkerton or Danielle Duffer, to be fished out of the ocean immediately. Rudy thought he might be left in the ocean to drown or get chewed up by sharks. The crowd didn't know what was going on and the whole thing made for wildly entertaining content. When Rudy Pinkerton was fished out and returned to the Platform the crowd erupted with cheers! He was no longer up to his neck in the water – but Rudy was still up to his neck in gambling debts.

"Rudy, Rudy, Rudy!" the crowd chanted — even though he lost the match he remained a popular and charismatic figure.

The event was a smashing success, both in terms of drama and revenue. Rudy Pinkerton exclaimed "Oh thank God," when the coast guard saved him — but a few minutes later he muttered "I couldn't even beat a fucking-God-damned-tranny at horseshoes. Now how in the hell am I gonna be able to pay off my bookie?"

The day after the Horseshoe Bonanza, Maddox Malone flew home to the northern outskirts of Phoenix. He felt incredibly relaxed. He felt warm inside. Strangely, it wasn't so much the money that he made on the event that made him feel so good. Instead, it was the feeling of success, of creating enjoyable, even whimsical, content, of creating a good, simple brand of popcorn and running an almost totally Pozz-free event — a little Pozz snuck in when, against all odds, a tranny was randomly selected for the Horseshoe contest. But there was no other Pozz. Otherwise, it was just a good old-fashioned Horseshoe challenge — that gave Maddox such a fount of positive energy.

The money didn't hurt, either. The ticket sales alone had netted two and a half million dollars and the online streaming brought in another three million dollars. Additionally, popcorn sales were over twenty-five thousand dollars.

Of course, Danielle Duffer had received her million dollar prize from Maddox and the Platform. Danielle planned to use exactly half of the money to treat her ongoing mental health issues and the remaining half to purchase street drugs, with a strong emphasis on meth. And, Maddox had to pay Nathan Lawsin his million dollars, which he did. Maddox also had to pay Grover Giles back for the rape hush money loan that Maddox eventually used on the Platform, which he did. Additionally, running the event itself had cost five hundred thousand dollars for staff and security and streaming and promotion and everything else. He gave over five hundred thousand dollars to the technology addiction recovery charity he had selected before the event. That group was most likely another Pinkerton Clinic - Maddox was pretty sure it wouldn't work - but it felt okay to try to help out. Chris Black, Omar, the Puddle Bear and Bart all received hefty bonuses for their hard work, as each bonus was approximately one hundred and fifty thousand dollars.

After all of that, Maddox still had more than two million dollars sitting in the Platform account. He paid himself a bonus so he could get caught up on the expenses he had been neglecting during the lead up to the Horseshoe Bonanza.

He decided that he would put on another original Platform event in six months or so. No Platform event format would ever be repeated, because each event was designed to take place in the moment. He wanted the next one to have something to do with music. A good, old fashioned music show. Maybe some Outlaw Country. Maybe some oldschool Rock and Roll. But he would take a couple weeks before he decided. He hadn't made up his mind as of yet exactly what the event would be.

He went home to Phoenix with hopes that he could arrange a good chunk of time to see Thomas, Chester and Felicia. He missed them terribly! He and Laura had not been getting along at all, which, he told himself, was to be expected. They didn't see eye to eye in divorce any more than they did while they were married. Maddox still needed to work on controlling his temper, his anger, the angry twin. There was no more unified interest and the trust was long gone – on both sides.

ii

It was a Sunday, but Maddox had no desire to waste his time watching football and the accompanying Pozz-ed football television advertisements. He was limiting the Pozz as much as he could. It was unseasonably cool in the northern outskirts of Phoenix. The day before, April Tilney, Pepe Soliz's rape victim, had killed herself. It happened after four p.m. April hanged herself with a belt in the closet of her apartment just outside of Saint Cortana, California. The hush money that she had received from Pepe Soliz's new agency – Big Time Superior Sports Agency – didn't make the whole thing feel better. The money let her buy some stuff and party but it didn't allow her to move on from the attack.

She couldn't escape her demons.

She couldn't escape her feeling of vulnerability after the rape. She went through every day thinking, at least once, of the destruction that Pepe, the rapey and horny Poobah, had unleashed on her balloon-knot butt-hole with his stubby, soda can of a copulatory apparatus. Many days, she spent sixty or seventy dollars of the hush money from Pepe on shittier vodka and a pile of marijuana. She tried to escape. She tried to numb herself. She tried to forget. But she couldn't escape from her thoughts the way she needed to. So, she had strapped the belt around her neck, had a brief thought about her mom and her sister, both of whom she loved, and then she kicked her little size six feet off of the stool that had propped her up. She gagged and choked, and then she died. April Tilney was gone and she wasn't coming back.

iii

April's tawdry death provided such a contrast to Pepe Soliz's still-glamorous life. Yes, Pepe's life was meaningless and empty, but most people didn't realize that. They didn't realize it, at all. In fact, they thought the opposite. He was a professional sport ball player! He was a Sunny Grove Big Boy! He had fans! He signed autographs! He had money! At this point in time, he had eight confirmed daughters with eight different women. And there were almost certainly more that were unconfirmed. He was famous! He was partying, drinking tequila two shots at a time. While Pepe enjoyed his celebrity status, April couldn't even muster up the strength to go on. How could she, what with a broken will and a busted-out anus? Ultimately, the persistent after-effects of the rape stripped her of her life. The event just proved to be too much to bear. She gave up.

Maddox found out about April's death via a text message from his contact in the police department. The same high school friend, one of Maddox's best friends, who had e-mailed him the police report from the encrypted Donald Keyballs e-mail account sent him a text message letting him know that April had committed suicide.

Maddox just sat there for a minute, staring at the text message, staring at his trusty little flip phone screen. He didn't even send a text message back because he didn't know what to say, and the texting interface on the flip phone required a lot of buttons be pressed. April's death, April's suicide, didn't seem right to Maddox. It didn't seem fair. But the news brought some closure, finally. Maddox stayed lost in his thoughts. His mind flashed back to that day at LegoLand. Things had been so different then! He remembered walking in the sun with his children, with his entire family in the park, enjoying the beautiful day in California. Maddox Malone could remember exactly how things looked on that day! The golden-blue light that reflected a soft and subtle glow. He remembered his conversation with Chester about the park. He remembered that it was warm, but not too warm.

"Ah," he thought, "in those days I was so fucking invincible!"

It had seemed as if nothing could harm him or his family! In some ways, the news of April's death felt like a way to bring closure to the chain of events that seemed, to Maddox anyway, to start on that day when Maddox's old smart phone — the one that now rested at the bottom of the San Francisco Bay — buzzed with the call from the Slug.

But the closure brought about by April's death didn't make Maddox feel good. He put the thoughts out of his head — he was getting much better at that now with passing time. He used to let thoughts consume him. They ate him up, sometimes. Sometimes thoughts alone made him boil with hatred and anger. Now, he controlled his thoughts much better and he moved on when he had to.

Other things were happening that were bringing closure as well. Maddox and Laura had finalized their divorce, for example. Maddox had hired karma as his lawyer — instead of showing up to divorce court, which was a kangaroo court rigged for ex-wives anyway — and Maddox had lost so much in the near term as a result. Karma was a shitty lawyer — Karma couldn't keep specific appointments! Karma was always late. Always out of town. Always busy with something else. But the strange thing was that Maddox didn't really care about Karma's performance as a lawyer. He figured it for more of a long-term approach, more of a long term deal. He felt like hiring a lawyer and showing up with lawyers to court for the divorce process would have crushed his soul. It would have damaged him further. It was gross and dirty — it's not that he had anything against the lawyers doing their jobs - he just felt that way in his case, in his life. He felt that in his heart. He was still working through disappointment, anger, and even some bitterness. It just wasn't worth it to go and subject himself to that stuff, not to Maddox Malone.

He wasn't up for attending the hearing, so he didn't go. Instead, he went to the gym and got coffee. Then he ate some grilled salmon with a Mediterranean salad. He finished that particular night by reading more Seneca who told Maddox that the highest good is a mind which despises the accidents of fortune, and takes pleasure in virtue. Maddox wanted that - but he admitted to himself that he had work to do. He knew that in some ways he had been a shitty husband. Sometimes, he was hard to be around. He was brooding! He was obsessed with the Malone Agency! He had often excluded Laura from his thoughts. He always excluded her from tough decisions! He thought he could handle everything on his own, without help. He also focused on his kids, to the exclusion of his marriage. Laura was outside the circle, on the periphery, looking in. His communication habits sucked! He knew that. He felt like he was always one day behind on his visits, phone calls, text messages and e-mails. It was a horrible, desperate feeling. Sometimes, he thought "what the fuck is wrong with me?" But he also knew he had a good heart. He would find someone eventually, he told himself, and he would try again. He wasn't looking, though; he wasn't in a rush.

By the time he moved out, the only thing he cared about was the custody of his children, and Maddox and Laura had already agreed that would be a fifty-fifty split. "Fuck the rest of it," Maddox thought. Besides the kids, I don't really give a fuck what Laura says or does. How could he?

iv

Paul McCartney, the Grasshopper, was just a ways away from Maddox Malone in North Scottsdale, hopping around while trying to do three or four things at once. He was scrolling on the same website he always seemed to use to find his hookers. He snorted a quick bump of cocaine, right off his thumb. He rejoiced while looking at his laptop computer because he could tell he had found the perfect companion for the evening, a blonde woman named Savannah who advertised four points of entry. Four? The Grasshopper had a feeling that she would be perfect for him. He thought about his finger and clenched his sprat for a second before grabbing his shiny Endless Content smart phone and unlocking it by taking a digital facial.

The 'Hopper dialed a phone call on his Endless Content Super Duper 6G phone. This call was to Charlie Corkoran. Charlie was a young, relatively inexperienced entrepreneur who had started a very successful race car driving instruction school in South Phoenix.

"Hello, Charlie?"

"Yes, this is Charlie," he said as he answered his Super Duper with the press of a digital button.

"Ah, yes, hello Charlie. My name is Paul McCartney and I wanted to call and introduce myself. Congratulations on your establishment of a very successful driving school in Phoenix. Double C Driving! That's so cool. It's really so impressive. My close friend Frank, who owns the professional baseball team here in Phoenix, took your course and loved it. Take no prisoners!"

The owner of the baseball team, Frank Goldman, barely knew Paul McCartney and had just mentioned the course in passing when they spoke for a couple minutes in the coffee shop they both frequented in North Scottsdale.

"Thank you."

"Yes, Charlie, well, the reason that I'm calling is that I would love to get involved with your driving school. I have all the resources we need to really expand it. Money is not an issue! Would you like to have your own race track?"

"Really?" asked Charlie. Charlie had dreamed of this exact plan before. His own track! His face glowed with excitement! He looked like he was in for the ride of his life!

"How about you provide the driving school and the expertise, and I will provide funding to purchase some land and we can develop a race track there. Three million dollars should do it. It will be the biggest thing in sports! We will have the most valuable company in racing, just watch! I inherited a company, you see, from my Grandfather. It's called PartDok. Core Values!"

"I would love to do that," said Charlie. "I've always wanted my own race track — and I think that can really help me grow my driving school. We can get more students and really grow my business. I'm in! Let's call it something simple, something clean. Maybe 'SPEED' or 'DRIVEN'" said Charlie, excitedly.

"Fantastic! Ha-ha-ha-ha. This is great. I can't wait to get started. We can use Roland Stanton, a lawyer from Philadelphia, to help us set up the company. I'll have him follow up with you. Let's do this!" said the Grasshopper.

v

Maddox decided to work on his new back patio for the rest of the day. He wanted to try to make some real progress while it was cool and on a day where he didn't have access to his kids. He was going to pick the kids up in a couple days, but not today. After the divorce, he had retreated to a little condo fifteen minutes to the north of his old house. He didn't hate the condo. It was okay, in fact. He wanted to work on the patio to take his mind off of Thomas, Chester and Felicia. His ex-wife just had better access to his kids than he did. She was tucked away in the old house, where the kids were comfortable, where they grew up. She knew more of the kids' classmates and their parents. Maddox was boxed out in many ways. At times he felt outmaneuvered. It was very hard for him to maintain the connection that he used to have with his boys and with Felicia. It made Maddox angry. But he knew that anger over not seeing his children all the time, like he had in the past, would be enough to consume him if he let it. He couldn't let that happen! He couldn't go through all of this and then collapse at the end. Sometimes he slipped and his anger broke through and controlled him. Sometimes he melted down. Once in a while he complained in frustration or felt intense anger or hatred, but he tried to resist that. When it happened, he eventually calmed himself and tried to stay on an even keel. He felt disconnected but told himself to be patient, things would work out. They would be okay.

The work outside, on his back patio felt so good and it took his mind off of everything. He and his dog, Abel, went to the home improvement store three times, and trudged back and forth from his truck all day, dumping about twenty buckets of fill dirt and topping it with about fifteen bags of sand before putting down about two or three hundred pavers, planting a palm tree, a cactus, and a nectarine tree. He also built a fire pit and a brick barbeque. All in all he spent almost twelve hours out back, working nonstop.

His little patio was looking great!

It was smaller and definitely much more humble than Maddox's old McMansion, but it was a better space for him for some reason. He just wanted to take a few months to rebuild himself, to lift weights and read books and drink his iced coffee, wait to see his kids and, once in a while come up with a great idea for an event to host on his Platform. He figured he would do one or two events a year.

That particular day, Maddox had had drank black coffee and ate a couple hard-boiled eggs - plus at one point drank down water mixed with fiber seeds to kill his appetite — but, after hours of work, he finally acknowledged that he was starving. Starving! He wrapped up at about nine o'clock and decided to leave his dog Abel in the bedroom instead of the crate, jump in his truck and find some food. Things were quiet, as expected, on a late spring Sunday night.

As he drove off, it struck Maddox that he was finally feeling right, most of the time. He felt good. He realized that he had been that way for a few weeks. He was experiencing life in the present. It used to be that he would bounce back and forth between a furious, overworked, and frantic past few hours or few days and the hopes for a happy, or happier, future. But, before, he never quite found himself wide awake in the present. He was always chasing something for his future, something for the Malone Agency. Then when the future arrived, or seemed like it was about to arrive, it was gone again and he was off chasing something else. The future he worked for never, ever arrived. When he thought about all of this, he felt like he was in a daze. He felt like his life had been a dream.

Maddox, who had sold his fancy sports car, rolled his lifted black pickup truck down Cave Creek road, north of Phoenix, while scanning around in search of a place to eat. He passed a massive, boxy bar and grill on the right. He had been there a couple times and it was okay but the menu was tough to pick from. It seemed like mostly fried food, bar style. He didn't want that. He saw a place for ribs but decided he didn't want to go there. Same with a little old style burger and chicken place — the grilled chicken sandwiches there was a decent option, but he wasn't in the mood. He pulled into a bar and grill that was on the right side of the street and tucked back a bit. He parked. "Fuck it," he thought, "it can't be worse than those other places." He thought he might even have a vodka and soda with a lime, after the long work day. He hadn't been drinking vodka at all unless he was traveling - and he hadn't been traveling recently. He didn't want to get back into that habit. Not like he was before. But tonight, he would have one, he decided.

It looked like a decent dive bar and there was a guy on the patio playing live music. Maddox hadn't showered, but had thrown a bandanna on to hold back his hair and give cover to his face, which had been soaked in sweat for most of the day. He had on some black pants and some tan tactical boots, which he had used all day for the patio work. They were his best work boots. His shirt was a simple blue tee-shirt that he had bought from a cheap department store. It said "All or Nothing" on the front and was blank on the back. His forearms and hands were fatigued from the full day's work, and the muscles were still pumped up. He had cut several of his fingers open and had a big scratch on his left forearm. He looked tired but strong. He felt good. He sat down at the bar on the outside edge and relaxed. The crowd was small because it was Sunday, but it was fun and boisterous. A couple folks were visibly drunk, but still laughing and having fun. A big muscular guy with a bunch of tattoos rode around on a motorized mini-bike and everyone laughed.

Maddox pulled the bandanna off his head as he walked in and put it in his back pocket. The bartender, a tall and pretty blonde girl, was busy in the middle of the bar but came over after a couple minutes and paused while she looked at Maddox. She blinked a couple of times. Maddox looked up, with a smirk on his face.

"What can I get you to drink?" she said with a nice smile.

"Can I get a vodka and soda with a lime?" Maddox asked. Maddox hadn't had a vodka since the last time he traveled for Malone Agency work.

"Of course," said the girl with a smile.

"Also, if you have the chance is it possible for me to look at a menu?"

"Let me grab one."

The bartender came back and said, "I didn't realize this but the cook shut down the kitchen early ... but there's a place across the street that is still open, I have the menu right here and you can call and order food then pick it up and bring it back here, your drink will be waiting for you right here. Here's the phone number. I'm gonna buy your drink because I'm really sorry that he shut the kitchen down early."

During the whole speech, the young woman never took her eyes off him and he stared at her. She rattled all that off and Maddox laughed inside but kept his face expression-less. Most times he would have just said thanks and left since he couldn't eat. After all, that's what he had come there to do. The vodka and soda with a lime was incidental, this time, not a focus.

Maddox's first instinct was that task involved too much. He could abandon the vodka and soda and go eat at the burger place across the street if it was the only place open. Why come back? Harold's also could serve vodka and soda. But that thought quickly faded as he saw the girl turned around, working on a tab and dancing to the music. She was tall, about five-foot-eleven or so, with blonde hair, nice-looking boobs with a round butt. Her shorts covered her butt, but the uniform requirements for the bar were that they be form fitting. No complaint from Maddox.

When she turned around and looked at Maddox he said, "okay, I'm gonna do that. I'm gonna be right back. Hold my drink if you would." He felt a buzz of good energy, not from the drink but from his interaction with the girl.

The bartender put the drink behind the bar. Maddox rolled across the street, grabbed a burger, bumped into his real estate agent. They visited for fifteen minutes, and then Maddox went back to the bar and grill. The bartender saw him and put his vodka and soda back in front of him with a smile.

"Thanks," said Maddox.

"Did you get your food?" she asked.

"Yeah, I ate it over there because I bumped into someone I knew and was visiting for a minute."

"Okay, great."

He felt good with some food in his belly and half the vodka and soda down – his first one in what seemed like ages. He didn't want to get back into "the habit" but he was enjoying the cocktail after a long day. He breathed. He had brought his sturdy, trusty little flip phone with him. It hadn't rang much that day, which was nice. And there was no digital media or social media on that phone. No Pozz, no pozz-ed corporate media conglomerates trying to push shit-tier media into his face, . There were a few couples. A few people just watching the band play music. A couple of old timers, regulars, down at the right side of the bar. He kept breathing, enjoying the music, people watching.

Maddox lifted his head when he heard the bartender say "hey, do you want another drink?"

Their eyes met just for a brief second. Maddox didn't react visibly, but when their eyes met he felt like she kicked his doors down! He hadn't felt that way in quite a while. "What's going on here?" he thought.

He had a bit left in his first cocktail but was enjoying the music and the upbeat environment so he said "yeah, sure."

She served him another vodka and soda with a lime. She was still dancing around, acting upbeat, smiling. He finished the previous drink and pushed it to the back of the bar. He looked around. He was in a good mood. Despite that fact, Maddox kept to himself for the most part. He just listened to the live music and relaxed. He was also watching the pretty girl serve drinks and dance, just a little.

"Love your tattoo... What's that say? 'Courage?'" she asked.

"Yeah, thanks."

"Why did you get that? Any particular reason?" she asked.

"No reason, I always wanted it."

Maddox didn't want to go into it, not now. But in his own mind, he knew that he got it for himself during a tough period in his life. He had his own reasons. He got the Courage tattoo a month or two after his divorce was finalized. He had just been through the Pepe Soliz million-dollar-rape-gauntlet, the Platform had collapsed, the TENACIOUS hoax had run its course, and he had been interviewed by the FBI about the illegal payments Zaine made to Major O and Obadiah and the others. His previous life was in a shambles when he got it done. At the time, he was bust. He felt rootless, aimless. He needed

Things were such a mess at the time! That flower pot! He had to rebuild himself. At the time, things felt incredibly menacing and totally devoid of intimacy. He couldn't believe it. Things felt inhuman. He wanted to be more responsible. More balanced. More practical. More thoughtful. He wanted to be precisely himself, and not like all the other people, many of whom were exactly the same. He wanted to think more carefully about what he was doing in life and why he was doing it. It wasn't easy, but nothing good is. He knew, all of that would require courage. And that's why he got the 'Courage' tattoo, for his own reasons, nothing else – shit, his mom hated tattoos and she would have killed him if she knew about it. But it was for him, no one else. He thought of all that, but kept it to himself.

"You always wanted courage, or the tattoo? Ha-ha," she laughed. Something had struck her as funny.

"Both," said Maddox with a smile.

"Oh, but why?"

"Well, I don't know, it's better than being a pussy. I always wanted to do something really special. I always wanted to do something original. I'm not talking about the tattoo, I'm talking about being my own man, being myself. Making my own way."

The girl just stared at him while he talked.

"But, things don't always work out right away, I learned that. I wouldn't say that I've pulled off special, not yet. Not even sure that I've come close. I've had some things go pretty haywire, recently."

"Haywire? Oh, really? I can't wait to hear about that. What happened?"

"Just a bunch of stuff. You wouldn't believe it anyway."

"Well, is everything still haywire or did you fix it?"

"I fixed some stuff and I'm still working on other stuff."

"How'd you do that?"

"I ditched my smart phone and bought a Platform," Maddox said while noticing how pretty the girl's eyes were. Her eyes sparkled.

"You ditched your smart phone? What kind did you have?" she asked, before she noticed his trusty little flip phone.

"I had the Endless Content Super phone. The six."

"You ditched it, huh?"

"Yeah. I threw it off the Golden Gate Bridge. I just stopped seeing the value in it. I'm not going to buy anymore products from Endless Content," Maddox said with a knowing smile.

"No way. Really? You're like the only person who's not going to have the Super Duper 6G, then," said the girl.

"Yeah, really," said Maddox. He thought, but did not say, "I'm not taking a digital facial, not anytime soon."

"What kind of Platform did you buy?"

"It's a big Platform in the Pacific Ocean. We just had an event a little bit ago. The Horseshoe Bonanza. We sell locally-sourced popcorn with a patented butter delivery system, too. It's called GoodPop."

"Horseshoes? I love horseshoes. I grew up playing. Popcorn is good, too."

"You do?"

"Yeah. Bet I could beat you," she said.

"Not a chance. You don't look like you're very coordinated. You're too tall for a girl. Your left foot looks bigger than your right. That will throw your balance off, your knee will buckle, and all the horseshoes will go wide left. You have no chance," Maddox said. He made the thing about her foot up, completely, just to mess with the girl. Her feet were perfectly sized.

The beautiful girl gave a sarcastic-looking frown and went to pour a drink for another customer and check on the bar. She came back a few minutes later.

"Well, are you courageous?" she asked.

"I try to be," said Maddox, with a hint of amusement.

"I think you seem courageous."

"You do? How would you know? You don't know anything."

"I'm looking right at you."

They paused.

"Where are you from, by the way?"

"I'm from California but I live here now, right down the road. This feels like home to me now. California is too different than it was - that place is a mess. And so what if you're looking at me?" said Maddox.

"Well, I think I know what courage is. Also, I'm from Northern California too," said the girl.

"A bartender who says she knows what courage is? This is going to be interesting," thought Maddox.

Maddox paused and looked at the girl.

"What is courage, then?" asked Maddox.

"It's a strong man who will stand and fight. Or, a woman standing firm through tough times."

"Okay, but what if the smarter thing to do is to not fight at all or to fight later? I think that decision can still be courageous."

"Well I don't know," said the girl. She seemed impulsive but Maddox sensed that she was trying to push herself to be logical. He also sensed that she was having difficulty with that.

"For example, it might be brave to run into a fight but if it's a fight you can't win is that really courage? I think it has to be combined with something else, not fighting wildly. Running into a bad fight is dangerous," said Maddox.

"Yeah that makes sense because if you run into a fight randomly you might get hurt or killed. That's just stupid. That's not courage."

"I think good people are always gonna lose the fight, eventually. Evil ebbs and flows but never stops pressing. The glory is in going down fighting, though. The victory is in actually fighting. The victory is the fight itself," said Maddox. "But you have to fight smart or bad shit will happen to you. Fighting smart is courage."

Maddox smiled and laughed. She was right and he had spent years charging forward in a direction that, in hindsight, didn't make sense. Chasing deals, chasing money. He shook his head very slightly and moved on from that thought.

"I think there has to be other characteristics to courage like justice and good judgment."

Maddox sipped on his vodka and soda and the bartender went to refill a beer for a fat, bearded biker. She came back. She had pretty blue eyes. She had a baseball cap on backwards with blond hair underneath.

The girl's face, as she looked at Maddox, looked very expressive. She was giving him really good energy, very engaging. Her face suggested that she thought that Maddox was cool, that he was successful, and that he was interesting. Maddox wondered what she was thinking.

The girl knew nothing of his failed marriage with Laura.

She didn't know about the angry twin, the disconnection Maddox sometimes felt from even his closest friends and his family.

She didn't know about the hour of failure.

She didn't know anything about the Poobah or the Grasshopper.

She never met the rotting Tick, the Bedbug, the Dung Beetle, the Slug and the Silverfish.

She didn't know how disappointed Maddox was, how frustrated and disappointed he felt, on the days when he didn't or couldn't see his boys and Felicia.

She didn't know the adversity that Maddox had faced the last couple years. Of course she didn't, you couldn't see it on his face. Yes, he had been lifting weights and looked fit and came across as charismatic. He looked happy, he looked just fine. He looked handsome, he looked like he had a good soul.

"To act with courage you have to overcome fear. Sometimes, I get afraid," the girl said.

"Afraid of what?" asked Maddox.

"Well, for example, I want to be a sing— oh, never mind," she said.

"No, say it," said Maddox.

"Well, I really want to sing. I love music."

Maddox didn't say anything about his next event. He didn't want to mix business into this particular conversation.

"That's cool. What kind of music?"

"Outlaw Country. I like rock and roll, too."

Maddox made a mental note, but changed the subject back to the previous one after nodding to acknowledge what the girl said.

"Well, it seems like the way you use courage to overcome fear is by allowing hope to thrive. You really have to give yourself over to hope. But you can't be stupid about that and hope for something that isn't realistic. I've done that before," said Maddox, thinking back about TENACIOUS and the hoax perpetrated by the Grasshopper.

"Ha-ha, are you afraid now?" she teased.

"Nah, that's not what I mean but it's smart to be afraid of some stuff. You have to learn from experience. You have to look around and notice things," he said.

Maddox sipped his vodka and soda — but had decided that this would be his last one. He felt good and wasn't looking to go on a bender.

"It's funny because I think to be truly courageous you can't only be focused on future events. You have to understand the past and the present."

"That's cheating, though. If you know everything about the past and present, how could you ever make a mistake?"

There was silence for a moment, but neither face suggested that the silence was awkward.

"I didn't say 'know everything.' You said that," replied the girl with a little laugh.

"It seems like you turned courage and acting in a certain way into something way more than that. Like courage plus justice plus wisdom plus acting in a good way. You did that."

They both laughed and looked at each other. Maddox felt the sharp pain and bitter loss of time gone by that could have been better spent. Maddox felt a need. A longing. Not a need for the girl, just generally. A need.

Maddox thought about everything he had gone through, and the fact that he was here, now, talking to this girl. All the events that didn't turn out as he hoped or as he planned. He felt a relentless, nagging claim on his life. Lost time. Lost opportunity. Modern times! But, lately, he felt as if he were clawing back.

Maddox Malone had no idea that the girl was having the exact same thoughts. How could he know?

"Well maybe that's why I like courage. It helps you keep going, no matter what."

"I like that," she said. "Say that again, for me."

"Courage helps you keep going, no matter what," said Maddox.

"I'm Maddox by the way."

"Nice to meet you," said the girl. "You said your name was Maddox? I like that name."

"Yeah, it's Maddox. Maddox Malone. Nice to meet you, too. What's your name?"

"I'm Kalli."

***

ABOUT THE AUTHOR

Forrester C. Fox, a pen name for Ryan William Morgan, is an American from California. He cites his literary influences as Xenophon, Plato, Thucydides, Milton, Keats & the Bard. In his spare time, he enjoys practicing his marksmanship, weight lifting, hunting, swimming in open water, vegetables & barbeque steak, translating Ancient Greek texts, writing song lyrics, going to music concerts (rock'n'roll & outlaw country) & visiting with friends & family. Fox, sans pen name, can be found tweeting from time to time under the handle @RealRWM, unless banned for wrong-think by big-tech.

Made in the USA
San Bernardino, CA
27 February 2019